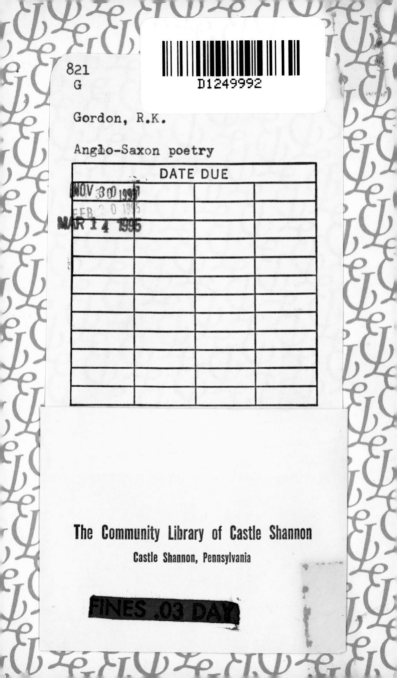

DATE DUE			
NOV 30 1993			
FEB 2 0 1995			
MAR 14 1995			

The Community Library of Castle Shannon
Castle Shannon, Pennsylvania

FINES .03 DAY

Anglo-Saxon Poetry

SELECTED AND TRANSLATED BY
R. K. GORDON, M.A.
Professor Emeritus of English Literature,
University of Alberta

DENT: LONDON
EVERYMAN'S LIBRARY
DUTTON: NEW YORK

NO. 794

ISBN: 0 460 00794 7

INTRODUCTION

THIS book contains translations of English poetry which was composed, roughly speaking, between A.D. 650 and 1000, or, in other words, from *Widsith*, which is perhaps the oldest English poem, to *Maldon*, which is the last great poem before the Norman Conquest. The coming of the French brought such great changes in language and in literary fashions that the older poetry seems somewhat remote from us.

English poetry before the Conquest may be roughly divided into two classes, heroic and Christian. The heroic poems deal for the most part with Germanic legend and history. About these poems there is nothing distinctively English except the language. The stories they tell or mention, the kings and warriors they refer to, were known to all the Germanic peoples, not merely to the tribes which came over to Britain. The Christian poetry adapts and paraphrases the biblical narrative, records the lives of saints, or uses verse for general moralizing. These religious themes were as much the subject of poetry after the Norman Conquest as before. Chaucer tells us the life of St Cecilia as Cynewulf tells us the life of St Juliana. The Conquest changed the language and metre of the religious poetry, but the substance remained the same.

Of the heroic poetry we can form no final estimate, because we do not know the extent or worth of what has been lost. The ravages of the Danes from the end of the eighth century onward blotted out a flourishing literature in the north of England. Monastic libraries were destroyed. Practically the only Northumbrian poetry preserved has survived in a West Saxon translation and not in its native dress. There are indications that *Beowulf* was originally a Northumbrian poem. *Beowulf* has survived complete, not because it was necessarily the best of the old poems, but merely because it was luckier than its fellows. *Waldhere* and *Finnesburh*, of which we have only fragments, were probably in some ways better poems.

The heroic poems, *Beowulf*, *Finnesburh*, *Waldhere*, *Deor*, and *Widsith*, probably took their present form in the course of the seventh century. Their substance, however, comes from an earlier time, from the age which had just closed, extending from the fourth to the sixth century and generally known as the Age of National Migrations, or, more briefly, as the Heroic Age. These poems reflect the tradition and spirit of that past time, and we can learn from them something about conditions of life in the Heroic Age, just as we see in the *Iliad* and *Odyssey* the Heroic Age of Greece. The way of living pictured in these English poems is not without nobility, and the impression they leave is a corrective to the brief historical annals of the time which tell largely of treachery and lust and bloodshed. No virtue is more insisted on in the poems than the loyalty a warrior owes his liege lord. This creed is well expressed in the words of Wiglaf when he exhorts his comrades to stand by Beowulf against the fire-dragon:

'I remember that time when we were drinking mead, when in the beer hall we promised our lord who gave us these rings, that we would requite him for the war gear, the helms and sharp swords, if need such as this came upon him. He chose us among the host of his own will for this venture; he reminded us of famous deeds, and gave me these treasures, the more because he counted us good spear-warriors, bold bearers of helmets, though our lord, the protector of the people, purposed to achieve this mighty task unaided, because among men he had wrought most daring deeds, daring ventures. Now the day has come when our lord needs the strength of valiant warriors. Let us go to help our warlike prince, while the fierce dread flame yet flares. God knows, that, as for me, I had much rather the flame should embrace my body with my gold-giver. It does not seem fitting to me that we should bear shields back to our dwelling, if we cannot first fell the foe, guard the life of the prince of the Weders. I know well that, from his former deeds, he deserves not to suffer affliction alone among the warriors of the Geats, to fall in fight; sword and helmet, corslet and shirt of mail, shall be shared by us both.'

This personal allegiance is strengthened by the lord's generosity, and the poems are full of praise for the lord who knows how to give freely. He is called 'the giver of rings,' 'the bestower of treasure,' 'the gold-friend of men.' Hrothgar is praised for his liberality to his followers and to Beowulf; and one of the reproaches brought against Heremod, of whom Hrothgar speaks, is that 'he gave not rings to the Danes.' The minstrels, Widsith and Deor, both receive grants of land from their masters. The sad exile in *The Wanderer* recalls 'how in his youth his gold-friend was kind to him at the feast.'

The poems reflect also another side of life in the Heroic Age—the frequency of feuds. *Beowulf* has many references to bitter tribal fights. The feud of Hrothgar the Dane and Ingeld the Heathobard is settled by Hrothgar giving Freawaru his daughter in marriage to Ingeld, but Beowulf tells Hygelac how the feud will break out again. There is, too, the tale of Finn of which Hrothgar's minstrel sings in hall and of which we have another glimpse in the *Finnesburh* fragment. Hygelac is slain in an expedition against the Franks and Frisians, and his son Heardred is killed fighting against the Swedes. Nor do the poems refer only to tribal strife. There is frequent mention of quarrels between kinsmen. Unferth is taunted by Beowulf with having slain his brothers and the treachery of Hrothulf is clearly foretold in *Beowulf*. Men were driven abroad by such feuds, or by the love of adventure and gain. So Beowulf goes to the Danish court to cleanse the hall of the monster Grendel and is rewarded with princely gifts.

Some of the pleasantest passages in *Beowulf* are those which describe the daily life of princes and warriors. The scenes in Hrothgar's great hall, Heorot, where men talk and drink mead and listen to the minstrel's song, and where the queen Wealtheow moves with courtesy among her guests, are full of simple dignity.

The style of these poems has a just claim to be called epic. It differs from that of the Homeric poems in degree but not in kind. The range of style is considerable. It can be swift and grim, as in Beowulf's struggle with Grendel or the great fight in the hall of Finn; or it can possess a strange beauty as in the picture of the mere where Grendel's mother lives. The voyage of Beowulf and his men to Hrothgar's court is a good example of steady, dignified narrative. The elegiac note also is often heard. 'There is no joy of the harp, delight of the timbrel, nor does the good hawk sweep through the hall, nor the swift steed stamp in the court. Violent death has caused to pass many generations of men.' One mark of the style is the comparative absence of similes but the frequency of descriptive phrases, known as Kennings, as, for example, when Beowulf's boat is called 'the foamy-necked floater.' These are sometimes of great beauty, and sometimes show the same kind of ingenuity which appears in a more expanded way in the *Riddles*.

The best introduction to the Christian poetry is the famous story of Cædmon told by Bede. 'This man had lived a secular life till he had reached old age, and had never learned a song. And so often at the feast, when it was decreed for the sake of mirth that each in turn should sing to the harp, when he saw the harp coming near him, then in shame he rose from the banquet and went home to his house. One time when he had done this, and had left the house where the feasting was, and had gone out to the cattle-stall, for the care of them was entrusted to him that night, and had duly laid his limbs to rest there and fallen asleep, there appeared a man unto him and hailed him and saluted him and called him by his name: "Cædmon, sing me something." Then he answered and said: "I cannot sing, and so I left the feasting and came hither because I could not." He who spoke to him again said: "Nevertheless, thou canst sing to me." He said: "What am I to sing?" He said: "Sing me the Creation." When he received that answer, then straightway he began to sing in praise of God, the Creator, verses and words which he had never heard before. This is the order of them:

> Now must we render praise to the Ruler of heaven,
> To the might of God and the thought of His mind,
> The glorious Father of men, since He, the Lord everlasting,
> Wrought the beginning of all wonders.
> He, the holy Creator, first fashioned
> The heavens as a roof for the children of earth.
> Then this middle-earth the Master of mankind,
> The Lord eternal, afterwards adorned,
> The earth for men, the Prince all-powerful.

Then he rose up from sleep and clearly remembered all he had sung while he slept, and straightway added in the same metre many words of the song worthy of God.' He was received into the monastery of Whitby under the Abbess Hilda, and there he passed his life in making poetry. 'He sang first of the creation of the world and the beginning of mankind and all the story of Genesis—that is the first book of Moses—and afterwards of the Israelites leaving the land of Egypt and of their entrance into the promised land, of many other stories from the holy scriptures and of Christ's incarnation and of His passion and His ascension into heaven, and of the coming of the Holy Ghost and the teachings of the Apostles. And afterwards of the fear of the judgment to come and of the terror of punishment in torment and of the sweetness of the heavenly kingdom he made many songs; and likewise also he wrought many others of divine benefits and judgments.' He died in 680.

Although the poems *Genesis*, *Exodus*, *Daniel*, and *Christ and Satan* were for long ascribed to Cædmon, it is probable that the nine lines quoted by Bede are all that we have of his work. But, though Cædmon's work is lost, Bede's description of it applies very well to the extant religious poems, to their scope and their spirit. The story brings out vividly the difference between the production of the old heroic poems and the new Christian verse, between Cædmon, the poet-monk alone in his cell, and Hrothgar's minstrel singing the tale of Finn to the warriors at their mead.

But the break between the religious poetry and the earlier work is not complete. The old devices of style are carried on and adapted to the new subjects. So, for example, the fallen Satan in *Genesis*—B, with his loyal band of followers, is described in terms that would suit a Germanic chieftain. Abraham's rescue of Lot and the fight at the opening of the *Elene* are told in the phrases of the old battle poetry. Moses leading the Israelites is called 'the glorious hero.' The poet who described St Andrew's mission to the strange land of Mermedonia knew and remembered Beowulf's mission to Hrothgar. In *The Dream of the Rood*, the most beautiful of all the religious poems, Christ is described as 'the young Hero' and the disciples are faithful warriors.

The religious poetry is of very unequal value. The *Later Genesis* (*Genesis*—B) and *The Dream of the Rood* are as good as anything in Old English poetry, but too often we get merely lifeless moralizing in conventional phrases. Except for the group of poems formerly thought to be by Cædmon, most of the religious poetry has at one time or another been ascribed to Cynewulf. He is the undoubted author of the works he has signed, *Elene*, *Juliana*, part at least of the *Christ*, and *The Fates of the Apostles*. The following poems—*Guthlac*, *The Phoenix*, *Andreas*, *The Dream of the Rood*, *Physiologus*, *Riddles*—have all been attributed to him. In spite of a great deal of discussion nothing has been certainly discovered as to his identity. He was probably born about 750 and was a Northumbrian or Mercian. Cynewulf is as deliberate and conscious an artist as Tennyson. His grace and his mastery of rhetoric are different from and inferior to the more solid qualities of *Beowulf*, which presents dramatic situations and human character.

But English poetry had not lost the power to deal well with great simple heroic themes. The poem on the battle of Maldon, written only a few years before A.D. 1000, shows the old strength and nobility. There is no sign of weakness or exhaustion.

Among the most interesting poems in Anglo-Saxon are the lyrics, or, more properly perhaps, the elegies—*The Seafarer*, *The*

Wanderer, The Wife's Lament, The Husband's Message, The Ruin, and *Wulf and Eadwacer.* These pieces have much in common, for with the exception of *The Husband's Message* they are sorrowful in mood, and the speaker looks back to happier times which have vanished. *The Ruin,* mutilated though the text is, is perhaps the finest of them.

Practically all the old poetry is written in the same kind of verse. The main principles of the metre are simple. Each line is made up of two half-lines which are separated by a caesura and joined by alliteration. Each half-line has normally two feet, and each foot is made up of an accented part and a varying number of unaccented syllables. The alliteration which links the two half-lines falls on these accented syllables. Words beginning with the same consonant alliterate in Old English, and a word beginning with any vowel alliterates with any other word beginning with a vowel.

The following lines will illustrate the structure of the verse:

Him se yldesta		ondswarode,
(*Him the eldest*		*answered,*)
Werodes wisa		word-hord onleac.
(*Of the troop the leader*		*word-hoard unlocked.*)

This alliterative metre was conquered by the rhyming measures brought in by the Normans. Strangely enough, it made a glorious reappearance in the fourteenth century in *Piers Plowman* and other poems, but the revival was not lasting. Its supremacy had gone.

There are four manuscript books which contain the greater part of Anglo-Saxon poetry.

1. *Beowulf* is preserved in a manuscript, written about A.D. 1000 and now in the British Museum. The manuscript was once in the possession of Lawrence Nowell, a sixteenth-century pioneer in Anglo-Saxon studies. He has written his name on the manuscript and the date 1563. Of its earlier history we know nothing. In the seventeenth century the manuscript found its way into the collection formed by Sir Robert Cotton. In 1705 Wanley, in his *Catalogue of Anglo-Saxon Manuscripts,* mentioned the poem, and said it described wars between a Dane, Beowulf, and the Swedes—a description which shows that the real contents of the poem were not yet understood. About a quarter of a century later the poem was nearly destroyed by fire. Thorkelin, an Icelander, near the close of the eighteenth century came to England, copied the manuscript himself and caused

another copy to be made. He spent years in preparing an edition only to have his translation and notes destroyed during the English bombardment of Copenhagen in 1807. The copy, however, of the manuscript escaped, and in 1815 his edition at last appeared. Among the other contents of the Beowulf manuscript is *Judith*.

2. *Genesis, Exodus, Daniel, Christ and Satan,* are contained in a manuscript in the Bodleian Library. It once belonged to Archbishop Usher, who gave it to Franz Junius, a Huguenot scholar who came to England in 1620. Junius printed the poems in 1655, and afterwards presented the manuscript to the University of Oxford.

3. The *Exeter Book* was given by Leofric, Bishop of Devon and Cornwall and Chancellor to Edward the Confessor, to Exeter Cathedral, where it still remains. Wanley was the first scholar to give an account of the book. The *Exeter Book* was not printed until 1842. The following poems form part of the contents of the *Exeter Book*: *Christ, Juliana, Guthlac, The Pheonix, Whale, Panther, Riddles, The Wanderer, The Seafarer, The Arts of Men, The Fates of Men, Gnomic Verses* (in part), *The Soul's Address to the Body* (Part 1), *Widsith, Deor, The Wife's Lament, The Husband's Message, The Ruin.*

4. The *Vercelli Book* is preserved in the cathedral library at Vercelli in Northern Italy. It has probably been there for six or seven centuries. How this book of Anglo-Saxon writings found its way to Italy we do not know. The manuscript contains the following poems: *Andreas, The Fates of the Apostles, The Soul's Address to the Body, The Dream of the Rood, Elene.*

R. K. GORDON.

SELECT BIBLIOGRAPHY

TEXTS, etc. *Beowulf*, the unique MS. autotyped and transliterated, ed. J. Zupitza, 1882. There are many later editions. Among them are those by A. J. Wyatt, 1894; 2nd edition, 1898; new edition, with introduction and notes by R. W. Chambers, 1914; revised 1920; Klaeber, 3rd edition, 1950; C. L. Wrenn, 1953; E. V. K. Dobbie, 1953.

Among many translations may be mentioned those by Earle, 1892; Clark Hall, 1901; Gummere, 1909; Scott-Moncrieff, 1921; C. W. Kennedy, 1940; Gavin Bone, 1945.

Beowulf, an introduction to the study of the poem, 1921, by R. W. Chambers, is indispensable for study of questions related to the poem.

There is a new translation, *Beowulf and its Analogues,* with a section on Archaeology, by Professor G. N. Garmonsway, Jacqueline Simpson and Dr Hilda Ellis Davidson, 1969.

Junius Manuscript, ed. G. P. Krapp, 1931. *Exodus* and *Daniel* in the *Junius MS.* have been edited together by Blackburn, 1907.

EXETER BOOK. *Codex Exoniensis* (with translation), ed. B. Thorpe, 1842. *The Exeter Book* (with translation). Part I, ed. I. Gollancz, 1895, Part II, ed. W. S. Mackie, 1933. *The Exeter Book* has also been edited by G. P. Krapp and E. V. K. Dobbie, 1936. Among editions of single poems in *The Exeter Book* are *The Christ* (with translation), ed. Gollancz, 1892, ed. A. S. Cook, 1900; *The Riddles of the Exeter Book*, ed. F. Tupper, 1910, ed. A. J. Wyatt, 1912; *Juliana*, ed. W. Strunk, 1904; *Advent Lyrics of the Exeter Book*, ed. J. J. Campbell, 1959.

VERCELLI BOOK. *Vercelli Codex: The Poetry of the Codex Vercellensis* (with translation), ed. J. M. Kemble, 1843. Later edition by G. P. Krapp, 1932.

CHARMS. *Leechdoms, Wortcunning, and Starcraft of Early England*, ed. T. O. Cockayne, 3 vols., 1864–6. 'Anglo-Saxon Charms' (*Journal of American Folklore*, vol. 22, 1909, pp. 106–237), by Felix Grendon.

MISCELLANEOUS. *Anglo-Saxon Minor Poems*, ed. E. V. K. Dobbie, 1942; *Deor*, ed. Kemp Malone, 1933; *Waldere*, ed. F. Norman, 1933; *The Battle of Maldon*, ed. E. V. Gordon, 1949; *Anglo-Saxon Poetry, an essay with specimen translations in verse*, by Gavin Bone, 1943; *Earliest English Poetry, a critical survey of the poetry written before the Norman Conquest, with illustrative translations*, by C. W. Kennedy, 1943; *Early English Christian Poetry*, translated with critical commentary, by C. W. Kennedy, 1952.

GENERAL LITERATURE. Stopford Brooke: *History of Early English Literature to the Accession of King Alfred*, 1892; *English Literature from the Beginning to the Norman Conquest*, 1898; *Cambridge History of English Literature*, ed. A. W. Ward and A. R. Waller, vol. i, 1907; W. P. Ker: *Epic and Romance*, 1897; 2nd edition, 1908; *The Dark Ages*, 1904; new edition, 1955; H. M. Chadwick: *The Origin of the English Nation*, 1907; K. Sisam: *Studies in the history of Old English literature*, 1953.

CONTENTS

BEOWULF

[A summary of the plot of *Beowulf* sounds like a nursery tale of marvels. The fight with Grendel in the hall, the slaying of Grendel's mother beneath the mere, and the encounter with the fire-breathing dragon belong to the same family as the adventures of Jack the Giant Killer. Parallels to Beowulf's exploits exist in written literature and in folklore. One of the most interesting is in the Icelandic saga about the famous outlaw Grettir. Two episodes in the saga bear such a strong resemblance to the fights with Grendel and Grendel's mother that it is clear they come from the same original story. (See *Saga of Grettir the Strong*, translated by G. A. Hight, Everyman's Library, No. 699, pp. 86–100, 170–7.) But a bare summary of the plot of *Beowulf* gives a wrong impression of the style and spirit of the poem. It has epic dignity and reality in spite of the fantastic character of the main story. Some of the events and persons referred to in the poem are historical. Hygelac was a real king who fell in battle near the mouth of the Rhine between A.D. 512 and 520. His people, the Geats, probably lived in a part of what is now southern Sweden. There is, however, no evidence that Beowulf the Geat, the hero of the poem, ever existed. There is good reason to suppose that the Swedish kings and princes mentioned in the poem—Eadgils, Onela, Ohtere, Ongentheow—are historical. Accounts in Scandinavian literature of the wars between the Geats and Swedes (their neighbours to the north) correspond to what is told us in *Beowulf* of the struggle. The Danish king Healfdene and his descendants are also probably historical, and their great hall Heorot almost certainly stood at Leire in the island of Seeland. There is, however, no evidence that Healfdene's ancestors—Scyld Scefing and Beowulf (not to be confused with the hero of the poem)—are anything but mythical figures. Scyld Scefing may mean Scyld son of Sceaf or Scef, or Scyld with the sheaf. The story told here of Scyld coming mysteriously over the sea as a child is told later in England (by Ethelwerd in the tenth century and by William of Malmesbury in the twelfth) not of Scyld, but of Scef or Sceaf. In William of Malmesbury's account a handful of corn is at the child's head in the boat; and this gave him his name Sheaf. Sceafa appears also in the catalogue of kings in *Widsith*. The Scandinavian records place Scyld at the beginning of the genealogies of the Danish kings, but do not mention the story of the child in the boat. It is probable, then, that that story originally belonged to Sceaf, and that in *Beowulf* it has somehow been transferred to Scyld.

In this poem are many references to Christianity. Some of these seem strangely incongruous. Hrothgar's minstrel sings a religious poem about the Creation, and yet Beowulf is cremated with pagan ceremonies. This mixture of pagan and Christian usages and beliefs has been explained in several ways. Some think that the Christian passages were not in the poem at first but were added by a later hand. We cannot be certain, but it is possible that they were the work of the original poet. Christianity did not at once drive out the older faith and ideas. The Christian king Alfred loved to listen to the old Saxon songs. For a time the old and the new existed side by side in England, as they do in this English poem. A little later, Old English poetry dealt almost entirely with Christian subjects, and the monk in his cell turned poet and replaced the minstrel in hall.]

1

GENEALOGIES

DANISH ROYAL FAMILY

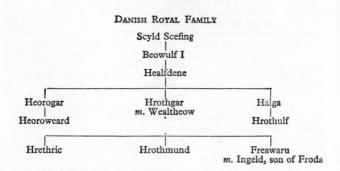

Scyld Scefing
|
Beowulf I
|
Healfdene
|
Heorogar   Hrothgar   Halga
| *m.* Wealtheow |
Heoroweard   Hrothulf

Hrethric   Hrothmund   Freawaru
                                     m. Ingeld, son of Froda

GEAT ROYAL FAMILY

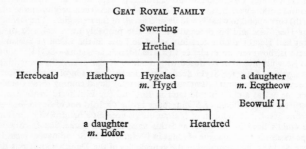

Swerting
|
Hrethel
|
Herebeald   Hæthcyn   Hygelac   a daughter
                         m. Hygd   *m.* Ecgtheow

                                            Beowulf II

          a daughter   Heardred
          m. Eofor

SWEDISH ROYAL FAMILY

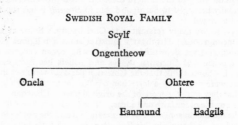

Scylf
|
Ongentheow
|
Onela   Ohtere

          Eanmund   Eadgils

I

Lo! we have heard the glory of the kings of the Spear-Danes in days gone by, how the chieftains wrought mighty deeds. Often Scyld Scefing wrested the mead benches from troops of foes,[1] from many tribes; he made fear fall upon the earls. After he was first found in misery (he received solace for that), he grew up under the heavens, lived in high honour, until each of his neighbours over the whale road must needs obey him and render tribute. That was a good king! Later a young son was born to him in the court, God sent him for a comfort to the people; He had marked the misery of that earlier time when they suffered long space, lacking a leader. Wherefore the Lord of life, the Ruler of glory, gave him honour in the world.

Beowulf, son of Scyld, was renowned in Scandinavian lands—his repute spread far and wide. So shall a young man bring good to pass with splendid gifts in his father's possession, so that when war comes willing comrades shall stand by him again in his old age, the people follow him. In every tribe a man shall prosper by glorious deeds.

Then at the fated hour Scyld, very strong, passed hence into the Lord's protection. Then did they, his dear comrades, bear him out to the shore of the sea, as he himself had besought them, whilst as friend of the Scyldings he had power of speech, as loved lord of the land long held sway. There at the haven stood the ring-prowed ship, covered with ice and eager to set forth, the chieftain's vessel. Then they laid down the loved lord, the bestower of rings on the bosom of the barge, the famous man by the mast. Many treasures and ornaments were there, brought from afar. I never heard of a sightlier ship adorned with weapons of war and garments of battle, swords, and corslets. Many treasures lay on his bosom that were to pass far with him into the power of the flood. Not at all did they furnish him with lesser gifts, with great costly stores, than did those who sent him forth in the beginning while he was still a child alone over the waves. Further they set a golden banner high over his head; they let the ocean bear him; they surrendered him to the sea. Sad was their mind, mournful their mood. Men cannot tell for a truth, counsellors in hall, heroes under the heavens, who received that burden.

[1] That is, conquered.

II

Then Beowulf of the Scyldings, beloved king of the people, was famed among peoples long time in the strongholds—his father had passed hence, the prince from his home—until noble Healfdene was born to him; aged and fierce in fight, he ruled the Scyldings graciously while he lived.   From him, the prince of hosts, four children sprang in succession, Heorogar, and Hroth-gar, and Halga the good; I heard that Sigeneow was Onela's queen, consort of the war-Scylfing.[1]   Then good fortune in war was granted to Hrothgar, glory in battle, so that his kinsmen gladly obeyed him, until the younger warriors grew to be a mighty band.

It came into his mind that he would order men to make a hall building, a mighty mead dwelling, greater than ever the children of men had heard of; and therein that he should part among young and old all which God gave unto him except the nation and the lives of men.   Then I heard far and wide of work laid upon many a tribe throughout this world, the task of adorning the place of assembly.   Quickly it came to pass among men in due time that it was perfect; the greatest of hall dwellings; he whose word had wide sway gave it the name of Heorot.[2]   He broke not his pledge, he bestowed bracelets and treasure at the banquet.   The hall towered up, lofty and wide-gabled; it endured the surges of battle, of hostile fire.   The time was not yet come when the feud between son-in-law and father-in-law was fated to flare out after deadly hostility.[3]

Then the mighty spirit who dwelt in darkness angrily endured the torment of hearing each day high revel in the hall.   There was the sound of the harp, the clear song of the minstrel.   He who could tell of men's beginning from olden times spoke of how the Almighty wrought the world, the earth bright in its beauty which the water encompasses; the Victorious One established the brightness of sun and moon for a light to dwellers in the land, and adorned the face of the earth with branches and leaves; He also created life of all kinds which move and live.   Thus the noble warriors lived in pleasure and plenty, until a fiend in hell began to contrive malice.   The grim spirit was called Grendel, a

[1] The Scyldings are Danes; the Scylfings, Swedes.
[2] Heorot means Hart.   The name probably refers to the antlers on the roof.
[3] Referring to the feud between Hrothgar and Ingeld (see Sections xxix and xxx).

famous march-stepper, who held the moors, the fen, and the fastness. The hapless creature sojourned for a space in the sea monsters' home after the Creator had condemned him. The eternal Lord avenged the murder on the race of Cain, because he slew Abel. He did not rejoice in that feud. He, the Lord, drove him far from mankind for that crime. Thence sprang all evil spawn, ogres and elves and sea monsters, giants too, who struggled long time against God. He paid them requital for that.

III

He went then when night fell to visit the high house, to see how the Ring-Danes had disposed themselves in it after the beer banquet. Then he found therein the band of chieftains slumbering after the feast; they knew not sorrow, the misery of men, aught of misfortune. Straightway he was ready, grim and greedy, fierce and furious; and seized thirty thanes on their couches. Thence he departed homewards again, exulting in booty, to find out his dwelling with his fill of slaughter.

Then at dawn with the breaking of day the war might of Grendel was made manifest to men; then after the feasting arose lamentation, a loud cry in the morning. The renowned ruler, the prince long famous, sat empty of joy; strong in might, he suffered, sorrowed for his men when they saw the track of the hateful monster, the evil spirit. That struggle was too hard, too hateful, and lasting. After no longer lapse than one night again he wrought still more murders, violence, and malice, and mourned not for it; he was too bent on that. Then that man was easy to find who sought elsewhere for himself a more remote resting-place, a bed after the banquet, when the hate of the hall visitant was shown to him, truly declared by a plain token; after that he kept himself further off, and more securely. He escaped the fiend.

Thus one against all prevailed and pitted himself against right until the peerless house stood unpeopled. That was a weary while. For the space of twelve winters the friend of the Scyldings suffered affliction, every woe, deep sorrows; wherefore it came to be known to people, to the children of men, sadly in songs, that Grendel waged long war with Hrothgar; many years he bore bitter hatred, violence, and malice, an unflagging feud; peace he would not have with any man of Danish race, nor lay aside murderous death, nor consent to be bought off. Nor did any of the councillors make bold to expect fairer conditions from the hands of the slayer; but the monster, the deadly creature, was hostile to warriors young and old; he plotted and planned. Many nights he held the misty moors. Men do not know whither the demons go in their wanderings.

Thus the foe of men, the dread lone visitant, oftentimes wrought many works of malice, sore injuries; in the dark nights he dwelt in Heorot, the treasure-decked hall. He might not approach the throne, the precious thing, for fear of the Lord, nor did he know his purpose.[1]

That was heavy sorrow, misery of mind for the friend of the Scyldings. Many a mighty one sat often in council; they held debate what was best for bold-minded men to do against sudden terrors. Sometimes in their temples they vowed sacrifices, they petitioned with prayers that the slayer of souls should succour them for the people's distress. Such was their wont, the hope of the heathen. Their thoughts turned to hell; they knew not the Lord, the Judge of deeds; they wist not the Lord God; nor in truth could they praise the Protector of the heavens, the Ruler of glory. Woe is it for him who must needs send forth his soul in dread affliction into the embrace of the fire, hope for no solace, suffer no change! Well is it for him who may after the day of death seek the Lord, and crave shelter in the Father's embrace!

IV

Thus the son of Healfdene was ever troubled with care; nor could the sage hero sweep aside his sorrows. That struggle was too hard, too hateful and lasting, which fell on the people— fierce hostile oppression, greatest of night woes.

Hygelac's thane, a valiant man among the Geats, heard of that at home, of the deeds of Grendel. He was the greatest in might among men at that time, noble and powerful. He bade a good ship to be built for him; he said that he was set on seeking the warlike king, the famous prince over the swan road, since he had need of men. No whit did wise men blame him for the venture, though he was dear to them; they urged on the staunch-minded man, they watched the omens. The valiant man had chosen warriors of the men of the Geats, the boldest he could

---

[1] An obscure passage, admitting of many interpretations, none of them very satisfactory.

find; with fourteen others he sought the ship. A man cunning in knowledge of the sea [1] led them to the shore.

Time passed on; the ship was on the waves, the boat beneath the cliff. The warriors eagerly embarked. The currents turned the sea against the sand. Men bore bright ornaments, splendid war trappings, to the bosom of the ship. The men, the heroes on their willing venture, shoved out the well-timbered ship. The foamy-necked floater like a bird went then over the wave-filled sea, sped by the wind, till after due time on the next day the boat with twisted prow had gone so far that the voyagers saw land, the sea-cliffs shining, the steep headlands, the broad sea-capes. Then the sea was traversed, the journey at an end. The men of the Weders [2] mounted thence quickly to the land; they made fast the ship. The armour rattled, the garments of battle. They thanked God that the sea voyage had been easy for them.

Then the watchman of the Scyldings whose duty it was to guard the sea-cliffs saw from the height bright shields and battle equipment ready for use borne over the gangway. A desire to know who the men were pressed on his thoughts. The thane of Hrothgar went to the shore riding his steed; mightily he brandished his spear in his hands, spoke forth a question: 'What warriors are ye, clad in corslets, who have come thus bringing the high ship over the way of waters, hither over the floods? Lo! for a time I have been guardian of our coasts, I have kept watch by the sea lest any enemies should make ravage with their sea raiders on the land of the Danes. No shield-bearing warriors have ventured here more openly; nor do ye know at all that ye have the permission of warriors, the consent of kinsmen. I never saw in the world a greater earl than one of your band is, a hero in his harness. He is no mere retainer decked out with weapons, unless his face belies him, his excellent front. Now I must know your race rather than ye should go further hence as spies in the land of the Danes. Now, ye far-dwellers, travellers of the sea, hearken to my frank thought. It is best to tell forth quickly whence ye are come.'

[1] Meaning probably Beowulf.
[2] Another name for the Geats.

V

The eldest answered him; the leader of the troop unlocked his word-hoard: 'We are men of the race of the Geats and hearth companions of Hygelac. My father was famed among the peoples, a noble high prince called Ecgtheow; he sojourned many winters ere he passed away, the old man from his dwelling. Far and wide throughout the earth every wise man remembers him well. We have come with gracious intent to seek out thy lord, the son of Healfdene, the protector of his people. Be kindly to us in counsel. We have a great errand to the famous prince of the Danes. Nor shall anything be hidden there, as I think. Thou knowest if the truth is, as indeed we heard tell, that among the Scyldings some sort of foe, a secret pursuer, works on the dark nights evil hatred, injury, and slaughter, spreading terror. I can give Hrothgar counsel from a generous mind, how he may overcome the enemy wisely and well, if for him the torment of ills should ever cease, relief come again, and the surges of care grow cooler; else he shall ever after suffer a time of misery and pain while the best of houses stands there in its lofty station.'

The watchman spoke, the fearless servant, where he sat his steed—a bold shield-warrior who ponders well shall pass judgment on both words and deeds: 'I hear that this is a troop friendly to the prince of the Scyldings. Go forth and bear weapons and trappings; I will guide you. Likewise I will bid my henchmen honourably guard your vessel against all enemies, your newly tarred ship on the sand, until once more the boat with twisted prow shall bear the beloved man over the sea-streams to the coast of the Weders; the brave ones to whom it shall be vouchsafed to escape unscathed from the rush of battle.'

They went on their way then. The ship remained at rest; the broad-bosomed vessel was bound by a rope, fast at anchor. The boar images shone over the cheek armour, decked with gold; gay with colour and hardened by fire they gave protection to the brave men. The warriors hastened, went up together, until they could see the well-built hall, splendid and gold-adorned. That was foremost of buildings under the heavens for men of the earth, in which the mighty one dwelt; the light shone over many lands.

The man bold in battle pointed out to them the abode of brave men, as it gleamed, so that they could go thither. One of the warriors turned his horse, then spoke a word: 'It is time for me to go. The Almighty Father guard you by His grace safe in your venture. I will to the sea to keep watch for a hostile horde.'

VI

The street was paved with stones of various colours, the road kept the warriors together. The war corslet shone, firmly hand-locked, the gleaming iron rings sang in the armour as they came on their way in their trappings of war even to the hall. Weary from the sea, they set down their broad shields, their stout targes against the wall of the building; they sat down on the bench then. The corslets rang out, the warriors' armour. The spears, the weapons of seamen, of ash wood grey at the tip, stood all together. The armed band was adorned with war gear. Then a haughty hero asked the men of battle as to their lineage: 'Whence bear ye plated shields, grey corslets, and masking helmets, this pile of spears? I am Hrothgar's messenger and herald. I have not seen so many men of strange race more brave in bearing. I suppose ye have sought Hrothgar from pride, by no means as exiles but with high minds.'

The bold man, proud prince of the Weders, answered him, spoke a word in reply, stern under his helmet: 'We are Hygelac's table companions; Beowulf is my name. I wish to tell my errand to the son of Healfdene, the famous prince, thy lord, if he will grant that we may greet him who is so gracious.' Wulfgar spoke—he was a man of the Wendels; his courage, his bravery, and his wisdom had been made known to many: 'I will ask the friend of the Danes, the prince of the Scyldings, the giver of rings, the renowned ruler, about thy venture as thou desirest, and speedily make known to thee the answer which the gracious one thinks fit to give me.' He turned quickly then to where Hrothgar sat, aged and grey-haired, amid the band of earls; the bold man went till he stood before the shoulders of the Danish prince; he knew courtly custom. Wulfgar spoke to his gracious master: 'Men of the Geats, come from afar, have travelled here over the stretch of the ocean. The warriors call the eldest one Beowulf. They request, my lord, that they may exchange words with thee. Refuse them not thy answer, gracious Hrothgar. They seem in their war gear worthy of respect from the noble-born. Of a truth the leader is valiant who guided the heroes hither.'

VII

Hrothgar spoke, the protector of the Scyldings: 'I knew him when he was a youth. His aged father was called Ecgtheow; to him Hrethel of the Geats gave his only daughter in marriage. His son has now come here boldly, has sought a gracious friend. Furthermore, seafaring men who brought precious gifts hither as a present from the Geats said that he, mighty in battle, had the strength of thirty men in the grip of his hand. May Holy God in His graciousness send him to us, to the West-Danes, as I think, against the terror of Grendel. I shall offer treasures to the valiant one for his courage. Do thou hasten, bid them enter to see the friendly band all together; tell them also with words that they are welcome to the people of the Danes.' Then Wulfgar went toward the door of the hall, spoke a word in the doorway: 'My victorious lord, prince of the East-Danes, bade me tell you that he knows your lineage, and that ye, bold in mind, are welcome hither over the sea-surges. Now ye may go in your war gear under battle helmets to see Hrothgar; let your battle shields, spears, deadly shafts, await here the issue of the speaking.'

The mighty one rose then, around him many a warrior, excellent troop of thanes. Some waited there, kept watch over their trappings, as the bold man bade them. They hastened together, as the warrior guided, under the roof of Heorot; the man, resolute in mind, stern under his helmet, went till he stood within the hall. Beowulf spoke—on him his corslet shone, the shirt of mail sewn by the art of the smith: 'Hail to thee, Hrothgar: I am Hygelac's kinsman and thane. I have in my youth undertaken many heroic deeds. The affair of Grendel was made known to me in my native land. Seafarers say that this hall, the noblest building, stands unpeopled and profitless to all warriors, after the light of evening is hidden under cover of heaven. Then my people counselled me, the best of men in their wisdom, that I should seek thee, Prince Hrothgar: because they knew the power of my strength, they saw it themselves, when I came out of battles, blood-stained from my foes, where I bound five, ruined the race of the monsters, and slew by night the sea beasts mid the waves, suffered sore need, avenged the wrong of the Weders, killed the foes—they embarked on an unlucky venture. And now alone I shall achieve the exploit against Grendel, the monster, the giant. I wish now at this time to ask

thee one boon, prince of the Bright-Danes, protector of the
Scyldings: that thou, defence of warriors, friendly prince of the
people, wilt not refuse me, now I have come thus far, that I and
my band of earls, this bold troop, may cleanse Heorot unaided.
I have also heard that the monster in his madness cares naught
for weapons; wherefore I scorn to bear sword or broad shield,
yellow targe to the battle, so may Hygelac my lord be gracious
to me; but with my grip I shall seize the fiend and strive for his
life, foe against foe. There he whom death takes must needs
trust to the judging of the Lord. I think that he is minded, if he
can bring it to pass, to devour fearlessly in the battle hall the
people of the Geats, the flower of men, as he often has done.
Not at all dost thou need to protect my head, but if death takes
me he will have me drenched in blood; he will carry off the
bloody corpse, will think to hide it; the lone-goer will feed
without mourning, he will stain the moor refuges. No longer
needst thou care about the sustenance of my body. Send to
Hygelac, if battle takes me off, the best of battle garments that
arms my breast, the finest of corslets. That is a heritage from
Hrethel, the work of Weland.[1] Fate ever goes as it must.'

VIII

Hrothgar spoke, the protector of the Scyldings: 'Thou hast
sought us, my friend Beowulf, dutifully and kindly. Thy father
achieved the greatest of feuds; he became the slayer of Heatholaf
among the Wulfings; then the race of the Weders would not
receive him because of threatening war. Thence he sought the
people of the South-Danes, the honourable Scyldings, over the
surging of the waves. Then I had just begun to rule the Danish
people and, young as I was, held a wide-stretched kingdom, a
stronghold of heroes. Then Heregar was dead, my elder
kinsman, the son of Healfdene had ceased to live; he was better
than I. Afterwards I ended the feud with money; I sent old
treasures to the Wulfings over the back of the water; he swore
oaths to me. It is sorrow for me in my mind to tell any man
what malice and sudden onslaughts Grendel has wrought on
Heorot with his hostile thoughts. Thinned is my troop in hall,

[1] The famous smith of Teutonic legend. He is mentioned in *Waldhere*
and in *Deor's Lament*. His name is connected with a cromlech known as
Wayland Smith in Berkshire. If a traveller left his horse there with a piece
of money and came again presently, he would find his horse shod. (See
Scott's *Kenilworth*.)

my war-band.   Fate has swept them away to the dread Grendel.
God may easily part the bold enemy from his deeds.

'Full often did warriors drunken with beer boast over the
ale cup that they would await Grendel's attack with dread blades
in the beer hall.   Then in the morning, when day dawned, this
mead hall, the troop hall, was stained with blood; all the bench-
boards drenched with gore, the hall with blood shed in battle.
I had so many the less trusty men, dear veterans, since death had
carried off these.   Sit down now at the banquet and speak thy
mind, tell the men of victorious fame, as thy mind prompts.'

Then a bench was cleared in the beer hall for the men of the
Geats together; there the bold-minded ones went and sat down,
proud of their strength.   A thane who bore in his hands the
decked ale cup performed the office, poured out the gleaming
beer.   At times the minstrel sang clearly in Heorot; there was
joy of heroes, a great band of warriors, Danes and Weders.

IX

Unferth spoke, son of Ecglaf, who sat at the feet of the prince
of the Scyldings.   He began dispute—the journey of Beowulf,
the brave seafarer, was a great bitterness to him, because he did
not grant that any other man in the world ever accomplished
greater exploits under heaven than he himself: 'Art thou that
Beowulf who strove with Breca, contended on the wide sea for
the prize in swimming, where ye two tried the floods in your
pride, and boastfully risked your lives in the deep water from
presumption?   Nor could any man, friend or foe, prevent the
sorrowful journey; then ye two swam on the sea, where ye plied
the ocean streams with your arms, measured the sea paths,
threw aside the sea with your hands, glided over the surge; the
deep raged with its waves, with its wintry flood.   Seven nights
ye toiled in the power of the water; he outstripped thee in
swimming, had greater strength.   Then in the morning the sea
bore him to the land of the Heathoremes.[1]   Thence, dear to his
people, he sought his loved country, the land of the Brondings,
the fair stronghold, where he ruled over people, castle and rings.
The son of Beanstan in truth fulfilled all his pledge to thee.
Wherefore I expect a worse fate for thee, though everywhere
thou hast withstood battle rushes, grim war, if thou durst await
Grendel throughout the night near at hand.'

[1] Near the modern Oslo.

Beowulf spoke, son of Ecgtheow: 'Lo! thou hast spoken a great deal, friend Unferth, about Breca, drunken as thou art with beer; thou hast told of his journey. I count it as truth that I had greater might in the sea, hardships mid the waves, than any other man.

'We arranged that and made bold, while we were youths— we were both then still in our boyhood—that we two should risk our lives out on the sea; and thus we accomplished that. We held naked swords boldly in our hands when we swam in the ocean; we thought to protect ourselves against the whales. In no wise could he swim far from me on the waves of the flood, more quickly on the sea; I would not consent to leave him. Then we were together on the sea for the space of five nights till the flood forced us apart, the surging sea, coldest of storms, darkening night, and a wind from the north, battle-grim, came against us. Wild were the waves; the temper of the sea monsters was stirred. There did my shirt of mail hard-locked by hand stand me in good stead against foes; the woven battle garment, adorned with gold, lay on my breast. A hostile deadly foe drew me to the depths, had me firmly and fiercely in his grip; yet it was granted to me that I pierced the monster with my point, my battle spear. The rush of battle carried off the mighty sea monster by my hand.

X

'Thus oftentimes malicious foes pressed me hard. I served them with my good sword, as was fitting. They had not joy of their feasting, the evildoers, from devouring me, from sitting round the banquet near the bottom of the sea; but in the morning they were cast up on the shore, wounded with swords, laid low by blades, so that no longer they hindered seafarers on their voyage over the high flood. Light came from the east, bright beacon of God. The surges sank down, so that I could behold the sea-capes, the windy headlands. Fate often succours the undoomed warrior when his valour is strong.

'Yet it was my fortune to slay with the sword nine sea monsters. I have not heard under the arching sky of heaven of harder fighting by night, nor of a sorer pressed man in the streams of ocean. Yet I escaped with my life from the grasp of foes, weary of my venture. Then the sea bore me, the flood with its current, the stormy surges, to the land of the Finns.

'I have not heard such contests told of thee, terror of swords; never yet did Breca or either of you two in the play of battle perform so bold a deed with gleaming blades—I do not boast of the struggle—though thou camest to be the murderer of thy brother, thy near kinsman. For that thou must needs suffer damnation in hell, though thy wit is strong. Forsooth, I tell thee, son of Ecglaf, that Grendel, the fearful monster, had never achieved so many dread deeds against thy prince, malice on Heorot, if thy thoughts and mind had been as daring as thou thyself sayest. But he has found out that he need not sorely dread the feud, the terrible sword battle of your people, the victorious Scyldings; he takes pledges by force, he spares none of the Danish people, but he lives in pleasure, sleeps and feasts; he looks for no fight from the Spear-Danes. But soon now I shall show him battle, the might and courage of the Geats. He who may will go afterwards, brave to the mead, when the morning light of another day, the sun clothed with sky-like brightness, shines from the south over the children of men.'

Then glad was the giver of treasure, grey-haired and famed in battle; the prince of the Bright-Danes trusted in aid; the pro-tector of the people heard in Beowulf a resolute purpose. There was laughter of heroes; there were cheerful sounds; words were winsome.

Wealtheow went forth, Hrothgar's queen, mindful of what was fitting; gold-adorned, she greeted the warriors in hall; and the free-born woman first offered the goblet to the guardian of the East-Danes; bade him be of good cheer at the beer banquet, be dear to his people. He gladly took part in the banquet and received the hall-goblet, the king mighty in victory. Then the woman of the Helmings went about everywhere among old and young warriors, proffered the precious cup, till the time came that she, the ring-decked queen, noble-hearted, bore the mead-flagon to Beowulf. She greeted the prince of the Geats, wise in speech she thanked God that her wish had been fulfilled, that she might trust to some earl as a comfort in trouble. He, the warrior fierce in fight, took that goblet from Wealtheow, and then, ready for battle, uttered speech.

Beowulf spoke, son of Ecgtheow: 'That was my purpose when I launched on the ocean, embarked on the sea boat with the band of my warriors, that I should surely work the will of your people to the full, or fall a corpse fast in the foe's grip. I shall accom-plish deeds of heroic might, or endure my last day in the mead hall.'

Those words, the boasting speech of the Geat, pleased the woman well. Decked with gold, the free-born queen of the people went to sit by her prince. Then again as before there was excellent converse in hall, the warriors in happiness, the sound of victorious people, till all at once Healfdene's son was minded to seek his evening's rest. He knew that war was destined to the high hall by the monster after they could no longer see the light of the sun, and when, night growing dark over all, the shadowy creatures came stalking, black beneath the clouds. The troop all rose.

Then one warrior greeted the other, Hrothgar Beowulf, and wished him success, power over the wine hall, and spoke these words: 'Never before did I trust to any man, since I was able to lift hand and shield, the excellent hall of the Danes, except to thee now. Have now and hold the best of houses. Be mindful of fame, show a mighty courage, watch against foes. Nor shalt thou lack what thou desirest, if with thy life thou comest out from that heroic task.'

XI

Then Hrothgar went his way with his band of heroes, the protector of Scyldings out of the hall; the warlike king was minded to seek Wealtheow the queen for his bedfellow. The glorious king had, as men learned, set a hall guardian against Grendel; he performed a special task for the prince of the Danes, kept watch against the giant. Truly the prince of the Geats relied firmly on his fearless might, and the grace of the Lord. Then he laid aside his iron corslet, the helmet from his head, gave his ornamented sword, best of blades, to his servant, and bade him keep his war gear.

Then the valiant one, Beowulf of the Geats, spoke some words of boasting ere he lay down on his bed: 'I do not count myself less in war strength, in battle deeds, than Grendel does himself; wherefore I will not slay him, spoil him of life by sword, although I might. He knows not the use of weapons so as to strike at me, hew my shield, though he may be mighty in works of malice; but we two shall go without swords in the night, if he dare to seek war without weapons, and afterwards the wise God, the holy Lord, shall award fame to whatever side seems good to Him.' The bold warrior lay down, the earl's face touched the bolster; and round him many a mighty sea-hero bent to his couch in the hall. None of them thought that he should go thence and ever again seek the loved land, the people or stronghold where he was fostered; but they had heard that murderous death had ere now carried off far too many of Danish people in the wine hall. But the Lord gave them success in war, support and succour to the men of the Weders, so that through the strength of one, his own might, they all overcame their foe. The truth has been made known, that mighty God has ever ruled over mankind.

The shadowy visitant came stalking in the dark night. The warriors slept, who were to keep the antlered building, all save one. That was known to men that the ghostly enemy might not sweep them off among the shadows, for the Lord willed it not; but he, watching in anger against foes, awaited in wrathful mood the issue of the battle.

<h2 style="text-align:center">XII</h2>

Then from the moor under the misty cliffs came Grendel, he bore God's anger. The foul foe purposed to trap with cunning one of the men in the high hall; he went under the clouds till he might see most clearly the wine building, the gold hall of warriors, gleaming with plates of gold. That was not the first time he had sought Hrothgar's home; never in his life-days before or since did he find bolder heroes and hall-thanes. The creature came, bereft of joys, making his way to the building. Straightway the door, firm clasped by fire-hardened fetters, opened, when he touched it with his hands; then, pondering evil, he tore open the entry of the hall when he was enraged. Quickly after that the fiend trod the gleaming floor, moved angry in mood. A baleful light, like flame, flared from his eyes. He saw in the building many heroes, the troop of kinsmen sleeping together, the band of young warriors. Then his mind exulted. The dread monster purposed ere day came to part the life of each one from the body, for the hope of a great feasting filled him. No longer did fate will that after that night he might seize more of mankind. The kinsman of Hygelac, exceeding strong, beheld how the foul foe was minded to act with his sudden grips.

Nor did the monster think to delay, but first he quickly seized a sleeping warrior; suddenly tore him asunder, devoured his body, drank the blood from his veins, swallowed him with large bites. Straightway he had consumed all the body, even the feet and hands. He stepped forward nearer, laid hold with his hands of the resolute warrior on his couch; the fiend stretched his hand towards him. Beowulf met the attack quickly and propped himself on his arm. Forthwith the upholder of crime found that he had not met in the world, on the face of the earth among other men, a mightier handgrip. Fear grew in his mind and heart; yet in spite of that he could not make off. He sought to move out; he was minded to flee to his refuge, to seek the troop of devils. His task there was not such as he had found in former days.

Then the brave kinsman of Hygelac remembered his speech in the evening; he stood upright and seized him firmly. The fingers burst, the monster was moving out; the earl stepped forward. The famous one purposed to flee further, if only he might, and win away thence to the fen strongholds; he knew the might of his fingers was in the grip of his foe. That was an ill journey when the ravager came to Heorot. The warriors' hall resounded. Terror fell on all the Danes, on the castle-dwellers, on each of the bold men, on the earls. Wroth were they both, angry contestants for the house. The building rang aloud.

Then was it great wonder that the wine hall withstood the bold fighters; that it fell not to the ground, the fair earth-dwelling; but it was too firmly braced within and without with iron bands of skilled workmanship. There many a mead bench decked with gold bent away from the post, as I have heard, where the foemen fought. The wise men of the Scyldings looked not for that before, that any man could ever shatter it, rend it with malice in any way, excellent and bone-adorned as it was, unless the embrace of fire should swallow it in smoke. A sound arose, passing strange. Dread fear came upon each of the North-Danes who heard the cry from the wall, God's foe sounding a lament, a song of defeat; the hell-bound creature, crying out in his pain. He who was strongest in might among men at that time held him too closely.

XIII

The protector of earls was minded in no wise to release the deadly visitant alive, nor did he count his life as useful to any man.

There most eagerly this one and that of Beowulf's men brandished old swords, wished to save their leader's life, the famous prince, if only they could.   They did not know, when they were in the midst of the struggle, the stern warriors, and wished to strike on all sides, how to seek Grendel's life.   No choicest of swords on the earth, no war spear, would pierce the evil monster; but Beowulf had given up victorious weapons, all swords.   His parting from life at that time was doomed to be wretched, and the alien spirit was to travel far into the power of the fiends.

Then he who before in the joy of his heart had wrought much malice on mankind—he was hostile to God—found that his body would not follow him, for the brave kinsman of Hygelac held him by the hand.   Each was hateful to the other while he lived. The foul monster suffered pain in his body.   A great wound was seen in his shoulder, the sinews sprang apart, the body burst open.   Fame in war was granted to Beowulf.   Grendel must needs flee thence under the fen-cliffs mortally wounded, seek out his joyless dwelling.   He knew but too well the end of his life was come, the full count of his days.   The desire of all the Danes was fulfilled after the storm of battle.

Then he who erstwhile came from afar, shrewd and staunch, had cleansed the hall of Hrothgar, freed it from battle.   He rejoiced in the night-work, in heroic deeds.   The prince of the Geat warriors had fulfilled his boast to the East-Danes; likewise he cured all their sorrow and suffering, which they endured before and were forced to bear in distress, no slight wrong. That was a clear token when the bold warrior laid down the hand, the arm, and shoulder under the wide roof—it was all there together—the claw of Grendel.

XIV

Then in the morning, as I have heard, around the gift hall was many a warrior; leaders came from far and near throughout the wide ways to behold the wonder, the tracks of the monster. His going from life did not seem grievous to any man who saw the course of the inglorious one, how, weary in mind, beaten in battle, fated and fugitive, he left behind him on his way thence to the mere of the monsters marks of his life blood.   There the water was surging with blood, the foul welter of waves all mingled with hot gore; it boiled with the blood of battle.   The death-doomed one dived in, then bereft of joy in his fen refuge he laid down his life, his heathen soul, there hell received him. Thence again old comrades went, also many a young man, from the joyous journey, brave men riding on horses from the mere, warriors on shining steeds. There Beowulf's fame was proclaimed. Oftentimes many a one said that neither south nor north between the seas, over the wide earth, under the vault of the sky, was there any better among warriors, more worthy of a kingdom. Nor in truth did they blame their friendly lord, gracious Hrothgar, for that was a good king.

At times the men doughty in battle let their chestnut horses run, race against one another, where the land-ways seemed fair to them, known for their good qualities; at times the king's thane, a man proud of exploits, mindful of treasures, he who remembered a great number of the old tales, made a new story of things that were true. The man began again wisely to frame Beowulf's exploit and skilfully to make deft measures, to deal in words. He spoke all that he had heard told of Sigemund's mighty deeds, much that was unknown, the warfare of the son of Wæls, the far journeys, the hostility and malice of which the children of men knew not at all, except Fitela who was with him when he was minded to say somewhat of such things, the uncle to his nephew; for they were always in every struggle comrades in need. They had felled with their swords very many of the race of giants. There sprang up for Sigemund after his death no little fame when the man bold in battle killed the dragon, the guardian of the treasure. Under the grey stone he ventured alone, the son of a chieftain, on the daring deed; Fitela was not with him. Yet it was granted to him that that sword pierced the monstrous dragon, so that it stood in the wall, the noble blade. The dragon died violently. The hero had brought it to pass by his valour that he could use the ring-hoard as he chose. The son of Wæls loaded the sea boat, bore to the ship's bosom the bright ornaments. The dragon melted in heat.

He was by far the most famous of adventurers among men, protector of warriors by mighty deeds; he prospered by that earlier, when the boldness, the strength, and the courage of Heremod lessened.[1] He[2] was betrayed among the Eotens into the power of his enemies, quickly driven out. Surges of sorrow pressed him too long; he became a deadly grief to his people, to all his chieftains. So also many a wise man who trusted to him as a remedy for evils lamented in former times the valiant one's

---

[1] The meaning seems to be that as Heremod lost fame through his cruelty Sigemund surpassed him in reputation. Heremod is a Danish king; he is mentioned here and later in the poem as an example of all that a hero should not be.　　　　　　　　　　　　　　　　[2] Heremod.

journey, that the prince's son was destined to prosper, inherit his father's rank, rule over the people, the treasure and the prince's fortress, the kingdom of heroes, the land of the Scyldings. There did he, the kinsman of Hygelac, become dearer to all men and to his friends than he. Evil possessed him.[1]

At times in rivalry they measured the streets of brown sand with their horses. Then the light of morning had quickly mounted up. Many a retainer went bold-minded to the high hall to behold the rare wonder; the king himself also, the keeper of ring-treasures, came glorious from his wife's chamber, famed for his virtues, with a great troop, and his queen with him measured the path to the mead hall with a band of maidens.

XV

Hrothgar spoke—he went to the hall, stood on the doorstep, looked on the lofty gold-plated roof and Grendel's hand—'For this sight thanks be straightway rendered to the Almighty. I suffered much that was hateful, sorrows at the hands of Grendel; ever may God, the glorious Protector, perform wonder after wonder.

'That was not long since when I looked not ever to find solace for any of my woes, when the best of houses stood blood-stained, gory from battle; woe widespread among all councillors who had no hope of ever protecting the fortress of warriors against foes, against demons, and evil spirits. Now the warrior has performed the deed through the Lord's might which formerly all of us could not contrive with our cunning. Lo! a woman who has borne such a son among the peoples, if she yet lives, may indeed say that the ancient Lord was gracious to her in the birth of her son. Now I will love thee in my heart as my son, Beowulf, best of men; keep well the new kinship. Thou shalt lack none of the things thou desirest in the world which I can command. Full often have I for less cause bestowed reward on a slighter warrior, a weaker in combat, to honour him with treasures. Thou hast brought it to pass for thyself by deeds that thy glory shall live for ever. The All-Ruler reward thee with good things as He has done till now.'

Beowulf spoke, son of Ecgtheow: 'We accomplished that heroic deed, that battle, through great favour. We risked ourselves boldly against the might of the monster. I had rather

[1] Heremod.

that thou couldst have seen him, the fiend in his trappings, weary unto death. I thought to bind him speedily with strong clasps on his deathbed, so that he must needs lie in his death-agony by my handgrip, unless his body should slip away. I could not, since the Lord willed it not, prevent his passing out. I did not hold him closely enough, the deadly enemy; the foe was too mighty in going. Nevertheless, to save his life he left his hand, arm, and shoulder to serve as a token of his flight. Yet the wretched creature won no solace there; no longer lives the malicious foe pressed by sins, but pain has embraced him closely with hostile grasp, with ruinous bonds. There the creature stained with sin must needs await the great doom, what judgment the bright Lord will award him.'

Then the son of Ecglaf was a more silent man in boasting of war deeds, when the chieftains beheld by the strength of the earl the hand, the fingers of the monster, stretching up to the high roof; each at its tip, each of the strong nails, was like steel, the claw of the heathen fighter, horrible, monstrous. Everyone said that no well-tried sword of brave men would wound him, would shorten the monster's bloody battle fist.

XVI

Then it was quickly commanded that Heorot should be decked within with hands. There were many there, men and women, who made ready the wine building, the guest hall. Woven hangings gleamed, gold-adorned, on the walls, many wondrous sights for all men who look on such things. That bright building was all sorely shattered, though firm within with its iron clasps; its door hinges burst. The roof alone survived all scatheless, when the monster stained with evil deeds turned in fight, despairing of life. That is not easy to avoid—let him do it who will—but he must needs seek the place forced on him by necessity, prepared for all who bear souls, for the children of men, for the dwellers on earth, where his body sleeps after the banquet fast in its narrow bed.

Then was the time convenient and fitting that Healfdene's son should go to the hall; the king himself wished to join in the banquet. I have not heard of a people who showed a nobler bearing with a greater troop about their giver of treasure. The famous ones then sat down on the bench, rejoiced in the feast; in seemly fashion they took many a mead goblet; brave-minded

kinsmen were in the high hall, Hrothgar and Hrothulf.   Heorot
within was filled with friends.   Not yet at this time had the
Scyldings practised treachery.[1]

The son of Healfdene gave then to Beowulf a golden ensign
as a reward for victory, an ornamented banner with a handle, a
helmet and corslet, a famous precious sword.   Many saw them
borne before the warrior.   Beowulf took the goblet in hall;
he needed not to be ashamed in front of the warriors of the
bestowing of gifts.

I have not heard of many men giving to others on the ale
bench in more friendly fashion four treasures decked with gold.
Around the top of the helmet a jutting ridge twisted with wires
held guard over the head, so that many an old sword, proved
hard in battle, could not sorely injure him, when the shield-
bearing warrior was destined to go against foes.   Then the
protector of earls commanded eight horses with gold-plated
bridles to be led into the hall, into the house; on one of them lay
a saddle artfully adorned, decked with costly ornament.   That
was the war seat of the noble king, when the son of Healfdene
was minded to practise sword-play.   Never did the bravery of
the far-famed man fail in the van when corpses were falling.
Then the protector of the friends of Ing [2] gave power over both
to Beowulf, over horses and weapons; he bade him use them well.
Thus manfully did the famous prince, the treasure-keeper of
heroes, reward the rushes of battle with steeds and rich stores,
so that he who wishes to speak truth in seemly fashion will never
scoff at them.

XVII

Further the lord of earls bestowed treasure on the mead bench,
ancient blades, to each of those who travelled the ocean path with
Beowulf; and he bade recompense to be made with gold for the
one whom Grendel before murderously killed.   So he was
minded to do with more of them, if wise God and the man's
courage had not turned aside such a fate from them.   The Lord
ruled over all mankind as He still does.   Wherefore under-
standing, forethought of soul, is everywhere best.   He who

[1] Hrothulf, as we know from Scandinavian sources, later proved a traitor.
He deposed and slew Hrethric, and was himself slain by Heoroweard.   His
hall was burnt over his head.   The phrase ('surges of battle, of hostile fire')
in Section ii probably refers to this family feud.
[2] Ing was a Danish king.   'The friends of Ing' means the Danes.

sojourns long in the world in these days of strife must needs suffer much of weal and woe.

There was song and music mingled before Healfdene's chieftain; the harp was touched; a measure often recited at such times as it fell to Hrothgar's minstrel to proclaim joy in hall along the mead bench. Hnæf of the Scyldings, a hero of the Half-Danes, was fated to fall in the Frisian battle-field when the sudden onslaught came upon them, the sons of Finn. 'Nor in truth had Hildeburh cause to praise the faith of the Eotens; sinless, she was spoiled of her dear ones at the shield-play, a son and a brother; wounded with the spear, they fell in succession. She was a sorrowing woman. Not without cause did the daughter of Hoc lament her fate, when morning came when she might see the slaughter of kinsmen under the sky. Where erstwhile he had had greatest joy in the world, war carried off all the thanes of Finn except a very few, so that in no wise could he offer fight to Hengest in the battle-field, nor protect by war the sad survivors from the prince's thane; but they offered them conditions, that they would give up to them entirely another building, the hall and high seat; that they might have power over half of it with the men of the Eotens, and that the son of Folc-walda would honour the Danes each day with gifts at the bestowal of presents, would pay respect to Hengest's troop with rings, just as much as he would encourage the race of the Frisians in the beer hall with ornaments of plated gold. Then on both sides they had faith in firm-knit peace. Finn swore to Hengest deeply, inviolably with oaths, that he would treat the sad survivors honourably according to the judgment of the councillors, that no man there should break the bond by word or deed, nor should they ever mention it in malice, although they had followed the slayer of their giver of rings after they had lost their leader, since the necessity was laid upon them; if then any one of the Frisians should recall to mind by dangerous speech the deadly hostility, then must the edge of the sword settle it.

'The oath was sworn and rich gold taken from the treasure. The best of the heroes of the warlike Scyldings was ready on the funeral fire. On that pyre the blood-stained shirt of mail was plain to see, the swine-image all gold, the boar hard as iron, many a chieftain slain with wounds. Many had fallen in the fight. Then Hildeburh bade her own son to be given over to the flames at Hnæf's pyre, his body to be burned and placed on the funeral fire. The woman wept, sorrowing by his side; she lamented in measures. The warrior mounted up. The greatest of funeral fires wound up to the clouds, it roared in front of the mound. Heads melted, wounds burst open, while blood gushed forth from the gashes in the bodies. The fire, greediest of spirits, consumed all those of both peoples whom war carried off there. Their mightiest men had departed.

XVIII

'The warriors went then, bereft of friends, to visit the dwellings, to see the land of the Frisians, the homes, and the stronghold. Then Hengest dwelt yet in peace with Finn, though very unhappily, for a winter stained with the blood of the slain; he thought of his land though he could not drive the ring-prowed ship on the sea (the ocean surged with storm, rose up against the wind; winter bound the waves with fetters of ice), till another year came into the dwellings; as those still do now who ever await an opportunity, the bright clear weather. Then winter was past; the bosom of the earth was fair; the exile purposed to depart, the guest out of the castle; he thought rather of vengeance for sorrow than of the sea journey, if he could bring the battle to pass in which he might show he remembered the sons of the Eotens. So he let things take their course when Hunlafing laid in his bosom the gleaming sword, best of blades. Its edges were famed among the Eotens. Even so did deadly death by the sword come upon brave Finn in his own home, when Guthlaf and Oslaf after their sea journey sorrowfully lamented the grim attack; they were wroth at their manifold woes; their restless spirit could not be ruled in their breast. Then was the hall reddened with corpses of foes, Finn slain likewise, the king mid his troop, and the queen taken. The warriors of the Scyldings bore to the ships all the house treasure of the king of the land, whatever they could find at Finn's home of ornaments and jewels. They bore away on the sea voyage the noble woman to the Danes, led her to her people.' [1]

The song was sung, the gleeman's measure. Joy rose again, bench music rang out clear, servants gave out wine from

[1] From this passage and from the fragment of the Old English poem on the subject (*Finnesburh*) it is not easy to make out all the details of the story of Finn. Finn is King of the Frisians, who may or may not be the same as the Eotens. He quarrels with Hnæf, the brother of his Danish wife Hildeburh. Hnæf is killed, and so is Hildeburh's son. Finn and Hengest, who commands the Danes after Hnæf's death, agree to a peace. The winter passes; in the spring more Danes arrive, led apparently by Guthlaf and Oslaf. Vengeance is taken on Finn, and Hildeburh is carried back to her people.

wondrous goblets. Then Wealtheow, under her golden circlet, came forth where the two valiant ones were sitting, uncle and nephew. At that time there was peace yet between them, each true to the other. Likewise Unferth sat there as a squire at the feet of the prince of the Scyldings. Each of them trusted his heart, that he had a noble mind, though he had not been faithful to his kinsmen at the play of swords. Then spoke the queen of the Scyldings: 'Receive this goblet, my prince, giver of treasure. Rejoice, gold friend of warriors, and speak to the Geats with kindly words, as it is fitting to do. Be gracious to the Geats, mindful of gifts; far and near now thou hast peace. They said that thou wast minded to take the warrior for son. Heorot is cleansed, the bright ring hall; be generous with many rewards while thou mayst, and leave to thy kinsmen subjects and kingdom, when thou must needs go forth to face thy destiny. I know my gracious Hrothulf, that he will treat the young men honourably, if thou, friend of the Scyldings, pass from the world before him. I think that he will richly reward our children, if he forgets not all the favours we formerly showed him for his pleasure and honour, while he was still a child.' [1]

She turned then towards the bench where her sons were, Hrethric and Hrothmund, and the sons of heroes, the young men together; there the valiant one, Beowulf of the Geats, sat by the two brothers.

XIX

To him was the flagon borne and a friendly invitation offered with words and the twisted gold vessel graciously presented; two bracelets, a corselet and rings, greatest of necklaces, of those which I have heard of on earth.

I have not heard of a better treasure-hoard of heroes under the sky since Hama carried off to the gleaming castle the necklace of the Brosings, the trinket and treasure; he fled the malicious hostility of Eormenric; [2] he chose everlasting gain. [3] Hygelac of the Geats, grandson of Swerting, had the ring on his last

[1] See note on Hrothulf in Section xvi.
[2] Eormenric or Ermanaric died about A.D 375. He became a famous figure in romance and legend (see *Widsith* and *Deor's Lament*). The necklace of the Brosings is celebrated in Scandinavian literature. Hama appears in many books but may not be historical; he is referred to in *Widsith*.
[3] The meaning of this is uncertain. It may mean 'he died,' or 'he entered a monastery.'

expedition, when beneath his banner he defended the treasure, guarded the booty of battle. Fate took him off, when in his pride he suffered misfortune in fight against the Frisians; the mighty prince bore the ornament, the precious stones over the sea; he fell under his shield. Then the king's body passed into the power of the Franks, his breast garments and the ring also; less noble warriors stripped the bodies of the men of the Geats after the carnage of war; their bodies covered the battle-field.[1] The hall rang with shouts of approval.

Wealtheow spoke, she uttered words before the troop: 'Enjoy this ring happily, dear young Beowulf; and use this corslet, the great treasures, and prosper exceedingly; make thyself known mightily, and be to these youths kindly in counsel. I will not forget thy reward for that. Thou hast brought it about that far and near men ever praise thee, even as far as the sea hems in the home of the winds, the headlands. Blessed be thou while thou livest, nobly born man. I will grant thee many treasures. Be thou gracious in deeds to my son, thou who art now in happiness. Here each earl is true to the other, gentle in mind, loyal to the lord. The thanes are willing, the people all ready, noble warriors after drinking. Do as I ask.'

She went then to the seat. There was the choicest of banquets; the men drank wine; they knew not fate, dread destiny, as it had been dealt out to many of the earls. Afterwards came evening, and Hrothgar went to his chamber, the mighty one to his couch. A great band of earls occupied the hall, as they often did before; they cleared away bench-boards; it was spread over with beds and bolsters. One of the revellers, ready and fated, sank to his couch in the hall. At their heads they placed the war shields, the bright bucklers. There on the bench was plainly seen above the chieftains the helmet rising high in battle, the ringed corslet, the mighty spear. It was their custom that often both at home and in the field they should be ready for war, and equally in both positions at all such times as distress came upon their lord. Those people were good.

[1] Hygelac's expedition against the Frisians, here referred to, belongs to authentic history. Gregory of Tours (d. 594) tells how the Danes under their king Chlochilaicus invaded the kingdom and carried many captives and much plunder to their ships. Chlochilaicus, delaying on shore, was killed by the Franks, who defeated the Danes in a naval battle and recovered the booty. Chlochilaicus of the Danes is the same person as Hygelac of the Geats. These events took place between 512 and 520. There are three other references in *Beowulf* to the expedition—Sections xxxiii, xxxv, and xl.

XX

They sank then to sleep. One sorely paid for his evening rest, as had full often come to pass for them, when Grendel held the gold-hall, and did wickedness until the end came, death after sins. That was seen, widely known among men, that an avenger, Grendel's mother, a she-monster, yet survived the hateful one, a long while after the misery of war. She who was doomed to dwell in the dread water, the cold streams, after Cain killed his only brother, his father's son, forgot not her misery. He departed then fated, marked with murder, to flee from the joys of men; he dwelt in the wilderness. Thence sprang many fated spirits; Grendel was one of them, a hateful fierce monster; he found at Heorot a man keeping watch, waiting for war. There the monster came to grips with him: yet he remembered the power of his strength, the precious gift which God gave him, and he trusted for support, for succour and help, to Him who rules over all. By that he overcame the fiend, laid low the spirit of hell. Then he departed, the foe of mankind, in misery, reft of joy, to seek his death-dwelling. And his mother then still purposed to go on the sorrowful journey, greedy and darkly minded, to avenge her son's death.

She came then to Heorot where the Ring-Danes slept through-out that hall. Then straightway the old fear fell on the earls there, when Grendel's mother forced her way in. The dread was less by just so much as the strength of women, the war terror of a woman, is less than a man's, when the bound sword shaped by the hammer, the blood-stained blade strong in its edges, cuts off the boar-image on the foeman's helmet. Then in the hall was the strong blade drawn, the sword over the seats; many a broad buckler raised firmly in hand. He thought not of helmet nor of broad corslet, when the terror seized him.

She was in haste, was minded to go thence and save her life when she was discovered. Quickly she had seized one of the chieftains with firm grip; then she went to the fen. That was the dearest of heroes to Hrothgar among his followers between the seas, a mighty shield-warrior, whom she slew on his couch, a noble man of great fame. Beowulf was not there, but another lodging had been set apart for him earlier, after the giving of treasure to the famous Geat. There was clamour in Heorot. She had carried off the famous blood-stained hand. Care was created anew, brought to pass in the dwellings. That was no good bargain which they had to pay for in double measure with lives of friends. Then the wise king, the grey battle warrior, was troubled in heart, when he knew that the noble thane was lifeless, that the dearest one was dead.

Beowulf was quickly brought to the castle, the victorious warrior. At dawn that earl, the noble hero himself with his comrades, went to where the wise man was waiting to see whether the All-Ruler would ever bring to pass a change after the time of woe. Then the man famous in fight went with his nearest followers along the floor (the hall wood resounded) till he greeted the wise one with words, the prince of the friends of Ing; he asked if, as he hoped, he had had a peaceful night.

<h2 style="text-align:center">XXI</h2>

Hrothgar spoke, protector of the Scyldings: 'Ask thou not after happiness. Sorrow is made anew for the Danish people. Æschere is dead, Yrmenlaf's elder brother, my counsellor and my adviser, trusted friend, in such times as we fended our heads in war, when the foot-warriors crashed together and hewed the helms. Such should an earl be, a trusty chieftain, as Æschere was.

'That disturbed slaughterous spirit slew him with her hands in Heorot. I know not whither the monster, made known by her feasting, journeyed back exulting in the corpse. She avenged the fight in which last night thou didst violently kill Grendel with hard grips because too long he lessened and slew my people. He fell in combat, guilty of murder, and now another mighty evil foe has come; she was minded to make requital for her son, and she has heavily avenged the hostile deed, as it may seem to many a thane who grieves in mind for the giver of treasure with heavy heart-sorrow. Now low lies the hand which was ready for all your desires.

'I heard dwellers in the land, my people, counsellors in hall, say that they saw two such great march-steppers, alien spirits, hold the moors. One of them was, as far as they could certainly know, the likeness of a woman; the other wretched creature trod the paths of exile in man's shape, except that he was greater than any other man. Him in days past the dwellers in the land named Grendel; his father they know not; nor whether there were born to him earlier any dark spirits.

'They possess unknown land, wolf-cliffs, windy crags, a

dangerous fen path, where the mountain stream falls down under the darkness of the rocks, a flood under the earth. That is not a mile hence where the mere stands; over it hang rime-covered groves; the wood firm-rooted overshadows the water. There each night a baleful wonder may be seen, a fire on the flood. There is none so wise of the children of men who knows those depths. Though the heath-stepper hard pressed by the hounds, the hart strong in antlers, should seek the forest after a long chase, rather does he yield up his life, his spirit on the shore, than hide his head there. That is an eerie place. Thence the surge of waves mounts up dark to the clouds, when the wind stirs up hostile storms till the air darkens, the skies weep.

'Now once more help must come from thee alone. Thou dost not yet know the lair, the dangerous place, where thou mayest find the sinful creature; seek if thou darest. If thou comest away alive, I will reward thee for that onslaught, as erst-while I did, with treasures, old precious things, twisted gold.'

XXII

Beowulf spoke, son of Ecgtheow: 'Sorrow not, wise warrior. It is better for each to avenge his friend than greatly to mourn. Each of us must needs await the end of life in the world; let him who can achieve fame ere death. That is best for a noble warrior when life is over. Rise up, guardian of the realm; let us go quickly hence to behold the track of Grendel's kinswoman. I promise thee she shall not escape under covering darkness, nor in the earth's embrace, nor in the mountain forest, nor in the water's depths—go where she will. Have thou, as I expect from thee, patience for all thy woes this day.'

The aged one leaped up then; thanked God, the mighty Lord, for what the man spoke. Then Hrothgar's horse was bitted, the steed with twisted mane. The wise prince went forth in splendour; the foot-troop of shield-bearing warriors stepped forward. The tracks were wisely seen along the forest paths, the course over the fields. Away over the dark moor she went; she bore the best of thanes, reft of life, who with Hrothgar ruled the land. Then the son of princes strode over the high rocky cliffs, the narrow paths, the straitened tracks, the unknown road, the steep crags, many a monster's abode. He with a few other wise men went ahead to spy out the land, until suddenly he found the mountain trees, the dreary wood hanging above the

grey rock. The water beneath lay blood-stained and troubled.
All the Danes, the friends of the Scyldings, were mournful in
mood; many a thane had to suffer; there was sorrow for all of the
earls, when they found Æschere's head on the cliff by the mere.

The flood surged with blood, with hot gore; the people beheld
it. At times the horn sang its eager war song. The troop all
sat down; then they saw along the water many of the dragon
kind, strange sea-dragons moving over the mere, also monsters
lying on the rocky headlands; such as those who in the morning
often go on a perilous journey on the sail road, dragons and wild
beasts. They fell away bitter and angered; they heard the clang,
the war horn sounding. The prince of the Geats with his bow
parted one of them from life, from the struggle of the waves, so
that the stout war-shaft stood in his heart. He was the more
sluggish at swimming in the water, because death carried him off.
Speedily the wondrous wave-dweller was hard pressed in the
waves with boar spears of deadly barbs, beset by hostile attacks
and drawn out on the headland. The men beheld the dread
creature.

Beowulf clad himself in warrior's armour; he lamented not his
life. The war corslet, hand-woven, broad, cunningly adorned,
must needs try the water; it knew how to guard his body so that
the grip of war might not wound his heart, the malicious clutch
of an angry foe his life. And the gleaming helmet, which was to
mingle with the depths of the mere, to seek the welter of the
waves, decked with treasure, circled with diadems, as the smith
of weapons wrought it in days long past, wondrously adorned it,
set it round with boar-images, guarded his head so that no sword
or battle blades could pierce it. That was not the least then of
mighty helps that Hrothgar's squire lent him in his need. That
hilted sword was called Hrunting; it was an excellent old
treasure; the brand was iron, marked with poisonous twigs,[1]
hardened in the blood of battle. It never failed any men in war
who seized it with their hands, who ventured to go on dire
journeys, to the meeting-place of foes. That was not the first
time that it was to accomplish a mighty deed.

In truth the son of Ecglaf mighty in strength did not remember
what erstwhile he spoke when drunken with wine, when he lent
the weapon to a better sword warrior. He himself durst not
risk his life beneath the tossing of the waves, accomplish heroic
deeds. There he forfeited fame, repute for might. Not so was
it with the other when he had clad himself for war.

[1] The markings on the sword had been made by the use of acid.

XXIII

Beowulf spoke, son of Ecgtheow: 'Consider now, famous son of Healfdene, wise prince, gold-friend of warriors, now I am ready for the venture, what we spoke of awhile since; if I should depart from life in thy cause, that thou shouldst ever be in the place of a father when I am gone. Be thou a guardian to my followers, my comrades, if war takes me. Likewise, dear Hrothgar, do thou send the treasures thou hast given me to Hygelac. The lord of the Geats may then perceive by that gold, the son of Hrethel may see when he looks upon that treasure, that I found an excellent good giver of rings, that I took joy while I could. And do thou let Unferth have the ancient blade, the far-famed man have the precious sword with wavy pattern and sharp edge; I shall achieve fame for myself with Hrunting, or death will carry me off.'

After those words the prince of the Weder-Geats hastened exceedingly; he would in no wise wait for an answer. The surge of waters received the war hero. Then there was a spell of time ere he might behold the bottom of the mere.

She who had held for fifty years the domain of the floods, eager for battle, grim and greedy, discovered straightway that a man was seeking from above the dwelling of monsters. She reached out against him then, seized the warrior with dread claws; nevertheless she injured not the sound body; the ring-mail guarded it round about so that she could not pierce the corslet, the locked mail-shirt, with hostile fingers. When she came to the bottom, the sea-wolf bore the prince of rings to her lair, so that he could not (yet was he brave) use weapons; and too many monsters set upon him in the water, many a sea beast rent his war corslet with battle-tusks; they pursued the hero. Then the earl noticed he was in some kind of hostile hall, where no water in any way touched him, nor could the sudden clutch of the flood come near him because of the roofed hall; he saw the light of fire, a gleaming radiance shining brightly.

Then the valiant one perceived the she-wolf of the depths, the mighty mere-woman; he repaid the mighty rush with the battle sword; the hand drew not back from the stroke, so that the sword, adorned with rings, sang a greedy war chant on her head. Then the stranger found that the sword would not bite or injure life, but the edge failed the prince in his need. It had endured in times past many battles, often had cut through the

helmet, the mail of a doomed man. That was the first time for
the costly treasure that its repute failed.

Once again the kinsman of Hygelac was resolute, mindful of
heroic deeds, no whit lax in courage. Then the angry warrior
cast down the sword with its twisted ornaments, set round with
decorations, so that it lay on the ground, strong and steel-edged.
He trusted in his strength, his mighty handgrip. Thus a man
must needs do when he is minded to gain lasting praise in war,
nor cares for his life.

Then the prince of the War-Geats seized Grendel's mother
by the hair; he feared not the fight. Then stern in strife he
swung the monster in his wrath so that she bent to the ground.
She quickly gave him requital again with savage grips, and
grasped out towards him. Weary in mood then she overthrew
the strongest of fighters, the foot-warrior, so that he fell down.
Then she sat on the visitor to her hall, and drew her knife, broad
and bright-edged; she was minded to avenge her child, her only
son. The woven breast net lay on his shoulder; that guarded
his life; it opposed the entrance of point and edge. Then the
son of Ecgtheow, the hero of the Geats, would have found death
under the wide waters if the war corslet, the stout battle net, had
not afforded him help, and if holy God, the wise Lord, had not
achieved victory in war; the Ruler of the heavens brought about
a right issue with ease, when once more he stood up.

XXIV

He saw then among weapons a victorious blade, an old sword
of giants, strong in its edges, the glory of warriors. That was
the choicest of weapons; save only it was greater than any other
man could bear to the battle-play, trusty and splendid, the work
of giants. The hero of the Scyldings, angered and grim in
battle, seized the belted hilt, wheeled the ring-marked sword,
despairing of life; he struck furiously, so that it gripped her hard
against the neck. It broke the bone-rings; the blade went
straight through the doomed body. She fell on the floor. The
brand was bloody; the man rejoiced in his work.

The gleam was bright, the light stood within, just as the candle
of the sky shines serenely from heaven. He went along the
dwelling; then he turned to the wall; Hygelac's thane, raging
and resolute, raised the weapon firmly by its hilts. The sword
was not useless to the warrior, but he was minded quickly to

requite Grendel for the many onslaughts which far more than once he made on the West-Danes, when he slew Hrothgar's hearth companions in their sleep, devoured fifteen men of the Danish people while they slumbered, and bore away as many more, a hateful sacrifice. He, the furious hero, avenged that upon him there where he saw Grendel lying, weary of war, reft of life, as erstwhile the battle at Heorot dispatched him. The body gaped wide, when after death it suffered a stroke, a hard battle-blow: and then he hewed off its head.

Straightway the wise men who gazed on the mere with Hrothgar saw that the surge of waves was all troubled, the water stained with blood. Grey-haired old men spoke together of the valiant man, that they did not expect to see the chieftain again, or that he should come as a conqueror to seek the famous prince. Then it seemed to many that the sea-wolf had slain him. Then came the ninth hour of the day. The bold Scyldings forsook the headland; thence the gold-friend of men departed homewards. The strangers sat sick at heart, and stared at the mere; they felt desire and despair of seeing their friendly lord himself.

Then that sword, the battle-brand, began to vanish in drops of gore after the blood shed in fight. That was a great wonder, that it all melted like ice when the Father loosens the bond of the frost, unbinds the fetters of the floods; He has power over times and seasons. That is the true Lord.

The prince of the Weder-Geats took no more of the precious hoardings in those haunts, though he saw many there, save the head and with it the treasure-decked hilts. The sword had melted before, the inlaid brand had burned away, so hot was that blood and so poisonous the alien spirit who died in it. Straightway he fell to swimming; he, who before in the struggle survived the fall of foes, dived up through the water. The wave-surges were all cleansed, the great haunts where the alien spirit gave up his life and this fleeting state.

Then the protector of seamen, brave-minded, came swimming to land; he took pleasure in the sea booty, in the mighty burden which he bore with him. They went to meet him, the excellent troop of thanes; they thanked God; they rejoiced in the prince, that they could behold him safe and sound. Then helm and corslet were loosed with speed from off the brave man; the lake lay still, the water under the clouds, stained with the blood of battle.

They set out thence on the foot-tracks, joyous at heart; they paced the path, the well-known street. Men nobly bold bore the head from the cliff with toil for each of the very brave ones. Four men with difficulty had to carry Grendel's head to the gold-hall on the battle spear, until of a sudden the fourteen brave warlike Geats came to the hall; their lord trod the fields about the mead hall with them, fearless among his followers.

Then the prince of thanes, the man bold in deeds, made glorious with fame, the hero terrible in battle, came in to greet Hrothgar. Then Grendel's head was borne by the hair into the hall where the men were drinking—a dread object for the earls and the queen with them; the men looked at the wondrous sight.

XXV

Beowulf spoke, son of Ecgtheow: 'Lo! son of Healfdene, prince of the Scyldings, we have brought thee with pleasure, as a token of glory, these sea trophies which thou beholdest here. Scarcely did I survive that with my life, the struggle beneath the water, barely did I accomplish the task, the fight was all but ended, if God had not protected me.

'I could do naught with Hrunting in the fight, though that weapon is worthy, but the Ruler of men vouchsafed that I should see a huge old sword hang gleaming on the wall—most often He has guided those bereft of friends—so that I swung the weapon. Then in the struggle I slew the guardians of the house when the chance was given me. Then that battle-brand, the inlaid sword, burned away as soon as the blood spurted out, hottest battle gore. Thence from the foes I carried off that hilt; I avenged, as was fitting, the deeds of malice, the massacre of the Danes.

'So I promise thee that thou mayest sleep in Heorot, free from sorrow with the band of thy warriors and all the thanes among thy people, the youths and veterans; that thou, prince of the Scyldings, dost not need to dread death for the earls from the quarter thou didst formerly.'

Then the gold hilt, the ancient work of giants, was given into the hands of the old warrior, the grey-haired leader. It came into the possession of the prince of the Danes, the work of cunning smiths, after the death of the monsters, and after the creature of hostile heart, God's foe, guilty of murder, and his mother also had left this world. It came into the power of the best of mighty kings between the seas who dealt out money in Scandinavia.

Hrothgar spoke; he beheld the hilt, the old heirloom. On

it was written the beginning of a battle of long ago, when a flood, a rushing sea, slew the race of giants; they had lived boldly; that race was estranged from the eternal Lord. The Ruler gave them final requital for that in the surge of the water. Thus on the plates of bright gold it was clearly marked, set down and expressed in runic letters, for whom that sword, the best of blades, was first wrought with its twisted haft and snake-images.

Then the wise man spoke, the son of Healfdene. All were silent. 'Lo! he who achieves truth and right among the people may say that this earl was born excellent (the old ruler of the realm recalls all things from the past). Thy renown is raised up throughout the wide ways, my friend Beowulf, among all peoples. Thou preservest all steadfastly, thy might with wisdom of mind. I shall show thee my favour, as before we agreed. Thou shalt be granted for long years as a solace to thy people, as a help to heroes.

'Not so did Heremod prove to the sons of Ecgwela,[1] the honourable Scyldings; his way was not as they wished, but to the slaughter and butchery of the people of the Danes. Savage in mood he killed his table companions, his trusty counsellors, until he, the famous prince, departed alone from the joys of men, although mighty God had made him great by the joys of power, and by strength had raised him above all men. Yet there grew in his heart a bloodthirsty brood of thoughts. He gave out no rings to the Danes according to custom; joyless he dwelt, so that he reaped the reward of his hostility, the long evil to his people. Learn thou by this; lay hold on virtue. I have spoken this for thy good from the wisdom of many years.

'It is wonderful to tell how mighty God with His generous thought bestows on mankind wisdom, land, and rank. He has dominion over all things. At times He allows man's thoughts to turn to love of famous lineage; He gives him in his land the joys of domain, the stronghold of men to keep. He puts the parts of the world, a wide kingdom, in such subjection to him that he cannot in his folly conceive an end to that. He lives in plenty; nothing afflicts him, neither sickness nor age; nor does sorrow darken his mind, nor does strife anywhere show forth sword hatred, but all the world meets his desire.

[1] Ecgwela was apparently a king of the Danes.

XXVI

'He knows nothing worse till within him his pride grows and springs up. Then the guardian slumbers, the keeper of the soul—the sleep is too heavy—pressed round with troubles; the murderer very near who shoots maliciously from his bow. Then he is stricken in the breast under the helmet by a sharp shaft—he knows not how to guard himself—by the crafty evil commands of the ill spirit. That which he had long held seems to him too paltry, he covets fiercely, he bestows no golden rings in generous pride, and he forgets and neglects the destiny which God, the Ruler of glory, formerly gave him, his share of honours. At the end it comes to pass that the mortal body sinks into ruin, falls doomed; another comes to power who bestows treasures gladly, old wealth of the earl; he takes joy in it. Keep thyself from such passions, dear Beowulf, best of warriors, and choose for thyself that better part, lasting profit. Care not for pride, famous hero. Now the repute of thy might endures for a space; straightway shall age, or edge of the sword, part thee again from thy strength, or the embrace of fire, or the surge of the flood, or the grip of the blade, or the flight of the spear, or hateful old age, or the gleam of eyes shall pass away and be darkened; on a sudden it shall come to pass that death shall vanquish thee, noble warrior.

'Thus have I ruled over the Ring-Danes under the heavens for fifty years, and guarded them by my war power from many tribes throughout this world, from spears and swords, so that I thought I had no foe under the stretch of the sky. Lo! a reverse came upon me in my land, sorrow after joy, when Grendel grew to be a foe of many years, my visitant. I suffered great sorrow of heart continually from that persecution. Thanks be to God, the eternal Lord, that I have survived with my life, that I behold with my eyes that blood-stained head after the old struggle. Go now to the seat, enjoy the banquet, thou who art made illustrious by war; very many treasures shall be parted between us when morning comes.'

The Geat was glad in mind; straightway he went to seek out his seat as the wise man bade him. Then again as before the meal was fairly spread once more for men in hall famed for their courage. The covering night grew dark over the noble warriors. The veterans all rose up; the grey-haired aged Scylding was minded to seek his bed. It pleased the Geat, the mighty shield-warrior, exceeding well to rest. Forthwith a hall thane, who

ministered in fitting fashion to all the needs of a thane which the
warlike seafarers should have that day, guided him forth, weary
as he was from his journey, come from afar. The great-hearted
man took his rest: the building towered up wide-gabled and
gold-plated; the guest slumbered within till the black raven
merrily proclaimed the joy of heaven.

Then came the bright light gliding after the shadow. The
warriors hastened, the chieftains were ready to go again to their
people, the stout-hearted sojourner was minded to seek the boat
far thence. Then the brave man, the son of Ecglaf, bade him
bear Hrunting, take his sword, his dear blade; he thanked him for
the gift; said that he counted him a good friend in battle, mighty
in war; in no wise did he belittle the sword's edge: that was a
brave warrior. And the men of war then, ready in war
trappings, were about to depart; the chieftain, dear to the Danes,
went to the throne where the other was, the hero dreaded in
battle; he greeted Hrothgar.

XXVII

Beowulf spoke, son of Ecgtheow: 'Now we seafarers, come
from afar, wish to say that we purpose to seek Hygelac. We
have been as kindly treated here as we could wish; thou hast
been good unto us. If I can in any way on earth win a greater
love from thee, lord of men, for warlike deeds than I have yet
done, I am ready forthwith. If beyond the compass of the
floods I hear that thy neighbours press upon thee with dread
war, as at times foes have done to thee, I shall bring to thy help
thousands of thanes and heroes. I know that Hygelac, the lord
of the Geats, protector of the people, though he is young, will
aid me in words and deeds to support thee well and bear a spear
to thy aid, mighty succour, if thou hast need of men. If
Hrethric, a prince's son, betake himself to the court of the Geats,
he may find many friends there. For him who trusts his own
merit it is better to visit distant lands.'

Hrothgar spoke to him in answer: 'The wise Lord has sent
those speeches into thy mind. I have not heard a man of such
young age discourse more wisely. Thou art strong in might and
wise in mind, prudent in speeches. It is my expectation, if it
comes to pass that the spear, grim war, sickness, or steel should
carry off the son of Hrethel, thy prince, the protector of the
people, and thou art still alive, that the Sea-Geats will have no
better king to choose, treasure guardian of heroes, if thou wilt

rule the kingdom of thy kinsmen. Thy mind pleases me the better as time goes on, dear Beowulf. Thou hast brought it to pass that there shall be peace between the peoples, the men of the Geats and the Spear-Danes, and that strife shall cease, the treacherous hostility they formerly suffered; while I rule over the wide realm treasures shall be in common; many a man shall greet another with gifts across the gannet's bath; the ring-prowed ship shall bear offerings and love-tokens over the sea. I know the people to be of firm mind towards friend and foe, wholly blameless in their ancient tradition.'

Then, moreover, the protector of earls, the son of Healfdene, gave him in the house twelve treasures; he bade him seek his dear people in safety with those offerings, come again speedily. Then the king of noble race, the prince of the Scyldings, kissed the best of thanes, and fell upon his neck: tears fell from him, the grey-haired man. There was the chance of two things for him, the old man full of years, but more of one, that they should not see one another again, brave men in talk together. That man was so dear to him, that he could not stifle the trouble in his heart, but, fast bound in the thoughts of his heart, the secret longing for the loved man burned in his blood. Thence Beowulf strode over the grass meadow, the warrior proud of his gold, glorying in treasure. The sea-goer riding at anchor awaited its lord. Then Hrothgar's gift was often praised on the voyage. That was a king blameless in all ways, till old age, which has done hurt to many, robbed him of the joys of strength.

XXVIII

Then the troop of exceeding brave warriors came to the flood; they bore ring-woven corslets, locked shirts of mail. The watchman spied the return of the earls as erstwhile he did.

He did not salute the strangers from the edge of the cliff with insult, but rode towards them; he told the people of the Weders that the warriors with gleaming armour went welcome to the ship. Then the spacious ship on the sand was laden with war garments, the ring-prowed vessel with horses and treasures; the mast towered aloft above Hrothgar's precious hoardings.

He gave to the guardian of the ship a sword bound with gold, so that afterwards on the mead bench he was the more esteemed for the treasure, the ancient sword. He embarked on the ship, to plough the deep water; left the land of the Danes. Then by the mast was a sea-cloth, a sail bound by a rope. The timbers creaked; the wind over the billows did not force the wave-floater from her course. The sea-goer went on her way, the foamy-necked one floated forth over the waves, the boat with bound prow over the ocean streams, till they could see the cliffs of the Geats, the well-known headlands. The boat drove ashore; urged by the wind it rested on the land.

Quickly the haven watchman, who for a long time had gazed out afar at the waters expecting the dear men, was ready by the sea. He bound the broad-bosomed ship to the sand firmly with anchor-bonds, lest the might of the waves should drive away the winsome vessel. Then he bade the treasure of chieftains, adorn-ments and beaten gold, to be carried up. He had not far to go thence to seek the giver of treasure, Hygelac, son of Hrethel, where he dwells at home, himself with his comrades near the sea wall.

The house was splendid, the ruler a mighty king in the high hall, Hygd very young, wise, high-minded, although she, the daughter of Hæreth, had lived few years in the stronghold. Yet was she not petty, nor too grudging in gifts and treasures to the people of the Geats. She, the splendid queen of the people, had not the pride or the dread hostility of Thryth.[1] No brave one of the dear comrades, except the mighty prince, durst venture to look upon her openly with his eyes; but he might count upon deadly bonds hand-woven made ready for him. Quickly after that he was seized and destined to the sword, so that the inlaid brand might give judgment, might proclaim the deadly evil. Such is not queenly usage for a woman to practise, though she is splendid; that she who was meant to establish peace should seek the life of a dear subject because of fancied wrong. In truth the kinsman of Hemming detested that.

Men at their ale-drinking told another tale, that she brought less evils on the people, crafty acts of malice, as soon as she was given, gold-adorned, to the young warrior, to the brave chieftain, when by her father's counsel she sought in her journey the hall of Offa over the yellow flood, where afterwards on the throne she well employed while she lived what was granted her in life, a good famous woman. She kept a noble love towards the prince of heroes, the best, as I have heard, of all mankind, of the race of

---

[1] Thryth, the wife of Offa (King of the Angles on the Continent in the fourth century), is here contrasted with Hygd as Heremod was with Beowulf. After her marriage Hygd seems to have become less savage. Offa's father is Garmund, his son is Eomær.

men between the seas.   For Offa was a skilled spearman, widely honoured for gifts and victories; he ruled his realm with wisdom. From him sprang Eomær for a help to heroes, kinsman of Hemming, grandson of Garmund, mighty in onslaught.

XXIX

Then the bold man went himself with his troop along the sand to tread the meadow by the sea, the wide shores.   The world candle shone, the sun bright from the south.   They went on their way; quickly they marched till they heard that the protector of earls, the slayer of Ongentheow,[1] the worthy young war king, was bestowing rings in the court.   Beowulf's arrival was quickly proclaimed to Hygelac, that the defender of warriors, the shield comrade, was come alive to the palace there, to the court, unscathed from the battle-play.

With speed, as the mighty one ordered, a space was cleared within the hall for the newcomers.   Then he who survived the combat sat down opposite him, kinsman opposite kinsman, when in solemn speech with chosen words he greeted his gracious lord.   The daughter of Hæreth went about throughout that hall building with mead vessels; she loved the people, bore the flagon to the hands of the Heath-dwellers.   Hygelac began graciously to question his companion in the high hall; desire to know the exploits of the Sea Geats was strong upon him.

'How fared ye on the voyage, dear Beowulf, when on a sudden thou hadst desire to seek combat afar over the salt water, warfare at Heorot?   Surely thou hast somewhat mended for Hrothgar, the famous prince, his wide-known sorrow?   In my heart's grief for that I was troubled with surgings of sorrow; I put no trust in my loved man's venture; long while I besought thee that thou shouldst have naught to do with the murderous monster, let the South-Danes themselves fight out the struggle with Grendel. I utter thanks to God, that it is granted me to behold thee unscathed.'

Beowulf spoke, son of Ecgtheow: 'That is known, my lord Hygelac, to many men, the famous encounter; what struggle there was between Grendel and me in that place, where he brought very many sorrows upon the victorious Scyldings, lasting oppression.   I avenged all that.   Thus none of Grendel's

---

[1] King of the Swedes.   The wars of Swedes and Geats are described later. (See Section xl.)

kin upon earth has cause to boast of that uproar at dawn, not he who lives longest of the loathly race, snared in sin.

'Even there did I come to that ring hall to greet Hrothgar. Straightway the famous son of Healfdene, when he knew my purpose, assigned me a seat beside his own son. His troop was making merry; I have never seen under the vault of heaven greater mead joy of men sitting in hall. At times the famous queen, she who establishes peace among the peoples, moved throughout the hall, encouraged the young men; often she gave a ring to a warrior ere she went to her seat. At times Hrothgar's daughter bore the ale flagon before the veterans, to the earls in the high places; then I heard men sitting in hall name Freawaru, where she bestowed the nail-studded vessel on the heroes; she, young, gold-adorned, is promised to the gracious son of Froda.[1] The friend of the Scyldings, the ruler of the realm, has brought that about, and counts it a gain that he should settle with the woman a part of his deadly feuds and struggles. It is always a rare thing, when a little while after the fall of the prince the murderous spear sinks to rest, even though the bride is of worth.

XXX

'That may rankle with the prince of the Heathobards and each thane among the people, when he goes in hall with the bride, that a noble scion of the Danes should tend the warriors. On him gleams the armour of his forefathers, hard and ring-marked, the treasure of the Heathobards, whilst they were able to wield those weapons, until they led their dear comrades and themselves to ruin at the shield-play.

'Then an old spear-warrior who gazes on the treasure, who bears in mind all the slaughter of men, speaks at the beer-drinking—grim is his heart—he begins in mournful mood to test the thoughts of the young warrior by the musings of his mind, to stir up evil strife—and he utters these words:

'"Canst thou, my friend, recognize the sword, the precious blade, thy father bore to battle, where the Danes slew him when

[1] Beowulf foretells here the feud between Hrothgar and his son-in-law Ingeld, the Heathobard. A previous quarrel between the Danes and the Heathobards, in which Ingeld's father, Froda, had been killed, has been ended by Hrothgar's daughter marrying Ingeld. But some young Dane, Beowulf foresees, will proudly wear in Ingeld's hall treasures won from the Heathobards in the former fight. Some old unforgiving warrior will urge Ingeld to revenge such insult; the young Dane will be killed, and the feud will break out again. (See *Widsith* for reference to the story of Ingeld.)

under his helmet for the last time; the bold Scyldings held the field when Withergyld lay low, after the fall of heroes. Now some youth or other of those murderers exulting in his adornments walks here in the hall; boasts of the slaughter and wears the treasure, which thou shouldst rightfully own."

'Thus at all times he admonishes and stirs up memories with baneful words till the season comes when the bride's thane slumbers, stained with blood after the sword stroke, his life forfeited because of her father's deeds. The other escapes with his life, he knows the country well. Then on both sides are broken the solemn oaths of earls. Afterwards deadly hatred surge up against Ingeld, and his love for his wife grows cooler from his anguish of mind. Wherefore I look not for the goodwill of the Heathobards, nor for much loyalty, void of malice, to the Danes, nor firm friendship.

'I shall speak once again about Grendel, that thou, the giver of treasure, mayest know well what was later the issue of the hand-struggle of heroes.

'After the jewel of the sky glided over the fields, the monster came raging, the dread night foe, to seek us out, where safe and sound we held the hall. There was war fatal to Hondscio, a violent death to the doomed man. He was the first to fall, the girded warrior. Grendel devoured him, the famous liege man; he swallowed the whole body of the loved man. Nevertheless the bloody-toothed slayer, his thought set on evil, was not minded to go out again from the gold-hall empty-handed; but, strong in his might, he pitted himself against me, laid hold with ready hand. A pouch hung wide and wondrous, made firm with artful clasps; it was all cunningly devised by the power of the devil and with dragon skins. He, the savage worker of deeds, purposed to put me into it, though guiltless, with many others: it could not come to pass thus when I stood upright in my wrath.

'It is too long to tell how I gave requital to the people's foe for every ill deed. There, my prince, did I bring honour on thy people by my deeds. He escaped forth; for a short space he enjoyed the pleasures of life; yet his right hand remained in Heorot for a token of him; and he, departing thence wretched, sank down, sad in mind, to the bottom of the mere.

'When morning came and we had sat down to the banquet, the friend of the Scyldings rewarded me richly for the deadly onslaught with beaten gold, with many treasures. There was singing and merriment. An aged Scylding of great experience told tales of long ago. At times one bold in battle drew sweetness from the harp, the joy-wood; at times wrought a measure true and sad; at times the large-hearted king told a wondrous story in fitting fashion. At times again an old warrior bowed down with age began to speak to the youths of prowess in fight; his heart swelled within him, when, old in years, he brought to mind many things.

'Thus we took our pleasure there the livelong day, till another night came to men. Then forthwith again Grendel's mother was ready to avenge her grief; sorrowful, she journeyed. Death, the hostility of the Weders, had carried off her son. The monstrous woman avenged her child, she slew a warrior in her might. There life went out from Æschere, a wise councillor through many years. Nor, when morning came, might they, the men of the Danes, consume with fire him who had been made powerless by death; nor lay the loved man on the pyre. She bore off that body in a fiend's embrace under the mountain stream. That was to Hrothgar the heaviest of the sorrows which for a long while had laid hold on the prince of the people. Then the prince, lamenting, entreated me by thy life, that, in the press of the floods, I should perform a deed of prowess, should hazard my life, should achieve a heroic exploit. He promised me reward. Then I found the grim, terrible guardian of the depths of the surging water, who is known far and wide. There for a space was hand-to-hand grappling; the water welled with blood, and in that hall in the depths I cut off the head of Grendel's mother with a gigantic sword; with violence I tore her life from her; I was not yet doomed to death, but the protector of earls, the son of Healfdene, gave me again many a treasure.

XXXI

'Thus did the king of the people live as was fitting; in no way did I lose the rewards, the guerdon of my strength; but he, the son of Healfdene, gave me treasures into my own keeping. Them I will bring and gladly proffer to thee, king of warriors. Once more all favours come from thee. I have few close kinsmen save thee, Hygelac.'

Then he commanded to be brought in the boar-image, the banner, the helmet riding high in battle, the grey corslet, the splendid war sword. Afterwards he spoke:

'Hrothgar, the wise prince, gave me this battle garment;

he expressly bade that I should first declare his goodwill to thee. He said that King Heorogar, prince of the Scyldings, had it, the breast-armour, for a long space; that nevertheless he would not give it to his son, the bold Heoroweard, though he was loyal to him. Use all things well.'

I heard that four horses, reddish yellow, every whit alike, came next in order; he gave him possession of steeds and stores; thus must a kinsman do, and not weave a cunning net for another, prepare death for a comrade with secret guile. To Hygelac, stout in fight, his nephew was very loyal, and each was mindful of the other's pleasure.

I heard that he presented to Hygd that neck-band, the precious, wondrous treasure, which Wealtheow, the prince's daughter, gave him, together with three steeds full of grace and furnished with gleaming saddles. When she had taken the ring her breast was made fair.

Thus the son of Ecgtheow, a man famous in battle, was bold in brave deeds; he lived honourably; never did he slay his hearth companions in his drunkenness; his was not a savage mind, but, fearless in fight, he guarded the precious gift which God had given him with the greatest strength among men. Long was he despised, for the men of the Geats accounted him worthless; nor was the lord of troops minded to do him much honour on the mead bench; they thought indeed that he was slothful, an unfit chieftain. A recompense came to the famous man for every slight.

Then the protector of earls, the king mighty in battle, bade them bring in the sword of Hrethel, decked with gold; there was not at that time with the Geats a better treasure among swords; he laid that in Beowulf's bosom, and gave him seven thousand measures of land, a house, and princely rank. To them both in that country inherited land, domain, ancestral claims, had come by natural right, but more to Hygelac, a wide realm, in that he was the more illustrious.

It came to pass in later days among the warriors, when Hygelac was laid low and battle swords slew Heardred under cover of his shield, after the bold battle heroes, the warlike Scylfings, sought him mid his victorious troop, pressed hard in fight the nephew of Hereric, that then the wide realm came under Beowulf's sway. He ruled well for fifty years—he was then an aged king, an old guardian of the land—till a dragon which guarded treasure in a burial mound, a steep rock, began to show his might on the dark nights. A pathway lay beneath, unknown to men; some man

entered there, greedily seized the pagan hoard. He took the
flagon with his hand, large, bright with jewels; nor did he (the
dragon) hide the act, though he had been tricked while he slept
by thievish cunning. And thus the people, the neighbouring
folk, come to know he was enraged.

XXXII

He who did him (the dragon) sore hurt did not violate the
dragon's hoard eagerly of his own free will; but some thane of the
sons of heroes was fleeing in great distress from hostile blows,
and pressed down by his guilt, lacking a shelter, the man took
hiding there. Straightway he looked in . . . dread of the
monster lay upon him, yet in his misery . . . then the sudden
attack seized him. . . .

There were in the cave many such ancient treasures, which in
days gone by some men carefully hid there, great relics of a noble
race, precious store.

Death took them all off in past times, and still that one veteran
of the people who tarried there longest, a watchman wearying
for his friends, looked toward the like fate, that but for a short
space he might have sway over the long-gathered treasures.
The barrow stood all ready on open ground, hard by the waves,
newly raised near the headland, strong in artful barriers. Into
it the guardian of the rings bore the precious heap of the treasures
of earls, of beaten gold. Few words he spoke:

'Now, earth, do thou hold, now that heroes cannot, the wealth
of earls! Lo! valiant men erstwhile took it from thee. Death
in war, a sweeping slaughter, took off each of the men, my
people, who gave up this life; they had seen joy in hall. I have
no one who can wield the sword or polish the golden vessel, the
precious flagon; the old warriors have departed. The stout
helmet adorned with gold must be reft of its beaten plates. The
polishers slumber who should make splendid the battle masks;
and the corslet likewise, which endured the stroke of swords in
war mid the cracking of shields, follows the warrior to decay.
The coat of mail cannot journey afar by the side of heroes after
the passing of the warrior. There is no joy of the harp, delight
of the timbrel, nor does the good hawk sweep through the hall,
nor the swift steed stamp in the court. Violent death has caused
to pass many generations of men.'

Thus, sad in mind, the latest left of all lamented his sorrow;

day and night he wept joyless, till the surge of death touched his heart. The old twilight foe, the naked hostile dragon, who seeks out barrows, flaming as he goes, who flies by night compassed with fire, found the costly treasure standing unguarded. Him the dwellers in the land greatly fear. He must needs seek the hoard in the earth, where, old in years, he holds possession of the pagan gold; nor shall he profit one whit by that.

Thus did the people's foe guard that mighty treasure-house in the earth for three hundred years, till a man angered him in mind. He bore the plated goblet to his master, begged his lord for protection. Then the treasure was found, the hoard of rings was lessened; the boon was granted to the unhappy man. For the first time the prince beheld the ancient work of men.

Then the dragon awoke, wrath was rekindled; he sprang along the rock; brave in heart, he came upon the enemy's foot-track; he had stepped with stealthy craft near the dragon's head. Thus may a man, not destined to fall, who relies on the Almighty's protection, easily survive sorrow and exile.

The treasure guardian, sore and savage in mind, made eager search along the ground; was set on finding the man, him who had done him scathe while he slept; often he made a whole circuit of the mound outside. There was no man in that waste place. Yet he was keen for the conflict, the work of war; at times he turned to the barrow, sought the treasure. Forthwith he found that some man had ransacked the gold, the rich stores. With difficulty did the treasure guardian delay till evening came; then wrathful was the warden of the barrow; the foul creature was determined to avenge with fire the precious flagon.

Then day had departed, as the dragon desired; no longer would he wait on the wall, but went forth with fire, furnished with flame. The first onslaught was terrifying to the people in the land, even as it was speedily ended with sorrow for their giver of treasure.

Then the monster began to belch forth flames, to burn the bright dwellings. The flare of the fire brought fear upon men. The loathly air-flier wished not to leave aught living there. The warring of the dragon was widely seen, the onslaught of the cruel foe far and near, how the enemy of the people of the Geats wrought despite and devastation. He hastened back to the hoard, to his hidden hall, ere it was day. He had compassed the dwellers in the land with fire, with flames, and with burning; he trusted in the barrow, in bravery, and the rampart. His hope deceived him.

XXXIII

Then quickly the terror was made known to Beowulf according to the truth, that his own abode, the best of buildings, the gift-throne of the Geats, was melting in the surges of flame. That was sorrow to the good man's soul, greatest of griefs to the heart. The wise man thought that, breaking established law, he had bitterly angered God, the Lord everlasting. His breast was troubled within by dark thoughts, as was not his wont.

The fire-dragon had destroyed with flames the stronghold of his subjects, the land by the sea from without, the countryside. The warlike king, the prince of the Weders, gave him requital for that. Then the protector of warriors, the lord of earls, bade an iron shield, a splendid war targe, to be wrought for him. Full well he knew that wood could not help him; linden wood against fire. The chieftain long famous was fated to endure the end of fleeting days, of life in the world, and the dragon with him, though for long space he had held the treasure store.

Then the prince of rings scorned to seek the far-flier with a troop of men, with a great host. He feared not the fight, nor did he account as aught the valour of the dragon, his power and prowess; because ere this, defying danger, he had came through many onslaughts, wild attacks, when he, the man of victory, purged Hrothgar's hall, and in war killed with his grip the kin of Grendel, the hateful race.

That was not the most paltry of hand-to-hand struggles, where they slew Hygelac, when the king of the Geats, the friendly prince of the peoples, the son of Hrethel, died in the rushes of battle in the land of the Frisians, his blood shed by the sword, beaten down by the brand. Beowulf came thence by his own strength; swam over the sea. Alone he held on his arm thirty suits of armour when he set out on the sea. The Hetware, who bore the linden shields forward against him, had no cause to boast of the battle on foot. Few escaped from that battle hero to seek their home. The son of Ecgtheow swam over the stretch of the gulfs, the hapless solitary man back to his people, where Hygd tendered him treasure and kingdom, rings and the throne; she did not trust her son, that he could hold his fatherland against hostile hosts, now that Hygelac was dead.

Yet the unhappy man could in no way win the chieftain's consent that he would be lord over Heardred, or that he would elect to rule the realm. Nevertheless he upheld him among the people with friendly counsel, graciously with support, until Heardred grew older; he ruled the Weder-Geats. Exiles, the sons of Ohtere, sought him over the sea.[1] They had risen against the protector of the Scylfings, the best of sea-kings who gave out treasure in Sweden, a famous prince. That ended his life. Deadly wounds from sword slashes he, the son of Hygelac, gained there for his hospitality; and the son of Ongentheow departed again to seek his home when Heardred was laid low; he let Beowulf hold the throne, rule over the Geats. That was a good king.

XXXIV

In after days he forgot not requital for the prince's fall; he became a friend to the wretched Eadgils. He aided the son of Ohtere over the broad sea with a troop, with warriors and weapons. He took vengeance afterwards with cold, sad marches; he deprived the king of life.

Thus he, the son of Ecgtheow, had survived every onslaught, dread battles, mighty ventures, until that day when he was to encounter the dragon. The lord of the Geats went then with eleven others, raging with anger, to behold the dragon. He had heard then whence the feud arose, the sore affliction of men; the famous costly vessel came into his possession through the hand of the finder.

He who brought about the beginning of that strife, fettered, sad in mind, was the thirteenth man in the troop; he was forced, though in misery, to show the way. He went against his will, till he could spy that cave, the barrow under the ground, hard by the surge of the waters, the struggle of the waves. Within, it was full of jewels and wire ornaments. The monstrous guardian, the ready fighter, grown old beneath the earth, held the treasures. That was no easy matter for any man to enter there.

The king, mighty in onslaught, sat down then on the headland, whilst he, the gold friend of the Geats, saluted his hearth companions. His mind was sad, restless, brooding on death; fate exceeding near which was destined to come on the old man, to

[1] Eanmund and Eadgils rebel against their uncle Onela, King of Sweden, and flee to the Geats, where Heardred shelters them. Onela follows with an army, attacks and kills Heardred. It is in this battle that Weohstan kills Eanmund (Section xxxvi). Onela returns to Sweden, leaving Beowulf undisturbed as Heardred's successor. Later Beowulf befriends Eadgils, who, after conquering and killing Onela, becomes King of Sweden.

seek the treasure of his soul, to part asunder life from the body. Not for long after that was the chieftain's spirit clothed in flesh.

Beowulf spoke, son of Ecgtheow: 'In my youth I came through many rushes of war, times of combat. I remember all that. I was seven years old when the prince of treasures, the friendly ruler of the peoples, took me from my father; King Hrethel brought me up and fostered me, bestowed on me treasure and banqueting, bore in mind our kinship; in his life I was no less loved by him, a child in the court, than any of his children, Herebeald and Hæthcyn, or my Hygelac. For the eldest a bed of death was made ready by deeds not fit for a kinsman, when Hæthcyn smote him with curved bow, his friendly prince with an arrow; he missed his mark and shot his kinsman, one brother the other with bloody shaft. That was a violent deed not to be atoned for by gifts, cunningly wrought, weighing sore on the heart. Yet in spite of that the chieftain must needs pass from life unavenged.

'In like manner it is sad for an aged man to endure, that his son in his youth should swing from the gallows. Then he makes a measure, a song of sorrow, when his son hangs, a delight for the raven, and he, aged and full of years, can in no way bring him help. He is ever reminded each morning of his son's death; he cares not to await the birth of another son in his court after the one has made acquaintance with evil deeds by the agony of death. Sorrowful he gazes on his son's room, the deserted wine hall, a resting-place for the winds, reft of noise. The horsemen slumber, the heroes in their graves; there is no music of the harp, joy in the palace, as there was of yore.

XXXV

'He goes then to his sleeping-place, sings a song of sorrow, one man for another; his lands and dwelling seemed all too spacious for him. Thus did the protector of the Weders bear surging sorrow in his heart for Herebeald; he could no whit avenge the murderous deed on the slayer. Nor could he work hurt to the warrior, though he was not dear to him. Then with that grief which came sorely upon him, he forsook joy of men, chose God's light; left to his sons, as a worthy man does, land and cities, when he departed from life.

'Then guilt and strife came to be the portion of Swedes and Geats [1] over the wide water, a bitter hostility after Hrethel died, and Ongentheow's sons were brave and bold in fight. They did not wish to keep up friendship over the lakes, but often they contrived dread slaughter near Hreosnaburh. That did my friendly kinsmen avenge, the feud and the outrage, as was well known, though one of them paid for it at a dear price with his life. To Hæthcyn, lord of the Geats, war proved fatal. Then I heard that in the morning one brother avenged the other on the slayer with the sword edge. There Ongentheow seeks out Eofor. The war helmet was shattered, the aged Scylfing fell mortally stricken; the hand forgot not the feud; it drew not back from the deadly blow.

'With gleaming sword I repaid in war, as chance was given me, the treasures he bestowed on me. He gave me land, domain, an ancestral seat. There was no need for him to seek among the Gepidæ, or the Spear-Danes, or in the kingdom of the Swedes for less worthy warriors, to buy them with treasure. Ever I wished to be before him on foot, alone in the van, and so shall I do battle while my life lasts, while this sword endures that early and late has often followed me. Afterwards I slew Dæghrefn, the champion of the Hugas,[2] in the presence of the veterans. He was not able at all to bring adornments, breast ornaments, to the king of the Frisians, but the keeper of the banner, the chieftain in his might, fell amid the warriors. The sword was not the slayer, but my battlegrip crushed the surges of his heart and his body. Now the edge of the sword, the hand and the keen blade, shall wage war for the treasure.'

Beowulf spoke, he uttered words of boasting for the last time: 'In my youth I passed through many battles; yet I, aged protector of the people, wish to seek the fight, to achieve the heroic deed, if the foul foe comes out of his cave to face me.'

Then for the last time he greeted each of the men, brave bearers of helmets, dear comrades: 'I would not bear a sword, a weapon against the dragon, if I knew how else I could make good my boast against the monster, as erstwhile I did against Grendel; but here I expect hot battle flame, a blast of breath, and poison. Wherefore I bear shield and corslet. I will not give back the space of a foot before the keeper of the barrow, but the fight shall be between us at the wall, as Fate, the master of every man, shall decide for us. I am brave in mind, so that I can keep from boasting against the winged fighter. Do ye, clad in corslets,

_____
[1] See Section xl.   [2] A name for the Franks.

warriors in battle array, bide on the barrow to see which of us two can better survive wounds after the deadly onslaught. This is not your venture, nor is it in any man's power, except mine alone, to strive with his strength against the monster, to perform heroic deeds. With my might I shall gain the gold; or war, a perilous death, shall carry off your prince.'

Then with his shield the strong warrior arose, stern under his helmet; he bore the battle corslet under the rocky cliffs; he trusted in the strength of a single man. Such is no coward's venture.

Then he, excellent in virtues, who had survived very many combats, wild attacks, when foot-warriors crashed together, saw a stone arch standing by the wall, a stream gushing out thence from the barrow. The surge of the spring was hot with battle fires; by reason of the dragon's flame he could not endure for any time unburnt the recess near the treasure. The prince of the Weder-Geats, when he was angered, let a word go out from his breast; the strong-hearted man was wrathful; his voice loud in battle went in resounding under the grey stone.

Hate was roused, the treasure guardian heard the speech of a man; that was no time for seeking of friendship; first the monster's breath, hot sweat of battle, issued out from the stone; the earth resounded. The warrior, lord of the Geats, swung his shield under the barrow against the dread creature. Then the heart of the coiling dragon was ready to seek strife. The valiant warlike king first brandished the sword, the ancient blade, not dull in its edges. Each of the two hostile-minded ones felt fear of the other. The ruler of friends stood staunchly against his high shield, when the dragon quickly coiled together; he waited in his war gear. Then striding amid flames, contorted he went, hastening to his fate. The shield guarded life and body well for the famous prince less time than he wished. There then for the first time he had to show his strength without Fate allotting him fame in battle. The lord of the Geats raised up his hand, he struck the dread gleaming monster with the precious sword, so that the bright edge turned on the bone; it bit less keenly than its king, hard pressed by trouble, has need. Then after the battle stroke the guardian of the treasure was in savage mood; he cast forth deadly fire; far leaped the war flames. The gold-friend of the Geats boasted not of famous victories; the naked battle blade failed at need, as it should not have done, the long-famous brand. That was no easy step for the famous son of Ecgtheow to consent to yield that ground; against his will he must needs inhabit a dwelling elsewhere; thus must every man forsake fleeting days.

It was not long till the fighters closed again. The treasure guardian took heart anew. His breast laboured with breathing. He who before held sway over the people suffered anguish, ringed round with fire.

No whit did his comrades, sons of chieftains, stand about him in a band with valour, but they took to the wood, they hid for their lives. In one of them the mind was roused to face sorrows. In him who well considers nothing can ever stifle kinship.

XXXVI

He was called Wiglaf, son of Weohstan, a valued shield-warrior, prince of the Scylfings, kinsman of Ælfhere; he saw his lord suffering the heat under his war helm. Then he called to mind the favour which formerly he had bestowed on him, the rich dwelling-place of the Wægmundings, all the rights his father possessed. He could not then hold back; his hand seized the shield, the yellow linden wood, drew the ancient sword, that was among men a relic of Eanmund, son of Ohtere. Weohstan slew him in battle with the edge of the sword, a friendless exile, and bore off from his kin the bright gleaming helm, the ringed corslet, the gigantic old sword that Onela gave him, his kinsman's war trappings, ready battle equipment. He spoke not of the feud, though he had killed his brother's child.[1] Many years he held the adornments, brand, and corslet until his son could achieve mighty deeds like his old father. Then when he departed from life, old in his passing hence, he gave among the Geats an exceeding number of battle garments.

That was the first time that the young warrior was to stand the rush of battle with his prince. His spirit did not weaken, nor did his father's sword fail in the fight. The dragon discovered that when they had come together. Wiglaf spoke, uttered many fitting words to his comrades; his mind was sad: 'I remember that time when we were drinking mead, when in the beer hall we promised our lord who gave us these rings, that we would requite him for the war gear, the helms and sharp swords,

---

[1] Weohstan, at this time a retainer of Onela, offers his lord the war gear of Eanmund. Onela refuses it, because he does not wish openly to approve of his nephew's slaying. 'He [Onela] spoke not of the feud, though he [Weohstan] had killed his brother's child.'

if need such as this came upon him. Because of this he chose us among the host of his own will for this venture, he reminded us of famous deeds and gave me these treasures, the more because he counted us good spear-warriors, bold bearers of helmets, though our lord, the protector of the people, purposed to achieve this mighty task unaided, because among men he had wrought most famous deeds, daring ventures. Now the day has come when our lord needs the strength of valiant warriors. Let us go to help our warlike prince, while the fierce dread flame yet flares. God knows that, as for me, I had much rather the flame should embrace my body with my gold-giver. It does not seem fitting to me, that we should bear shields back to our dwelling, if we cannot first fell the foe, guard the life of the prince of the Weders. I know well that, from his former deeds, he deserves not to suffer affliction alone among the warriors of the Geats, to fall in fight; sword and helmet, corslet and shirt of mail shall be shared by us both.'

He went then through the deadly reek, bore his helmet to the aid of the prince, few words he spoke: 'Dear Beowulf, achieve all things well, as thou saidst long ago in thy youth, that thou wouldst not let thy repute fail while life lasted; now, resolute chieftain, mighty in deeds, thou must guard thy life with all thy strength; I will help thee.'

After these words the dragon came raging once more, the dread evil creature, flashing with surges of flame, to seek out his foes, the hated men. The shield was burnt away to the rim by waves of fire. The corslet could not give help to the young shield-warrior; but the youth fought mightily beneath his kinsman's buckler, when his own was consumed by the flames. Then again the warlike king was mindful of fame; he struck with his battle sword with mighty strength, so that, urged by the force of hate, it stuck in his head. Nægling burst apart; Beowulf's sword, ancient and grey, failed in fight. It was not granted to him that the edges of swords might aid him in the struggle. His hand was too strong, he who, as I have heard, tried every sword beyond its strength, when he bore to battle the weapon hardened by blood of wounds. It profited him nothing.

Then for the third time the enemy of the people, the bold fire-dragon, was set on fighting; he rushed on the mighty man, when a chance offered, hot and fierce in fight; he clutched his whole neck with sharp teeth; Beowulf grew stained with his lifeblood; the gore welled out in surges.

XXXVII

Then I heard that, in the peril of the people's prince, the exalted earl showed courage, strength, and daring, as was his nature. He guarded not his head, but the brave man's hand burned when he helped his kinsman, so that he, the man in his armour, beat down a little the hostile creature; and the sword sank in, gleaming and plated; and the fire after began to abate. Then once more the king himself was master of his thoughts; he brandished the battle knife, keen and sharp for the fray, which he wore on his corslet; the protector of the Weders cut through the dragon in the midst. They felled the foe; force drove out his life; and then they both had slain him, the noble kinsmen. Such should a man be, a thane in time of need.

That was the last victory for the prince by his own deeds, the end of his work in the world. Then the wound which erstwhile the earth-dragon dealt him began to burn and swell. He found forthwith that the poison was working with pestilent force within his breast. Then the chieftain went till, taking wise thought, he sat down on a seat by the wall; he gazed on the work of giants, saw how the eternal earth building held within stone arches, firm fixed by pillars. Then with his hands the exceeding good thane bathed him with water, the blood-stained famous prince, his friendly lord, wearied with battle; and loosed his helm.

Beowulf spoke, he talked of his wound, of the hurt sore unto death; he knew well that he had ended his days, his joy on earth. Then all his length of days was passed away, death was exceeding close: 'Now I would give armour to my son, if it had been so granted that any heir, sprung from my body, should succeed me. I have ruled this people for fifty years. There was no people's king among the nations about who durst come against me with swords, or oppress me with dread. I have lived the appointed span in my land, guarded well my portion, contrived no crafty attacks, nor sworn many oaths unjustly. Stricken with mortal wounds, I can rejoice in all this; wherefore the Ruler of men has no cause to blame me for the slaughter of kinsmen, when my life passes out from my body. Now, dear Wiglaf, do thou go quickly to behold the hoard under the grey stone, now that the dragon lies low, sleeps sorely wounded, spoiled of the treasure. Haste now that I may see the old riches, the golden treasure, may eagerly gaze on the bright gems of artful work, so that, after winning the great store of jewels, I may the more easily leave life and land, which long I have guarded.'

XXXVIII

Then I heard that the son of Weohstan after these words quickly obeyed his wounded lord, stricken in battle, bore his ringed corslet, his woven shirt of mail, under the roof of the barrow. Then, exulting in victory, the brave kinsman-thane, as he went by the seat, beheld many costly ornaments, gold gleaming along the ground, wondrous work on the wall, and the lair of the dragon, the old flier at twilight; vessels standing, goblets of olden time, lacking a furbisher, reft of their ornaments. There was many a helm, ancient and rusty, many bracelets cunningly bound. Treasure, gold on the ground, may easily madden any man; conceal it who will!

Likewise he saw a banner all gilt lying high above the hoard, greatest of wonders wrought by hand, cunningly woven in stitches. A gleam shone forth from it so that he might see the floor, behold the jewels. There was no trace of the dragon there, for the sword had carried him off. Then I heard that one man rifled the hoard, the old work of giants in the mound, laid in his bosom flagons and dishes at his own will; took also the banner, brightest of beacons. The sword of the old chieftain—its edge was iron—had earlier laid low him who long while was guardian of the treasures; he bore with him to guard the treasure a dread hot flame, blazing out in battle at midnight, till violently he perished. The messenger was in haste, eager to return, urged on by the treasures. Desire was strong on him to know whether he, the courageous one, should find the mortally wounded prince of the Weders alive in that place where erstwhile he left him.

Then with the treasures he found the famous prince, his lord bleeding, at the end of his life. Again he began to dash water upon him, until speech came from him. Then the warrior spoke, the aged man in his pain; he gazed on the gold:

'I give thanks in words to the Prince of all, the King of glory, the eternal Lord, for the adornments which I behold here, that I have been able to win such for my people before my death-day. Now have I sold my old life for the hoard of treasures; attend ye now to the need of my people. No longer may I tarry here. Bid the men famed in battle raise at the sea headland a gleaming mound after the burning. It shall tower high on Hronesness, a reminder to my people, so that seafarers may afterwards call it Beowulf's barrow when from afar the ships drive over the dark sea.'[1]

The prince of brave mind took from his neck a golden ring, gave to the thane, the young spear-warrior, his helm bright with gold, his ring and corslet; bade him use them well: 'Thou art the last of our race, of the Wægmundings. Fate has swept all my kinsmen away to their destiny, earls in their might; I must needs follow them.'

That was the last word from the old man's thoughts, before he sought the pyre, the hot, fierce surges of flame. His soul passed from his breast to seek the splendour of the saints.

XXXIX

Then was it sorrow for the young man to see on the earth the man he loved best, his life closed, lying there helpless. The slayer also lay low, the dread earth-dragon, reft of life, vanquished by violence. No longer could the coiled dragon keep guard over the treasure-stores, but iron blades, sharp battle-notched swords, forged by hammers, had carried him off, so that the wide-flier sank to the ground near the treasure-house, still from his wounds. No more did he wheel in his flight through the air at midnight, no more displayed himself exulting in costly possessions; but he fell to the earth because of the warrior's handiwork. Few of a truth among men, among those of might in the land, as I have heard, though they were eager for all exploits, have succeeded in rushing against the blast of the venomous foe, or seizing with hands the hall of rings, if they found the guardian on watch dwelling in the barrow. Beowulf had paid with his death for the many costly treasures; each had gone to the end of fleeting life.

It was not long then till the cowards left the wood, weak failers in loyalty, the ten together, who durst not before wield spears in their lord's great need; but shamefully they bore their shields, the war gear, where the old man lay; they looked at Wiglaf. He, the foot-warrior, sat wearied, hard by the prince's shoulders, tried to recall him with water. No whit did he succeed; he could not, though dearly he wished, keep life in the prince on earth; nor alter the will of the Almighty. The might of God

[1] Compare the description of the burial of Achilles in the *Odyssey* (Book xxiv).

was pleased to show its power over all men by its deeds, as He yet does now.

Then a grim speech came readily from the youth to those who erstwhile had lost their courage. Wiglaf spoke, son of Weohstan, a man sad at heart; he looked at the hated men: 'Lo! he, who wishes to tell the truth, can say that the lord who gave you treasures, warlike adornments, wherein ye stand there, when on the ale bench he often bestowed on men sitting in hall, a prince to his thanes, helmet and corslet, the most excellent he could anywhere find far or near, that doubtless he miserably cast away the garments of war, when battle beset him. The people's king had indeed no cause to boast of his comrades in fight; yet God, the Disposer of victories, granted that he alone with his sword avenged himself, when he had need of might. Small protection to his life could I afford him in the fight, and yet I tried to aid my kinsman beyond my power. When with the sword I smote the deadly foe, he grew ever weaker, his fire surged out less strongly from his breast. Too few protectors pressed round the prince, when the time came upon him. Now the receiving of jewels, giving of swords, all the splendid heritage, and life's necessities, shall pass away from your race. Every man of the people shall wander, stripped of his rights in the land, when chieftains from afar hear of your flight, the inglorious act. Death is better for all earls than a shameful life.'

XL

He bade then the battle be proclaimed in the entrenchment, up over the sea-cliff, where that troop of earls, bearing their shields, sat sad in mind the whole morning, expecting both issues, the death and the return of the loved man. He who rode up to the headland held back little of the late tidings, but truthfully he told them all:

'Now is the giver of delights among the people of the Weders, the lord of the Geats, fast in his deathbed, he bides in his slaughterous couch by the deeds of the dragon. By his side lies the deadly foe stricken with knife wounds; he could not in any way deal a wound to the monster with a sword. Wiglaf, son of Weohstan, sits over Beowulf, the earl over the other lifeless one; reverently he keeps watch over friend and foe.

'Now there is prospect of a time of strife for the people, when the fall of the king becomes widely known to Franks and Frisians.

The harsh strife with the Hugas was brought about when Hygelac went to the land of the Frisians with a navy, where the Hetware laid him low in battle; they did mightily with their greater numbers, so that the corslet-warrior was forced to yield; he fell mid his troops; the prince gave no adornments to his veterans. To us ever since the goodwill of the Merovingian king has been denied.

'Nor do I expect any peace or good faith from the people of Sweden; for it was widely known that Ongentheow robbed Hæthcyn, son of Hrethel, of life near Ravenswood, when the warlike Scylfings first sought in their pride the people of the Geats. Straightway the aged father of Ohtere, old and terrible, dealt him a blow in return, killed the sea-guide, the old man freed the bride, the wife reft of her gold, the mother of Onela and Ohtere;[1] and then he followed his deadly foes till with difficulty they escaped, leaderless, to Ravenswood. Then he besieged with a mighty host those who had escaped the sword, wearied from wounds; often through the livelong night he threatened the wretched band with misery; he said that in the morning he would do them hurt with the edge of the sword; some on the gallows-tree for the sport of the birds. With dawn came relief again to the woeful, when they heard Hygelac's horn and the blare of the trumpet, when the valiant one came on the track of the warriors of the people.

XLI

'The blood trail of Swedes and Geats, the deadly attack of men, was widely noted, how the men roused strife between one another. Then the valiant one departed with his kinsmen, the old man very sad, to seek his stronghold. The earl Ongentheow went on further; he had heard of Hygelac's skill in battle, of the proud man's war strength; he relied not on resistance to check the seamen, to defend treasure, children and wife against the sea raiders; the aged man turned thence once more behind a rampart. Then chase was given to the men of the Swedes, the banner to Hygelac. Upon that they overran the stronghold after the people of Hrethel had penetrated the fastnesses. There the grey-haired Ongentheow was constrained to tarry by the edge of the sword, so that the people's king had to suffer the might of Eofor alone. Wulf, son of Wonred, angrily struck

[1] The wife of Ongentheow whom Hæthcyn had captured.

him with the sword, so that after the blow the blood gushed from
the veins under his hair. Yet was he not daunted, the aged
Scylfing, but quickly repaid that deadly stroke with a worse in
exchange, as soon as he, the people's king, turned thither. The
strong son of Wonred could not give a blow in return to the old
man, for he first clove his helmet on his head, so that, stained
with blood, he had to give back: he fell on the ground: he was
not doomed yet, but he revived, though a wound had stricken
him. The bold thane of Hygelac, when his brother was laid
low, caused his broad sword, old gigantic brand, to crash the
massive helmet over the wall of shields: then the king sank down,
the protector of the people; he was stricken unto death. Then
were there many who bound up his kinsman; they lifted him
speedily when space was cleared for them, so that they might hold
possession of the battle-field. Then one warrior spoiled
another, took from Ongentheow his iron corslet, his sharp hilted
sword, and his helm also; bore the trappings of the old man to
Hygelac. He received the adornments, and graciously promised
him rewards amid the people, and thus did he fulfil it; the lord
of the Geats, the son of Hrethel, when he came to his home,
rewarded Eofor and Wulf with exceeding rich treasures for
that onslaught; to each of them he gave a hundred thousand
measures of land and twisted rings; men on earth had no cause to
blame him for the gifts, when they fought heroically; and then to
Eofor he gave his only daughter, to adorn his dwelling, as a
pledge of goodwill.[1]

'That is the feud and the hostility, the deadly hatred of man,
which I look for, of Swedish men who will come upon us, when
they learn that our prince is dead, who erstwhile guarded
treasure and kingdom, the bold Sea-Geats, against foes after the
fall of heroes, did what was best for the people, and performed
heroic deeds more and more.

'Now haste is best, that we should gaze there upon the people's
king, and bring him, who gave us rings, on his way to the pyre.
No solitary thing shall be consumed with the brave man, but
there is store of treasures, untold gold dearly gained, and now,
at the last, rings bought with his own life; the flame shall devour,
the fire enfold them; the earl shall not wear the treasures as a

---

[1] The narrative of the battle is somewhat hard to follow. Ongentheow,
the Swedish king, attacks Hæthcyn, king of the Geats, and slays him. The
leaderless Geats retreat to Ravenswood, where they are rescued by Hygelac.
Ongentheow now retires to some sort of fortification, where he is attacked by
the Geats. He is assailed by the brothers Eofor and Wulf: he deals Wulf a
heavy stroke, but Eofor strikes Ongentheow down.

memorial, nor shall the fair maid bear on her neck the adornment of a circlet, but sad in mind, reft of gold, shall walk in a strange land, not once but oftentimes, now that the leader of the host has done with laughter, joy, and merriment. Wherefore many a spear, cold in the morning, shall be grasped with fingers, raised aloft with hands; the sound of the harp shall not rouse the warriors, but the dark raven, ready above the fallen, shall speak many things, shall tell the eagle how he sped at the feasting, when with the wolf he spoiled the slain.'

Thus the bold man told evil tidings; he lied not at all in his forecasts and words. The troop all rose up, sadly they went under Earnanæss, with tears welling up, to behold the wonder. Then they found him lifeless on the sand, keeping his helpless couch, him who in former times gave them rings. Then the last of days had come to the valiant one, on which the warlike king, the prince of the Weders, perished a wondrous death. First they saw there a stranger creature, the hateful dragon lying opposite on the ground there: the fire-dragon, the grim dread monster, was scorched with flames; he measured fifty feet long as he lay: often he had taken his pleasure in the air at night; he had come down again to visit his lair; and now he was firm bound by death; he had taken his last delight in the earth-caves. By him stood goblets and flagons, dishes lay there and costly swords eaten through by rust, as if they had remained there a thousand years in the earth's embrace. Moreover, that mighty heritage, gold of men of olden time, had a curse laid upon it, so that none among men might touch that ring hall, unless God Himself, the true King of victories—He is the helper of men—granted to whom He would to lay open the hoard; even to that man who seemed good unto Him.

XLII

Then it was clear that the way of them, who had wrongfully hidden the jewels under the wall, had not prospered. First the guardian slew one; then the feud was fiercely revenged. It is unknown where an earl, mighty in valour, may come to the end of life, when he may no longer sit on the mead bench with his kinsmen. Thus was it with Beowulf, when he sought out the guardian of the barrow and battle; he knew not himself in what way his passing from the world should come about.

Thus did the famous princes, who stored that there, lay a

heavy ban upon it till doomsday, so that the man who should plunder the place should be guilty of sins, confined in cursed places, fast in bonds of hell, smitten with plagues. He would rather not have beheld the gold-treasure, the owner's might.

Wiglaf spoke, son of Weohstan: 'Often must many an earl suffer sorrow through the will of one, as has come upon us. We could not counsel the dear prince, the protector of the kingdom, not to approach the guardian of the gold, but to let him lie there, where long he had been; bide in his dwelling till the end of the world. We have suffered sore fortune; the hoard is seen, grimly won; that fate was too hard which drew the people's king thither. I was within and beheld all that, the stores of the building, when the chance was granted me; in no pleasant way was a passage opened to me in under the earth-wall. In haste I seized a mighty burden of precious treasures in my hands; bore them out hither to my king; he was still living then, wise and clear in mind; the old man in his agony spoke many things, and bade me greet you; asked that ye should raise on the site of the pyre a high barrow, great and famous, befitting his exploits, even as he was among men the most renowned warrior far and wide throughout the earth, whilst he could enjoy wealth in his castle. Let us now hasten to behold and seek once more the heap of rare gems, the wondrous sight beneath the wall. I will guide you, so that ye may see the rings and broad gold near at hand. Let the bier be made ready, speedily wrought, when we come out and bear then our prince, the loved man, where long he shall wait in the Almighty's keeping.'

Then the son of Weohstan, the hero bold in battle, bade orders be given to many of the men who were owners of dwellings, that they, the leaders of bands, should bring from afar wood for the funeral fire to where the valiant man lay: 'Now shall the fire consume—the dark flame shall tower up—the ruler of warriors, him who often endured the iron shower when the storm of arrows, urged with might, darted over the shield-wall, when the shaft did its office; fitted with feathers, it aided the barb.'

In truth the wise son of Weohstan called out the king's thanes from the troop, the best seven together; he went with the seven under the hostile roof of the foemen; one who went in front bore in his hand a torch. It was not settled by lot then who plundered that hoard when the men saw any part unguarded remaining in the hall, lying there perishing; little did any of them mourn that they bore out quickly the precious treasures; also they shoved the dragon, the monster, over the cliff; they let the wave take him, the flood embrace the guardian of the treasures. There was twisted gold wholly beyond measure loaded on the wagon; the chieftain, the grey-haired warrior, was borne to Hronesness.

XLIII

Then the people of the Geats made ready for him a pyre firm on the ground, hung round with helmets, battle targes, bright corslets, as he had craved; then the sorrowing men laid in the midst the famous prince, their loved lord.   The warriors began to rouse on the barrow the greatest of funeral fires; the wood-reek mounted up dark above the smoking glow, the crackling flame, mingled with the cry of weeping—the tumult of the winds ceased—until it had consumed the body, hot to the heart.   Sad in heart, they lamented the sorrow of their souls, the slaying of their lord; likewise the old woman with bound tresses sang in sadness a dirge for Beowulf, declared heavily that she sorely dreaded the onset of evil days, many slayings, a warrior's terror, his humiliation and captivity.   The sky swallowed up the smoke.

Then the people of the Weders wrought a mound, which was lofty and broad, at the edge of the headland, visible far and wide to seafarers; and in ten days they finished the beacon of the man mighty in battle; the ashes they compassed round with a wall, as exceeding wise men might most worthily devise it.   They laid on the barrow rings and ornaments, all such adornments as men, eager for combat, had erstwhile taken from the hoard; they let the earth keep the treasure of earls, the gold in the ground, where it yet lies, as useless to men as it was before.   Then men bold in battle, sons of chieftains, twelve in all, rode about the mound; they were minded to utter their grief, to lament the king, to make a chant and so speak of the man; they exalted his heroic life and praised his valorous deed with all their strength.

Thus it is fitting that a man should extol his friendly lord in words, should heartily love him, when he must needs depart from his body and pass away.   Thus did the men of the Geats, his hearth companions, bewail the fall of their lord; they said that among the kings of the world he was the mildest of men and most kindly, most gentle to his people and most eager for praise.

FINNESBURH

[This fragment was found written on a single leaf in the library of Lambeth Palace by George Hickes and was printed by him in 1705. Since then the manuscript has unfortunately been lost. The story told in the fragment can be made out fairly plainly. A young king guarding a hall, apparently with a companion, is startled by moonlight gleaming on the armour of approaching enemies. He rouses his men. Sigeferth and Eaha station themselves at one door; Ordlaf, Guthlaf, and Hengest at the other door. We then turn to the assailants. Garulf is about to lead the attack. Guthere tries to dissuade him from risking his life at the beginning of the fight. But Garulf advances to the door and asks who holds it. Sigeferth replies and the fight begins. Garulf is the first to fall. For five days the hall is held without loss to the defenders. Finally the attackers draw off and reckon their losses. So much is clear, but the poem presents many difficulties. Garulf is called son of Guthlaf. Among the defenders there is also a Guthlaf. Possibly the two Guthlafs are the same, and the story involves the tragic opposition of son and father. The chief problem is the relationship of the fragment to the story of Finn as told in *Beowulf* (Sections xvii and xviii). There is no agreement on this matter. One view which has a good deal to recommend it is as follows: The fragment deals with the treacherous attack made by Finn upon his Danish guests. The young king would then be Hnæf. Ordlaf and Guthlaf, mentioned among the defenders of the hall, are probably the same as Oslaf and Guthlaf in the *Beowulf* account.]

. . . the gables are never burning.' Then the king young in war spoke: 'This is neither the dawn from the east, nor does a dragon fly hither, nor are the gables of this hall here burning, but they are launching a sudden attack; the birds are singing; the grey corslet rings; the spear clashes; shield answers to shaft. Now gleams the wandering moon beneath the clouds; now dire deeds come to pass which will enact the hatred of this people. But awake now, my warriors, grasp your shields, be mindful of courage, strive in the front of the fight, be resolute.'

Then rose up many a gold-decked thane, girded on his sword; then to the door went the excellent warriors, Sigeferth and Eaha, drew their swords; and Ordlaf and Guthlaf at the other door, and Hengest himself came behind them.

Then Guthere exhorted Garulf that he in his armour should not risk so noble a life at the first onslaught on the doors of the hall, since one bold in attack [1] was minded to take it away; but

---

[1] That is, Sigeferth.

he, the daring minded hero, openly asked over all who it was held the door.

'Sigeferth is my name,' said he, 'I am a warrior of the Secgan, a hero widely known. Many trials have I undergone, stern conflicts; now is decreed for thee here what thou shalt gain from me.'

Then by the wall there was uproar of deadly struggles; shields must needs be in the hands of the bold men, the helmet must burst—the floor of the fortress rang—until Garulf, son of Guthlaf, fell in the fight, first of all the dwellers in the land; round him many valiant men. The flying raven circled over the the bodies; dusky and dark brown, it wheeled; there was gleaming of swords as if all Finnesburh was in flames. Never have I heard of sixty triumphant warriors bearing themselves better, more worthily in the battle of men, nor ever of youths making better requital for sweet mead than his liege men yielded to Hnæf.

Five days they fought without any of the warriors falling, but they held the doors. Then the hero departed wounded; he said that his corslet was broken, his battle-dress useless, and his helmet also was pierced. Then the protector of the people straightway asked him how their warriors had survived their wounds, or which of the young men . . .

WALDHERE

[In 1860 two leaves of Anglo-Saxon manuscript were discovered at Copenhagen. These two fragments are all that survive in English of what was apparently a poem of considerable length. The story was well known on the Continent and is told in a spirited Latin poem by Ekkehard of St Gall (*d.* 973). Its main outlines are as follows: Hildegund, a Burgundian princess, Walter of Aquitaine, and Hagen, a warrior of the Franks, are hostages with Attila, king of the Huns. They remain together at the court of Attila until Hagen escapes to join Gunther, the new king of the Franks. Walter and Hildegund, who are lovers, also escape, and flee to the west, taking with them great store of treasure. Gunther, hearing of their flight, is eager to rob them, and persuades the unwilling Hagen to join him in the cowardly enterprise. With eleven other warriors, they come upon Walter and Hildegund in a narrow pass. Walter's offers of rings are refused, and the onset begins. The Franks come forward one by one up the path and all except Hagen and Gunther are slain. So the day's fighting ends. The next morning Gunther and Hagen attack Walter, and in the struggle Gunther loses a leg, Hagen an eye, and Walter his right hand. The fight ends.

The first fragment of the Old English *Waldhere* is part of a speech by Hildegund encouraging Walter.

The second fragment opens with the end of a speech, apparently by Gunther, and then gives Walter's reply.]

A

. . . she encouraged him eagerly: 'Surely the work of Weland will fail not any of men, of those who can hold stout Mimming.[1] Often in the battle one warrior after another has fallen bloodstained and stricken with the sword. Best warrior of Attila, let not thy might now perish to-day, thy valour fail. Now the day has come, when thou, son of Ælfhere, must do one of two things—lose thy life or achieve lasting glory among men. Never shall I blame thee in words, my friend, that I saw thee at the sword-play flee from any man's onset as a craven, or fly to the wall to save thy life, though many foes cut thy corslet with swords. But thou soughtest ever to press the fight further. Wherefore I feared for thy fate, that thou shouldest seek the fight too keenly, battle with another man on the field. Win fame by valiant deeds, and may God guard thee the while.

[1] The most famous of the swords made by Weland. Compare *Beowulf* (Section vii), where Beowulf's corslet is called 'the work of Weland.'

Have no misgivings for thy sword; the choicest of treasures was
given to thee for help to us two. With it thou shalt break the
boast of Guthhere, since he first sought the battle wrongly;
he refused the sword and the treasures, the many rings; now
must he needs depart from this battle bare of rings; the lord
must seek his old domain, or here die before, if he then . . .'

B

'. . . a better sword except the one which I also have laid at rest
in its scabbard set with stones. I know that Theodric thought
of sending it to Widia himself and also much treasure with the
sword, and of decking much beside it with gold. The kinsman
of Nithhad, Widia, son of Weland, received the meed for past
deeds, because he had delivered him from durance. Through
the domain of the monsters he hastened forth.'

Waldhere spoke, daring warrior; he had in his hand the help in
battle, the piercing war sword; he spoke in measured words:
'Lo, surely, thou didst think, friend of the Burgundians, that
Hagen's hand would prevail against me and remove me from
combat; come and take, if thou darest, the grey corslet from me,
who am thus weary of battle. The heirloom of Ælfhere lies here
on my shoulders good and broadly woven, adorned with gold, no
mean dress for a prince to bear, when his hand protects his life
against foes; it will not turn against me when evil kinsmen make
a new onset, meet with swords, as ye did to me. Yet He can
give victory who is ever prompt and wise in every matter of
right; he who trusts to the Holy One for help, to God for aid,
finds it ready there, if he takes thought before how to deserve it.
Then may the proud give wealth, rule over possessions; that
is . . .'

WIDSITH

[*Widsith* or *Farway* was probably composed in the seventh century, but seems to have received later additions, such as the passage referring to the Medes, Persians, and Hebrews. The poem is thus one of the oldest, if not the oldest, in our language. It is the song of a wandering minstrel who tells with pride of the rulers, the peoples, and the heroes he has known. *Widsith* is not to be taken as the record of the actual travels of a real gleeman. A minstrel who had been at the court of Eormanric who died A.D. 375 could not have been in Italy with Ælfwine (Alboin) who invaded Italy in 568. *Widsith* is a record of the tribes and heroes of the age of the barbarian invasions of Italy, and its author was a man who loved the old stories of dead kings and warriors. He gives a catalogue of heroic lore, the repertoire of stories which an English minstrel of his day had at his command. For a full treatment of the allusions in the poem, see R. W. Chamber's *Widsith* (Cambridge University Press).]

WIDSITH spoke, unlocked his word-hoard, he who of men had fared through most races and peoples over the earth; often he had received in hall precious treasure. His ancestors sprang from the Myrgings.[1] He with Ealhhild, gracious weaver of peace, first, from Angel in the east, sought the home of the Gothic king Eormanric, the savage faithless one.[2] He began then to speak many things:

'I have heard of many men ruling over the peoples; every prince must needs live fittingly; one earl after another must rule the land, he who wishes his throne to prosper. Of these Hwala was for a time the best and Alexander mightiest of all the race of men, and he prospered most of those of whom I have heard tell throughout the earth. Ætla[3] ruled the Huns, Eormanric the Goths, Becca[4] the Banings, Gifica the Burgundians. Cæsar ruled the Greeks and Cælic the Finns, Hagena the Island-Rugians and Heoden[5] the Glommas. Witta ruled

---

[1] Probably between the Eider and the Elbe. Most of the tribes in the poem lived on the shores of the North Sea or of the Baltic.

[2] Eormanric's wolfish mind is mentioned in *Deor*. Ealhhild is probably his wife. The story is that he murdered her.

[3] Attila.

[4] Eormanric sent his son and Becca to woo Swanhild (probably the same as Ealhhild) on his behalf. Becca proved traitor both to Eormanric and to the son.

[5] Heoden carried off Hagena's daughter Hild.

the Swabians, Wade[1] the Hælsings, Meaca the Myrgings, Mearchealf the Hundings. Theodric[2] ruled the Franks, Thyle the Rondings, Breoca[3] the Brondings, Billing the Wærnas. Oswine ruled the Eowan, and Gefwulf the Jutes, Fin Folc-walding[4] the race of the Frisians. Sigehere ruled the Sea-Danes for a very long time, Hnæf[5] the Hocings, Helm the Wulfings, Wald the Woingas, Wod the Thuringians, Sæferth[6] the Secgan, Ongentheow[7] the Swedes, Sceafthere the Ymbras, Sceafa the Longobards, Hun the Hætwere, and Holen the Wrosnas. Hringweald was called king of the pirates. Offa ruled Angel, Alewih the Danes: he was bravest of all these men, yet he did not perform mighty deeds beyond Offa; but Offa, first of men, while still a youth, gained the greatest of kingdoms; no one of the same age achieved greater deeds of valour in battle: with his single sword he fixed the boundary against the Myrgings at Fifeldor.[8] Afterwards the Angles and Swabians held it as Offa had won it. Hrothwulf and Hrothgar kept peace for a very long time, uncle and nephew, when they had driven away the race of the Vikings and overcome the array of Ingeld, destroyed at Heorot the host of the Heathobards.[9] Thus I travelled through many foreign lands, through this wide world; good and evil I suffered there, cut off from kinsmen, far from those of my blood; I served far and wide.

'Wherefore I may sing and utter a measure; recite before the company in the mead hall how the noble ones were liberal to me in their generosity. I was with the Huns and with the glorious Goths, with the Swedes and with Geats and with South-Danes. With the Wendlas I was and with the Wærnas and with the Vikings. With the Gefthas I was and with the Wends and with the Gefflegas. With the Angles I was and with the Swabians and with the Ænenas. With the Saxons I was and with the Secgan and with the Sweordweras. With the Hronas I was and with the Danes and the Heathoremes.

[1] Father of Weland. He helped Heoden to carry off Hild. He was credited with power over the sea and with great strength.

[2] The historical Theodoric I of the sixth century. He became a famous figure in later medieval poetry. His son Theodebert conquered Hygelac (see *Beowulf*).

[3] Apparently the Breca of *Beowulf*.

[4] The Finn of *Beowulf* and *Finnesburh*.

[5] See *Beowulf*.

[6] The Sigeferth of *Finnesburh*.

[7] See *Beowulf*.

[8] Offa is mentioned in *Beowulf* as the husband of Thryth; here as the champion of the Angles against the Myrgings. Fifeldor is the Eider.

[9] See *Beowulf*.

With the Thuringians I was and with the Throwendas and with the Burgundians, where I received an armlet; Guthhere[1] gave me there a splendid jewel in reward for my song; that was no sluggish king! With the Franks I was, and with the Frisians and with the Frumtings. With the Rugas I was, and with the Glommas and with the Romans. Likewise I was in Italy with Ælfwine; he had, I have heard, the promptest hand among mankind to gain praise, a heart most generous in giving of rings, gleaming armlets, the son of Eadwine.[2] I was with the Saracens and with the Serings. With the Greeks I was and with the Finns and with Caesar who had festive cities in his power, riches and things to be desired, and the kingdom of Welshland. With the Scots I was, and with the Picts, and with the Scride-Finns. With the Lidwicings I was and with the Leonas and with the Longobards, with the Hæthnas and with the Hærethas and with the Hundings. With the Israelites I was and with the Assyrians, with the Hebrews and the Jews and with the Egyptians. With the Medes I was and with the Persians and with the Myrgings and the Mofdings and against the Myrgings and with the Amothingas. With the East Thuringians I was and with the Eolas and with the Iste and with the Idumingas.

'And I was with Eormanric all the time; then the king of the Goths treated me well; he, prince of the city-dwellers, gave me a ring in which there was reckoned to be six hundred pieces of pure gold counted by shillings; I gave it into the keeping of Eadgils,[3] my protecting lord, when I came home, as reward to the dear one because he, the prince of the Myrgings, gave me land, my father's dwelling-place; and then Ealhhild, the daughter of Eadwine, a queen noble in majesty, gave me another. Her praise was spread through many lands, whenever it fell to me to tell in song, where under the sky I best knew a gold-adorned queen bestowing gifts. When Scilling and I with clear voice raised the song before our victorious lord—loud to the harp the words sounded in harmony—then many men proud in mind, of full knowledge, said they had never heard a better song. Thence I passed through all the land of the Goths; I sought ever the best of companions, that was the household of

---

[1] Same as the Guthhere of *Waldhere*; historical king of the Burgundians in fifth century. For centuries he remained a famous figure in poetry. In the *Nibelungen Lied* he appears as Gunther.

[2] Ælfwine and his father Eadwine are the Alboin and Audoin (*d.* 565) of history, kings of the Lombards.

[3] Not the Eadgils of *Beowulf*.

Eormanric. Hethca I sought and Beadeca and the Harlungs, Emerca and Fridla;[1] and East-Gota,[2] wise and good, father of Unwen. Secca I sought and Becca, Seafola and Theodric,[3] Heathoric and Sifeca,[4] Hlithe and Incgentheow. Eadwine I sought and Elsa, Ægelmund and Hungar and the proud band of the Withmyrgings. Wulfhere I sought and Wyrmhere:[5] full often there war did not fail when the army of the Goths with their strong swords must defend their ancient domain against the people of Ætla by the Vistula-wood. Rædhere I sought and Rondhere, Rumstan and Gislhere, Withergield[6] and Frederick,[7] Wudga and Hama;[8] those were not the worst companions though I am to name them last. Full often from that band the yelling spear flew screaming against the hostile people; Wudga and Hama, wanderers, had sway there over men and women by twisted gold. So I ever found it in my faring, that he is most dear to dwellers in a land to whom God gives power over men to hold while he lives here.

Thus the minstrels of men go wandering, as fate directs, through many lands; they utter their need, speak the word of thanks; south or north, they always meet one wise in measures, liberal in gifts, who wishes to exalt his glory before the warriors, to perform valorous deeds, until light and life fall in ruin together: he gains praise, he has lofty glory under the heavens.

[1] Emerca and Fridla were nephews of Eormanric.

[2] Ancestor of Eormanric.

[3] Probably Theodoric the Goth, not Theodoric the Frank mentioned earlier. Seafola was his retainer.

[4] A traitor whose evil advice led Eormanric to put his sons to death.

[5] Hlithe, Incgentheow, and Wyrmhere are probably heroes of the wars between the Huns and Goths.

[6] Probably the same as the Withergyld of *Beowulf* (Section xxx).

[7] Probably the son of Eormanric.

[8] Wudga is a Gothic hero. He is mentioned in *Waldhere* as receiving a reward for helping Theodric. Hama is spoken of in *Beowulf* as having robbed Eormanric.

DEOR

[*Deor* is the lament of a minstrel who has been supplanted in his lord's favour by a rival singer. He seeks comfort by recalling 'old, unhappy, far-off things,' and in the refrain, which is found only here and in *Wulf and Eadwacer* in Old English poetry, he expresses his hope that his trouble may pass as the troubles of men before him have done.

The poem is interesting not only because of the refrain, but also because it refers to stories which were well known in England, but which have not been preserved for us in English poems.

Weland, the famous smith of Teutonic legend, was carried into captivity by Nithhad, but he avenged himself and escaped. Beadohild, the daughter of Nithhad, was outraged by Weland, but bore a mighty son Widia. Widia is referred to in *Waldhere* as receiving a reward for aiding Theodric. The Geat's love for Mæthhild is apparently one of the many stories which have been lost. Among the stories which gathered round the historical Theodoric was a story of his thirty years' exile. Probably the passage in *Deor* refers to this. The rule of Eormanric was oppressive to men, but death ended his sovereignty.

Thinking of these old tales, Deor hopes that he may not always be an unhappy wanderer.]

WELAND, the resolute warrior, had knowledge of exile; he suffered hardships; sorrow and longing he had for companions, wintry cold exile. Often he found woes after Nithhad put compulsion upon him, supple bonds of sinew upon a more excellent man.

That passed away, so may this.

Her brothers' death was not so sore upon Beadohild's mind as her own state, when she had clearly seen that she was with child. She could never think with a light heart of what must come of that.

That passed away, so may this.

Many of us have heard that the Geat's love for Mæthhild grew boundless, that his grievous passion wholly reft him of sleep.

That passed away, so may this.

Theodric ruled for thirty years the stronghold of the Merovingians; that was known to many.

That passed away, so may this.

We have heard of the wolfish mind of Eormanric; he held wide sway in the kingdom of the Goths; he was a savage king. Many a warrior sat, bound by sorrow, expecting woe, often wishing his kingdom should be overcome.

That passed away, so may this.

The sad-minded man sits bereft of joys; there is gloom in his mind; it seems to him that his portion of sufferings is endless. Then he may think that throughout this world the wise Lord brings many changes; to many a man He grants honour, certain fame; to some a sorrowful portion.

I will say this of myself, that once I was a minstrel of the Heodeningas, dear to my lord. Deor was my name. For many years I had a good office, a gracious lord, until now Heorrenda, a man skilled in song, has received my land that the protector of warriors formerly gave me.

That passed away, so may this.

THE WANDERER

[*The Wanderer* is an elegy uttered by one who had formerly known happiness and honour in his lord's hall. Now his lord is dead, and he has lost his post. He has become a wanderer who knows that 'sorrow's crown of sorrow is remembering happier things.']

OFTEN the solitary man prays for favour, for the mercy of the Lord, though, sad at heart, he must needs stir with his hands for a weary while the icy sea across the watery ways, must journey the paths of exile; settled in truth is fate! So spoke the wanderer, mindful of hardships, of cruel slaughters, of the fall of kinsmen:

'Often I must bewail my sorrows in my loneliness at the dawn of each day; there is none of living men now to whom I dare speak my heart openly. I know for a truth that it is a noble custom for a man to bind fast the thoughts of his heart, to treasure his broodings, let him think as he will. Nor can the weary in mood resist fate, nor does the fierce thought avail anything. Wherefore those eager for glory often bind fast in their secret hearts a sad thought. So I, sundered from my native land, far from noble kinsmen, often sad at heart, had to fetter my mind, when in years gone by the darkness of the earth covered my gold-friend, and I went thence in wretchedness with wintry care upon me over the frozen waves, gloomily sought the hall of a treasure-giver wherever I could find him far or near, who might know me in the mead hall or comfort me, left without friends, treat me with kindness. He knows who puts it to the test how cruel a comrade is sorrow for him who has few dear protectors; his is the path of exile, in no wise the twisted gold; a chill body, in no wise the riches of the earth; he thinks of retainers in hall and the receiving of treasure, of how in his youth his gold-friend was kind to him at the feast. The joy has all perished. Wherefore he knows this who must long forgo the counsels of his dear lord and friend, when sorrow and sleep together often bind the poor solitary man; it seems to him in his mind that he clasps and kisses his lord and lays hands and head on his knee, as when erstwhile in past days he was near the gift-throne; then the friendless man wakes again, sees before him the dark waves, the sea-birds bathing, spreading their feathers; frost and snow falling mingled with hail. Then heavier are the wounds in his heart, sore for his beloved; sorrow is renewed. Then the memory of kinsmen crosses his mind; he greets them with songs; he gazes on them eagerly. The companions of warriors swim away again; the souls of sailors bring there not many known songs.[1] Care is renewed in him who must needs send very often his weary mind over the frozen waves. And thus I cannot think why in this world my mind becomes not overcast when I consider all the life of earls, how of a sudden they have given up hall, courageous retainers. So this world each day passes and falls; for a man cannot become wise till he has his share of years in the world. A wise man must be patient, not over-passionate, nor over-hasty of speech, nor over-weak or rash in war, nor over-fearful, nor over-glad, nor over-covetous, never over-eager to boast ere he has full knowledge. A man must bide his time, when he boasts in his speech, until he knows well in his pride whither the thoughts of the mind will turn. A wise man must see how dreary it will be when all the riches of this world stand waste, as in different places throughout this world walls stand, blown upon by winds, hung with frost, the dwellings in ruins. The wine halls crumble; the rulers lie low, bereft of joy; the mighty warriors have all fallen in their pride by the wall; war carried off some, bore them on far paths; one the raven bore away over the high sea; one the grey wolf gave over to death; one an earl with sad face hid in the earth-cave. Thus did the Creator of men lay waste this earth till the old work of giants stood empty, free from the revel of castle-dwellers. Then he who has thought wisely of the foundation of things and who deeply ponders this dark life, wise in his heart, often turns his thoughts to the many slaughters of the past, and speaks these words:

'"Whither has gone the horse? Whither has gone the man? Whither has gone the giver of treasure? Whither has gone the place of feasting? Where are the joys of hall? Alas, the bright cup! Alas, the warrior in his corslet! Alas, the glory of the prince! How that time has passed away, has grown dark under the shadow of night, as if it had never been! Now in the place of the dear warriors stands a wall, wondrous high, covered with serpent shapes; the might of the ash-wood spears has carried off the earls, the weapon greedy for slaughter—a glorious fate; and storms beat upon these rocky slopes; the falling storm binds the earth, the terror of winter. Then comes darkness, the night

[1] An obscure passage.

shadow casts gloom, sends from the north fierce hailstorms to the terror of men. Everything is full of hardship in the kingdom of earth; the decree of fate changes the world under the heavens. Here possessions are transient, here friends are transient, here man is transient, here woman is transient; all this firm-set earth becomes empty.'"

So spoke the wise man in his heart, and sat apart in thought. Good is he who holds his faith; nor shall a man ever show forth too quickly the sorrow of his breast, except he, the earl, first know how to work its cure bravely. Well is it for him who seeks mercy, comfort from the Father in heaven, where for us all security stands.

THE SEAFARER

[*The Seafarer* is taken by some critics to be a dialogue in which an old sailor tells of the lonely sufferings of life at sea, and is answered by a youth who urges that it is the hardness of the life which makes it attractive. The poem, however, may be a monologue in which the speaker tells of his sufferings, but also admits the fascination of the sea. The mood of contempt for the luxuries of land and his yearning to set forth on the voyage lead him to think of the future life and the fleeting nature of earthly pomps and joys.]

I CAN utter a true song about myself, tell of my travels, how in toilsome days I often suffered a time of hardship, how I have borne bitter sorrow in my breast, made trial of many sorrowful abodes on ships; dread was the rolling of the waves. There the hard night-watch at the boat's prow was often my task, when it tosses by the cliffs. Afflicted with cold, my feet were fettered by frost, by chill bonds. There my sorrows, hot round my heart, were sighed forth; hunger within rent the mind of the sea-weary man. The man who fares most prosperously on land knows not how I, careworn, have spent a winter as an exile on the ice-cold sea, cut off from kinsmen, hung round with icicles. The hail flew in showers. I heard naught there save the sea booming, the ice-cold billow, at times the song of the swan. I took my gladness in the cry of the gannet and the sound of the curlew instead of the laughter of men, in the screaming gull instead of the drink of mead. There storms beat upon the rocky cliffs; there the tern with icy feathers answered them; full often the dewy-winged eagle screamed around. No protector could comfort the heart in its need. And yet he who has the bliss of life, who, proud and flushed with wine, suffers few hardships in the city, little believes how I often in weariness had to dwell on the ocean path. The shadow of night grew dark, snow came from the north, frost bound the earth; hail fell on the ground, coldest of grain. And yet the thoughts of my heart are now stirred that I myself should make trial of the high streams, of the tossing of the salt waves; the desire of the heart always exhorts to venture forth that I may visit the land of strange people far hence. And yet there is no man on earth so proud, nor so generous of his gifts, nor so bold in youth, nor so daring in his deeds, nor with a lord so gracious unto him, that he has not always anxiety about his seafaring, as to what the Lord will bestow on him. His thoughts are not of the harp, nor of receiving rings, nor of delight in a woman, nor of joy in the world, nor of aught else save the rolling of the waves; but he who sets out on the waters ever feels longing. The groves put forth blossoms; cities grow beautiful; the fields are fair; the world revives; all these urge the heart of the eager-minded man to a journey, him who thus purposes to fare far on the ways of the flood. Likewise the cuckoo exhorts with sad voice; the harbinger of summer sings, bodes bitter sorrow to the heart. The man knows not, the prosperous being, what some of those endure who most widely pace the paths of exile. And yet my heart is now restless in my breast, my mind is with the sea-flood over the whale's domain; it fares widely over the face of the earth, comes again to me eager and unsatisfied; the lone-flier screams, resistlessly urges the heart to the whale-way over the stretch of seas.

Wherefore the joys of the Lord are more inspiring for me than this dead fleeting life on earth. I have no faith that earthly riches will abide for ever. Each one of three things is ever uncertain ere its time comes; illness or age or hostility will take life away from a man doomed and dying. Wherefore the praise of living men who shall speak after he is gone, the best of fame after death for every man, is that he should strive ere he must depart, work on earth with bold deeds against the malice of fiends, against the devil, so that the children of men may later exalt him and his praise live afterwards among the angels for ever and ever, the joy of life eternal, delight amid angels.

The days have departed, all the pomps of earth's kingdom; kings, or emperors, or givers of gold, are not as of yore when they wrought among themselves greatest deeds of glory, and lived in most lordly splendour. This host has all fallen, the delights have departed; weaklings live on and possess this world, enjoy it by their toil. Glory is laid low; the nobleness of the earth ages and withers, as now every man does throughout the world. Old age comes on him; his face grows pale; grey-haired he laments; he knows that his former friends, the sons of princes, have been laid in the earth. Then, when life leaves him, his body can neither taste sweetness, nor feel pain, nor stir a hand, nor ponder in thought. Though he will strew the grave with gold, bury his brother with various treasures beside dead kinsmen, that will not go with him.[1] To the soul full of sins the gold

[1] An obscure passage.

which it hoards while it lives here gives no help in the face of God's wrath.   Great is the fear of God, whereby the earth turns; He established the mighty plains, the face of the earth, and the sky above.   Foolish is he who fears not his Lord; death comes to him unexpected.   Blessed is he who lives humbly; mercy comes to him from heaven; God establishes that heart in him because he trusts in his strength.

One must check a violent mind and control it with firmness, and be trustworthy to men, pure in ways of life.

Every man should show moderation in love towards a friend and enmity towards a foe. . . .   Fate is more strong, God more mighty than any man's thought.   Let us consider where we possess our home, and then think how we may come thither, and let us then also attempt to win there, to the eternal bliss, where life springs from God's love, joy in heaven.   Thanks be for ever to the Holy One because He, the Prince of glory, the Lord ever-lasting, has honoured us.   Amen.

THE WIFE'S LAMENT

[*The Wife's Lament* is a monologue by a woman parted from her husband. Her husband has left his country, perhaps driven out by a feud. In his absence the wife has been persecuted and forced to dwell in the wilderness, apparently by her husband's enemies. She throws all the blame on the foe and calls down a curse on him, praying that he may know the wretchedness of exile and loneliness. It is possible that there is a connection between this poem and *The Husband's Message*.]

I MAKE this song of my deep sadness, of my own lot. I can say that since I grew up I have not endured miseries new or old more than now. Ever I suffer the torment of my exile. First my lord went hence from his people over the tossing waves. I had sorrow at dawn as to where in the land my lord might be. Then I set out, a friendless exile, to seek helpers in my woeful hard straits. The man's kinsmen began to plot in secret thought to part us, so that we should live most wretchedly, most widely sundered in the world, and a yearning came upon me. My lord bade me take up my dwelling here; few dear loyal friends had I in this place; and so my mind is sad, since I found the man most mated to me unhappy, sad in heart, cloaking his mind, plotting mischief with blithe manner. Full often we two pledged one another that naught but death should divide us; that is changed now. Our friendship now is as if it had not been. I must needs endure the hate of my dear one far and near. They bade me dwell in the forest grove under the oak-tree in the earth-cave. Old is this earth-hall; I am filled with yearning. Dim are the valleys, high the hills, harsh strongholds o'ergrown with briers, dwellings empty of joy. Full often the departure of my lord has seized cruelly upon me. There are loving friends alive on the earth; they have their bed; while alone at dawn I pass through this earth-cave to beneath the oak-tree, where I sit a long summer's day. There I can mourn my miseries, many hardships, for I can never calm my care of mind, nor all that longing which has come upon me in this life. Ever may that youth be sad of mood, grievous the thought of his heart; may he likewise be forced to wear a blithe air and also care in his breast, the affliction of constant sorrows. May all his joy in the world depend on himself only; may he be banished very far in a distant land where my friend sits under a rocky slope chilled by the storm, my friend weary in mind, girt round with water in a sad dwelling. My friend suffers great grief; too often he remembers a happier home. Ill is it for him who must suffer longing for his loved one.

THE HUSBAND'S MESSAGE

[*The Husband's Message* is spoken by the letter itself which comes to assure
the faithful, waiting wife of her husband's faith. He has prepared a new
home for her abroad and calls on her to sail thither in the spring when the
cuckoo's song is heard.

The poem resembles the *Riddles* in its device of making inanimate objects
speak. The runic letters at the end of the poem are perhaps a kind of secret
sign from the husband understood by the wife.]

Now I will tell thee apart my lineage as a tree. I grew up in my
youth elsewhere in the land; a voyage took me over the salt
streams. Very often in the boat's bosom I sought high dwel-
lings where my master sent me. Now I have come here in the
ship, and now thou shalt know how thou mayest think in thy
mind of my lord's love. I dare promise that thou wilt find there
firm faith.

Lo! he who engraved this wood bade me pray thee that thou,
treasure-adorned, shouldst call to thy mind the promises which
you two often spoke in earlier days, while yet you might have
your abode in the mead castles, live in the same land, enjoy
friendship. A feud drove him away from the victorious people;
now he himself has bidden me tell thee joyfully, that thou
shouldst cross the sea, when on the edge of the mountain thou
hast heard the sad cuckoo cry in the grove. After that let no
living man hold thee from the journey or hinder thy going.
Go seek the sea, the home of the gull! Board the ship, so that
south from here thou mayest find thy husband over the path of
the sea, where thy lord lives in hopes of thee. Nor may a wish in
the world come more to his mind, from what he said to me, than
that Almighty God should grant you two that together you may
afterwards give treasure, studded armlets, to warriors and
companions. He has enough treasures of beaten gold, though in
a foreign land he holds his dwelling, in a fair country. Many
proud heroes wait upon him, though here my friendly lord,
driven by necessity, launched his boat and was forced to go forth
alone on the stretch of the waves, on the way of the flood, to
furrow the ocean streams, eager for departure. Now the man
has overcome woe; he lacks not his desires, nor horses, nor
treasures, nor mead joys, none of the precious stores of earls on

the earth, O prince's daughter, if he enjoy thee in spite of the old threat against you two.　I put together S. R. EA. W. and D. to assure thee with an oath that he was there, and that he would perform, while he lived, the true faith which you two often spoke in earlier days.

WULF AND EADWACER

[This poem is very obscure and has been interpreted in various ways. It is found in the *Exeter Book* immediately preceding the *Riddles*, and the old view was that it was a riddle itself. By doing some violence to the text the solution *Cynewulf* was found, and this led to the theory that Cynewulf was the author of the *Riddles*. These conjectures are now discredited, and the poem is generally believed not to be a riddle at all, but a dramatic monologue such as *Deor* and *The Wife's Lament*. This view was first stated by Henry Bradley in 1888. Attempts have been made to connect the poem with Teutonic and with Norse legend but nothing has been proved. The main features of Bradley's view are as follows: The speaker is a woman, and apparently a captive in a foreign land. Wulf, whom she longs for, is her outlawed lover, and Eadwacer probably her tyrannous husband. There are difficult words and phrases in the text and any translation must be regarded as tentative. Like *Deor* the poem is remarkable for its use of a refrain.]

* * * * *

Is to my people as if one gave them an offering.
Will they feed him, if he should feel want?
       It is not so with us.
Wulf is on an island, I on another;
Closely begirt is that island with bog;
Cruel men are there on the island;
Will they feed him, if he should feel want?
       It is not so with us.
I waited for my Wulf with far-wandering yearnings,
When it was rainy weather and I sat weeping.
When the warlike man wound his arms about me,
It was pleasure to me, yet it was also pain.
Wulf, my Wulf, my yearnings for thee
Have made me sick, thy rare visits,
A woeful heart and not want of food.
Dost thou hear, Eadwacer? Our cowardly cub
Wulf shall bear off to the wood.
They can easily sunder that which was never joined together,
The song of us two together.

THE RUIN

[This elegy on a ruined city with its fallen walls and departed glory is taken by many to refer to the city of Bath. The text of the poem is unfortunately in a very imperfect condition and the meaning often uncertain, but the passionate regret with which it pictures the city,

'Where a multitude of men breathed joy and woe
Long ago,'

makes it one of the greatest of Old English poems.]

WONDROUS is this wall-stone; broken by fate, the castles have decayed; the work of giants is crumbling. Roofs are fallen, ruinous are the towers, despoiled are the towers with their gates; frost is on their cement, broken are the roofs, cut away, fallen, undermined by age. The grasp of the earth, stout grip of the ground, holds its mighty builders, who have perished and gone; till now a hundred generations of men have died. Often this wall, grey with lichen and stained with red, unmoved under storms, has survived kingdom after kingdom; its lofty gate has fallen . . . the bold in spirit bound the foundation of the wall wondrously together with wires. Bright were the castle-dwellings, many the bath-houses, lofty the host of pinnacles, great the tumult of men, many a mead hall full of the joys of men, till Fate the mighty overturned that. The wide walls fell; days of pestilence came; death swept away all the bravery of men; their fortresses became waste places; the city fell to ruin. The multitudes who might have built it anew lay dead on the earth. Wherefore these courts are in decay and these lofty gates; the woodwork of the roof is stripped of tiles; the place has sunk into ruin, levelled to the hills, where in times past many a man light of heart and bright with gold, adorned with splendours, proud and flushed with wine, shone in war trappings, gazed on treasure, on silver, on precious stones, on riches, on possessions, on costly gems, on this bright castle of the broad kingdom. Stone courts stood here; the stream with its great gush sprang forth hotly; the wall enclosed all within its bright bosom; there the baths were hot in its centre; that was spacious . . .

CHARMS

[The *Charms* preserve much superstition and folklore. In them Christian and pagan elements are curiously mingled. They show how the old beliefs and customs were gradually overlaid and transformed by the new faith. The Church won men away gradually, not abruptly. The clergy themselves were often credulous. Pope Gregory, in giving advice to the English missionaries, recommended them not to destroy the old temples, but merely the idols. Holy water should be sprinkled in the old places of worship and altars and relics placed there, 'that the nation, seeing that their temples are not destroyed, may remove error from their hearts, and knowing and adoring the true God, may the more familiarly resort to the places to which they have been accustomed.' Later the attitude towards heathen practices became less conciliatory, and laws were passed against the old usages. The *Charms* are difficult to date. They are preserved in manuscripts of the tenth century or later, but the passages in them untouched by Christian beliefs are probably among the oldest lines in the English language.]

FOR A SUDDEN STITCH

[This charm offers considerable difficulty. The first part describes the attack of the spirits which cause the pain. The exorcist hears and sees them from where he stands under the safety of his shield. He calls upon the pain to leave the sufferer by repeating the formula, 'Out, little spear, if herein thou be!' The exorcist has three retaliatory measures—the arrow, the knife forged by the smith, and the spears wrought by six smiths. Then having driven the pain forth he proceeds to heal the wound by naming its situation and author. Perhaps each formula is accompanied by application of the salve the ingredients of which are given at the beginning of the charm. Finally the pain is banished to the mountain. The last line is a final direction to the exorcist. The knife, it would seem, is to be used on a dummy representing the evil spirits.]

FEVERFEW and the red nettle which grows through the house and plantain; boil in butter—

Loud were they, lo! loud, when they rode over the hill,
Resolute were they when they rode over the land.
Fend thyself now, that thou mayest survive this violence!
Out, little spear, if herein thou be!
I stood under the targe, beneath a light shield,
Where the mighty women made ready their strength
And sent whizzing spears;

85

I will send them back another
Flying arrow in their faces.
Out, little spear, if herein it be!
The smith sat, forged his little knife,
Sore smitten with iron.
Out, little spear, if herein thou be!
Six smiths sat, wrought war spears.
Out, spear, not in, spear!
If herein be aught of iron,
Work of witch, it shall melt.
If thou wert shot in the skin, or if thou wert shot in the flesh,
Or if thou wert shot in the blood, or if thou wert shot in the
     bone,
Or if thou wert shot in the limb, thy life shall never be harmed.
If it were the shot of gods, or if it were shot of elves,
Or if it were shot of witch, now I will help thee.
This to relieve thee from shot of gods, this to relieve thee from
     shot of elves,
This to relieve thee from shot of witch; I will help thee.
Flee to the mountain-head,
Be thou whole; may the Lord help thee.

Take then the knife; plunge it into the liquid.

AGAINST A DWARF

[The dwarf, against whom the charge is directed, apparently represents some
     convulsive disease. The names invoked at the beginning are those of
     the Seven Sleepers whose influence may be expected to soothe a violent
     sufferer. The charm, it seems, is to be sung over the patient and then
     hung round his neck. The spider is most easily explained as identical
     with the dwarf. The creature lays its bonds on its victim, but its power
     is checked by the friendly effort of the beast's sister who takes the dwarf
     or spider away and leaves the sufferer's wounds to cool.]

You must take seven little wafers, such as one uses in worship,
and write these names on each wafer: Maximianus, Malchus,
Johannes, Martinianus, Dionysius, Constantinus, Serapion.
Then afterwards you must sing the charm which is given below,
first into the left ear, then into the right ear, then over the man's
head. And then let a maiden go to him and hang it upon his
neck, and do this for three days; he will straightway be better.

Here came a spider creature stalking in;
He had his dress in his hand.
He said that thou wert his steed.
He puts his bonds on thy neck.
They began to sail from the land.
As soon as they left the land,
They began then to cool.
Then came the beast's sister stalking in,
Then she made an end and swore these oaths:
That this should never hurt the sick,
Nor him who could acquire this charm,
Nor him who could chant this charm.
Amen, fiat.

AGAINST WENS

[In this charm the exorcist begins in a tone of command (lines 1–3); then (lines 4–5) he becomes persuasive. In lines 6–7 he is once more stern. The charm ends with a series of similes.]

WEN, wen, little wen,
Here thou shalt not build, nor have any abode.
But thou must pass forth to the hill hard by,
Where thou hast a brother in misery.
He shall lay a leaf at thy head.

Under the foot of the wolf, under the wing of the eagle,
Under the claw of the eagle, ever mayest thou fade.
Shrivel as coal on the hearth,
Shrink as muck in the wall,
And waste away like water in a bucket.
Become as small as a grain of linseed,
And far smaller also than a hand-worm's hip-bone,
And become even so small that thou become naught.

FOR A SWARM OF BEES

[The purpose of this charm is not so much to prevent a swarm as to keep the
bees from going too far when they do swarm. The man referred to may
be the sorcerer who is thought to have caused the swarm. The flattery
about his mighty tongue may be intended to mollify him, just as the
phrase 'victorious women' is meant to flatter the bees.]

TAKE earth, cast it with thy right hand under thy right foot, and
say:

> 'I put it under foot; I have found it.
> Lo, the earth can prevail against all creatures,
> And against injury, and against forgetfulness,
> And against the mighty tongue of man.'

Cast gravel over them when they swarm, and say:

> 'Alight, victorious women, descend to earth!
> Never fly wild to the wood.
> Be as mindful of my profit
> As every man is of food and fatherland.'

LAND-REMEDY

[In this charm Christianity and paganism stand side by side. The new faith
has partly transformed the old heathen beliefs and customs. First the
ceremonial is explained. This is followed by a prayer that the land may
be blessed. Then comes more ceremonial; and then the chief incanta-
tion—an address to Mother Earth. The first furrow is then to be made,
and Mother Earth again entreated. In the closing lines an attempt has
been made to offset the heathen tone of the charm by a Christian prayer.]

HERE is the remedy with which thou canst mend thy fields, if
they will not produce well, or if anything harmful is done to
them by sorcery or witchcraft.

Take then at night before dawn four sods from four sides of
the land and observe their former position. Then take oil and
honey and yeast and milk of all cattle which are on the land, and
part of every kind of tree which grows on the land, except hard
trees,[1] and part of every known herb, except burdock only; and
then put holy water thereon, and then let it[2] drop thrice on the

---

[1] Hard wood did not need sanctification.
[2] Probably this refers not only to the holy water, but also to the liquids
(oil, honey, etc.) mentioned above.

bottom of the sods,[1] and say then these words: 'Crescite grow, et multiplicamini and multiply, et replete and replenish, terram the earth. In nomine patris et filii et spiritus sancti sitis benedicti.' And Paternoster as often as the other.

And afterwards carry the sods to church, and let the mass-priest sing four masses over the sods, and let the green be turned to the altar, and later let the sods be brought ere sunset to where they were before. And let him have made four crosses of aspen wood and write on each end Matthew and Mark, Luke and John. Lay the cross on the bottom of the pit; then say: 'Crux Mattheus, Crux Marcus, Crux Lucas, Crux Sanctus Johannes.' Then take the sods and place them thereupon, and then say these words nine times: 'Crescite . . .' and as often a Paternoster, and then face east and bow humbly nine times, and then say these words:

'Eastward I stand, I pray for mercies;[2]
I pray the great Lord, pray the mighty God,
I pray the holy Guardian of heaven,
I pray earth and sky
And the righteous holy Mary
And the might of heaven and the lofty temple,
That this charm by the grace of God
I may utter; by strong resolve
Raise crops for worldly use,
Fill these fields by firm faith,
Make beautiful these meadows; as the prophet said
That he found favour here on earth who gave
Alms wisely, according to the will of God.'[3]

Then turn thrice with the course of the sun, then stretch thyself flat and repeat the litanies; and then say Sanctus, sanctus, sanctus, to the end. Then sing Benedicite with arms extended and Magnificat and Paternoster thrice, and entrust it to the praise and honour of Christ and holy Mary and the sacred cross and to the profit of him who owns the land, and of all those who are under him. When all that is done, let unknown seed be taken from beggars, and let there be given them double what was taken from them. And let him gather all his ploughing tools together; then bore the beam and put in incense and fennel

[1] The placing of things on the sods is a symbol of the desired fruitfulness; it is also intended to sanctify the samples of all the things the field produces.
[2] This may originally have been a pagan prayer to 'the maturing sun.'
[3] Up to this point the charm refers to pasture land; what follows, to ploughed land.

and holy soap and holy salt.   Then take the seed, place it on the
body of the plough, then say:

'Erce, Erce, Erce,[1] mother of earth,
May the Almighty, the Lord everlasting, grant thee
Fields growing and flourishing,
Fruitful and reviving,
Store of gleaming millet-harvests,
And broad barley-crops,
And white wheat-crops,
And all the crops of the earth.
May the Lord everlasting
And his saints who are in heaven
Grant him that his land be kept safe from all foes
And may it be guarded against all evils,
Witchcrafts sown throughout the land.
Now I pray the Ruler who wrought this world
That no witch be eloquent enough, nor any man powerful
     enough
To pervert the words thus pronounced.'

Then let the plough be driven forth and the first furrow made.
Then say:

          'Hail to thee, Earth, mother of men!
           Be fruitful in God's embrace,
           Filled with food for the use of men.'

Then take meal of every kind and let a loaf be baked as broad
as the inside of the hands and knead it with milk and holy water,
and lay it under the first furrow.   Then say:

'Field full of food for mankind,
Brightly blooming, be thou blessed
In the holy name of Him who created this heaven
And this earth we live on.
May God who wrought these lands grant us growing gifts,
So that every kind of grain may prove of use.'

Then say thrice, 'Crescite, in nomine patris sitis benedicti.'
Amen and Paternoster thrice.

          [1] Perhaps a meaningless formula.

A JOURNEY SPELL

[A charm to be recited by a man about to set out on a journey and intended to protect him from all dangers by land or sea. St Eligius (588–659) said in a sermon: 'But whether you are setting out on a journey, or beginning any other work, cross yourself in the name of Christ, and say the Creed and the Lord's Prayer with faith and devotion, and then the enemy can do you no harm.']

I GUARD myself with this rod and give myself into God's protection,
Against the painful stroke, against the grievous stroke,
Against the grim dread,
Against the great terror which is hateful to each,
And against all evil which may enter the land.
I chant a charm of victory, I bear a rod of victory,
Word-victory, work-victory. May they be of power for me;
That no nightmare hinder me, nor belly-fiend afflict me,
Nor ever fear fall upon my life;
But may the Almighty save me, and the Son and the Holy Ghost,
The Lord worthy of all glory,
And, as I heard, Creator of the heavens.
Abraham and Isaac, Jacob and Joseph,
And such men, Moses and David,
And Eve and Hannah and Elizabeth,
Sarah and also Mary, Christ's mother,
And also the brethren, Peter and Paul,
And also thousands of the angels,
I call upon to fend me against all fiends.
May they lead me, and guard me, and protect my path,
Wholly preserve me and rule me,
Shaping my work; may I have the hope of heaven,
A hand to guard my head, saints to shield me,
A company of conquering, righteous angels.
Glad in heart I pray to them all, that Matthew be my helm,
Mark my breastplate, gleaming life's covering,
Luke my sword, sharp and bright-edged,
John my shield, made beautiful in glory, Seraph of those who travel.
Forth I fare; I shall find friends,
All the inspiration of angels, the counsel of the blessed.
I pray now to the God of victory, to the mercy of God,
For a good journey, a mild and gentle
Wind from these shores. I have heard of winds
Which rouse whirling waters. Thus ever preserved

From all fiends may I meet friends,
So that I may dwell in the Almighty's protection,
Guarded from the enemy who seeks my life,
Set amid the glory of the angels,
And in the holy hand of the Mighty One of heaven,
Whilst I may live in this life.—Amen.

FOR THEFT OF CATTLE

MAY naught of what I own be stolen or hidden any more than
Herod might do to our Lord.   I thought of St Helena, and I
thought of Christ hanging on the cross; so I look to find this
cattle,[1] not to have them borne away, and to learn of them, not
to have them injured, and to have them cared for, not led off.

> Garmund, servant of God,
> Find those cattle and fetch those cattle,
> And have those cattle and hold those cattle,
> And bring home those cattle.
> So that he may never have land to lead them to,
> Nor ground to bear them to,
> Nor houses to keep them in.
> If any should do so, may he never thrive by it!
> Within three nights I shall know his powers,
> His strength and his skill to protect.
> May he wholly wither as fire withers wood,
> As bramble or thistle hurts thigh,
> He who may purpose to bear off these cattle,
> Or think to drive away these kine.

NINE HERBS CHARM

[Some lines in this charm are now meaningless.   It is clearly an old heathen
thing which has been subjected to Christian censorship.]

FORGET not, Mugwort, what thou didst reveal,
What thou didst prepare at Regenmeld.[2]
Thou hast strength against three and against thirty,
Thou hast strength against poison and against infection,
Thou hast strength against the foe who fares through the land.

[1] That is, may my cattle be saved as Christ was from Herod, and may I
recover them as St Helena did the cross of Christ.
[2] This and Alorford, mentioned later, are apparently names of places.

And thou, Plantain, mother of herbs,
Open from the east, mighty within,
Over thee chariots creaked, over thee queens rode,
Over thee brides made outcry, over thee bulls gnashed their teeth.
All these thou didst withstand and resist;
So mayest thou withstand poison and infection,
And the foe who fares through the land.

This herb is called Stime; it grew on a stone,
It resists poison, it fights pain.
It is called harsh, it fights against poison.
This is the herb that strove against the snake;
This has strength against poison, this has strength against infection,
This has strength against the foe who fares through the land.

Now, Cock's-spur Grass, conquer the greater poisons, though thou art the lesser;
Thou, the mightier, vanquish the lesser until he is cured of both.

Remember, Mayweed, what thou didst reveal,
What thou didst bring to pass at Alorford:
That he never yielded his life because of infection,
After Mayweed was dressed for his food.

This is the herb which is called Wergulu;
The seal sent this over the back of the ocean
To heal the hurt of other poison.

These nine sprouts against nine poisons.

A snake came crawling, it bit a man.
Then Woden took nine glory-twigs,
Smote the serpent so that it flew into nine parts.
There apple brought this to pass against poison,
That she nevermore would enter her house.

Thyme and Fennel, a pair great in power,
The Wise Lord, holy in heaven,
Wrought these herbs while He hung on the cross;
He placed and put them in the seven worlds
To aid all, poor and rich.

It stands against pain, resists the venom,
It has power against three and against thirty,
Against a fiend's hand and against sudden trick,
Against witchcraft of vile creatures.

Now these nine herbs avail against nine evil spirits,
Against nine poisons and against nine infectious diseases,
Against the red poison, against the running poison,
Against the white poison, against the blue poison,
Against the yellow poison, against the green poison,
Against the black poison, against the blue poison,
Against the brown poison, against the crimson poison,
Against snake-blister, against water-blister,
Against thorn-blister, against thistle-blister,
Against ice-blister, against poison-blister;
If any poison comes flying from the east or any comes from the
    north,
Or any from the west upon the people.

Christ stood over disease of every kind.
I alone know running water, and the nine serpents heed it;
May all pastures now spring up with herbs,
The seas, all salt water, be destroyed,
When I blow this poison from thee.

Mugwort, plantain which is open eastward, lamb's cress,
cock's-spur grass, mayweed, nettle, crab-apple, thyme and
fennel, old soap; crush the herbs to dust, mix with the soap and
with the apple's juice. Make a paste of water and of ashes; take
fennel, boil it in the paste and bathe with egg-mixture, either
before or after he puts on the salve. Sing that charm on each of
the herbs: thrice before he works them together and on the apple
likewise; and sing that same charm into the man's mouth and
into both his ears and into the wound before he puts on the salve.

GENESIS

[This was formerly thought to be one poem and to be the work of Cædmon. We now know that there are two poems and that probably neither was written by Cædmon. *Genesis* (A), probably written early in the eighth century by a monk in one of the northern English monasteries, begins with a prologue about the war in heaven, and then goes on to paraphrase the Book of Genesis (chaps. i–xxii). The writer follows, as a general rule, the biblical narrative very closely. His object is to give a faithful rendering of the story in English, not to write good poetry. One example of independent and stirring writing is the account of the capture and rescue of Lot. The translator remembers the old heroic poetry and echoes its phrases, and is not content to stick to the quiet biblical story (Genesis xiv. 1–16). In the middle of *Genesis* (A) are over six hundred lines, now known as *Genesis* (B), or the *Later Genesis* (probably ninth century). In 1875 the great German scholar Sievers showed that these lines differed from the rest of the *Genesis* poem in metre, style, and vocabulary, and, indeed, from any Old English poetry. His theory was that *Genesis* (B) was a translation of a lost German original. This theory was confirmed in 1894 by the discovery in the Vatican of part of the German poem. How *Genesis* (B) came to be interpolated in the other poem we do not know. The subject of the *Later Genesis* is that of *Paradise Lost*. The passionate and defiant character of Satan revealed, as in Milton, by his speeches, and the dramatic treatment of Eve's temptation, make the poem one of the most remarkable things in our literature. There is no evidence that Milton knew the poem, but it is not impossible. The manuscript was, in the middle of the seventeenth century, in the possession of the scholar Junius. He and Milton were in London at the same time, but we do not know that they ever met. The resemblances between the work of Milton and that of his unknown predecessor are very striking.]

A

IT is very right for us to praise with words and to love in our hearts the Lord of heaven, the glorious King of hosts. He is fullness of power, Head of all exalted creatures, Lord Almighty. Beginning or source was never wrought for Him, nor shall an end come now for the Lord everlasting, but for ever in high majesty He shall be mighty above the thrones of heaven. Righteous and strong, He has ruled the realms of the sky; far and wide they were established by God's power for the children of glory, for the keepers of souls. The companies of angels felt gladness and joy, radiant bliss, towards their Creator. Great was their happiness. Servants in glory worshipped the

95

Prince, gladly uttered praise of their Lord of life, glorified God; they were exceeding rich in blessings. They could not commit sins or crimes; but they lived in peace for ever with their Prince.

They performed naught in heaven save right and truth, till the leader of the angels in his pride fell into error. They would no longer follow their own way of life, but turned from the love of God. They made great boasting that they could share with God the glorious abode, wide and radiant, amid the splendour of the host. Grief came upon them there, envy and presumption and the pride of that angel who first began to work and weave and stir up that wickedness, when, thirsting for strife, he declared that he would possess a dwelling and throne in the northern part of the kingdom of heaven! [1]

Then God grew angry and wroth at that band whom before He had honoured with beauty and glory. He made for the faithless ones as reward for their work a wretched abode, the lamentations of hell, grievous afflictions. Our Lord, when He knew it well, commanded the keepers of souls to endure the abode of torments and miseries in the depths, reft of joys, surrounded with eternal night, filled with anguish, pierced by fire and sudden cold, by smoke and red flame. Then He bade terrors of torment to spread through that joyless dwelling. They had fiercely contrived crime against God; a grim guerdon came to them for that. They said in their zeal that they were minded to possess the kingdom, and that they could easily do so. Their hope played them false, when the Lord, the high King of heaven, raised His hand most high against that host. The reckless wicked ones could not share power with God, but the Glorious One put an end to their presumption, humbled their pride, when He grew wroth; He deprived the evildoers of victory and dominion, of glory and happiness; and reft His foe of rejoicing, of peace and all gladness, radiant glory; and strongly avenged His grief on His adversaries by their downfall through His own might and power. He had fiercely roused His stern mind; He seized his foes with hostile hands, and wrathful in heart, crushed His enemies in His bosom, reft of their home, of their heavenly possessions. Then our Creator passed judgment on the haughty race of angels, and drove them from heaven. The Lord sent the faithless host, the hostile army, the sad spirits, on a

---

[1] Lucifer is generally mentioned as having his seat in the north. Isaiah xiv. 13–14 may be the source of this belief. See Milton, *Paradise Lost*, v. 755–60.

long journey; their vaunting was humbled, their boast brought to naught and their glory laid low, their beauty marred. Afterwards they bided for a weary while in misery. They had no cause to laugh loudly, but they dwelt accursed in hell-torments and knew woes, grief, and sorrow; they suffered anguish, covered with darkness, severe retribution, because they strove against God.

Then was true peace in heaven as before, fair quiet; the Lord dear to all, the Prince to His servants. The glories flourished of those who were in bliss with God. They who dwelt in heaven, the glorious land, were then in harmony; strife, tribulation, and hostility had ceased among the angels after the warriors, reft of light, had departed from heaven. Then widely throughout God's realm there remained behind them thrones rich in glorious powers, abounding in grace, radiant and splendid, with none to sit in them, after the accursed spirits had gone in misery to the place of exile in prison. Then our Lord took counsel in mind, how He should again establish the glorious creation, the foundation, heavenly bright thrones for a better band, when they, His boastful foes, had departed from heaven on high. Wherefore holy God purposed that earth and sky and the wide water, earthly creatures, should be established for Him under heaven's embrace, in the place of His foes whom He had sent, rebellious, out of His protection.

Nothing had then been wrought here as yet save darkness, but this wide land stood, sunk and dark, remote from God, empty and useless. The resolute King looked thereon with His eyes, and beheld the place bare of joys, saw the dark mist brooding in eternal night, black under the heavens, sombre and waste, till at the command of the glorious King this creation came into being.

· · · · · ·

Then I heard that the prince of the Elamites, bold leader of the people, Orlahomor, declared war; Ambrafel went from Shinar to aid him with a great host. Then four kings with mighty power went south thence to seek Sodom and Gomorrah. Then was the land of men beside Jordan overspread with armies, with foes to the country. Many a pale-cheeked woman must go trembling to a stranger's bosom; the defenders of brides and treasures fell, smitten with wounds. Then against them went five kings in warlike fashion with troops from the south; they wished to guard Sodom against foes. For twelve years then they had had to yield tribute and pay tax to the Northmen, until the people would no longer support the prince of the Elamites with treasures of the people, but withdrew their allegiance from him. Then came together fierce bands of slaughter; the javelins rang aloud; the dark bird, dewy-feathered, sang among the spear-shafts, eager for the slain. Heroes hastened in great troops, mighty in heart, until the people, arrayed in helmets, had come together with a host from the south and from the north. There was stern play, exchange of deadly spears, great uproar of battle, loud clamour in the fight. Men drew swords adorned with rings, might in their edges, from their sheaths. There was plenty of fighting for an earl, for him who before had not known much of battle. The Northmen were treacherous to the people of the south; the men of Sodom and Gomorrah were reft in that battle of their loved giver of gold, their companion in arms. They fled from the field to save their lives, smitten by men; behind them fell sons of chieftains, eager companions, destroyed by the sword. The leader of the van of the Elamites gained the victory, he held the battle-field. Then the survivors went to seek a stronghold. Foes carried off gold, ravaged then with their host the treasure-place of men, Sodom and Gomorrah; then the famous city was emptied of joy; maidens, wives, and widows departed, bereft of friends, from their native city. Foes took away from the city of Sodom the kinsman of Abraham with his goods. We may tell truly further concerning what afterwards came to pass following that battle, the journey of warriors, those who took Lot and the goods of the people, the treasure of the Southmen; they boasted of victory.

Then a man, one who had escaped the spears, who had survived the battle, went journeying quickly to seek Abraham. He told the Hebrew earl of the fight, of the people of Sodom heavily slaughtered, the flower of the nation, and of Lot's fate. Then Abraham told those ill tidings to his friends; the faithful hero asked them, his comrades, for help, Aner and Mamre and thirdly Eshcol. He said he had grief in his heart, sorest of sorrows, that his nephew had suffered captivity; he asked the brave warriors to devise a plan so that his warlike kinsman should be rescued, the man with his wife. Then the three brothers in great haste healed his sorrow by their speech, valiant with bold words, and gave a pledge unto Abraham that they with him would avenge his wrong on his foes, or fall on the field of battle. Then the holy man commanded his trained servants to take arms; he found there three hundred and eighteen spear-bearing warriors, loyal to their lord, each of whom he knew could well bear a yellow targe into battle.

Then Abraham set out and the three earls who before had given him a pledge, with their host, brave men. He wished verily to deliver his kinsman Lot from durance. Strong were the warriors; they bore their shields forth stoutly on the journey. The men of battle had drawn nigh unto the camp; then he, the prudent man, the son of Terah, spoke in words to his chiefs— there was great need for them to make a show of battle, of stern combat, fiercely on two sides upon the foe—he said that the holy eternal Lord could easily grant them success in the struggle. Then I heard that heroes ventured to battle under cover of night; clashing of shields and spears arose in the camp, slaughter of bowmen, shivering of arrows; cruelly the sharp spears gripped men beneath their garments, the lives of foes; thickly they fell. There went warriors and comrades rejoicing in plunder. Victory departed again from the attack of the Northmen, war glory of men. Abraham gave battle as ransom for his nephew, in no wise twisted gold; he slew and slaughtered the foe in fight; the Lord of heaven struck to aid him. The four hosts were put to flight, the kings of the peoples, chiefs of men; the trained servants joyfully followed them and heroes were laid low; they encamped behind them who had spoiled Sodom and Gomorrah of gold, who had robbed the householders. Lot's uncle avenged that heavily upon them. The chief nobility of the Elamites, reft of glory, fled until they were nigh unto Damascus.

Then Abraham departed on the war-path to look on the retreat of the hostile men. Lot was delivered, the earl with his goods; women and wives rejoiced; far and wide they saw birds rending amid the slaughter the slayers of free men. Abraham brought back the treasure of men of the south and their wives, sons of chieftains near to their native land, maidens to their kinsmen. Never did any of all living men here who have attacked so great a host achieve a more glorious victory with a small company.

B (Fall of the Angels) [1]

'. . . but eat of all the rest, leave that one tree, beware of that fruit; ye shall not lack blessings.' Then devoutly they bowed their heads to the heavenly King, and gave thanks for all His

[1] The beginning of the poem is imperfect. God is speaking to Adam and Eve.

wisdom and counsel. He bade them cultivate that land. Then the holy Lord, the strong-souled King, returned to heaven. His creatures stood together on the earth; they knew naught of the sorrows they were to suffer if they should cease to obey God's will. They were dear to God while yet they were minded to keep His holy word.

The Ruler of all, the holy Lord, by the might of His hand had established ten tribes of angels in whom He greatly trusted to bear Him true allegiance, to work His will; wherefore He, the holy Lord, gave them intelligence and created them with His hands. Thus had He placed them in blessedness; one He had wrought very strong, very mighty in thought; He let him have sway over much, next under Himself in the kingdom of heaven. He had made him very radiant; very beautiful was his form in heaven that was given him by the God of hosts; he was like the shining stars. His it was to glorify the Lord, to praise His joys in heaven, and to thank his God for the guerdon He had granted him in this world. Then He let him possess his power for long, but he turned it to a worse issue, began to stir up strife against the most high Ruler of heaven who sits on the holy throne. Loved was he by our Lord, and it could not be hidden from Him that his angel began to be haughty against Him, rose up against his Master, sought hostile speech, words of boasting against Him, was not minded to serve God. He said that his body was bright and beautiful, white and radiant of hue. He could not find it in his heart to serve God, the Lord, with allegiance; it seemed to him that he had greater strength and skill than holy God, the Companion in war, could have. The angel uttered many words in his pride; thought how by his single strength he should set up for himself a stronger throne, higher in heaven. He said that his heart prompted him to work westwards and northwards; he set up a building; he said it seemed doubtful to him whether he would be God's disciple.

'Why am I to toil?' said he. 'I need have no master; I can work as many wonders with my hands. I have great power to prepare a more goodly throne, higher in heaven. Why am I to wait upon His favour, bow before Him with such homage? I can be a God as well as He. Strong comrades, bold-hearted heroes, stand by me, who will not fail me in the fight; they, brave men, have chosen me for their master. With such can a man lay a plan, carry it out with such companions in war. They are keen in their friendship to me, loyal in their hearts; I can be their leader, rule in this kingdom. Thus it seems not right to me that

I need flatter God any whit for any benefit; no longer will I be His follower.'

When the Ruler of all heard all this, that His angel began to set up great pride against his Master and that presumptuously he uttered haughty words against his Lord, he had to atone for the deed, suffer the affliction of war, and he must needs have his penalty, heaviest of all punishments; so does every man who tries to fight against his Ruler, wickedly against the glorious Lord. Then the Mighty One, the most high Ruler of heaven, was angered; He cast him off his lofty throne. He had won hate from his Master, he had forfeited His favour; the Righteous One was wroth at him in His heart. Wherefore he was doomed to seek the abyss of bitter hell-torment, because he warred against the Ruler of heaven. He rejected him then from His favour and hurled him to hell, to the deep valleys, where he became the devil, the fiend with all his followers. Then the angels fell from heaven on high into hell for as long as three nights and days, and the Lord transformed them all into devils. Because they would not honour His deed and word, therefore Almighty God set them, vanquished, in a darker place, down under the earth in swart hell. There in the evening for time beyond measure all the fiends feel fire new-kindled; then at dawn comes a wind from the east, frost exceeding chill; ever fire or the piercing cold.[1] Some must endure hard toil; it was dealt to them as a punishment; their way of life was changed; for the first time He filled hell with His foes. Henceforth angels who were true before to God's allegiance held the height of heaven. The other fiends lay in the fire, who before in such numbers had strife with their Ruler. They suffer torment, the hot fierce flame in the midst of hell, fire, and broad flames, likewise also the bitter fumes, vapour, and darkness, because they neglected the service of God. Their pride played them false, the angel's presumption; they were not minded to honour the word of the Ruler of all. They had heavy punishment; then they had fallen through their folly and pride to the depths of the fire in hot hell. They sought another land that was void of light and teeming with flame,[2] great peril of fire. The fiends saw that they had won countless torments through their haughty hearts and the might of God and most of all through pride.

[1] The origin of the belief that those in hell endured both cold and heat is the mention in the gospel of weeping, which was supposed to be in the fire, and of gnashing of teeth, which was supposed to be in the cold. The idea is to be found both in Dante and Milton.

[2] Flame which gives no light is also in Milton, *Paradise Lost*, I. 61 ff.

Then spoke the haughty king who once was the fairest of angels, most radiant in heaven and loved by his Master, dear to God, till they grew too proud, so that mighty God Himself became wrathful in heart at him because of his pride, cast him into that torment, down to that bed of death, and afterwards gave him a name; He said that the highest should henceforth be called Satan, bade him have charge of the depths of dark hell, by no means to strive with God.

Satan uttered speech; he who henceforth must needs dwell in hell, have the abyss in his keeping, spoke in sorrow—he was once God's angel, radiant in heaven, until his mind led him astray, and his pride most strongly of all, so that he would not honour the word of the Lord of hosts. Within him pride swelled about his heart, outside him was hot grievous torment. He spoke these words:

'This desolate place is very different from that other which once we knew, high in heaven, which my Lord gave me, though we could not hold it before the Ruler of all, possess our kingdom. Yet He has not done right to hurl us to the fiery abyss, to hot hell, reft of the heavenly realm; He has determined to people it with mankind. That to me is the greatest of griefs, that Adam, who was wrought from earth, shall hold my mighty throne, dwell in bliss, and we suffer this torment, affliction in this hell. Alas! had I but the strength of my hands, and could win free for one hour, but for a winter hour, then I with this host——! But around me lie iron bonds, the chain of the fetter is on me. I am powerless. The hard bonds of hell have seized me so closely. Here is a great fire above and beneath; never have I looked on a loathlier landscape; the fire ceases not, hot throughout hell. A chain of rings, a fetter severe, has barred my going, reft me of movement; my feet are bound, my hands pinioned. The passage through these doors of hell is closed; thus I cannot at all free my limbs from these bonds. Huge bars of hard iron, forged in the heat, lie around me; with them God has shackled me by the neck. So I know that He knew my thought, and the Lord of hosts knew also that Adam should strive with me for the kingdom of heaven, if I had the strength of my hands. But now in hell we suffer torments; there are darkness and heat—grim, bottomless; God Himself has whirled us away to these gloomy mists. Though He can convict us of no sin nor prove that we did Him hurt in that land, yet He has reft us of the light, hurled us into the greatest of all torments. We cannot work vengeance, requite Him with any hurt, for that He has reft us of the light.

He has now planned out a world where He has man, wrought after His image, with whom He will again people the kingdom of heaven with pure souls. We must earnestly plan to satisfy our vengeance on Adam and on his children together with him, if ever we can, to deprive Him there of his desire, if we can in any way devise it. No longer do I look to regain that light, that happiness, which He thinks long to enjoy with the host of his angels. We can never succeed in appeasing the wrath of mighty God. Let us snatch it from the sons of men, that heavenly kingdom, now that we may not have it, cause them to abandon His allegiance, to break the behest which He uttered. Then He will be angry at them in His heart, dismiss them from His protection; then they shall seek this hell and these dread depths; then we can have them for our followers, the sons of men, in these firm bonds. Put now your thoughts to the warlike venture. If of yore I gave princely treasures to any follower, whilst, blessed, we dwelt in that happy realm and held sway over our abodes, never at a time more desired could he pay back my gifts with offerings, if now any of my followers would be willing to pass out hence from this prison and had the strength to fly with pinions, wing his way up through the clouds, to where Adam and Eve stand created on the realm of earth with riches all round them, while we are hurled hither into these valleys profound. They are now far dearer to the Lord and may own the wealth which we should have in the heavenly kingdom, the realm rightly ours: that good fortune is decreed for mankind. It is this that is such a grief to me in my heart, that causes sorrow to my mind, that they should hold the kingdom of heaven for ever. If any of you can contrive in any way that they should forsake the command and teaching of God, straightway they will be the more hateful unto Him. If they observe not His charge, then He will grow angered against them, then will their weal suffer change and punishment be prepared for them, hard affliction. Do ye all ponder this, how ye may beguile them; afterwards I shall be able to rest at ease in these fetters, if that kingdom be lost to them. For him who achieves that the reward is afterwards ever ready, what henceforth we can gain of benefits in this fire. I will let him sit with myself, whosoever comes in this burning hell to say that they in word and deed have ignobly forsaken the counsel of heaven's King.'

Then God's foe began to prepare himself, ready in his trappings; he had a faithless heart. He set on his head a helmet which made its wearer unseen, and bound it full tightly, fastened it with clasps. He knew many speeches of wicked words. He winged his way thence, passed through the doors of hell; by the fiend's art the fire was cleft in two. He purposed to beguile God's followers, men, secretly by evil deeds, to mislead and allure them, so that they should grow hateful to God.

Then by fiend's art he went till on earth he found Adam, God's handiwork, ready, and his wife also, the fairest woman, wrought with wisdom, so that they knew how to do much good which the Lord of mankind Himself had appointed for His followers; and by them stood two trees which were laden with fruit, clothed with plenty, as mighty God, the high King of heaven, had established them with His hands, so that there the children of men, every man, might choose good and evil, weal and woe. Their growth was not alike. One was so pleasant, beauteous and bright, gentle and praiseworthy; that was the tree of life. Whoever ate of its fruit could afterwards live for ever in the world, so that thereafter old age nor grievous illness should do him hurt, but he could forthwith be in gladness for ever and possess his life, have the favour of the heavenly King here in the world. Glorious honours were destined for him in high heaven when he should pass hence. Then the other was all black, gloomy, and dark; that was the tree of death; it bore much bitterness. Every man who tasted what grew on that tree should know both evil and good in misery in this world, must ever after live in torment with toil and sorrows. Old age must deprive him of mighty deeds, delights, and power, and death must be his destiny. For a short space he shall enjoy his life, then seek the darkest of realms in the fire, shall serve the fiends for a long while, where is the greatest of all perils for men. The hostile, secret messenger of the devil, who strove against God, knew that well. He changed himself then into the shape of a serpent, and then with devilish art twined himself about the tree of death, took the fruit there, and departed again to where he knew was the handiwork of the King of heaven.

Then the foe with his first word began to question him with lies: 'Adam, dost thou desire aught from God? I am come hither from afar with His message. It was not long since that I sat with Himself. Then He bade me go on this journey, bade thee eat of this fruit. He said that thy strength and skill and thy mind would grow greater and thy body more beautiful by far, thy form fairer; He said that thou shouldst lack no possession in the world when thou hadst fulfilled the desire and gained the grace of heaven's King, served thy Master to His delight, made thyself dear unto God. I heard Him praise thy deeds and words in His brightness, and speak of thy life. Thus shalt thou obey the commands which His messengers bring hither to this land. There are green spaces far and wide in the world, and God rules in the highest heavenly kingdom, the All-Powerful above. He, the Lord of men, is not minded to have the trouble Himself of coming on this journey; but He sends his follower to speak with thee. Now in His message He bade me teach thee arts. Do thou perform His service with zeal; take this fruit in thy hand, bite it and taste it. Thy mind shall be made wider, thy stature fairer. The Lord God, thy Master, has sent thee this help from heaven.'

Adam spoke, where he stood on the earth, a man not born of woman: 'I heard the victorious Lord, mighty God, speak with stern voice then, and He bade me bide here, keep His commandments, and gave me this woman, this beauteous wife, and bade me beware that I should not come into the power of the tree of death and be too grievously led astray. He said that he who performed aught evil in his heart should dwell in dark hell. I know not whether thou comest with lies, with guileful intent, or whether thou art God's messenger from heaven. Lo! I cannot understand aught of thy precepts, of thy words or ways, of thy journey or speeches. I know what He Himself, our Saviour, commanded me when I last saw Him. He bade me honour and carefully observe His word, perform His teaching. Thou art not like any of His angels whom I have seen before, nor dost thou show me any sign which He, my Master, has graciously sent to me as a pledge. Therefore I cannot obey thee; but thou mayest go forth. I have a firm belief in Almighty God who created me here with His arms and with His hands. From His high kingdom He can endow me with every blessing, though He send not His servant.'

Angry in heart, he turned where he saw that woman, Eve, fashioned in fairness, standing on earth. He said that the greatest of injuries would afterwards fall upon all their children in the world: 'I know that Almighty God will be angered at you two, when I myself tell Him this message when I come from this journey over the long way, that ye two perform not well every command which He sends hither from the east at this time. Now He Himself shall come at your answer; His herald cannot enforce His message. Therefore I know that He, mighty in heart, will be angered at you two. Nevertheless, if thou, woman, wilt gladly hearken to my words, then thou mayest fully consider what counsel to give him. Think in thy heart that thou mayest ward off punishment from you both, as I will show thee. Eat this fruit. Then thy eyes will be so clear that thou wilt be able afterwards to see so widely over all the world, and the throne of thy Master Himself, and henceforth to have His favour. Thou canst guide Adam afterwards if thou hast his goodwill and he trusts thy words, if thou sayest to him truly what precept thou hast in thy heart, so that thou dost perform the command of God. He will forsake the hostile strife, the evil answer in his breast, if we two both speak to him for his good. Urge him earnestly to perform thy counsel, lest ye two should perforce grow hateful to God, your Ruler. If thou dost carry out that design, best of women, I will conceal from your Lord that Adam spoke so much insult, evil words, unto me. He accuses me of lies, says that I am a messenger zealous to work cruel injuries, not at all God's angel. But I know so well all the condition of angels, the high vaults of heaven. So long was the time that I have zealously served God, my Master, with loyal heart; I am not like a devil.'

Thus with lies he led her on, and with wiles won the woman to that evil, until within her the serpent's thought began to stir—God had assigned her a weaker mind—so that she began to yield her heart to those promptings. Wherefore against God's command she received the grievous fruit of the tree of death from the foe. A worse deed had not been decreed for men. It is a great marvel that eternal God, the Lord, would ever suffer it, that so many men should be led astray by lies when they sought for instruction. Then she ate the fruit, broke the command and will of the Ruler of all. Then she could see far and wide by the gift of the foe who had betrayed her with lies, secretly beguiled her, whereby through his acts it came to pass with her that heaven and earth seemed fairer to her and all this world more beautiful and God's work vast and mighty, though she saw it not by man's counsel. But the foe eagerly tricked her soul who before granted her sight, so that she could gaze so widely over the heavenly realm.

Then the forsworn one spoke in enmity; he taught her no good: 'Now mayest thou behold thyself, as I need not tell thee, good Eve, so that beauty and forms are different for thee since thou hast trusted my words, followed my counsel. Now light shines pleasantly before thee, which I brought from God, beauteous from heaven. Now thou mayest touch it. Tell Adam what power of sight thou hast through my coming. If even now he follows my counsels in modest virtue, then I will give him abundant light, even as I have decked thee with good. I blame him not for the evil speeches, though he is not worthy to be pardoned because he spoke much evil unto me. So shall his children afterwards live; when they do evil they shall gain love, make amends to their Lord for blasphemy, and have his favour henceforth.'

Then went unto Adam the fairest of women, most beauteous of wives, who should come into the world, because she was the handiwork of the King of heaven, though she was secretly led astray then, beguiled with lies, so that they should grow hateful to God by the intent of the foe, should forsake glory by the devil's cunning, should lose the favour of the Lord, the kingdom of heaven. Many a time shall the man have great sorrow that he did not refrain when he had the power. One she bore in her hand, one lay at her heart, the cursed apple, the fruit of the tree of death, which the Lord of lords had forbidden her before; and the Prince of glory spoke that command, so that men, His servants, should not need to endure that great death; but He, the holy Lord, gave a heavenly realm to all men, bountiful happiness, if they would leave that one fruit which that evil tree bore on its boughs filled with bitterness. That was the tree of death which God forbade them. He who was hostile to God in his hate of the King of heaven deceived them then with lies, and the heart of Eve, the weak mind of the woman, so that she began to trust in his words, to follow his counsels, and believed that he had brought the precept from God which he in his words declared to her so carefully. He showed her a sign and promised faith, his loyal intent.

Then she spoke to her lord: 'Adam, my master, this fruit is so sweet, pleasant in the breast, and this messenger so fair, the good angel of God; I see by his garb that he is the envoy of our Lord, the King of heaven. His goodwill is better for us to win than his enmity. If to-day thou didst speak aught injurious to him, yet he forgives it, if we will render him homage. What shall such hostile strife against the messenger of thy Lord do for thee? We need his goodwill. He can carry tidings of us to the almighty King of heaven. I can see from here where He Himself sits—it is to the south-east—begirt with blessedness, who wrought this world; I see His angels wheel about Him on their wings, greatest of all companies, most gladsome of hosts. Who could give me such understanding, if God, the Ruler of heaven, did not send it straight to me? I can hear far and see so

widely in all the world over this vast creation. I can hear the
celestial rejoicing in heaven. Such clearness has been within
and without my mind since I ate this fruit. Now, my good lord,
I have it here in my hand; eagerly I give it thee; I believe that it
has come from God, brought by His command, as this messenger
told me with careful words. It is like naught else on earth,
unless, as this envoy says, it has come straight from God.'

Often she spoke to him and urged him all day to the evil deed,
that they should depart from the desire of their Lord. The
hostile messenger stood there, incited desires in them, and urged
them with cunning, pursued them boldly. The fiend was very
near who had gone on that daring venture over the long way; he
plotted to cast mankind to mighty death, to mislead and delude
them, so that they should forsake the gift of God, the grace of the
Almighty, the possession of the heavenly kingdom. Lo! the foe
from hell knew well that they should suffer God's wrath and the
durance of hell, should perforce feel severe affliction, after they
had broken God's behest, when he with lying words seduced the
fair woman, the most beauteous of wives, to that wickedness, so
that she spoke according to his desire; the handiwork of God
was a help to him in beguiling them to hateful crime.

Then she, the fairest of women, spoke very often to Adam,
until the man's mind began to be swayed to trust in the promise
which the woman spoke to him in words. Yet she did it with
faithful intent; she knew not that so many injuries, terrible
sufferings for mankind, should follow that which she received in
her mind, so that she obeyed the counsels of the evil messenger;
but she thought that she was gaining the favour of the King of
heaven with those words, whereby she declared unto the man
such tokens and promised faith, until Adam within his breast
revolved his mind, and his heart began to turn to her desire.
From the woman he received hell and death, though it was not so
called, but it was to have the name of fruit. Yet it was the sleep
of death and the allurement of the devil, hell, and death, and the
destruction of men, the ruin of mankind, that they took for food
the evil fruit. When it entered into him, touched his heart, then
the messenger with bitter thoughts rejoiced and was glad, gave
thanks to his lord for both:

'Now I have gained thy favour decreed unto me and have
worked thy will! For full many a day men are led astray,
Adam and Eve. The disfavour of the Lord is decreed for them,
now that they have forsaken his command and counsels. Where-
fore no longer can they possess the heavenly kingdom, but they

must needs go to hell on that dark journey. Thus thou hast no cause to bear sorrow for him in thy breast where thou liest bound, to mourn in mind that here men dwell in high heaven, though we now endure injuries, misery, and a land of darkness, and though through thy mighty mind many have forsaken the lofty buildings in heaven, the goodly dwellings. God grew wroth at us because we were not minded to bow our heads in subjection to Him, the holy Lord in heaven. But it was not fitting for us that we should serve Him in allegiance. Wherefore the Lord grew wroth at us in His heart, stern in mind, and drove us into hell, hurled the greatest of hosts into that fire, and with His hands again set up the celestial thrones in heaven, and gave that kingdom to mankind. Blithe be thy heart in thy breast, for here both things are brought to pass, that the children of men, mankind, shall forsake the kingdom of heaven and pass to thee, burning, into that fire; also despite, grief of heart, has been dealt unto God. Whatsoever we suffer here of torment, it is now all requited to Adam by the hatred of the Lord and the ruin of men, to men by the pain of death. Wherefore my mind is healed, the thoughts of my heart are lightened. All our wrongs are avenged, the evil we long have suffered. Now once more I will draw near the fire, I will seek Satan there. He is in dark hell, bound with fettering of rings.'

The most bitter messenger descended again; he was destined to seek the far-spreading flames, the gates of hell, where his master lay bound with chains. Adam and Eve both grieved, and often words of sorrow passed between them. They dreaded the hate of God, their Lord; greatly they feared the enmity of the King of heaven. They thought His command had been changed. The woman grieved; with sad heart she lamented—she had forsaken the favour and counsels of God—when she saw that light depart elsewhere who had showed her a sign by perfidy, who had brought suffering on them by his advice, so that they should have the affliction of hell, numberless injuries. Wherefore sorrows burned in their breasts. At times they fell to prayer, man and wife together, and greeted the Lord of victory as good, and called on God, the Lord of heaven, and prayed Him that they might have punishment from Him, that they might eagerly undergo it, now that they had broken God's behest. They saw that their bodies were bare; they had no fixed dwellings as yet in the land, nor did they know aught of the sorrows of toil; but they could live well in the land, if they would always follow the teaching of God. Then they uttered many words of sorrow together, man and wife. Adam spoke and said unto Eve:

'Lo! thou, Eve, hast marked the fate of us both with evil. Dost thou not see dark hell, greedy and ravening? Now thou canst hear it raging from here. The kingdom of heaven is not like that fire; but this is the best of lands which we might possess by our Lord's intent, if thou hadst not hearkened to him who brought this harm on us by his counsel, so that we broke the command of the Lord, the King of heaven. Now in grief we may sorrow for His coming. Wherefore He Himself charged us that we should guard ourselves against torment, the greatest of injuries. Now hunger and thirst cruelly tear my breast, by both of which we were at all times untroubled before. How shall we live now or dwell in this land, if wind comes here from west or east, from south or north, if a cloud rises, if a shower of hail comes driving from heaven, if frost comes in the midst, which is cold unto men, if at times this bright sun shines hotly, gleams from heaven, and we stand here naked, unprotected by clothes? We have naught before us for defence against storms, nor have we any store set aside for food, but mighty God, the Ruler, is angry in heart at us. What shall become of us now? Now I may regret that I prayed the God of heaven, the good Ruler, that He should create thee here from my limbs, since thou hast led me astray into the displeasure of my Lord. So now I may regret for ever that I saw thee with my eyes.'

Then Eve, fairest of women, most beauteous of wives, spoke once more—she was created by God, though she had come then into the devil's power: 'My friend, Adam, thou mayest blame me for it with thy words; yet thou canst not sorrow more deeply for it in thy mind than do I in my heart.'

Then Adam answered her: 'If I knew the will of the Lord, what punishment I was to have from Him—if thou hadst but seen more quickly—though the God of heaven should now bid me go hence on the sea, journey on the flood, it would not be so deep for men, the ocean so vast, that ever my heart would doubt Him, but I would go to the depths, if I could work God's will. I have no heart for my service on earth, now that I have forfeited the favour of my Lord, so that I cannot have it. But we can no wise be both thus naked together. Let us go into this wood, into the covering of this forest.'

They both went aside; grieving, they went their ways into the green wood; they sat apart to await the decrees of the King of heaven Himself, when they could no longer have that which

Almighty God formerly gave them. Then they covered their bodies with leaves; they clothed themselves with the foliage; they had no garments. But they fell to prayer, both together, every morning; they prayed the Mighty One that Almighty God should not forget them, and that the good Lord should show them how henceforth to live in the light.

EXODUS

[This is not a lifeless paraphrase of the biblical narrative. The poet centres his attention on the coming out of Egypt, on the situation of the Israelites trapped between their foes and the sea, and on the overwhelming of the pursuing host.]

Lo! we have heard far and near over the world of the judgments of Moses, the wondrous laws for the generations of men, of recompense in heaven after death for the evils of life for all the righteous, enduring benefit for all the living. Let him who will, hearken! The Lord of hosts, the true King, honoured him in the wilderness by his own might, and the eternal Ruler of all gave him power to do many marvels. He, the prince of the people, shrewd and wise guide of the host, bold leader, was loved by God. He afflicted the race of Pharaoh, God's foe, when the Lord of victories delivered the life of his kinsmen to the brave leaders, the occupation of the land to the sons of Abraham. Great was the guerdon, and the gracious Lord gave him mighty weapons against the assault of foes; he overthrew in battle the power of many hostile kinsmen. Then was the first time [1] that the God of hosts addressed him in words, when He told him many marvels, how the wise Lord had wrought this world, the orb of the earth, and in His triumph had established the heavens, and His own name [2] which the children of men, the wise race of fathers, knew not before, though they knew much. Then by true powers He had strengthened and honoured the prince of the host, [3] the foe of Pharaoh, in his departure, when not long before the greatest of nations had been stricken with bitter torments, with death. Mourning was renewed at the fall of their keepers of treasure; joys in hall passed away with the loss of possessions; at midnight He had boldly struck down the evil-doers, many first-born children, had slain the watchmen; the destroyer stalked far and wide, the hated foe of the people; dark grew the land with bodies of the slain. The host set forth; there was lamenting far and wide, little rejoicing. The hands of

[1] The meaning seems to be that while Moses was in the wilderness God told him the story of Creation.
[2] See Exodus iii. 13–14.
[3] Moses.

112

laughter-makers were bound; the people were allowed to go forth, a nation on the march. The fiend was robbed, the hosts in hell; lamentation arose there; the idols fell down. That day was famed over the world when the multitude went forth which for many years had endured captivity and been in bondage to the wicked Egyptians, because they thought to refuse for ever, if God had allowed them, to the kinsmen of Moses their constant desire for the cherished journey. The host was made ready; brave was he who led their nation, a prince unafraid; with the people he passed many strongholds, the land and the king of hostile men, strait narrow ways, an unknown road, till they bore their war gear to the Ethiopians.[1] Their lands were shrouded with a covering of cloud; then Moses led the army past border dwellings hard by the moors, past many hindrances.

Then after two nights He ordered the glorious hero, when they had escaped from their foes, to encamp about the city of Etham in the border lands with the surging army, with the whole host, the great multitude. They pressed on northwards; they knew that south of them lay the land of the Sun-Folk, burnt hills, people dark from the sun's heat. There holy God guarded the people against the great heat;[2] He overcast the burning sky with a canopy, the hot air with a holy net. The cloud in its wide embraces had truly divided earth and heaven; it guided the host. The flame was quenched, bright in its heat; the men were amazed, most joyful of multitudes. The shelter of the day-shield moved over the sky; wise God had covered the course of the sun with a sail,[3] though men, dwellers on earth, knew not the rigging, nor could behold the sail-yard by any skill, how the greatest of tents was made fast. After He had gloriously honoured the faithful ones, then came the third encampment as a solace to the people; all the army saw how the holy sails towered up there, bright marvel of the sky; the people, the host of Israelites, saw that the Lord, the God of hosts, came there to lay out the camp. Fire and cloud went before Him, two pillars in the sky, each of which had an equal share in the high services of the holy spirit, in the journey of the brave-hearted by day and night. Then I heard that in the morning the valiant in soul lifted up a glorious sound with the loud notes of the war-trumpet. The host all rose up, the army of brave men, as

[1] The literal meaning of the word here translated by 'Ethiopians' seems to be 'war-dark.' It may, however, mean 'warlike borderers.'

[2] The idea of the cloud as a protection against heat is not in the biblical narrative.

[3] The cloud is here called a sail; a little later the Israelites are called sailors.

Moses, the famous leader, bade them, the people of God. The band, all alert, saw the leader of life going forward on the road to safety; the sail guided their course; the sailors followed on the road to the sea; the people were joyful.

There was loud clamour in the army. The heavenly sign arose every evening; the other marvel wondrous after sunset, the burning pillar, failed not to shine with its fire over the men. The bright flames stood gleaming above the warriors, the shields shone; the shadows shrank away; their hiding-places could not conceal close the deep night shadows, heaven's candle burned. The new night guardian must perforce abide over the troops, lest ever the desert terror, the grey heath, should in stormy weather put their souls to flight with sudden fear. The pillar in front of them had fiery tresses, gleaming columns; it threatened the host with terror of fire, with hot flame, that it would consume the multitude in the wilderness, unless they in their boldness obeyed Moses. The gleaming host shone; shields glittered; the shield-warriors kept the straight road in view; the banner above the troops, alert on its advance, guarded the army to the sea-fastness at the land's end. Camp was pitched; they rested in weariness; servants approached the brave warriors with food; they mended their strength. The sailors were spread along the hills in their tents, when the trumpet sang; then was the fourth camp, the resting-place of the shield-warriors by the Red Sea. There on their army fell sudden tidings, a pursuit from inland. Fears came upon them, terror of death among the troops; the fugitives awaited the hostile pursuer who, bent on injury, had for long before laid oppression and suffering upon the homeless ones. They recked not of the promise though the elder king [1] had given one before, when he became heir of the peoples and lord of men's treasures, so that thereby he prospered exceedingly. The people of the Egyptians forgot all that, when they grew oppressive in war; then they did violence to his kinsmen, worked wrong, broke their promise.

The surges of battle filled their hearts, the strong passion of men, owing to treachery. They were resolved to requite the gift of life with deceit, so that the people of Moses would have paid for that day's work with blood; if mighty God had prospered the Egyptians in their journey of destruction. Then the hearts of men lost hope when they saw Pharaoh's host come

[1] The Pharaoh who befriended Joseph, through whose advice he became 'heir of the peoples.' (See Genesis xlvii.) The 'gift of life' referred to a few lines later is the saving of Egyptian lives by Joseph's shrewdness.

sweeping on from the south, bearing their shields, the troops gleaming—spears were strong, battle drew nigh, shields shone, trumpets sang—banners reaching aloft, the host treading the road. Birds of prey, greedy for battle, dewy-feathered, dark lovers of carrion, screamed in wheeling flight over the corpses. The wolves sang their dread evensong in hope of the feasting; savage beasts behind the foemen awaited, unsorrowing, the fall of the host; the watchers of the ways cried out at midnight. The fated soul took flight; the people were hemmed in!

At times proud warriors from the host paced the roads on the backs of steeds. There the king, prince of men, rode ahead with his troop, hard by the banner; the captain of men fastened his helmet, the king his chin-guard, to make ready for battle—the standards shone—he shook his corslet; he bade his cohorts carefully hold firm their order of battle. The foemen beheld with eyes of hate the advance of the men of the land. Around him moved fearless fighters; old wolves of the sword welcomed war, thirsting for the press of battle, loyal to their leader. He had chosen two thousand famed warriors of the people for the high duty, who were leaders and kinsmen, esteemed for their rank. Wherefore each of them led out all the male warriors he could find at the time. All the leaders were together in a band. The horn often made it known in the host whither the warriors, the army of men, were bearing their war gear. So there they led unending swarthy hosts, foeman after foeman, a mighty army; they were on their way thither in thousands. It had been the resolve of those troops to destroy with swords the race of the Israelites at dawn in revenge for their brothers; wherefore in the camp lamentation was raised, a dread evensong; terrors came upon them; deadly nets enclosed them. When the uproar came, bold speeches fled. The foe was resolute; the host shone in armour, till the mighty angel, who guarded the multitude, cut them off in their pride, so that the foemen could no longer see one another; their advance was broken.

The fugitives had the space of a night, though foes lurked about them on all sides, the army or the sea. They had no other way out; they had no hope of their heritage. They sat among the hills in shining dress awaiting their woe; all that host of kinsmen waited, watching together for the greater army, till Moses commanded the leaders to summon the people at dawn with brazen trumpets, the warriors to rise up, to don their corslets, to think of valour, to bear bright gear, to call the troop near the shore with signals. Quickly the watchers heeded the war signal; the host was made ready. The sailors moved with their tents over the hills; they obeyed the trumpets; the army was in haste. Then they told off twelve tribes, brave in heart, in the van to meet the dread onslaught; their might was roused up. In each were fifty companies chosen of warriors of noble race, bearing their shields; each company of the famous host had a thousand spear-bearers, glorious warriors. That was a warlike multitude; the leaders of the host received no weaklings into that number, who by reason of youth could not yet guard with their hands under the shield the breast-net of men against the wily foe, or who had not suffered grievous hurt over the edge of the targe, the mark of a wound, warfare of the spear. Old men, grey-haired warriors, could not be of service in battle, if their strength grew less in the bold hosts, but they chose the warriors by stature, considering how valour would honourably acquit itself among the people, how also the power of strength would grasp the spear-shaft. Then the army of brave men was gathered together, ready to march onward. The standard rose into the air, brightest of pillars; they all waited yet, until the guide, bright above the shields, hard by the sea-currents, moved forward in the air.

Then in front of the men the war-herald leaped up; the bold leader raised aloft his shield, bade the captains make quiet the army, whilst many hearkened to the brave man's speech. The prince was minded to speak with holy voice to the troops; the leader of the host spoke nobly: 'Be ye not the more fearful, though Pharaoh should bring vast armies of sword-warriors, a countless host of men; this day by my hand mighty God will requite them all for their deeds, so that no longer they may live to vex with suffering the race of the Israelites. Fear not dead troops, doomed bodies; their time of fleeting life is at an end. God's teaching has deserted your breasts. I give better counsel, that ye should honour the Prince of glory and pray the Lord of life for favour, for triumphant victories, when ye march forth. This is the everlasting God of Abraham, the Lord of Creation, fearless and famed for might, who guards this army with His strong hand.'

Then before the hosts the prince of men raised up his voice when he spoke to the people 'Lo! dearest of peoples, now behold a marvel with your eyes, how I myself and this right hand have struck the abyss of the sea with the green symbol;[1] the wave mounts up, swiftly makes the water a wall; dry are all the

[1] The rod of Moses.

roads, grey are the highways; the sea swept aside, the ancient
foundations, which never before in the world have I heard of
men faring over, shining fields, the buried sea-bottoms, which
hitherto the waves have always covered. The south wind has
swept away the storming of the sea; the water is parted; the sand
has caused the sea to ebb. Well do I know the truth, that
mighty God has shown mercy unto you, ye men bright in
armour. Haste is best, that ye may escape from the clutch of
your foes, now that the Lord has raised up the red waves as a
rampart. The bulwarks are fairly built up to the vault of the
sky, a wondrous way through the sea.'

After these words the host all rose up, the army of brave men;
the sea remained quiet. The troops raised their white shields,
the standards on the shore. The wall of waters mounted up;
upright it stood hard by the Israelites for the space of a day; the
band of men was resolute; the wall of waves held them in safety
in its firm embraces.

[A passage of about 150 lines follows of little interest. An
account of the order in which the tribes marched through the
Red Sea is begun, but is interrupted rather suddenly by a
description of Noah's flood and the story of Abraham. The
narrative is then resumed with a vivid picture of the Egyptians'
overthrow.]

Panic fell on the people; the terror of the flood beset their sad
souls. The abyss threatened death. The mountainous waters
were bedewed with blood; the sea spewed forth gore; there was
uproar in the waves, the water full of weapons; a deadly mist
mounted up. The Egyptians were turned back again; they fled
in fear; they felt sudden terror; panic-stricken they wished to
seek out their homes; less blithe was their boasting. The dread
rush of the waves grew dark upon them, nor did any of that host
come again home, but fate blocked the road behind them with
water. Where erstwhile the roads lay, the sea raged; the host
was engulfed. The waves mounted up, the storm rose high to
the heavens, the mightiest outcry of an army. The foemen
screamed aloud with doomed voices; the air grew dark above
them; blood stained the flood. The protecting walls were
pulled down; the greatest of drownings scourged the sky.
Brave men perished, kings in their pomp; their chance of return
was lost at the border of the sea. Battle shields shone high over
the men; the wall of waters rose up, the raging sea. The army
was fettered fast in death, with no chance of escape, bound by

their war gear. Drowning was dealt to the doomed host, when the surge of the billows, the cold sea, naked messenger of distress, hostile traveller which overwhelmed the foes, came back to everlasting foundations, as it was wont, with its wandering salt waves. The blue sky was blent with blood; the bursting sea threatened with terror of death the journey of the sailors, till the true Lord by the hand of Moses loosed its fury. Far and wide it swept along, rushed with deadly clutches; the flood foamed; the fated men fell; water rushed on the land; the air was in turmoil. The walls gave way; the waves burst; the towering seas flowed down, when the Mighty One, the Keeper of heaven, smote with His holy hand the warriors, the proud people. They could not restrain the course of the rescuing waters, the rage of the sea, but He destroyed many with screaming terror. The ocean raged, it drew itself up, it glided upon them. Terrors were there; wounds gushed forth. The handiwork of God fell on the fatal road, high from the heavens; the foamy-bosomed one smote the guardian barriers, the unavailing wall, with an ancient sword, so that the hosts, the troop of the sinful, perished by that death-blow; closely hemmed in, they lost their souls, the army aghast at the flood, when on them fell the greatest of raging waves dark with its mass. The whole host perished when it overwhelmed the warriors of the Egyptians, Pharaoh with his people; when God's foe sank he quickly found that the wall of the sea was greater in might, that, wrathful and terrible, it was verily minded to decide the battle by its embraces. Full requital was dealt to the Egyptians for that day's work; wherefore of all that countless host there came not one survivor home to tell their fate, to proclaim through the cities to the waves of men the greatest of evil tidings, the fall of princes, but drowning with its power devoured the hosts, the messengers, destroyed the boasting of men; they fought against God.

Thereupon Moses, the noble man, uttered to the Israelites on the seashore with holy speech enduring wisdom, deep teaching; they name the day's work,[1] as yet people find in the scriptures every law which the Lord laid upon them with true words on that journey. If the interpreter of life, bright in the bosom, the keeper of the body, will unlock the great benefits by the keys of the spirit, the mystery will be made clear, wisdom will come forth.[2] It has wise words in its bosom, it will be a

---

[1] An obscure passage. The reference may be to the decalogue.
[2] 'The keeper of the body' is the mind which will reveal the mystery and wisdom of the Bible.

strong teacher of souls, so that we shall not lack God's instruction, the mercy of the Lord. He will reveal more unto us, now that wise men declare more lasting joys of the sky. This is fleeting happiness, cursed with sins, granted to exiles, the waiting of the unhappy. Homeless, they abide in this guest hall in sorrow; they grieve in soul; they know the place of punishment is fixed under the earth, where are fire and the worm, a pit ever open for all that is evil. Whether now great sinners have as their lot old age or early death, requital shall come, greatest of glories over the world, a day which shall punish deeds. God Himself in the place of meeting shall pass judgment on many. Then He shall lead the souls of the righteous, the blessed spirits, to heaven, where are light and life, and also abundance of mercy. People in bliss will praise God, the glorious King of hosts, for ever and ever.

Thus, with loud voice, spoke the meekest of men, mindful of counsel, strengthened in might. The host awaited in quietness the will of the appointed leader, the good counsel of the brave man; they had witnessed a wonder. He spoke to a great number: 'Mighty is this multitude, strong the Captain, greatest of helpers, who leads this march. He has from on high delivered to us the races of Canaan, the cities and treasures, their broad realm. The Lord of angels will now perform what long since in days past He promised with an oath to our forefathers, if ye keep his holy commandment, so that henceforth ye overcome all enemies. In triumph ye shall occupy the banquet halls of men; great shall be your glory.'

After these words the host was joyful; the trumpets of victory sang; the standards stood amid the fair melody. The people were on land; the glorious pillar had led the multitude; the holy bands, in God's protection. They rejoiced in life, when they had escaped alive from the power of foes, though they had ventured boldly, the men under the vault of waters; they saw the walls stand there. All the seas seemed bloody to them, through which they had borne their war gear. They were jubilant with a war song, when they escaped. The troops lifted up loud voices; they praised the Lord for that day's work; men and women one to another, greatest of hosts, chanted with reverent voices a song of glory, a hymn of battle, about the many marvels.

Then was easy to find the African maiden [1] on the seashore,

[1] Possibly Miriam (Exodus xv. 20–21), but it is not clear why she should be called African. Possibly the passage refers to drowned Egyptian women cast up on the shore and plundered by the Israelites, but the Egyptians would hardly have their women with them.

decked with gold.   They raised their hands in thanksgiving for
safety; they were glad; they beheld their deliverance; they forgot
not the booty; their bondage was broken.   On the shore they
began to divide among the standards the spoils cast up by the sea,
ancient treasures, clothing and shields.   They divided justly the
gold and precious cloth, the treasure of Joseph, the possession
of men.   They who had owned them had been laid low in the
place of death, the greatest of hosts.

DANIEL

[The poem follows its biblical source fairly closely. It is much less interesting than *Exodus*, but the description of the deliverance from the furnace has beauty, and the song of praise is not without eloquence.]

I HAVE heard that the Hebrews lived in wealth in Jerusalem, distributed treasure, held sway, as was natural to them, after, by the Lord's might, an army had been given to the hand of Moses, a multitude of warriors, and they had left the Egyptians with a great host. They were a proud people, whilst they could rule the realm and had power over cities; glorious prosperity was theirs, whilst the people were minded to keep the covenant of their father;[1] God was their guardian, the Keeper of heaven, the holy Lord, the Ruler of Glory, the Lord of all creatures, who gave to the host courage and power, so that often they did hurt to many peoples, to captains of armies, who were not friendly to Him,[2] until pride with its crimes came upon them at the banquet, drunken thoughts. Then they forsook all the teachings of the law, the power of the Lord, in a way that no man should do, dividing the love of his soul for God. Then I beheld the nation fall into error, the people of Israel work evil, practise sins; that was a grief unto God. Often He, the Guardian of heaven, sent counsel unto the people, holy spirits, who proclaimed wisdom to the multitude. For a little while they held that wisdom as truth, till desire of earthly delight defrauded them of eternal wisdom, so that at last they themselves forsook the laws of the Lord, chose the might of the devil. Then was the Prince of the kingdom wroth, harsh to the people to whom He had given power. In the beginning He had pointed out the path to the lofty city to them who at first ere that were dearest of mankind to God, most valued of nations, most loved by the Lord; to the men from a strange land He had shown their heritage, where Salem stood, defended by its walls, beautified by its barriers.[3] Thither the warriors went, the race of the Chaldeans, onwards to the city, where were the possessions of the Israelites, guarded

[1] Abraham.
[2] A reference to the conquest and settlement of the promised land.
[3] This sentence means that God has shown the Israelites, on their leaving Egypt, the way to Jerusalem.

by ramparts. Thither went that host, renowned army, eager
for violence.

[The poem follows the account in *Daniel* of the capture and
plunder of Jerusalem by Nebuchadnezzar and his training of
some of the younger captives for public service. The king's
dream of the image and Daniel's interpretation of it are briefly
told. The story of the golden image follows, and then the ordeal
of the furnace is described in the most vigorous passage of the
poem.]

Then the king, set in his purpose, grew angry; he bade the
furnace be heated for the torment of the youths, because they
opposed his power. When it was made hot as fiercely as might
be with the cruel flame of the fire, then he summoned the people
thither, and the ruler of Babylon, grim and savage, ordered God's
servants to be bound. Then he commanded his men to thrust
the youths, the young men, into the blaze. He who aided them
was at hand; though they were forced so fiercely into the embrace
of the blazing fire, yet the mighty protection of God saved their
lives, as many have heard; afforded them holy help there. God,
the Guardian of men, sent them from high heaven the holy
spirit; an angel passed into the furnace, where they were suffering
torment; under the fiery vault he covered the noble youths with
his embraces. The darting of the flickering flame could do no
hurt to their beauty, when the Sovereign saved them. Savage
was the heathen prince, bade them be straightway burned. The
flame was large beyond measure. Then the furnace was heated,
the iron was hot throughout; many servants there cast wood into
it, as they were commanded; they bore brands of gleaming fire
to the blaze. The wolfish-hearted king was minded to heat the
iron wall round about the righteous men, till the flame rose over
the loved ones, and gladly it slew far more than had been pur-
posed. Then the fire turned on the hostile men, on the heathen,
away from the holy. The youths were glad in heart; the ser-
vants were burned round the furnace without; the flame became
a scourge to the evil ones, where the prince of Babylon gazed.
The men of the Hebrews rejoiced; with zeal in their gladness
they praised the Lord; they showed their delight at the saving of
their lives as well as they could within the furnace. Men in
their happiness did honour to God under the cover of that which
had been driven away, the fierce heat of the fire. The noble
youths were freed from the assaults of the flame, nor did they do
them any hurt there. To them the roaring was no more grievous

than the light of the sun; nor did the fire threaten the men who were in peril, but the flame fell upon those who wrought the wickedness, turned on the heathen caitiffs away from the holy youths, destroyed the beauty of the accursed ones who took delight in that work. Then the proud king saw, when he trusted his senses, a marvel which had come to pass in the place of torment; that seemed wondrous unto him. Unscathed, the youths moved in the hot furnace, all the three righteous men. An angel of the Almighty was also visible to him there. Nothing harmed them there, but it was therein just as when the sun shines in summer, and the dew-fall in the daytime is scattered by the wind. It was glorious God who saved them from that hate.

Then Azariah in his holiness, zealous in works, spoke earnestly through the hot flame; the man unspotted by sins praised the Lord, and uttered these words: 'Lord of all creatures, lo! Thou art strong in Thy powers to save men; Thy name is renowned, fair and glorious among the nations; every day Thy judgments are righteous and strong and triumphant, as Thou Thyself also art. Ruler of the heavens, what Thou desirest in Thy power is right and great. Now, Creator of souls, holy Lord, give us good aid and graciously help us. Now we in our woes and oppressions and humiliations pray Thee for mercies, encompassed as we are with fire. We earned that in the world while we lived; our fore-fathers also wrought evil in their pride, broke thy laws while yet they dwelt in their city, scorned the way of holy life. We are scattered throughout the wide world, broken up in bands, reft of protection; despised is our life through many lands and a byword to many peoples, who have driven us forth into the power of the worst of earth's kings, into slavery with cruel men, and now we endure the oppression of the heathen. Thanks be to Thee, glorious King of hosts, for that Thou hast laid this punishment upon us. Because of Thy mercy which men look for in Thee, and because of the covenant which Thou, Saviour of men, un-changing in glories, Creator of souls, didst make with Abraham and Isaac and Jacob, forsake us not, Thou only eternal Lord. Thou didst promise to them in speech in days long gone that Thou wouldst multiply their race, so that after them it should continue through generations, and the multitude should be famed, a race to be raised up, as the stars of heaven wheel their wide course, or as the sand of the sea-coast, of the shores of ocean, lies beneath the salt waves, so that in many years their race should grow to be numberless. Fulfil now the promise, though few of them are living; make good Thy speech and Thy glory on us; show forth strength and might, that the Chaldeans and many peoples, who live as heathens under the heavens, may learn that Thou art the only eternal God, Ruler of hosts, of creatures in the world, Maker of victories, righteous Lord.'

Thus the holy man praised the Lord's mercy and set forth in speech the abundance of His power. Then an angel all radiant was sent from on high, a being fair of face from his glorious home, who came to comfort them and save their lives with love and mercy; he, holy and heavenly bright, scattered the blaze of the hot fire, swept it away and made vanish by his strong might the glare of the fire, so that no harm was done to their bodies, but in wrath he hurled the fire against their foes for their evil deeds. Then in the furnace, when the angel entered, it was windy and winsome, like to the weather when in summer season the dropping of rain is sent in the day-time, warm shower of the clouds. As is the fairest weather, so was it in the fire by the might of the Lord to succour the holy men; the hot flame was scattered and quenched when the bold ones passed through the furnace and the angel with them, the saviour of their lives, who was the fourth there.   Hananiah and Azariah and Mishael, there the three men, daring in heart, praised the Prince in their thoughts, prayed the eternal Lord, the Ruler of nations, to bless the children of Israel, all the creatures of earth.   Thus they three, wise in mind, uttered words in unison:

'May the beauty of worldly skill and all works, heavens and angels, bless Thee, gracious Father! And clear waters which by just decree abide in glory above the heavens, they honour Thee; and all creatures, the stars bright in the sky which keep their course, the sun and moon, may each by itself in its degree praise Thee, almighty! And the stars of heaven, the dew and dear rain, may they glorify Thee! And may souls praise Thee, mighty God! Burning fire and bright summer praise the Saviour, night together with day, and may all lands, light and darkness, together with heat and cold, praise Thee in their degree! And may frosts and snows, bitter winter weather and the course of the clouds praise Thee on high, mighty Lord! And lightning flashes, gleaming and swift, may they bless Thee! All the face of the earth, the hills and the plains and the high mountains, the salt waves, the flood and surge of the billows, the gushing of springs, they honour Thee, eternal Lord, righteous God.   Whales praise Thee, and fowls of the air in their flight; may they who move in the floods, in the world of waters, and wild beasts and all cattle bless Thy name! And the children of men love Thee in their hearts, and the Israelites in their degree praise Thee, the Creator of all we have, their Lord. And the strength of holy men's hearts, the souls and spirits of every righteous man, praise the Prince of life, the eternal Lord, who gives reward to all. May Hananiah and Azariah and Mishael glorify Thee, O God, in the thoughts of their hearts! We bless Thee, Lord of all peoples, Father almighty, true Son of God, Saviour of souls, Helper of men, and we honour Thee who art in glory, holy spirit, wise God. We praise Thee, holy Lord, and extol Thee in prayers; Thou, high King of heaven, source of light and life, art blessed, Thy life raised in honour above earth's summit by Thy holy powers, over all lands.'

Then the prince Nebuchadnezzar spoke of that with his people, with his nearest nobles: 'Many of you beheld that, my lords, that we sent three, committed them to the fire, into the burning blaze of the flame. Now verily I behold four men there; my senses do not trick me.' Then he who was counsellor of the king, wise and sage in words, spoke: 'That is a great wonder which we behold there with our eyes. Consider, my lord, what becomes thee; understand clearly who bestowed that gift on the young men. They praise God, the One, Eternal, and with zeal call wholly upon Him by every name; with bold words they thank Him for His majestic power; they declare Him to be the one Almighty God, wise, glorious King of the world and the heavens. Prince of the Chaldeans, call the men out of the furnace; it is nowise good that they should be in torment longer than thou canst help.'

Then the king bade the youths come to him. The bold young men obeyed the command; the excellent men went as they were bidden; the young men came before the heathen. The bonds had been burned which lay on their bones, the harmful device of the king of the people, and their bodies unharmed; their faces were not marked, nor any injury done to their garments, nor their hair singed by fire, but they, men wise-hearted, walked gladly out of the dread terror in the Lord's keeping, in the protection of the spirit. Then the angel ascended to seek eternal joys in the high vault of the kingdom of heaven, a high servant and loyal to holy God. By that miracle he had done honour to those who deserved it. The youths exalted the Lord in the presence of the heathen people; they uttered praise with true speeches and told him many true signs, until he himself believed that He who had delivered them from the darkness was

the mighty God.   Then the bold ruler of Babylon in his stern-
ness charged his people that he should forfeit his life who should
deny that He who had delivered them from death was in truth
the great mighty God.   He restored to Him then the remnant of
his people who had been led away, and granted to his old foes
that they should be honoured; they were prosperous in Babylon
after they had passed through the fire; throughout the nation
their glory was proclaimed after they had obeyed the Lord;
mighty was their counsel after the Ruler of the heavens, the holy
Guardian of the heavenly kingdom, had shielded them from
harm.   Then I heard that the ruler of Babylon, after he had
beheld the miracle of the burning of the fire, sought to know in
true words how the three youths had survived the great terror
of the fire, of the hot furnace, and had passed through the surging
flame, so that the fierce hate of the fires, of the cruel blaze, no
whit harmed them, God's messengers, but the Lord's protection
shielded their lives against the dread terror.   Then the prince
caused a meeting to be held, summoned then his people together,
and then in the hearing of the host in the assembly declared the
event which had come to pass and God's miracle, which was
revealed in the youths.

'Consider now the holy power, the wise miracle of God.
We saw Him deliver from death, from the darting flame, the
young men in the furnace, those who exalted His praise.   Where-
fore He is the only eternal Lord, almighty, who gave glory, trium-
phant success unto them who hear His message.   Therefore by
many a marvel He makes Himself known to holy spirits who have
chosen His favour.   It is well known that Daniel told me the
truth of a secret dream, which before exceedingly perplexed
many of my people in mind, because the Almighty sent a wise
spirit into his mind, skill of wisdom.'

Thus the king of the multitude, the ruler of Babylon, spoke in
words, when he had seen the sign, God's clear token.

[The remainder of the poem, under three hundred lines,
relates Nebuchadnezzar's dream of the tree, Daniel's interpreta-
tion of it, and gives an incomplete account of Belshazzar's feast.]

CHRIST AND SATAN

[*Christ and Satan* is in three parts; or perhaps it comprises three poems. The first deals with the Fall of the Angels. Satan here is a very different figure from the Satan of the other Old English poem on the Fall of the Angels (*Genesis*—B). We have here a sentimental lamenting outcast, reproached by his followers, and stretching his hands in entreaty to the light above him. In the other poem we see Satan surrounded by loyal though suffering comrades, lifting his hands in defiance, and showing

'the unconquerable will,
And study of revenge, immortal hate,
And courage never to submit or yield.'

The second poem is on Christ's Harrowing of Hell. The story of Christ's triumphant invasion of the underworld during the interval between His crucifixion and resurrection was no doubt inspired by passages in the New Testament such as 1 Peter iii. 19. It was a favourite subject in medieval art and literature. Its dramatic possibilities made it a common theme for miracle plays. References to Christ's Descent occur in *Elene*, *Christ*, and other Old English poems. The subject of the third poem is Christ's Temptation. The first poem and part of the second are translated here.]

It became known to dwellers on earth that God had might and power when He established the regions of earth. He Himself placed sun and moon, stones and earth, the current out in the sea, water and cloud, by His wondrous might. God in His power encompasses the deep circuit of ocean and the whole world. He Himself, God's own Son, can look through the sea, through the ocean depths, and He can count every drop of the rain showers. He Himself appointed by His true power the number of days, when the Creator by His glorious spirit on high in heaven devised and established in six days the regions of the earth, the deep sea. Who possesses pure intelligence save eternal God? He gave delights, powers, and language to Adam first and that noble lineage to the chief of angels who afterwards fell to ruin. It seemed to them in their hearts that it might be that they themselves should be the rulers of heaven, the sovereigns of glory. A worse fate befell them, when one after the other they set up their abode in hell, in that dread den, where they were doomed to bide in surge of fire, in sore grief, not at all to possess celestial light on high in heaven; but they were doomed to be plunged in the deep surge down under the headlands in the low abyss, insatiate and ravening. Only God knows how He condemned that guilty host.

Then the ancient one cries out from hell, utters speeches with a voice of misery, in terrible tone: 'Where has gone the glory of angels we were wont to possess in heaven? This is a dark abode, strongly bound in by fetters of fire; the ground is venomously aflame with surging fire. For no short time must we suffer torments together, woes and damnation; not at all possess glorious light in heaven, the happiness of thrones. Lo! in the presence of God we had delights of yore, singing in heaven in happier times, where now around the Eternal stand the noble ones about the throne and praise the Lord in words and deeds; and I must needs bide, fettered in agony, and because of my pride never have hope of a better abode.'

Then the dread spirits, dark and sinful, whelmed in torment, answered him: 'Thou didst prompt us by thy lying not to obey the Saviour. To thee alone it seemed that thou hadst sway over all, over heaven and earth; that thou wert holy God, the Creator Himself. Now art thou a wretched wrongdoer, fast bound in the grip of fire. Thou didst think in thy glory that thou and we angels with thee did own the world, and had power over all things. Dread is thy aspect; foully have all of us fared because of thy falsehoods. Thou didst tell us as truth that the Lord of mankind was thy son; now hast thou greater torment.'

Thus the wicked ones blamed their leader with treacherous words, with sorrowful speeches. Christ had driven them forth bereft of joys; in their pride they had forsaken God's light on high; the regions of hell, burning agony, were their joy. The dark demons went forth transformed; the evildoers, unhappy creatures, wandered throughout that dread den because of their presumption which erst they displayed. Once again the leader of the fiends spoke; he was yet more terrible when he felt the greatness of the torment. He gave out sparks of fire and venom, when he began to speak; that was no pleasant joy when he vented words in his torments:

'Of yore I was a holy angel in heaven, loved by the Lord; I possessed great joy with God, in the Lord's presence, and this host likewise. Then I thought in my heart that I would overthrow the glorious light, the Sons of God; that I and this unhappy band which I have brought to its abode in hell should have the sway of the strongholds wholly in our possession. Remember that clear token and the suffering when I was driven forth from heaven down under the headlands into the deep abyss. Now I have brought you all from your abode to a place of bondage; here is no glory of the Blessed One, wine hall of the proud, nor worldly joy, nor company of angels; nor may we possess heaven on high. This dread dwelling is aflame with fire; I am God's foe. For ever at the gates of hell dragons stand on guard with glowing breasts; they cannot help us. This abode of sorrow is filled with anguish; we have not darkness to hide ourselves in this deep gloom. Here is the hiss of adders, and serpents have here their dwelling. This tormenting bond is fast fettered; fierce are the fiends, gloomy and dark; day shines not here, the light of the Creator, because of the shadow's gloom. Of yore I had sway over all heaven before I was forced to await in this dread domain what the Lord God may be pleased to decree for me, doomed in the abyss; now I have come, bringing a host of devils to this dark abode. But I and more of you, who established the beginning of pride, shall at some time seek out abodes, winging our way in flight. We need not hope that the King of heaven will ever give us an abode, a domain to possess, everlasting power, as aforetime He did; God's Son has sway over all heaven and torments. Wherefore I, hapless and wretched, must wander more widely, go on the paths of exile, deprived of glory, bereft of blessings, possess no joy on high with the angels, whereof I spoke before, so that I myself should be lord of heaven, ruler of creatures; but a worse fate has come upon me.'

Thus the accursed spirit, guilty of sins, poured forth all his sufferings—a fiery glare blended with venom was spread through that dread den! 'I am of such stature that I cannot lie hidden in this vast hall, stricken with sins. At times both heat and cold are mingled; at times I hear the creatures of hell, the sorrowing race bemoaning the abysses down under the headlands; at times naked men strive amid serpents; this windy hall is all filled with evil. I may not enjoy a happier home, city or dwelling, nor may I ever again with my eyes gaze on the radiant creation. It is now worse for me that I ever knew the glorious light on high with the angels, singing in heaven, where all the youths themselves surrounded the blessed Son of God with song. Nor may I do hurt to any souls of the blessed, save only those which He cares not to own. Them I may bear to a home in bondage, bring to a dwelling in the dread abyss. We are all changed from when aforetime we had beauty and honour in heaven. Full often the sons of God bore heavenly harmony in their breasts, where we all, as limbs around the Precious One, raised songs of praise, spoke unto God. Now I am stained with deeds, stricken with guilt; now I must bear this fetter of torment burning upon my back, hot in hell, empty of joy.'

Then the guardian of sins, the dread creature from hell, wearied by torments, spoke many things further.   Speech flew with sparks, like venom, when he drove it forth: 'O glory of the Lord!   O Guardian of the people!   O power of God: Alas the world!   Alas the glittering day!   Alas the gladness of God! Alas the host of angels!   Alas heaven on high!   Alas that I am wholly cut off from eternal joy, so that with my hands I may not reach heaven, nor gaze up to it with my eyes, nor even with my ears ever hear the sound of the clearest trumpet because I purposed to drive out the Son of God, the Lord, from His dwelling and make myself master of joy, of glory and gladness! A worse fate came upon me there than the delight which was mine aforetime.   Now I am banished from that bright band, driven from the light to a hateful dwelling.   I cannot think how I, stained with sins, have been cast from heaven into this deep place of darkness.   I know now that he who is minded not to obey the King of heaven, to please the Lord, is wholly cut off from eternal joy.   I must endure woe and agonies and misery by this torment, bereft of blessings, stained with guilt of past deeds, because I purposed to drive God, the Lord of hosts, from His dwelling.   Now, troubled with grief I must go on the paths of exile, on far journeys.'

Then God's foe passed to hell, when he had been vanquished. His followers did likewise, insatiate and ravening, when God drove them into that hot abode whose name is hell.   Wherefore every man must be careful not to offend the Son of God; let him take as an example how the dark fiends all perished in their pride.   Let us take the Lord of hosts for our joy, heavenly, everlasting gladness, the Ruler of angels.   He showed that He had strength, mighty powers, when He drove out the host, captives from the high dwelling.   Let us remember holy God eternal in heaven.   Let us choose an abode in heaven with the Author of all created things, with the King of all kings, who is called Christ.   Let us bear glad thoughts in our breasts, peace and wisdom; let us forget not truth and right, when we purpose to bow to the throne and ask mercy of the Ruler of all.   Then he who lives here in the joys of the world will need to shine in beauty when afterwards he seeks another life a far fairer land than is this earth.   There it is beauteous and winsome; plenty gleams brightly in the cities; there is a wide land, home of the joyous, dear to Christ in heaven.   Let us turn thither where He

Himself, the Lord of victories, sits, God the Saviour, in the precious home; and around that throne stand troops of angels and blessed ones in radiance. Holy heavenly bands praise God in words and deeds; their beauty shines for ever and ever with the King of heaven.

[A passage of about 150 lines follows, consisting of further lamentation on Satan's part, and of conventional moralizing, in which the joys of heaven are contrasted with the torments of hell. Then comes a description of Christ's Harrowing of Hell.]

In former days in God's kingdom that angel was called Lucifer, the bearer of light. Then he roused hostility in heaven because he was minded to have pride of place. Guiltily Satan purposed to set up a throne in heaven on high with the Eternal One. He was their leader, the creator of evil. Afterwards he repented of that, when he was doomed to descend to hell and his followers with him, to fall under the Saviour's sternness, and never again might they gaze on the Eternal One.

Then fear fell upon him; there was clamour because of the Judge, when He broke and overcame the gates in hell. Bliss came to men when they beheld the Saviour's head. Then the loathly one, whom erstwhile we named, and the doomed people, were terror-stricken in heart; then far and wide throughout the windy dwelling they were all cowed by fear; they uttered words: 'This is terrible, now that this storm, the Prince with His host, the Lord of angels, has come; a fairer light goes before Him than we have ever seen before with our eyes, save when we were on high with the angels. Now by His glorious strength He will scatter our torments now that this dread might has come, the loud noise of the Lord; this sorrowful host shall straightway now suffer anguish. It is the Son of God Himself, the Lord of angels; He will take the souls up hence, and we afterwards shall for ever endure humiliation because of His wrath.'

Then God by His might entered hell to the sons of men; He was minded to bring forth many thousands of men up to His home. Then came a sound of angels, a noise at dawn. The Lord Himself had laid low the fiend; the struggle was yet to be seen at daybreak; then the dread strength was made manifest. Then He caused the blessed souls, the race of Adam, to rise up; and Eve could not yet look upon heaven till she uttered words: 'I angered Thee once, eternal God, when Adam and I through the serpent's malice ate two apples, as we should not have done. The loathly one, who now burns ever in bonds, taught us that we should have happiness, a holy dwelling, heaven in our possession.   Then we trusted in the accursed one's words, took the gleaming fruit on the holy tree with our hands.   Bitter was our requital for that, when we had to pass into this hot pit and afterwards bide there many thousand years in dreadful flame.   Now, Lord of heaven, I beseech Thee by the followers Thou bringest hither, the troops of angels, that I may rise hence with my people.   And three nights ago the Saviour's servant came home to hell—he is now firm in fetters, accursed in torments, even as the King of heaven grew wroth at him for his pride—he told us truly that God Himself purposed to descend to the abode of dwellers in hell.   Then all rose up, and raised themselves on their arms, leaned upon their hands.   Though the terror of hell seemed dreadful, all were exceeding glad that their Lord was minded to seek their abode to aid them.'

Then she stretched her hands to the heavenly King, prayed God for mercy by Mary: 'Lo! Thou, Lord, wert born into the world by my daughter to aid men.   Now is it manifest that Thou art God Himself, the eternal Author of all creatures.'

Then eternal God let the host rise up to heaven; He had laid fetters of torment upon the fiends and thrust them further into that deep darkness, hard oppressed.   There Satan, the hapless monster, and with him the loathly ones, accursed in torments, hold evil converse.   They can have no light of heaven, but the abyss of hell, nor can they ever have hope of escape, after the Lord God had grown wroth at the race of devils, laid dread bondage of torment upon them and dire terror, the dim and dark shadow of death, hot depths of hell, deadly fear.   Behold! that was gladsome when the company came up to their abode, and the Eternal One with them, the Lord of mankind into the glorious city.   Holy prophets, the race of Abraham, raised Him among them with their hands to His abode.   Then God Himself had overcome death, put the fiend to flight.   Prophets told of that in days gone by, that He would do thus.   This all came to pass at dawn, before daybreak, that the uproar came loud from heaven, when He broke and overcame the doors of hell; the fiends grew powerless when they saw so bright a light.

CHRIST

[The *Christ* is made up of three parts. Some have regarded these as separate poems by different authors and Cynewulf as the composer only of the part which contains his name in runic letters. The first part, which deals with the season of Advent, a period of devout expectancy and longing, is largely a free adaptation of some of the Church antiphons for Advent. The dialogue between Mary and Joseph is interesting as the earliest dramatic scene in English literature. The principal source for Part II, the Ascension, is a homily of Pope Gregory the Great. Part III with its powerful, though diffuse, description of Doomsday and Christ's passionate address to the sinners is based on various originals.]

PART I

I

. . . to the King.[1] Thou art the corner-stone which the builders rejected from the work; it befits Thee well that Thou shouldst be head of the glorious temple, and frame the wide walls, the unbreakable flint, with firm joint, so that all things with gazing eyes throughout the cities of earth may marvel for ever at the Lord of glory. Now do Thou, true and triumphant, show forth with skill Thy own work, and straightway leave standing stone upon stone. Now is there need in the work that the Craftsman come and the King Himself and then restore the house beneath the roof, since it is in ruins. He created that body, the limbs of clay; now the Lord of life will deliver the hapless host from their foes, the wretched ones from fear, as He has often done.

O Thou Ruler and Thou righteous King, who holdest the key, who openest life—gladden us with victory, with glorious success, denied to another if his work is not well done. Verily in distress we utter these words, we entreat Him who created man that He may not elect to declare the doom of hapless men, of us who sit in prison sorrowing for the sun's joyous journey, until the Lord of life reveal light to us, become a guardian to our soul and gird the feeble mind with glory. Make us worthy of this, us whom He hath admitted to glory when we were doomed in misery, reft of our home, to sojourn in this narrow world.

[1] Some lines are missing at the opening of the poem.

Wherefore he who tells truth may say that He delivered the race of men when it was froward. Young was the Virgin, a maid free from foulness, whom He chose for his mother; it was brought to pass without a man's embraces, that the Bride became great with the Child. There hath not come to pass in the world before nor since a woman's pregnancy like unto that; that was a hidden mystery of God. All spiritual grace overspread the earth; many matters, abiding teachings, prediction of the prophets, which before lay shrouded under shadow, were then made clear by the Author of life, when the Lord came who gives free course to the words of all those who in their wisdom zealously desire to praise the Creator's name.

O Vision of peace, holy Jerusalem, best of thrones, city of Christ, habitation of angels, and in thee the souls of righteous men alone rest eternally, rejoicing in glory. No mark of defilement shall ever be seen in that dwelling, but every transgression, cursing, and conflict shuns thee afar. Thou art gloriously filled with holy joy, according to thy name. Now lift up thine eyes to look widely about thee on all sides at this broad creation, also at the vault of the sky, how the King of heaven seeks thee in His course, and Himself comes, makes in thee His dwelling, as wise prophets long ago proclaimed, showed forth Christ's birth, spoke of solace for thee, most excellent of cities. Now that Child is come, born to transform the suffering of the Hebrews. He brings thee bliss, loosens the bonds imposed by sin; He knows the hard straits—how the hapless must needs look for mercy.

II

'O joy of women in heavenly glory, fairest maid on the whole face of the earth, of whom dwellers by the sea ever heard tell; make clear to us that mystery which came to thee from heaven, how thou didst ever conceive the Child, and knew no intercourse after the manner of men. In truth we have never heard of such thing happening in days past, such as thou didst receive by special grace, nor need we look for that event in time to come. Verily, exalted faith has dwelt in thee, since thou hast borne in thy bosom the Majesty of heaven, and thy great virginity was not destroyed. Even as all children of men sow in sorrows, so shall they reap again—bring forth in agony.'

The blessed Virgin, holy Mary, ever triumphant, spoke: 'What is this amazement with which ye wonder, and sorrowing lament with grief, thou son and thou daughter of Salem? Ask ye in curiosity how I have kept my maidenhood, my virginity, and yet become mother of the glorious Son of God? Verily that hidden thing is not revealed to men, but Christ made known in David's dear kinswoman that Eve's sin is all done away, the curse cast off, and the more lowly sex exalted. Hope has been won, that now blessing may abide with both men and women for ever and ever in the heavenly joy of angels, continually with the father of truth.'

O Rising Sun, most radiant of angels sent to men upon earth, and true beam of the sun bright beyond the stars—out of thyself thou dost ever enlighten all seasons. As Thou, God verily begotten of God, Son of the true Father, wast ever without beginning in the glory of heaven, so now Thine own handiwork in its distress beseeches Thee boldly to send us the bright sun, and to come Thyself, that Thou mayest bring light to those who long erstwhile have sat here covered with darkness and in gloom, enfolded by sins in eternal night, and who have had to endure the dark shadow of death. Now gladly we trust in salvation brought to multitudes through that Word of God, which in the beginning was co-eternal with God, the Father almighty, and then afterwards became flesh free from iniquities, which the Virgin bore for the succour of the sorrowful. God was seen sinless among us; the mighty Child of the Lord and the Son of man dwelt together in concord among men. Wherefore we can ever utter thanks to the Lord of victory for His deeds, because He was pleased to send us Himself.

O God of souls, how fitly wast Thou named aright by the name Emmanuel, as the angel first spoke it in Hebrew; that was afterwards fully interpreted according to its inner meaning: 'Now is the Guardian of the heavens, God Himself, with us'; thus men of old time long ago spoke truly of the King of all kings, and also of the pure Priest to come. In like manner the glorious Melchizedec, wise in soul, once revealed the divine majesty of the eternal Almighty. He was the Giver of law, Bringer of precepts, to those who long while hoped for His coming, even as it had been promised to them that the Son of God himself would purify the peoples of the earth, likewise by the might of the spirit seek also the abyss in his course.[1] Then patiently they bided in bonds till the Son of God should come to the sorrowful. Wherefore, made weak by sufferings, thus they spoke:

[1] Referring to Christ's descent to hell.

'Now do Thou, high King of heaven, come Thyself. Bring salvation to us wretched captives, worn out by weeping, by bitter burning tears. Succour for those in sore need can come from Thee alone. Seek hither the sad prisoners; leave not behind Thee so mighty a multitude when Thou returnest hence; but do Thou, Christ the Saviour, Prince of glory, royally manifest mercy upon us; let not the accursed have dominion over us. Grant us unending gladness in Thy glory, so that those whom erstwhile Thou didst create with Thy hands may honour Thee, glorious King of hosts. Thou dost dwell for ever on high with God the Father.'

III

(*Mary*.) 'O my Joseph, son of Jacob, descendant of David the glorious king, must thou now break off steadfast love, forsake my fondness?'

(*Joseph*.) 'I am this instant deeply distressed, reft of repute, because I have heard on thy account many words, great griefs, and taunts of contumely, and they speak scorn unto me, many a word of insult. Sad in soul, I must needs shed tears. God can easily heal the sorrow of my heart, comfort the hapless one. O young maiden, Virgin Mary!'

(*Mary*.) 'Why dost thou lament, lift up thy voice in trouble? I never found any fault, cause of complaint in thee for evil committed; and thou utterest these words as if thou thyself wert filled with all sins and iniquities.'

(*Joseph*.) 'I have borne too many miseries from child-bearing. How can I refute hateful talk, or find any answer against my foes? Far and wide it is known that gladly I received from the glorious temple of God a pure virgin, void of sin, and now by someone she is changed. It helps me not, either to speak or hold my peace. If I tell the truth, then the daughter of David shall die, slain by stones. Yet it is harder for me to cloak crime; a man forsworn shall afterwards live hated by all men, despised among the people.'

Then the maiden made known the mysteries, and thus she spoke: 'By the Son of God, the Saviour of souls, I speak the truth, that I have no knowledge yet by wedlock of any man anywhere on earth; but it was granted to me, still young in my home, that Gabriel, the archangel of heaven, gave me greeting; said truly that the heavenly Spirit should enlighten me with radiance; that I should bear the Glory of life, the excellent Son, the exalted Child of God, the resplendent King of glory. Now without guilt I have been made His temple; in me the Comforter has made His abode. Now do thou renounce all grievous sorrow. Utter never-ceasing thanks to the glorious Son of God that I have become His mother, and yet remain a maiden, and thou reputed by opinion His earthly father. Truly prophecy was to be fulfilled in Himself.'

O Thou true and peaceful King of all kings, Christ almighty, how wast Thou begotten as a child with Thy glorious Father by His power and might before all the multitudes of the world! There is no being now under heaven, no wise man, so sage that he can tell the dwellers by the sea, rightly set forth, how the Lord of the heavens took Thee at the beginning for His glorious Son. In the beginning it was brought to pass beneath the heavens first of those things which here the race of men have heard among the people, that wise God, the Author of life, divided, as Lord, light and darkness; and in Him was the power of judgment, and the Lord of hosts uttered the commandment: 'Now let the light remain gleaming henceforth for ever, a delight to all living creatures who may be brought forth in their generations.'

And then straightway it came about when thus it was ordained; the light shone on the races of men, bright with the stars according to the lapse of the seasons; He Himself ordained that Thou shouldst be the Son co-dwelling with Thy only Lord, before aught of this ever was wrought. Thou art the wisdom who didst make all this wide creation with Thy Lord. Wherefore there is none so wise or discerning who can clearly declare Thy descent to the children of men. Come now, Lord of victory, God of mankind, and in Thy graciousness show forth Thy mercy here; we all desire to know Thy lineage on the mother's side and its mysteries, for we can no whit explain from what father Thou art sprung. Do Thou, Saviour Christ, graciously gladden this world by Thy coming, and do Thou, supreme Lord of the heavens, bid the golden gates be opened, which in days past have stood locked full long erstwhile. And then visit us in lowly wise by coming Thyself to earth. We need Thy mercies. The accursed wolf, the dark shadow of death, has scattered Thy flock, O Lord, driven it far and wide; that which Thou boughtest aforetime with blood, O God, the evil one sorely oppresses, and takes into bondage against our desires. Wherefore, Saviour, we earnestly beseech Thee in the thoughts of our hearts speedily to send help to us sorrowful wretches; so that the tormenting

slayer may fall in misery into hell's abyss; and that Thy handi-
work may arise, Creator of men, and come according to right
to the excellent heavenly kingdom; whence erstwhile the malig-
nant spirit beguiled and misled us through desire after sin; so
that we, reft of glory, must needs suffer misery for ever without
end, except Thou, eternal Lord, living God, Protector of all
creatures, wilt save us the more speedily from the common foe.

IV

O thou glorious one of the world, purest woman ever wrought
on earth, how do all creatures endowed with speech, men
throughout the earth, glad in heart, rightly name thee, and say
that thou art the Bride of the most excellent Lord of heaven!
Likewise the highest servants of Christ in heaven do also say and
sing that thou by holy powers art Lady of the heavenly host, and
of earthly estates under heaven, and of dwellers in hell; because
thou alone of all mankind didst make that resolve nobly, with
courage, to bring thy virginity to God; to give it without guilt.
No such other has come, surpassing all men, a Bride bedecked
with rings, who has since sent the excellent offering to the
heavenly home with pure heart.   Wherefore the Lord of victory
bade His archangel fly hither from His angelic host, and straight-
way show thee the fullness of power, that thou shouldst bring
forth the Son of God, by a spotless birth in mercy to men, and
yet henceforth for ever preserve thyself, Mary, unpolluted.

Also we have heard what long ago in olden days a certain
true prophet, Isaiah, spoke of thee; that he was brought where in
the eternal home he beheld all the abode of life.   Thus then the
wise prophet gazed over the land till he fixed his eyes where was
set up a glorious doorway. The huge portal was all overlaid with
costly treasure, encompassed with wondrous bands.   Strong
was his belief that none among men could ever in eternity
unfasten bars so firmly fixed, or open the lock of the city gate,
before God's angel with gracious thought made known the
matter and spoke these words—'I can say unto thee that truly it
has come to pass that God Himself, the Father almighty, by
the strength of the spirit will yet at some time pass through these
golden gates, and come to earth through the firm barriers; and
then for ever eternally they shall stand thus shut behind Him,
so that no other except God the Saviour shall ever again unlock
them.'

Now that is fulfilled which the wise one then beheld there with his eyes. Thou art that door in the wall; through thee the Sovereign Lord once journeyed out to this earth; and Christ almighty found thee even so endowed with virtues, pure and elect; so the Lord of angels, the Giver of life, locked thee, wholly undefiled, after Him with a key. Manifest to us now the mercy which the angel Gabriel, God's messenger, brought thee. Verily we city-dwellers pray that thou wilt reveal comfort to the people, thine own Son. Then we shall be able, all with one accord, to rejoice, when we behold the Child on thy breast. Plead for us now with bold words that He may leave us no longer in this valley of death to hearken unto godlessness, but that He may carry us to the Father's kingdom, where we may henceforth dwell free from sorrow, in glory with the God of hosts.

O Thou holy Lord of heaven, Thou wast of old co-existent with Thy Father in the glorious home. As yet none of the angels had come into being, nor any of the mighty heavenly host who watch over the kingdom in the skies, the glorious abode of the Prince and His servants, when first Thou Thyself wast with the eternal Lord establishing this wide creation, the broad spacious lands. The holy spirit is common to you both. We do all pray thee in humbleness, O Christ the Saviour, O God our Deliverer, to hearken to the voice of Thy servants in bondage—how we are distressed by our own desires. Evil spirits, malicious fiends, have sorely fettered the outcasts, bound them with grievous cords. Help can come only from Thee alone, eternal God. Succour the sorrowful, so that Thy coming hither may comfort the wretched, though we have striven against Thee through lust of sins. Now show mercy to Thy servants, and forget not our sufferings—how we stumble with feeble heart, and miserably go astray. Come now, King of men; linger not too long. We have need of mercies—that Thou deliver us, and in righteousness give us salvation, so that thenceforth we may ever do better things among the people, Thy will.

V

O the fair heavenly Trinity, filled with glories, high and holy, blessed far and wide throughout the spacious plains, men endowed with speech, wretched earth-dwellers, shall rightly praise Thee exceedingly with all their might, now that God, the faithful Saviour, has revealed to us that we may know Him. Wherefore they, diligent, crowned with glory, the righteous race of the seraphim, ever uttering praise on high with the angels, sing with unwearied strength very loud, with a great voice, sweetly far and near. They have the best of ministries with the King. Christ granted them that their eyes may delight in His presence, brightly arrayed, worship the Lord ever continually far and wide; and with their wings they guard the presence of Almighty God, the Lord eternal, and throng about the throne all eagerly striving which of them in the courts of peace may in his flight flutter nearest to our Saviour. They laud the Loved One; and in the light utter these words to Him, and glorify the noble Author of all created things:

'Holy art Thou, holy, Lord of archangels, true Prince of victory; ever art Thou holy, Lord of lords; ever Thy glory shall endure on earth among men, honoured far and wide at all times. Thou art the God of hosts, for Thou, Refuge of warriors, Protector of all creatures, hast filled earth and skies with Thy glory. Everlasting hosanna be to Thee in the highest, and on earth praise, excellent among men. Abide, Thou blessed one, who didst come in God's name as a comfort to hapless men. To Thee in the heights be everlasting praise without end.'

O! what a marvellous new thing is this in the life of men, that the merciful Creator of mankind should receive from the Maiden, flesh without spot; nor knew she aught of man's embraces; nor did the Lord of victory come by the seed of any man on earth. But that was a greater marvel than all dwellers on earth could know by reason of its mystery, how He, the Glory of the skies, the Lord of heaven, brought help to mankind through His mother's womb. And the Saviour of the people, the Lord of hosts, continuing thus henceforth, bestows His bounty every day in aid of men. Wherefore let us, striving after glory, praise Him devotedly in deeds and words. That is excellent wisdom for every man who takes thought, that he should ever worship God most frequently and fervently and eagerly. He, the sacred Saviour Himself, will yield him reward for that love, even in that country where he never came before, in the bliss of the land of the living, where He shall dwell in happiness henceforth, abide for ever without end. Amen.

PART II

I

Now, famous man, seek earnestly with meditations, with shrewdness by wisdom of mind, that thou mayest truly know how that came to pass—when the Almighty was begotten in purity, when He chose the protection of Mary, the Flower of maidens, the glorious Virgin—that angels robed in white garments appeared not when the Prince came, the Chief to Bethlehem. Messengers were ready, who in speech showed forth to the shepherds, told the true gladness, that the Son of God was born into the world in Bethlehem. Yet it says not in books that they appeared there at that glorious time in white garments, as they afterwards did, when the famous Prince, the glorious Lord, summoned his band of disciples, the beloved company, to Bethany. They were not heedless on that glorious day of the words of the Master, their Giver of treasure. Straightway the heroes were ready with the Lord for the holy city, where the Giver of glory, the Protector of heaven, made known many mysteries unto them by parables, before the only begotten Son ascended, the Child co-eternal with his own Father, after the number of forty days since He rose out of the earth from death— then had He fulfilled by His sufferings the prophets' words even as they had sung before throughout the world. Disciples praised, gratefully glorified the Lord of life, the Father of created things. He later requited his loved companions dearly for that, and the Lord of angels, the mighty Prince, about to depart to His Father's kingdom, spoke these words:

'Be joyful in heart; I shall never leave you, but ever continue my love towards you, and give you power, and abide with you for ever and ever, so that by my grace ye shall never feel the want of God. Go now throughout all the wide earth, throughout distant regions; make known to multitudes, preach and proclaim the fair faith; and baptize people beneath the sky, turn them to heaven; cut down the idols, fell and destroy them; abolish hatred, sow peace in men's hearts by your fullness of power. I shall abide with you henceforth as a solace, and keep you in peace with steadfast strength in all places.'

Then suddenly a loud sound was heard in the sky; the company of heavenly angels, the glorious band, the messengers of heaven, came in a host. Our King passed through the roof of the temple where they were beholders—chosen disciples, they who still kept watch in the meeting-place over the Loved One's track. They saw the Lord, the Son of God, ascend from the earth to the heights. Mournful was their mind, a sorrowing spirit hot at their heart, because no longer could they behold beneath the sky Him whom they so loved. The heavenly heralds raised a song; they glorified the Prince, praised the Author of life; rejoiced in the light which shone from the Saviour's head. They saw two radiant angels, glittering nobly in their adornments about the first-born Child, the Glory of kings. They called with wondrous words from on high with clear voices over the host of men! 'Men of Galilee, what do ye await in a circle? Now ye clearly behold the true God, the Lord of victory, pass to heaven: the Chief of princes, the Ruler of all peoples, will ascend up hence to his dwelling, the royal seat of His Father, with these hosts of angels.

II

'With such a band will we bear the Lord, the best and noblest of all Sons of victory, over the vaults of heaven to the shining city with the glad host which here ye gaze upon and behold, glittering in their adornments in joy—nevertheless He Himself with a mighty host will once again seek the peoples of the earth, and then judge every deed which men have done beneath the skies.'

Then the Lord of heaven, the King of archangels, the Refuge of saints, was begirt by the clouds up above the heights. Joy was renewed, bliss in the cities, by the Prince's coming. The eternal Giver of joy sat in triumph at the right hand of His own Father.

Then the men, stout-hearted, sad in spirit, went on their way to Jerusalem, into the holy city, whence a short while since they had seen with their eyes God, their King, ascending on high. There was the cry of lamentation; constant love hot in the heart was whelmed in grief; their spirit was stirred within; their soul burned. The glorious disciples all waited there in the bright city yet ten nights for the Prince's promises, as the Lord of heaven Himself charged them ere the Ruler of all ascended into the protection of heaven. Shining angels came to meet men's Giver of happiness. It is well said, as the Scriptures set forth, that radiant angels came to meet Him at that hallowed time in troops descending from the sky. Then came to pass the greatest rejoicings in heaven. It is very fitting that disciples in dazzling raiment, a glorious band, should come to that joy in the Prince's city; they beheld the Lord of heaven, the Giver of life to peoples, the Lord of all the world and of the host of heaven, in his adornments, a welcome guest on the high throne.[1]

'Now the Holy One has despoiled hell of all the tribute which in days past they wrongfully engulfed in that place of strife. Now the devils' warriors are vanquished and humbled and bound in hell-torment, bereft of blessings in hell's abyss. His adversaries could not succeed in battle by casting of weapons, after the King of Glory, the Protector of the kingdom of heaven, made war by the might of One against His ancient foes. There He delivered from bondage the greatest of spoils, a vast host of people from the stronghold of the fiends, this same band which here ye gaze upon. Now the Saviour of souls, God's own Son, will seek the throne of spirits after the struggle. Now ye certainly know who the Lord is who leads this host. Now glad in heart go without faintness to meet friends. Ye gates, unclose; the Lord of all, the King, the Author of created things, with a mighty multitude will lead unto you, into the city, into the joy of joys, the people whom He took from the fiends by His own triumph. Henceforth for ever and ever there shall be peace between angels and men. There is a covenant between God and men, a sacred bond—love, the joy of life, and the gladness of all light.'

Lo! now we have heard how the Christ-child, the glorious Son of God, by His coming hither gave salvation again, set free and safeguarded the people under the heavens, so that now every living man while he bides here may choose as well the infamy of hell as the glory of heaven, as well the gleaming brightness as the grievous night, as well the fullness of majesty as the doom of darkness, as well delight with God as uproar among devils, as well torment among foes as glory among angels, as well life as death, according as he prefers, while body and soul abide in the world. May the Majesty of the Trinity have glory for that, unending gratitude.

---

[1] What follows is a hymn sung by angels to welcome Christ as He rises to heaven, bringing with Him the Old Testament saints whom He has redeemed from hell.

III

Fitting it is that nations should render thanks to the Lord for every good which He ever wrought for us late and early through the mystery of powers manifold. He gives us food and fullness of possessions, wealth over the wide earth, and soft weather under the shelter of the sky. Sun and moon, noblest of constellations, heaven's candles, shine upon all men on earth. Dew and rain descend; they bring to life blessings to sustain mankind; they add to worldly wealth. For all that we must needs render thanks and praise to our Prince, and specially for that salvation which He gave unto us for a hope, when at His ascension He made an end thereafter of the distress which erstwhile we endured, and when the only begotten King made settlement for mankind with the beloved Father of the greatest of feuds. Afterwards for the peace of souls He destroyed the decree which before was pronounced in wrathful mood to the sorrow of men: 'I framed thee on earth; upon it shalt thou live in suffering, abide in strife and endure misery, chant a song of death for the delight of fiends, and shalt turn to earth again, swarming with worms; thence from the earth thou shalt afterwards seek the flame of torment.' Lo! the Prince, when He took on Himself limbs and body and became the offspring of man, made this milder for us. When the Son of God, the Lord of Hosts, was minded to ascend on high to the home of the angels at that holy time, the wish arose to help us in our wretchedness.

Concerning that Job[1] made a proverb according to his knowledge; praised the Protector of men; glorified the Saviour; and lovingly fashioned a name for the Son of the Sovereign; and called Him a bird whom the Jews could not conceive in the strength of his divine spirit. The bird's flight was inscrutable and hidden from foes on earth, who bore a benighted understanding in their bosoms, a heart of stone. They would not acknowledge the glorious tokens which the noble Son of God wrought before them, many and various, throughout the world. Thus the dear bird assayed flight; sometimes undaunted, strong in his powers, he sought on high the abode of angels, the glorious home; sometimes he sank again to the ground; sought the face of the earth by grace of the spirit; came to the world. Of that the prophet sang: 'He, exalted and holy, was caught up in the clasps of the angels in His great fullness of power above the glory of the heavens.'

[1] Job xxviii. 7.

They who made denial of the ascension could not know of the bird's flight; and did not believe that the Author of life, holy from the earth, was raised up in man's image above the glorious hosts.

Then He who wrought the world, God's spiritual Son, did us honour, and bestowed gifts upon us, enduring habitations on high with the angels; and also sowed and planted throughout the souls of men manifold wisdom of mind.[1] To one He sends eloquence into the thought of his mind by the spirit of his mouth, noble understanding; he can sing and tell very many things; the excellence of wisdom is entrusted to his spirit. One can deftly with his fingers play the harp loudly before heroes, sweep the strings. One can set forth the righteous law of God. One can declare the course of the stars, the vast creation. One can write a discourse with skill. To one is given victory in battle, when the bowmen send a shower of darts over the shield, flying arrows. One can boldly drive the ship over the salt sea, stir the raging water. One can climb the towering upright tree. One can make a tempered sword, a brand. One knows the sweep of the plains, the far-reaching paths. Thus the Lord, the Son of God, grants His gifts to us on earth. He is not willing to give all wisdom of spirit to any one man, lest pride in the power of himself alone, raised above others, should do him hurt.

IV

Thus mighty God, King of all creatures, endows with gifts unstinted and with powers the offspring of earth; moreover on the blessed He bestows glory in heaven. He established peace for ever and ever for angels and men.

Thus He honours His handiwork. Of that the prophet said [2] that sacred gems, bright stars of heaven, the sun and moon, should be raised up on high. What are those gems so fair save God Himself? He is the true brightness of the sun, a glorious radiance to angels and earth-dwellers. The moon shines over the world, a spiritual star; thus the church of God brightly gleams by the union of truth and right—so it is written in books —after the Son of God, King of all creatures undefiled, ascended from the earth. Then the church here of the faithful ones

[1] Compare the following passage with the poems, *The Arts of Men* and *The Fates of Men*.
[2] Habakkuk iii. 11.

suffered persecution under the sway of heathen shepherds. Then the evildoers heeded not truth, the profit of the soul; but they broke and burned God's temple, made blood to be spilt, caused destruction and ruin. Yet by the grace of the spirit the glory of God's servants came forth after the ascension of the Lord everlasting.

Of that Solomon, the Son of David, the ruler of nations, skilled in measures, sang in his meditations,[1] and uttered these words: 'It shall be made known that the King of angels, the Lord great in might, shall go up the mount, leap upon the lofty downs, shall garb with His glory the hills and peaks, redeem the world, all dwellers on earth, by the noble leap.'

The first leap was when He passed into the Virgin, the spotless Maiden, and there took on man's form free from sin; that came to be a solace for all men on earth. The second leap was the Child's birth, when He, the Glory of all glories, was in a manger, swaddled in garments, in the form of a babe. The third leap, the bound of the heavenly King, was when He, the Father, the Comforter, was raised on the cross. The fourth leap was to the sepulchre, fast in the tomb, when He forsook the tree. The fifth leap was when He hurled down the host of hell to living torment, bound the king within, the fierce leader of the fiends, with fiery fetters, where yet he lies in prison, held fast in chains, shackled by sins. The sixth leap, the Holy One's joyful play, was when He ascended to heaven, to His former dwelling. Then the host of angels at that holy time grew blissfully joyous in their rapture. They saw the Majesty of glory, the Chief of princes, seek His home, the gleaming dwellings. Then the Prince's play became to the blessed ones of that city an endless delight.

Thus here on earth God's everlasting Son sprang in leaps over the lofty hills, unafraid along the mountains. So must we men spring in leaps in the meditations of our heart from power to power, endeavour after glorious deeds, so that we may by holy works ascend to the topmost height where are happiness and bliss, an excellent host of thanes. Sore need is there for us to seek salvation with our heart where we earnestly believe in spirit, so that the Christ-child, the living God, may ascend up hence with our body.

Wherefore we must ever despise vain desires, the wounds of sin, and delight in the better part. We have the Father almighty in heaven for a help to us. Thence in His holiness He will send His heralds hither from on high, who fend us against the grievous

[1] Song of Solomon ii. 8.

arrow-flights of foes, lest the fiends should deal wounds, when the author of evil sends forth a bitter shaft from his bent bow into God's people. Wherefore we must ever firmly and warily keep watch against a sudden shot, lest the poisonous point, the bitter dart, the guile of the fiends, should pierce into the body. That is a perilous wound, most livid of gashes. Let us then defend ourselves while we dwell on earth. Let us beseech the Father for protection, pray the Son of God and the merciful Spirit to shield us against the weapons of enemies, the wiles of foes; He gave us life, limbs, body, and spirit. Praise be to Him for ever, glory in heaven world without end.

V

No one on earth of the race of men need dread the darts of the devils, the spear-flight of foes, if God, the Lord of hosts, is his shield. The Judgment is at hand when we shall gain rewards according as we in our lives have laid up for ourselves by works throughout the wide earth. Books tell us how the Storehouse of might humbly came down into the world, the glorious Son of God into the Virgin's womb, holy from on high. Verily, I look for and also dread for myself a sterner doom—when the Prince of angels comes again—because I have not obeyed what my Saviour bade me in the Scriptures. For that I must needs look upon terror, the punishment for sin—this I take for the truth— where many shall be brought in a throng together before the presence of the eternal Judge.

Then the *Bold* (C) [1] shall tremble, he shall hear the King speak, the Sovereign of the skies utter stern words to those who before hearkened heedlessly to Him in the world, while *Misery* (Y) and *Distress* (N) could most easily find solace. There many a one accursed shall await in fear in that place what dread torments He will doom him according to his deeds. Gone is the *Gladness* (W) of earth's gauds. For long our *Possession* (U), our portion of life's pleasures, our *Fortune* (F) on earth, was overflowed by *Waterfloods* (L). Then shall gauds be burned in the blaze; the swift red flame shall rage brightly, rush far and wide

---

[1] In this and in three other passages (*The Elene, Juliana, Fates of the Apostles*) Cynewulf has signed his name in runic letters. The runic letters are used in two different ways. Sometimes they merely stand for letters of the alphabet, but sometimes (as in this passage) the runes represent not only letters but also words suggested by the letters. The exact meaning of this passage and of the other three is difficult to determine.

through the world in its fierceness. The plains shall perish, the strongholds burst asunder. The fire shall fare forth; the greediest of spirits shall eagerly consume ancient treasures which men formerly hoarded while pride was theirs upon earth.

Wherefore I wish to teach each loved one not to neglect the needs of the spirit, nor pour himself out in pride, while God is pleased that he should sojourn in the world and that the soul also should make its journey in the body, in its tenement. Every man must earnestly ponder on his past days, how the Ruler of might was merciful unto us at first according to the angel's word; when He comes again now He will be stern, severe, and just. The sky shall be troubled, and then the great estates of the world shall wail; then the radiant King shall make requital because they have lived on earth amid vile deeds, guilty of sins. For that they must needs long space, weary in soul, ringed round with surging flames, endure dire retribution in a sea of fire.

Then shall the King of hosts come to the assembly with the mightiest of multitudes; because of the sound from heaven great terror will be loudly heard, the outcry of those who lament; the joyless shall make wailing before the presence of the Judge everlasting, those who put faint trust in their works. Then shall a greater fear be shown than was ever heard of on earth since the creation. Then in that season, which shall come suddenly, each of the workers of iniquity would far rather be able to seek shelter in the triumphant host than have all this transitory creation, when the Lord of hosts, the Chief of princes, shall give to all, to friends and foes, to each man, reward according to what is right. Sorely do we need in this barren time before that horror earnestly to ponder on the beauty of the spirit.

Now it is as if we were faring in ships on the flood over the cold water, voyaging on ocean steeds, in vessels upon the wide sea. That flood is perilous, the waves exceeding great, the billows windy over the deep road on which we are tossed through this changeful world. Hard was the wayfaring ere we had won to land over the stormy, heaped waters; then help came to us, God's spiritual Son, who led us to the haven of salvation; and gave us grace, so that we may learn where we are to moor the sea steeds, the ancient wave-horses, firmly with anchors over the side of the ship. Let us fix our hope in that haven which the Sovereign of the skies prepared for us, in its holiness on high, when He rose to heaven.

PART III

I

Then suddenly at midnight the great day of the mighty Lord shall fall in its power upon dwellers on earth, upon fair created things, as often a stealthy robber, a thief in his daring, who goes forth in the darkness, in the black night, on a sudden surprises careless men wrapped in sleep: brings down misery on men unprepared.

So to Mount Sion a mighty multitude faithful to God shall come up together, gleaming and glad; to them shall glory be given. Then from the four corners of the world, from the uttermost ends of earth's domain, bright angels shall blow all together with a blare of the trumpet; the world shall quake, the ground beneath men's feet. They shall sound out together, steadfast and shining, to the course of the stars; they shall sing and make melody from south and north, from east and west, over all creation; they shall call from death to judgment warriors' sons, all mankind, in terror from the ancient earth, shall bid them rise up straightway from deep sleep. There one may hear people sorrowing, mournful in mind, sore disquieted, trembling, terrified, lamenting with wailing the deeds of their lifetime. That shall be the greatest of portents which before or after shall have ever appeared unto men. There shall be mingled whole throngs of angels and devils, bright and black; the coming of both, the white and the dark, shall be different as the abode of angels and devils is differently made.

Then suddenly to Mount Sion from the south-east the light of the sun shall come from the Creator shining more brightly than men can conceive in their minds, beaming brightly when the Son of God shall appear hither through the vaults of heaven. The presence of Christ, the splendour of the noble King, shall come out of the skies from the east, pleasant in heart to His people, stern to the sinful, wondrously different, unlike to blessed and wretched.

He shall be joyous in aspect to righteous men, fair and pleasant to the holy host—lovely in His gladness, friendly and gracious; sweet and mild shall it be for men He loves, to look upon the shining splendour, with delight upon the benign coming of the Lord, the mighty King, for those who pleased Him well before in heart by words and works. To the wicked He shall be dread and terrible to behold, to sinful men, to those who come forth there undone by iniquities.

That may be a warning of torment for him who thinks wisely, so that he shall fear naught. He shall not grow afraid in his heart with fear of that sight, when he sees the Lord of all creatures come before his face to the judgment of many with mighty wonders; and on every side of Him shall circle hosts of heavenly angels, a multitude of radiant ones, companies of saints, thronging in legions.

The vast creation shall resound, and the greatest of surging fires shall sweep before the Lord over the spacious earth; the hot flame shall go hurtling; the skies shall be riven; the stars, steadfast and shining, shall fall down. Then the sun, which had shone brightly over the ancient world upon the sons of men, shall be darkened to the colour of blood; the moon likewise shall fall down which erstwhile shed light upon men at night; and the stars also shall be scattered from heaven, buffeted by storms, in the mighty blast.

The Almighty, the Lord of great kings, the glorious Prince with his company of angels, will come to the concourse. The triumphant troop of his servants shall also be there. Holy souls shall go with their Lord, when the Protector of peoples Himself visits the nations of earth with dread punishment. Loud throughout the spacious earth the sound of the heavenly trumpet shall be heard; and on seven sides the winds shall howl; roaring, they shall blow with the greatest of clamours; they shall rouse and blight the world with their blast, fill the creatures of the earth with fear. Then a great crash shall be made manifest, loud, immense, deafening, and tremendous, greatest of noises, bringing fear upon men.

Then the accursed throngs of mankind shall pass in hosts to the far-spreading flame, some up, some down, smitten by the blaze, when the consuming fire finds them alive there. Then verily it shall come to pass that Adam's race, laden with cares, men in their sorrow, shall grieving lament, not for small miseries but for the sorest, when the lurid leaping of the flame, the dusky blaze, far and wide shall lay hold on all three together at the same time, the seas with their fish, the earth with her mountains, and high heaven shining with her stars. The destroying flame shall fiercely burn in its fury the three together at once. The whole world shall mourn in sorrow in that dread season.

II

Thus the greedy spirit shall go sweeping through the world, the ravaging flame through the lofty buildings; the far-famed blast, hot, devouring, shall hurl the world wholly to the ground by the terror of fire. City walls shall fall down all shattered. Mountains shall melt, and towering cliffs which erstwhile strongly guarded the land against the sea and the floods, firm and fixed on the shore, barriers against the billow, the heaving water. Then the deadly blaze shall seize all creatures, beasts and birds; the smoky flame, a warrior in his wrath, shall walk through the earth. Even as waters flowed before, whirling floods, then fish of the sea shall be burnt, cut off from the ocean; all sea monsters shall die in misery; water shall burn like wax. There shall be more marvels than any man can conceive in his mind—how the din and the tempest and the driving blast shall shatter creation far and wide. Men shall make wailing, weep and moan with wretched voices, hapless, sad at heart, troubled with sorrows. The lurid fire shall flame against those made foul by sin, and the blazes shall devour the adornments of gold, all the old treasure of the kings of the land. There shall be din and distress, and toil of the living, lament and loud weeping, the pitiful plaint of men, because of the sound in heaven. No one guilty of evil deeds can gain refuge from that, win free from the flame anywhere in the land; for in every region that fire shall stretch its grasp, shall fiercely ferret, eagerly seek out the corners of the earth within and without, till the flash of the flame has wholly consumed in its surging the foulness of earthly corruption.

Then mighty God shall come to the glorious mount with the greatest heavenly host; the King of angels, God the Ruler, shall shine in holiness, glorious above the multitudes; and round about Him the most excellent noble band, holy martial hosts, the blessed company of angels, shall brightly glitter; in their inmost thoughts they shall tremble, afraid with dread of the Father. Wherefore it is no wonder that the foul race of men, grieving in sorrows, should sorely fear, when the holy race, radiant and heavenly bright, the host of archangels, shall be struck with fear before that Presence; the creatures of brightness shall await in trembling the judgment of the Lord. The most terrible of days shall come upon the world, when the King of glory shall chasten all people with His power, shall bid men rise up from their graves in the ground, all folk, each one of mankind, to be gathered together.

Then quickly Adam's race shall be all clothed with flesh; there shall be an end of their rest in the earth and their sojourn.   Then each one must needs rise up living at Christ's coming, take on limbs and body, be made young again; he shall bear upon him all of good or of evil which in days gone by, in the course of the years, he garnered in his spirit.   He shall have body and soul joined together.   The countenance of his works, and the memory of his words and the meditation of his heart shall come to light before the King of heaven.

Then shall mankind be multiplied and made anew by God; a great multitude shall rise up to judgment, after the Author of life looses death's bond.   The sky shall be set on fire; the stars of heaven shall fall; the devouring flames shall destroy far and wide.   Spirits shall go to their eternal home.   The acts of men shall be laid open throughout the world; men can no whit hide their secrets, the thoughts of the heart, before the Ruler; deeds shall not be concealed from Him, but there on the great day it shall be known to the Lord how every man before had deserved life everlasting; and all which they have done in the world early or late shall be present.   Naught of men's meditations shall be covered there, but the famous day shall lay bare all the stored treasure of breasts, the thoughts of the heart.   He who purposes to bring unto God a shining presence when the fire, hot, consuming, searches out before the face of the Judge triumphant how souls have been kept from sins, must needs ere that ponder the needs of his soul.

Then the blare of the trumpet and the gleaming banner and the hot blaze and the host on high and the company of angels and the agony of terror and the stern day and the lofty cross set up erect as a sign of sovereignty shall summon the throng of men to the Presence, all souls of those who late or early have been clothed in the body with limbs.   Then the vastest of multitudes, moved by desire and necessity, eternal and made young again, shall pass into the presence of the Ruler called by name; they shall bear the store of their breasts, the treasures of life, before the Son of God.   The Father will note how his sons bring their souls unmarred from the land where they lived.   Then they who bring a shining presence to the Lord shall be of good courage; their strength and gladness shall be very plenteous as a reward for their souls, a glorious recompense for their deeds. Well shall it be for those who in that stern time can please God.

III

There sinful men in their sorrow shall gaze upon Him with the greatest grief. It shall not mean mercy for them that our Lord's cross shall stand before the face of all peoples, the brightest of signs bedewed with the blood of the King of heaven, with pure blood, wet with gore, that casts its light brightly over the wide creation. The shadows shall be driven off where the shining tree sheds its brightness on men. Yet that shall bring calamities and affliction on men, on them who, working iniquity, rendered not thanks unto God, that He was hanged on the hallowed cross for the sins of mankind, where He, the Prince, lovingly purchased life for mankind on that day with the ransom wherewith He redeemed us—He whose body wrought no evil, no sins of transgression. For all that He is minded to exact a return with rigour when the red cross shines brightly over all in place of the sun.

Dark workers of iniquity defiled by sins shall sorrowfully behold it in fear; they shall see as their affliction what would have been their highest weal, if they had been minded to look upon it as a source of good. And downcast in soul they shall also behold the ancient gashes and the gaping wounds in their God, even as His foes pierced His white hands and hallowed feet with nails, and likewise made blood run from His side, where blood and water issued forth together in the sight of all, flowing before the face of men, when He was on the cross. Then they may see all this manifest, revealed, that He suffered exceedingly for the love of men, the workers of sin. The sons of men can clearly know how faithless men denied Him in their thoughts, reviled Him with insults, and also cast their spittle in His face; they railed upon Him; and men destined for hell likewise smote the blessed face with their hands, their outstretched palms and also fists; and blind in their thoughts, besotted and beguiled, they twisted round about His head a grievous crown of thorns.

They beheld the dumb creation—the verdant earth and high heaven—sympathizing in fear with the Lord's sufferings; and though they had not life, they lamented with anguish when foes laid hold on their Creator with sinful hands. The sun was darkened, obscured by sufferings, when the people in Jerusalem saw the most excellent of precious cloths, which erstwhile the multitude were wont to gaze on as the adornment of the holy house, all rent from above, so that it lay on the earth in two pieces; the veil of the temple itself wrought of wondrous colours for the glory of the house was torn in twain, as if the keen edge of a knife had cut it. Many walls and stones fell wholly to the earth; and the earth also, troubled by terror, trembled in the uproar; and the broad sea showed the power of its strength, and burst forth from its confines in anger on the earth's bosom; and in their shining station the stars forsook their pleasant beauty. At the same time the heaven in its brightness looked upon Him who arrayed it exceeding resplendent with starry gems; wherefore it sent its messenger when the bright King of creation was first born.[1] Lo! guilty men also verily beheld a great marvel the same day on which He suffered—that the earth yielded up those who lay in it; those whom before it had closely confined, dead and buried, who kept God's commandment in their heart, rose up restored to life. Hell also, the avenger of sin, perceived that the Creator, God the Ruler, came, when it gave up that host, the horde from its hot breast. The minds of many men were made glad, sorrows vanished from souls. Lo! the sea also declared who set it in its vast bed, the King of glorious might; therefore it formed a floor for Him when God wished to go over its waves. The waterflood durst not whelm its Lord's feet with its wave. And trees also, in great numbers, proclaimed who created them with branches, when mighty God mounted one of them, where He suffered agonies for the sake of mankind, a hateful death for the succour of men. Then many a tree was wet under its bark with bloody tears, redly and plentifully; the sap turned to blood.[2] Earth-dwellers cannot explain by wisdom of mind how much the lifeless creatures who cannot feel were sensible of the Lord's agonies. Those who are the noblest of earth's races and the high buildings of heaven also—everything grew joyless, seized by fear, because of that alone. Though they had no understanding in their nature, yet were they wondrously conscious when their Lord departed from the body. People could not, men blind of heart, harder than flints, acknowledge the Lord—that the Prince, Almighty God, had delivered them by his holy powers from the torment of hell. Since the world's beginning far-seeing men, prophets of the Lord, sacred and sage in thought, in their wisdom of mind first told men often, not once, of that glorious Child—that the precious Stone, the Lord of glory, the Author of blessedness, was to be a defence and delight to the race of men in the world, by means of the glorious Woman.

[1] The reference seems to be to the star in the east at the birth of Christ.

[2] This belief was based on the apocryphal book of Esdras (II. Chap. V, 5): 'And blood shall drop out of wood and the stone shall give his voice, and the people shall be troubled.'

IV

What shall he look for who will not store in his mind the mild teaching of God and all the agonies He suffered for men, because He wished that we might for ever possess a dwelling-place in heaven? Thus it shall go hard on the stern day of the great judgment with them who, defiled by deadly sins, shall behold the scars, the wounds, and anguish of the Lord. With heavy heart they shall behold the greatest of sorrows; the King Himself with tender heart redeemed them from sins with His body, so that they might live free from iniquities, and enjoy for ever the blessedness of glory. They rendered no thanks to their Lord for that heritage; wherefore the unhappy ones to their sorrow shall behold tokens there, plain to be seen, in righteous men.

When Christ, the God of heavenly hosts, the Father almighty, the radiant Creator, shall sit on His throne, on His judgment seat, the Lord of the skies shall rightly apportion all things for all peoples according to their acts. Then on the right hand of Christ Himself the pure people shall be gathered together, chosen because of their virtues, who formerly in their life-days performed his behest with eager pleasure; and there the evil-doers shall be assigned to the left side in the Creator's presence; the true King of victories shall bid the host of the sinful depart to the left hand. There they shall lament and tremble, fearful before the face of the Lord, exposed in their sin, as foul as goats, a people impure; they look not for mercy. Then shall the doom of souls be determined for the generations of men before God, according as erstwhile they acted.

There in the blessed shall be manifest three marks together, for that in words and deeds they kept well their Lord's will.

The first one shall be plain there—that they shall gleam with light before men, with beaming and brightness above the dwellings of cities; in each of them their former deeds shall shine fairer than the sun.

The second also shall be likewise clear—that in glory they shall know God's grace, and gaze to the delight of their eyes, that they can possess pure joys in heaven blessed among the angels.

Then the third shall be—how that happy band shall behold that ruined one suffering agony in the misery of darkness as punishment for sins—the raging flame, and gnawing of worms with bitter jaws—the host of those who burn; whence happy delight shall spring up in them. When they see others enduring that agony which by God's mercy they have escaped from, then they thank God for glory and gladness the more earnestly because they behold both fortunes—that He preserved them from perdition, and also bestowed upon them pleasures which pass not away; to them hell shall be shut, the kingdom of heaven surrendered. Thus shall reward be made to those who erstwhile faithfully followed the will of God in love.

Then in different wise to the others shall their desire be granted. They shall be able to gaze on too many griefs in themselves, sins abounding, iniquities formerly wrought. Then distress, great dire affliction, shall cleave unto them in their sorrow in three ways.

One of them is that they shall see too many miseries, fierce hell-fire ready at hand to torment them, in which for ever bearing misery they must needs endure damnation.

Then the second affliction shall likewise be a shame to them in their guilt—that there, whelmed in ruin, they shall bear the greatest disgrace. God shall see in them many a loathsome iniquity; and the shining host of heaven's angels, and the sons of men, all dwellers on earth, and the fell demon shall also look upon that, upon their evil power, upon every pollution of sin. They can see in their souls wicked sins through their bodies—the sinful flesh shall be filled with abominations—as through that clear glass through which one can look without let most easily.

Then the third grief, wailful sorrow for the sufferers, shall be that they shall look upon the pure ones, how they rejoice in gladness because of their good deeds, which they, wretched creatures, scorned to do erstwhile, while their days continued; and weeping sorely for their works, that formerly they gladly wrought iniquity. They shall see the more righteous gleaming in glory. Not only their own afflictions shall be laid upon them for a punishment, but the blessedness of the others shall be a sorrow, because in days past they forsook joys so fair and excellent because of the false joys of the flesh, the vain lust of the vile body. There confounded, troubled with shame, they shall go wandering in giddiness; shall bear the burden of sin, deeds of iniquity; the peoples shall gaze thereon.

Better then had it been for them that they had sooner felt shame before a man for an evil deed, for every iniquity, for vile works, that they had told God's messenger that they knew to their sorrow there were evil deeds in them. The confessor cannot look through the flesh into the soul, whether a man tell him truth or falsehood when he confesses sins. Yet a man can cure any crimes, foul evil, if he tells it to a single man; and no one can cloak sin unatoned on that stern day; the multitude shall look upon it then.

Alas! if now we might see in our souls with our bodily eyes the horrible iniquities, the wounds made by sins, the foul thoughts, the impure imaginations! No man can tell another how eagerly each by every art would seek after life, fearfully strive to prolong his existence, purge away the rust of sin, and chasten himself, and heal the blemish of the old wound, for the short space which life lasts here; so that unashamed before the eyes of earth-dwellers he may enjoy his heritage among men free from blame, whilst body and soul may both abide together.

v

Now with zeal we must search our breasts shrewdly, the vices within, with the eyes of the heart. With the other eyes, the jewels of the head, we cannot at all see through the spirit of the thought, whether good or evil dwells beneath, so that it may be pleasing unto God at the dread time.

When He shall gleam in glory over all peoples with a pure flame from His high throne, then before angels and all nations He, heaven's high King, shall speak first to the most blessed, and shall graciously promise them peace, solace them sweetly with His sacred voice, and proclaim protection for them; He shall bid them enter into their heritage of the happiness of angels, unmarred and blessed, and enjoy it gladly for ever:

'Take now with your friends my Father's kingdom, which was winsomely prepared for you in ages past, glory amid gladness, the bright splendour of the heritage, against the time when ye might behold the bounty of life with those most beloved, the sweet joys of heaven. Ye earned that when ye gladly received with gentle heart poor men and needy. When they in my name humbly besought you for mercy, then ye helped them, and gave them lodging, food to the hungry, and raiment to the naked; and those who lay sick in pain and bound by disease, and suffered grievously, on whom ye fixed your thought in kindness with love of heart. Ye did all that unto Me when ye sought them with friendliness, and cheered their hearts henceforth with solace. For that ye shall long enjoy a reward gloriously with my loved ones.'

Then Almighty God shall begin to speak in other wise with fearful threatening to the wicked who stand at his left hand. They need look to the Lord for no mercy, life nor favours, but reward shall be paid there to men, to human creatures, according to their words and deeds; they must needs endure the one just doom though it bring dismay. The great mercy of the Almighty shall on that day be put away from mankind, when in his wrath He shall charge the perverse people with sins in stern words; shall bid them reveal before Him a reckoning of their lives which aforetime He gave unto them, sinful men, for their weal. He Himself, the Almighty Lord, shall begin to speak as if He addressed but one, and yet He shall mean them all, the people who have sinned:

'Lo, man, I first wrought thee with My hands, and gave thee understanding; I made thy limbs of clay; I bestowed on thee a living spirit; honoured thee above all creatures; caused thee to have a countenance, a form like unto Me. I gave thee also fullness of power, prosperity over all spacious lands. Thou knewest nothing of the misery and darkness thou wast to endure. Thou wast not grateful for that. When I had framed thee so fair, made thee winsome, and given thee prosperity, so that thou couldst have dominion over the world's creatures; when I placed thee on the fair earth to enjoy the bright plenty of Paradise gleaming with varied hues, then thou wouldst not follow the command of life, but didst break My behest at the word of thy destroyer; thou didst hearken to the faithless fiend, the mischievous foe, rather than to thy Creator. Now I leave that ancient tale, how at first thou didst devise evil, didst squander in iniquities that which I bestowed on thee for a benefit. When I had given thee so many good things, and to thy heart there seemed too little blessedness in all those things, save thou couldst enjoy equal fullness of power with God, then thou didst grow a stranger to that gladness, cast far away, to the delight of fiends. Sad at heart, sinful and joyless, bereft of all blessings and delights, thou wast forced by necessity to forgo the glory of Paradise, the abode of blessed spirits; and then thou wast driven forth into this dark world, where thou hast suffered since for a long space misery, pain and heavy tribulation and sombre death, and after life thou wast doomed to go down hapless to hell with none to help thee.

'Then I began to repent that My handiwork should pass into the power of the fiends, that mankind's offspring should behold destruction, should learn to know a forbidding abode, heavy trials.   Then I Myself came down, a Son conceived by a mother, though her maiden state was wholly unmarred.   I was born alone, as a solace to the people.   They swaddled Me with their hands, wrapped Me in a poor child's raiment; and then laid Me in the darkness, folded in sombre clothes—lo! I suffered that for the world!   I seemed small to the sons of men; I lay on the hard stone, a babe in the manger, because I wished to keep death from thee, the fiery agony of hell; I bore that misery that thou mightest shine in holiness, blessed in the life everlasting.

VI

'I did it not from pride, but in youth I endured distress, cruel torment, so that thereby I should be like thee, and that thou mightest grow after My image, purged of sin; and for the love of men My head suffered grievous smiting.   My face knew pain; often My countenance received spittle from the mouths of impious men, workers of iniquity.   They also mixed together for Me with bitterness a harsh drink of vinegar and gall.   Then in the presence of the people I bore the hatred of foes; they afflicted Me with outrages—they held not back from enmity— and smote Me with scourges.   In lowliness I bore all that agony for thee, scorn and reviling.   Then about My head they twined a sharp crown of pain, cruelly pressed it on; it was made of thorns.   Then I was hanged on the high cross, fastened to the rood.   Then forthwith they made blood flow from My side with a spear, gore to the ground, so that thou thereby shouldst be saved from the devil's tyranny.   Then I, free from sins, suffered torment, sore tribulations, till I sent forth from My body My living spirit alone.

'See now the deadly wounds which aforetime they made in My hands and in My feet also, by which I hung, cruelly made fast; thou mayest see here too in My side the bloody hurts still manifest.

'How unequal a reckoning was that between us two!   I bore thy agony, so that thou mightest happily enjoy in blessedness My kingdom; and with My death I bought for thee at a great price that lasting life, so that thou mightest afterwards dwell in light, fair, free from sins.   My body, which did hurt to none, lay buried in the ground, in the tomb, hidden deep down, so that thou mightest be in radiance on high in heaven, exalted among the angels.

'Why hast thou forgone that fair life which I graciously purchased in love for thee with My body to help thee in thy misery? So foolish hast thou become that thou hast not rendered thanks to the Ruler for thy redemption. I ask naught now for My bitter death which I endured for thee; but yield Me thy life for which long ago in martyrdom I laid down Mine as a ransom; I claim the life which to thy own shame thou hast ruined with sins. Why in thy uncleanness hast thou defiled of thy own will by sinful lusts and foul sin that tabernacle which I consecrated in thee to be a dear pleasure-house for Myself? And by evil-doing thou hast shamefully stained that body which I redeemed for Myself from the grasp of the fiends, and then forbade it to sin. Why dost thou hang Me on the cross of thy hands more painfully than long ago I hung? Lo! this seems harder to Me. Now the rood of thy sins, on which against My will I am bound, is more grievous unto Me than was that other, which aforetime I mounted of My own will, when thy trouble touched My heart most keenly, when I drew thee forth from hell—if thou hadst been willing to be watchful since.

'I was a pauper in the world, that thou shouldst have plenty in heaven; I was wretched in thy kingdom, that thou shouldst be blessed in Mine. Then for all that thou wast not any way grateful to thy Saviour.

'I charged you to cherish well My brothers in the world with those goods which I gave you on earth, to aid the wretched. Ill have ye done that; ye refused to allow the needy to come in under your roof, and with hard hearts wholly denied raiment to the naked, food to the hungry. Though weary, ailing, distressed, bereft of blessing, parched by thirst, they prayed in My name for water, for a drink, ye harshly denied them. Ye sought not the sorrowful, nor spoke to them a kindly word and consolation, so that thereby they might gain a gladder spirit in heart. Ye did all that to Me in scorn of the King of heaven. For that ye shall suffer sore torment for ever, endure misery among devils.'

Then the Lord of victories Himself shall pronounce over that doomed people a dread decree laden with torment—He shall speak to the host of sinful souls:

'Go now, ye cursed, cut off by your own will from the delight of angels, into the everlasting fire which was prepared, glowing and fierce, for Satan the devil and his companions and the host of darkness; therein shall ye fall.' Then, with naught to help them, they cannot scorn the command of the King of heaven;

they shall fall quickly into the dread abyss, who aforetime fought against God. Then the Lord of the kingdom shall be stern and powerful, angry and terrible. No foe on this earth shall be able to remain before His face.

VII

He shall swing the victor-sword with His right hand, so that the devils shall fall into the deep pit, the host of the sinful into the dark flame, the fated souls under the face of the earth, the multitude of the corrupt into the abode of fiends, those damned to destruction into the house of torment, the devil's hall of death. They shall not afterwards come to the Lord's mind; they shall not escape from sin; there they shall suffer death, stained with crimes, fettered by fire. Before their face the punishment of sin shall plainly appear; that is agony unending. That hot abyss will not be able to burn away in endless night the guilt from the dwellers in hell, nor ever the stain from their souls; but there the deep pit shall sustain the disconsolate; the bottomless abyss shall keep the souls in darkness, consume them with its ancient fire and with the dread frost, and with horrible worms and many torments, with terrible dread jaws it does hurt unto the people.

We can mark and forthwith declare and say truly, that he who cares not now whether his soul shall be wretched or blessed, when after death it shall be for ever settled, has lost the keeper of his soul, the wisdom of life. He, rash man, fears not to commit sin, nor has he any sorrow in his heart, that the holy Spirit should depart from him by reason of iniquities in this fleeting time.

Then the sinner shall stand in his darkness at the judgment afraid before God, and pale as death, accursed in sins; the faithless one, not worthy of life, shall be filled with fire, overwhelmed with fear before the face of God; ghastly and unsightly he shall have the colour of a man accursed, the mark of a guilty life. Then the children of sin shall shed tears when the season is past, lament their guilt; but too late they bring help to their souls, when the Lord of hosts will not heed how the evildoers at that time, which discloses all things, bitterly deplore what erst they held dear. That time of sorrow will not be granted to the people in order that he may find salvation then who will not now, whilst he lives here, secure safety for his soul. Grief shall not be made known to any good men there, nor weal to any of the wicked; but each shall bring there to the Presence his own deserts.

Wherefore he who wishes to gain life from God must needs bestir himself, whilst in him body and soul are joined together. Let him earnestly foster the fairness of his soul after the will of God, and grow heedful in words and deeds, in ways and thoughts, whilst this world moving on amid shadows can still be bright, so that in this fleeting time he shall not forfeit the fullness of his joy, and the number of his days and the fair face of his work, and his glorious reward, that the true King of heaven at that holy season gives as the guerdon of victory to those who gladly obey Him in spirit.

Then heaven and hell shall be filled with the children of men, with the souls of mankind. The abyss shall engulf God's enemies; the darting flame shall vex wicked men, doers of evil, and shall not let them go thence in gladness to salvation; but the fire shall fetter the firm-fixed host, shall trouble the children of sin. It seems to me perilous that these beings endowed with souls, men in their hearts, will take no heed, when they do sin, what punishment the Lord has set up for them, for evil people. Then the abodes of life and death shall receive souls; the house of torments shall be gaping and open for perjurers; men lustful after sin shall fill that with their dark souls. Then the host of the guilty, as a punishment for their sins, shall be set apart for destruction, the wretched from the holy. There thieves and malefactors, false men and fornicators, must not look for life, and men forsworn shall see the wages of sin, dire and dreadful. Then hell shall take the host of the faithless, and the Lord shall deliver them to the fiends for destruction; the guilty shall suffer dread mortal agony. Unhappy is he who will work iniquities, so that at the day of judgment he shall be cut off in his crime from his Creator down to death, into that hot fire among the race of hell, under the fetter of the flame. There they shall stretch out their limbs to be bound and burned, and to be scourged in punishment for sins. Then the Holy Ghost by the power of God, at the King's command, shall shut up hell, the greatest of houses of torment, full of fire and the army of fiends. That shall be the greatest of agonies for devils and men. That is a joyless dwelling. No one there can ever win free from cold bonds. They broke the King's behest, the excellent command of the Scriptures; therefore they who here mocked the majesty of the kingdom of heaven must needs abide in eternal night; stained with evil deeds they must henceforth endure torment ever-lasting.

Then the chosen shall bear bright adornments before Christ; their glory shall endure in the day of judgment; they shall have the joy of untroubled life with God which is vouchsafed to every saint in the kingdom of heaven. That is the fatherland which shall never pass away, but henceforth for ever there, free from sins, they shall enjoy bliss; encompassed by light, enfolded in peace, guarded from griefs, honoured with joys, held precious by God, they shall praise the Lord, the dear Protector of life; for ever and ever illustrious with grace they shall blissfully enjoy the fellowship of angels, worship the people's Protector. The Father shall have and hold dominion over all the hosts of the holy.

There shall be the song of angels, the delight of the blessed; there shall be the dear face of the Lord brighter than the sun for all the happy ones; there shall be the love of friends; life without death; a glad multitude of men; youth without age; the glory of the heavenly hosts; salvation without sorrow; rest without strife for those who did right; the glory of the blessed; day without darkness, radiant, full of splendour; gladness without griefs; peace henceforth without dissension between friends happy in heaven; love without enmity among the saints. There shall be neither hunger nor thirst there, sleep nor grievous sickness, nor the heat of the sun, nor cold nor care; but the band of the blessed, the most glorious of hosts, with the Lord of heaven shall ever enjoy there the grace of the King.

That will be the fairest of joys when they meet at first—the angel and the blessed soul; it will forsake the delights of this earth, leave these fleeting pleasures, and it will part from the body. Then the angel shall speak; he shall have a higher rank—one spirit will greet the other, declare unto it God's message: 'Now thou mayest go whither long and often thou hast turned thy desires; I shall lead thee. The paths shall be pleasant unto thee, and the light of heaven revealed in its radiance. Thou art now a wayfarer to the sacred home where sorrow never enters in, a refuge from miseries; but there is the joy of angels, peace and happiness, and rest for souls; and there for ever and ever they who perform His behests here on earth may make merry and rejoice with the Lord. He holds for them in heaven a reward everlasting, where the highest King of all kings rules the city. Those are the buildings which decay not, nor does life fail those who dwell therein by reason of miseries; but the longer their sojourn the better. They enjoy youth and God's mercy. Thither the souls of righteous men may come after death, those who before teach and follow Christ's law, and exalt His praise, vanquish the evil spirits, and win for themselves heavenly rest.' Whither soon or late shall the man's heart rise, if he foster his soul here, so that, pure of sins, he may pass into God's power?

JULIANA

[*Juliana* is a typical saint's life and less interesting than *Andreas* or *Guthlac*. It follows its Latin prose source fairly closely. The saint suffers the same torments, displays the same constancy, and wins the same glory of martyrdom as other saints whose lives were written and read throughout medieval Christendom.]

I

Lo! we have heard heroes declare, brave men announce, that which came to pass in the days of Maximian,[1] the cruel king, the heathen war-chief, who stirred up persecution throughout the world, slew Christian men, pulled down churches, spilled on the grassy plain the blood of the saints, the worshippers of God, the doers of right. Broad was his realm, wide and excellent among the nations, nearly covering the whole spacious earth. Fierce soldiers went through the cities as he had charged them; often they did violence, perverse in their deeds, they who in their sinful power hated the Lord's law; they roused enmity, they raised idols, killed the saints, destroyed the learned, burned the chosen ones, persecuted God's warriors with spear and fire.

One was a wealthy man of noble lineage, a powerful prefect; he commanded cities; held his abode most often in the city Nicomedia, possessed store of treasure. Often against God's word, frequently in his zeal, he sought false gods and idols. He was called Eleusius; he had great and famous power. Then his heart began to love a maiden, Juliana—desire was strong upon him. She bore in her spirit holy faith; she earnestly resolved to keep her virginity for the love of Christ unspotted by any sin.

Then the maiden with her father's consent was betrothed to the rich man; he knew not fully how things stood, how she, the young girl, scorned his affection in her soul. The fear of God was greater in her mind than all that treasure which was among the nobleman's possessions.

Then the rich man, wealthy in gold, was eager in heart for the wedding, that straightway the maiden should be prepared for him, the bride for his house. She firmly opposed the man's

[1] According to the legend, Juliana suffered martyrdom at Nicomedia in the reign of Galerius Maximianus.

love, though he had treasure in his coffer, unnumbered adorn-ments on earth; she despised all that; and among a multitude of men she spoke these words:

'I can tell thee thou needst not afflict thyself more; if thou dost love and believe the true God, and dost exalt His praise, dost recognize the Protector of souls, forthwith I am ready without wavering to be at thy will. Also, I tell thee, if through idols thou dost put thy trust in a worse god, dost vow a heathen tribute, thou mayest not have me nor win me by force for thy wife. Thou shalt never in thy fierce hatred prepare pain so sore of grievous torments as to turn me from these words.'

Then the nobleman grew furious in anger; he, stained with sinful deeds, heard the words of the maiden. Then brutal and blinded in mind he bade speedy messengers bring the holy maiden's father swiftly to counsel. There was sound of speech when they, the warriors, leaned their spears together. Both were pagans, father-in-law and son-in-law, stricken with sins.

Then the guardian of the kingdom, holding aloft his spear, spoke with fierce mind to the maiden's father: 'Thy daughter has shown me dishonour; she tells me outright that she esteems not my love or affection. The insults are most painful to my mind, that she so bitterly should assail me with calumny before this people; she bade me richly honour, praise with words, cherish in mind, a strange god above the others whom erstwhile we knew, else not have her.'

Then the maiden's father, stern-minded, grew wroth; swore at those words; he opened his breast: 'By the true gods I swear, so may I ever find favour with them, or, my lord, thy grace in the joyous cities, if these words which thou, dearest of men, tellest me are true, that I will not spare her, but, famous prince, give her up to destruction, into thy power. Doom her to death, if it seems good unto thee; or, if thou dost prefer, let her live.'

Then resolute and raging, furious with anger, he went straightway to speak with the maiden, where he knew the virgin had her abode in gladness. Then he uttered these words:

'Thou art my daughter, the dearest and the sweetest to my heart, my only one in the world, light of my eyes, Juliana! Thou hast madly by thy hostility taken a vain course against the judgment of wise men; too strongly dost thou oppose thy bride-groom by thy own counsel; he is better than thou, nobler in the world, more wealthy in treasures; he is good to have for a friend. Therefore it is meet that thou cast not aside the man's love, his lasting affection.'

II

Then the blessed Juliana made answer unto him—she had firmly fixed her love upon God: 'I will never agree to alliance with the prince, unless he worship the God of hosts more earnestly than he has yet done, love with offerings Him who created light, heaven and earth, and the vastness of the seas, the circuit of the regions; else may he not bring me to his abode; he with his wealth must needs look for bridal love from another woman; he shall have none here.'

Then her father bitterly made answer unto her in his anger; no whit did he promise her adornments: 'I shall bring it to pass, if my life lasts, if thou forsake not thy folly before, and if thou henceforth worship strange gods and leave those who are dearer to us, who stand as an aid to this people, that soon thou shalt suffer death, thy life being forfeit, by the rending of beasts, if thou wilt not consent to his pleading, to union with the brave man. Great and terrible is the venture for such as thee, that thou shouldst despise our lord.'

Then Juliana the blessed, wise and dear unto God, made answer unto him: 'I will speak the truth unto thee; while I live I will not tell a lie; I shall never fear thy judgments, nor are the terrors of torment, the alarms of battle, grievous unto me, which thou dost fiercely threaten me with in thy evil-doing, nor by thy delusion shalt thou ever cause me to turn from the worship of Christ.'

Then the father was furious, raging and wroth, terrible and and savage towards his daughter. Then he bade them scourge her, afflict her with torment, oppress her with tortures, and spoke these words: 'Alter thy mind and change the words which erstwhile thou didst speak in folly, when thou didst scorn the worship of our gods.'

To him the fearless Juliana made answer, prompted by her thought: 'Thou shalt never teach me to promise tribute to false things; to dumb and deaf idols, to the enemies of souls, to the worst servants of torments, but I honour the Lord of heaven, of the world and of the glorious host; and put all my trust in Him alone, that He will become my Protector, my Helper and Saviour against hellish foes.'

Then in his anger Africanus, the maiden's father, gave her to Eleusius, into the power of her foes. At daybreak, when light had come, he bade her be led to his judgment seat. The warriors, the host of people, marvelled at the maiden's beauty.

Then the nobleman, her bridegroom, first greeted her with glad words: 'My sweetest light of the sun, Juliana! What radiance hast thou, generous grace, the blossom of youth! If thou wilt yet propitiate our gods and seek protection for thyself from them in their mercy so great, grace from the holy ones, untold torments cruelly performed shall be turned away from thee, fierce pains which are prepared for thee, if thou wilt not sacrifice to the true divinities.'

The noble maiden made answer unto him: 'Never shalt thou compel by thy threats, nor prepare cruel torments so many, that I shall love thy fellowship, unless thou forsake false beliefs, the worshipping of idols, and wisely recognize the God of glory, the Creator of souls, the Lord of mankind, in whose power are all creatures for ever and ever.'

Then in fierce mood he spoke menacing words in front of the people; the lord of the people was exceeding wroth; and with hateful cruelty commanded the maiden to be stretched out naked, and, sinless as she was, to be lashed with scourges. Then the warrior laughed, uttered insulting speeches:

'This is the triumphant issue of our strife seized at the outset! I will still grant thee life, though thou hast uttered ere now many wild words, hast refused too strongly to love true gods. To thee in thy obstinacy torments shall afterwards be meted out as reward, unless beforehand thou make peace with them, and offer fit sacrifice after thy wicked speeches, and establish peace. Let be the strife, the hateful combat! If after this in thy folly thou dost longer follow delusion, then perforce, driven by thy enmity, I must avenge in the sternest way this blasphemy, the bitter speeches of insult with which in irreverence thou didst strive to assail the best and the kindest whom men know, whom this people among themselves have long worshipped.'

That noble soul spoke fearlessly unto him: 'Accursed foul foe, I fear not thy judgments, nor the harm of thy torments! I have the Guardian of heaven, the merciful Protector, the Lord of hosts, for my hope, who will defend me against thy delusion, from the grasp of fierce creatures, whom thou dost count as gods. They are void of all good, vain, useless, of no value; no man finds any benefit there, true peace, though he seek affection from them. He finds not virtue there among devils. I fix my mind on the Lord, who as Ruler of heaven for ever holds sway over all powers, over every victory; that is the true King!'

III

Then to the governor it seemed shameful that he could not turn the heart, the resolve of the maiden. He bade her be hanged and raised up by the hair on a high tree, where she, like to the sun in beauty, suffered strokes, very cruel agony for six hours of the day; and forthwith he, the hateful persecutor, bade her be taken down again, and ordered her to be led to prison. For her, mild in mind, the worship of Christ was firm closed in her breast, a power not to be broken.

Then the prison door, the work of hammers, was closed by a bar; there the saint dwelt steadfast. Ever in her heart she praised the King of glory, the God of the kingdom of heaven, the Saviour of men, in the dungeon, covered with darkness; the Holy Ghost was her constant companion. Then on a sudden into the prison came the foe of men, skilful in evil; the enemy of the soul, trained in tormenting, the captive of hell, had the form of an angel; he spoke to the saint:

'Dearest and most precious to the King of glory, our Lord, why dost thou suffer? This judge has prepared for thee the worst torments, endless pain, if thou wilt not prudently sacrifice and do pleasure to his gods. Do thou hasten, when he bids thee be led out hence, so that thou mayest quickly make an offering, a victorious sacrifice, before destruction take thee, death in the presence of the warriors. Thus shalt thou, blessed maid, win free from the wrath of the judge.'

Then she who was not afraid, dear unto Christ, straightway asked whence was his coming. The outcast replied to her: 'I am God's angel coming from above, an excellent servant, and sent to thee in holiness from on high. Cruel torments, wondrously murderous, are made ready for thee as a deadly punishment. God, the Son of the Ruler, bade thee be commanded to avert those things from thee.'

Then the maiden was terrified with dread at the sudden tidings, which the demon, heaven's foe, told her in words. Then the young maid in her innocence began to establish her soul with firmness, to call unto God: 'Now, Protector of men, everlasting, almighty, I will beg Thee by that noble creation which Thou, Father of angels, didst set up in the beginning, that Thou let me not leave worship of Thy grace according to the perilous tidings which this messenger announces, who stands before me. So I will pray Thee in Thy purity, Glory of kings, Guardian of splendour, to reveal unto me who this servant is

who flies in the air, who in Thy name urges me to an evil path.'
A glorious voice answered her from the clouds, uttered a speech:
'Seize that proud one and hold him fast, till he tell his whole
errand truthfully, from the beginning, what his lineage is.'

Then the glorious maiden's soul was rejoiced; she laid hold
on the devil . . .

[A leaf of the manuscript is missing at this point. The Latin
version enables us to conjecture what the missing passage con-
tained. Juliana makes the messenger confess he is a demon,
and that it was he who had tempted Adam, Eve, Cain, and others.
Lastly he admits he prompted Judas to betray Christ.]

. . . to give to death the King of all kings. Then moreover I
contrived that the soldier wounded the Lord—the multitude
looked on—so that blood and water both together there sought
the earth. Then, moreover, I incited Herod in his heart, so
that he commanded John's head to be hewn off, when the holy
man disturbed with speeches his love for his wife, his sinful
wedlock. Also I taught Simon[1] with crafty thoughts, so that he
strove to contend against Christ's chosen disciples and assail
with insult by deep delusion the holy men. He said they were
wizards. I ventured sharp tricks when I deluded Nero, so that
he bade Christ's disciples, Peter and Paul, to be put to death.
Pilate erstwhile by my promptings hanged on the cross the Lord
of the heavens, mighty God. Likewise also I taught Ægeas, so
that in his folly he bade Andrew the holy be hanged on a high
cross, so that from the cross he sent forth his spirit into the
splendour of heaven. Thus with my brothers I have brought to
pass many cruel evils, foul sins, that I cannot utter, fully declare;
nor can I know the number of hard thoughts of malice.' The
holy Juliana answered him by the grace of the spirit:

'Foe of mankind, still further shalt thou declare thy errand,
and who sent thee to me.' The demon made answer unto her in
fear, held fast, without hope of peace: 'Lo! my father, the king of
hell-dwellers, sent me hither on this journey to thee from the
close-pent abode; in the house of woe he is more eager than I for
all evil things. When he sends us to mislead the heart of the
righteous by deceit, to turn them from salvation, sad in thought
are we, fearful in soul. The dread prince is not a merciful
master unto us. If we have wrought no ill, then we dare not go
anywhere in his sight. Then he sends his followers forth from

[1] Simon Magus (Acts viii. 9–24). His dealings with the apostles Peter
and Paul are told in the apocryphal Acts of Peter.

the darkness throughout the wide world; he bids them persecute, bind us, and scourge us with torments in the surging fire if we are to be found on the earth, or discovered far or near. If the heart of the righteous, the thought of the holy, is not misled by stumbling-blocks, we suffer the harshest and most grievous torments by painful blows. Now thou thyself mayest know the truth in thy mind, that I perforce was compelled to this boldness, oppressed by misery, so that I sought thee.'

IV

Then still the saint questioned with words the foe of men, the worker of iniquity, the author of ancient sins: 'Enemy of souls, thou shalt tell me further, how thou, encompassed with wickedness, dost most hurt the righteous by their falling into sins.' The fiend, the perfidious outcast, answered her, uttered words:

'I can easily show thee the beginning and end of all the evils which I wrought by the wounds of sins no few times, so that thou thyself mayest know more clearly that this is true, no whit false. In my bold mind I expected and held it for certain that I by my single craft could without difficulty turn thee from salvation, so that thou shouldst oppose the King of heaven, the Prince of victories, and bow down to a worse god, sacrifice to the author of sins. Thus do I mislead the heart of the righteous by my changed aspect. Where I find he has fixed his heart on the will of God, forthwith I am ready to bring against him manifold vices of the mind, cruel thoughts, secret delusions; by a host of deceptions I sweeten for him the pleasures of sin, wicked affections; so that, lured by vices, he quickly obeys my teachings. So strongly do I inflame him with sins, that in his burning he ceases to pray, goes boldly forward. No longer can he remain firm in the place of prayer because of his love of vices. So I bring hateful terror on him to whom I grudge life and his shining faith. If he in the desire of his heart will hearken to my counsels and commit sin, afterwards he shall live stripped of good virtues. If I find any valiant brave warrior of the Lord opposing the attack of arrows, he who will not flee far thence from the fray, but wisely raises his buckler against me, the holy shield, the spiritual armour, who will not desert God, but, bold in prayer, stands at bay firm among his fellows, I must depart thence, hapless, reft of joys, to lament my sorrow in the clutch of the flames, that I could not prevail in war by the power of strength. But in sadness I must seek another warrior more weak, more feeble under the banner of war, whom I can excite with my prompting, impede in fighting. Though he strive in spirit for some good, I am ready forthwith to look through all his inward thought, to see how the soul is established within and resistance contrived. I open the gate of the wall by assault; when the tower is pierced, the portal opened, then first by a flight of arrows I send into his breast bitter thoughts by various desires of the mind, so that it seems better to him to perform sins, the lusts of the flesh, rather than the worship of God. Zealously do I teach that he, plainly turned from Christ's law, should live according to my evil habits, with his mind in my power led by corruption into the pit of sins. I care more for the soul's destruction, more eagerly for that of the spirit than that of the body which in its grave in the world, hidden in the ground, shall be a joy for the worm.' Then still the maiden spoke:

'Tell me, wretched impure spirit, how hast thou, ruler of darkness, forced thy way among the pure? Of yore thou didst strive and contend with Christ in thy rashness, didst plot against the Holy One. The pit of hell was dug below for thee, when, harassed by misery, thou didst seek thy abode because of thy presumption. I thought thou wouldst be the more wary and the more timid of such an encounter with the righteous, for through the King of heaven they often withstood thy intent.'

Then the accursed one, the hapless monster, replied to her: 'Tell me first how thou, daring in thy wisdom, didst become thus bold in combat beyond the whole race of women, so that thou hast bound me thus firmly, wholly helpless with fetters? Thou didst trust in thy God everlasting who sits in glory, the Lord of mankind, as I fix my hope on my father, the king of hell-dwellers. When I am sent against the righteous to turn by wicked deeds their minds, their hearts, their thoughts from salvation, at times my desire, my hope of success with the holy ones, is thwarted by resistance, as here sorrow befell me in my journey. Too late I have learned that myself! Now because of this I, a doer of evil, must long suffer shame. Wherefore I entreat thee by the power of the most High, by the grace of heaven's King, the Prince of glory who suffered on the cross, to have mercy on me in my distress, that I perish not wholly in misery, though daring and thus foolhardy I sought thee in my journey, where assuredly I had not looked for such a plight.'

v

Then the candle of glory, fair of countenance, spoke in words to the faithless one: 'Thou shalt confess more evil deeds, wretched spirit of hell, ere thou mayest fare hence, great acts of wickedness which thou hast performed by dark delusions to the hurt of the children of men.'   The devil answered her: 'Now by thy utterance I hear that I perforce shall be driven by thy enmity to lay open my mind, to suffer affliction, as thou dost bid me. Full harsh is the plight, calamity measureless.   I must needs suffer and endure all things at thy decree, disclose all the dark evil deeds which I have ever contrived.   Often have I taken sight away, blinded countless men with wicked thoughts, covered the light of eyes with a veil of mist in dark showers by my poisonous breath; and with evil snares have I broken to pieces the feet of some; sent some to burn in the fire's embrace, so that their traces were no more seen.   Also I have caused the bodies of some to spurt blood, so that suddenly they let forth their lives through the gush of the veins.   Some by my powers at sea were whelmed with waters while on their way, beneath the fierce flood on the ocean.   Some I have given to the cross, to yield their lives in misery on the high gallows.   Some I have led by counsels, brought them to strife, so that on a sudden, when drunk with beer, they revived old grudges; I proffered them enmity from the goblet, so that in the wine hall by the sword-stroke they, doomed to die, stricken with torments, let their souls hasten from their bodies.   Some whom I found without God's token, heedless, unblessed, boldly I have slain with my hands in craftiness by deaths of many kinds.   Though I should sit the length of a summer day I cannot tell all the distresses which I have wrought early and late in my wickedness, ever since heaven was set on high and the course of the stars, since the earth was established and the first beings, Adam and Eve, whose life I reft from them, and taught them to leave the love of God, everlasting grace, the bright splendid abode, so that on both and on their children also came misery for ever, darkest of crimes. Why should I further recount endless evil?   I have brought forth all those wicked enmities throughout the nations which from the beginning of the world have ever befallen mankind, men on the earth.   There was none of them who durst lay hands upon me as boldly as thou in thy holiness now; there was no man on earth brave enough through holy strength, none of the patriarchs nor prophets; though the God of hosts, the King of glory had disclosed to them the spirit of wisdom, measureless grace, yet I could have access to them. There was none of them who thus boldly put bonds upon me, afflicted me with miseries, before thou now didst vanquish, grasp firm, my great power, which my father, the foe of mankind, gave me when he, the prince, bade me leave darkness to make sin sweet unto thee. There sorrow came upon me, a heavy combat. After my tribulation I shall have no cause to rejoice among my fellows over this journey, when in misery I shall pay my penalty in the mournful abode.'

Then the prefect, the cruel man, bade Juliana, holy in heart, to be led out from the narrow dwelling to speak with the pagan at his judgment seat. Inspired in heart, she haled along the fiend fast in his bonds, the holy one the heathen. Then in sadness he began to lament his errand, to bewail his torment, to grieve at his plight. He uttered words: 'Lady mine, Juliana, I entreat thee, by the peace of God, to put no insults upon me, disgrace before men, more than thou hast done erstwhile, when in the darkness of prison thou didst defeat the most wise king of hell-dwellers in the stronghold of thy foes; he is our father, the wicked murderous lord. Lo! thou hast constrained me by painful blows; forsooth I know that I have found no woman in the world early or late like unto thee, of bolder thought nor more perverse, among the race of women. It is manifest to me that thou art become guiltless, wholly wise in soul.' Then after his time of punishment the maiden let him, the enemy of souls, go to seek the darkness in the gloomy abyss, to be destroyed by agonies. He, the announcer of evil, knew the more surely to tell his fellows, the servants of torment, how he had sped on his journey. . . .

[Another page or pages of the manuscript is missing here. Juliana is brought before the prefect, who asks her how she had survived the tortures. She replies that God had sent an angel to sustain her, and warns the judge that he will suffer eternally for his cruelty. Then Juliana is tortured on a wheel set with swords, but her faith remains firm. She is also tortured by fire, but an angel extinguishes the flames. Juliana prays God for deliverance. The executioners repent and are converted to belief in Juliana's God. They are all beheaded by command of Maximian. The prefect then orders Juliana to be burned alive. She prays for aid and an angel comes to scatter the fire.]

VI

... earnestly praised before on high and his holy work; they said truly that He alone over all creation controlled every victory, everlasting blessings.[1] Then came an angel of God, gleaming in adornments; and thrust aside the fire; freed and fended her who was untouched by wickedness, void of sins; and cast away the devouring flame where the saint, the chief of maidens, stood unharmed in the midst. That was a grief for the rich man to bear—if only he could change it in the eyes of the world. Stained with sins, he sought how he might devise her death most painfully by the worst torments. The demon was no laggard who so taught him that he ordered an earthen vessel to be wrought by wondrous skill, with warlike incantations, and to be set about with trees, with wood. Then the cruel man ordered that the earthen jar be filled with lead; and then commanded the greatest of pyres to be kindled, the funeral pile to be lighted. On all sides it was girt with fires; the bath boiled hotly. Then hastily, enraged with anger, he commanded her, void of sins, guiltless, to be thrust into the seething lead. Then the flame was parted and dispersed; the lead leaped out far, hot, devouring. The men were terrified, caught by its rush; seventy-five in number of the heathen host were there burnt up by the fire's blast. Still the saint stood with beauty unblemished; neither hem nor garment, neither hair nor skin, neither body nor limbs, was marked with fire. She stood in the blaze wholly unhurt, gave thanks for all to the Lord of lords. Then the judge grew fierce and savage, fell to rending his robe; likewise he showed his teeth and gnashed them together; he was maddened in mind like a wild beast; he raged in fury and blasphemed his gods, because they could not in their might withstand a woman's will. The glorious maiden was staunch and fearless, forgetting not her strength nor the will of God. Then the judge in his anger ordered the maiden holy in thought to be killed by a sword-blow, the chosen of Christ to have her head cut off. Her death profited him not, when he came to know the outcome.

VII

Then joy was renewed in the saint, and the maiden's heart greatly gladdened, when she heard men declare hateful counsel;

[1] These lines apparently form the conclusion of Juliana's prayer.

that her days of struggle were about to end, that her life was to be released. Then he, full of sins, commanded the pure and chosen one, void of crimes, to be led to death. Then on a sudden came the wretched spirit of hell; hapless and sorrowful, he sang a song of misery, the accursed one whom erstwhile she had bound and scourged with torments. Full of laments he called aloud before the host: 'Reward her now with pain because she scorned the strength of our gods and prevailed over me exceedingly, so that I confessed unto her. Let her gain harsh requital by the mark of the weapon. Do ye, stricken with sin, avenge your old enmity. I forget not my sorrow, how, fast in fetters, I suffered woes beyond number, distresses in one night, measureless evils.' Then the blessed Juliana beheld the monster before her; she heard the devil of hell cry forth his affliction. The enemy of mankind began then to flee in haste, to go to his torments, and uttered this speech: 'Woe is me, brought to ruin! Now I may well expect that she will again humble me in my misery with unhappy woes, as erstwhile she did.'

Then she was led near the border of the land and to the place where cruel men thought to kill her in hatred. Then she began to teach and to win the people from sins to worship; and she promised them solace, a path to heaven; she uttered this speech:

'Remember the Joy of warriors and the splendour of heaven, the Bliss of the saints, the God of the heavenly angels! He is worthy that nations and all the race of angels on high in the heavens, the mighty host, should praise Him, in whom is succour for ever and ever for him who shall obtain it. Wherefore, beloved people, I wish to teach you by doing righteousness, to establish your house lest the winds cast it down with fierce blasts; the strong wall shall stand the more stoutly against the assaults of storms, the promptings of sins. Do ye, stout of heart, fix firm the foundation on the living stone, with the love of peace, with clear belief; hold in your heart true faith and peace among you, holy mysteries cherished in your mind. Then the Father almighty will bestow mercy upon you, when after sorrows ye have greatest need of solace from the God of hosts; seeing that ye yourselves know not the passing hence, the end of life. Prudent it seems to me, that ye in your watchfulness keep guard against the dread onslaught of your foes lest adversaries bar your road to the city of heaven. Pray the Son of God that the Prince of angels, the Lord of mankind, the Bestower of victories, be merciful unto me! Peace be with you, true love for ever!'

Then her soul by a blow of the sword was borne away from the body to its lasting joy.

Then the wicked enemy Eleusius, affrighted, sought the sea on a ship with a band of evil men. Long time he was tossed upon the flood, on the swan road. Death with stern visitation swept off the whole troop of men and himself with them, ere they had reached land. Four-and-thirty of the race of warriors were reft of life there by the surge of the wave, luckless with their lord; void of joys, deprived of delights, they sought hell. Nor did it avail the thanes in that dark abode, the band of comrades in that low den, to look to the chieftain for treasures to be bestowed, that in the wine hall on the beer bench they should receive rings, embossed gold. Far otherwise was the body of the saint borne to the grave with chants of praise by a mighty throng, so that they, a great host, brought it within the city. There later, as the years passed, God's praise has been raised up with great glory among the people unto this day.

Sore is my need that the saint should give me aid, when two comrades, dearest of all, divide me, rend their kinship, their great affection. My soul must pass from the body on its journey, ignorant of its goal, myself I know not whither. From this abode I must go to seek another according to my former deeds, my old acts. Sadly mankind (CYN) will depart; the King will be wroth, the Bestower of victories, when the sheep (EWU) stained with sins await in terror what He will decree for them as life's guerdon according to their acts; the body (LF) will tremble, remain heavy with sorrow. I shall remember all the pain, the wounds of sins which early or late I wrought in the world. Weeping, I shall lament that with tears. Too slow was I at the fit time in repenting of my evil deeds, whilst spirit and body sojourned together, strong in their abode. Then I shall need mercies, that the saint may plead for me with the highest King. My distress warns me thereof, heavy heart-sorrow. I pray every man of human race, who may recite this poem, zealously and fervently to remember my name, and pray the Lord that the Protector of the heavens, the mighty Ruler, the Father, the Comforter, the Judge of deeds, and the beloved Son will afford me help on the great day, when the Trinity, gloriously throned in unity, will decree through the fair world reward to the race of men, to every man according to his deeds. God of hosts, grant us that we may find thy countenance merciful, Thou Joy of princes, at that great time. Amen.

THE FATES OF THE APOSTLES

[*The Fates of the Apostles* follows *Andreas* in the manuscript and possibly forms the epilogue to it. If it is part of *Andreas*, the runic signature shows Cynewulf to be the author of the whole work. The command to the disciples, 'Go ye therefore and teach all nations,' gave rise to stories of the wanderings and adventures of the different apostles. Here we have merely a list of the apostles with a brief indication of the work and death of each.]

Lo! weary of wandering, sad in spirit, I wrought this song, gathered it from far and wide, of how the heroes bright and glorious showed forth their courage. There were twelve, illustrious in acts, chosen by the Lord, beloved while they lived. Wide through the world spread the praise, might, and fame of the Master's servants, no mean majesty. Fate guided the sacred band where they should glorify the law of the Lord, make it manifest before men. Some in Rome, brave and warlike, Peter and Paul, laid down their lives through Nero's cruel cunning; widely are the apostles honoured among the nations.

Likewise Andrew in Achaia ventured his life before Ægeas; he feared not for the might of any monarch on earth, but chose eternal unending life, light everlasting, when amid the shouting of the multitude he lay on the cross after the conflict, fearless in the fight.

Lo! we have also heard men learned in the law tell of John's lineage. He was, as I know, because of his kindred, dearest to Christ among men of mortal nature, when the King of glory, the Prince of angels, the Father of mankind, came to earth through the womb of a woman. He constantly taught the people in Ephesus; journeying thence he sought the way of life, bright joys, the radiant glorious habitation. His brother was not backward, slow to set forth, but among the Jews by the stroke of the sword James was destined before Herod to part from life, the breath to leave his body. Philip was among the people of Asia; thence straightway he sought life everlasting by death on the rood, when in Hierapolis he was hanged on the cross by a warlike troop.

Verily, the event was openly known far and wide, that Bartholomew, a strong man in battle, ventured his life in India.

178

Astrages in Albania, heathen and blind in spirit, commanded
them to cut off his head because he would not bow down to
idolatry, honour an image. The bliss of glory was his, the riches
of eternal life, dearer than those possessions which pass away.
Likewise Thomas also boldly ventured in other parts of India
where the minds of many were enlightened, their hearts en-
couraged, by his holy word. Afterwards, bold in spirit, in the
presence of multitudes with marvellous power by God's might,
he awakened the king's brother, so that he rose up from death,
young and daring in battle, and his name was Gad; and then in
the struggle he gave his life to the people; a sword-blow from a
heathen hand took him off; there the saint fell, stricken before
the hosts. Thence his soul sought the glorious radiance as a
reward for victory.

Lo! we have heard through holy books that truth was made
manifest among the Ethiopians, the glorious power of God.
The dawning of day, of a joyous faith, appeared; the land was
purged by the glorious teaching of Matthew. Irtacus, murder-
ous monarch, enraged in heart, commanded him to be killed with
weapons. We heard that James [1] suffered death in Jerusalem
before the priests; unflinchingly he fell by the stroke of the staff,
the blessed man a prey to hate. Now in reward for his warfare
he has life everlasting with the King of glory. Those two were
not slow in the strife, in the shield-play; Simon and Thaddeus,
men bold in battle, ready to travel, sought the land of the
Persians. One day of death came to them both together; the
noble men were destined to endure tribulation from violent hate,
to seek the reward of victory, and true bliss, delight after death,
when life was parted from the body; and they scorned all these
transient treasures, vain riches. Thus the heroes met death,
twelve men of noble heart; they cherished undying glory in their
minds, servants of heaven.

Now then I ask the man who may love the study of this song,
that he will pray to the hallowed band for help, peace, and aid
for me in my sadness. Lo! I need friends, kindly ones on the
journey, when alone I must seek the long home, the unknown
country, leave the body, the earthly part, behind, my corpse to
remain as a delight to the worms.

Here can the man shrewd in perception, who delights in songs,
discover who wrought this measure. *Wealth* (F) comes at the

---

[1] James, brother of Jesus (Mark vi. 3). The tradition is that he was cast
from a pinnacle of the temple at Jerusalem and then beaten to death with a
staff.

end; earls enjoy it on earth; they may not always remain together, dwelling in the world; *Our* (U) *Pleasure* (W) on earth shall pass away; the fleeting adornments of the flesh shall afterwards perish, even as *Water* (L) glides away.   Then shall the *Bold Warrior* (C) and the *Wretched One* (Y) crave help in the anguish of the night; *Constraint* (N) lies upon them, the service of the king. Now mayest thou know who has been made manifest to men in these words.   Let the man who loves the study of this lay forget not to seek what shall succour and solace me.   I must go far hence, seek alone elsewhere a habitation, venture on a voyage out of this world, I myself know not whither; unknown are my new abodes, my land and home.   Thus will it be for every man unless he possess a holy spirit.

But let us the more earnestly call unto God, send our prayers to shining heaven, that we may enjoy that mansion, a home on high.   There is the greatest of joys, where the King of angels bestows on the pure reward everlasting.   Now His praise shall endure for ever, great and glorious; and His might shall remain, eternal and renewed in youth, over all creation.

ANDREAS

[The ultimate source of this poem is the Greek *Acts of Andrew and Matthias*, but probably the English poet worked from a Latin version. *Andreas*, if not by Cynewulf, belongs to his school. Like *Elene*, it is a romantic poem, consciously artistic, in which setting is of more importance than story or characters. Andrew and Matthew are not memorable as Beowulf and Hrothgar are. The poet misses no chance to expand his source. The description of the storm, elaborated with all the devices of rhetoric, not for its importance in the story but as an incidental beauty, is typical of the poem as a whole.]

I

Lo! we have heard in distant days of twelve glorious heroes, servants of the Lord, under the stars. Their majesty failed not in fight when banners clashed together, after they had disbanded, even as God Himself, the great King of heaven, laid their duty upon them. They were men renowned on earth, eager leaders and active in war, bold warriors, when on the field of battle, the place of war, shield and hand guarded the helmet. Matthew was one of them, who by wondrous power first began among the Jews to write the gospel in words; holy God appointed him his lot out on that island,[1] where as yet no stranger could enjoy the happiness of home. Often the hand of murderers did him grievous harm on the battle-field. That country, the land of men, the abode of heroes, was completely encompassed with crime, with the devil's treachery. There was no bread in the place to feed men, nor a drink of water to enjoy, but throughout the land they feasted on the blood and flesh, on the bodies of men, of those who came from afar. Such was their custom, that when they lacked meat they made food of all strangers who sought that island from elsewhere. Such was the savage nature of the people, the violence of the wicked, that they, fierce foemen, destroyed in their cruelty with the points of spears the sight of the eyes, the jewels of the head. Afterwards magicians by sorcery stirred together in hatred a murderous draught, which

[1] This apparently means a land bordering on the water and to be reached by travelling over the sea, rather than an island in the strict sense. Mermedonia is perhaps Scythia.

181

perverted the mind, the reason of men, the heart in the breast; their thoughts were changed, so that, now become bloodthirsty men, they mourned not for the joys of men, but hay and grass for lack of other food were an affliction to them in their weariness.

Then Matthew had come to that famed city, into that town. There was mighty tumult throughout Mermedonia, gathering of the wicked, thronging of the evil ones, when the servants of the devil heard of the hero's journey. They went out against him, equipped with spears, speedily under shields; they were not slow to the strife, angry bearers of spears. By the power of the devil they, men hastening to hell, bound and secured the saint's hands; and with the edge of the sword destroyed the sun of his head. Yet still in breast and heart he glorified the Lord of heaven though he received a dire drink of poison; blessed and bold, he still did honour mightily in words, with holy voice from prison, to the Prince of glory, the Lord of heaven; the praise of Christ was firmly planted in his breast. Then weeping with weary tears he addressed his victorious Lord, the Prince of men, the King of hosts, with sorrowful speech, with sad voice, and thus spoke in words:

'Lo! hostile people weave an evil chain, a snare for me! Ever at all times have I been eager in mind to follow Thy will in every way; now through tribulations I must suffer like the dumb cattle. Thou alone, Lord of mankind, knowest the thoughts of all men, the heart in the breast. If it be Thy will, Prince of glory, that faithless men should kill me with the edges of weapons, with swords, I am ready straightway to suffer what Thou, my Lord, generous Master of angels, Hero of warriors, wilt appoint for me in this strange land. Grant me in mercy, Almighty God, light in this life, lest I, reft of sight in the city, now that the swords have done their hateful work, endure forthwith scornful speech for longer space through the blasphemy of bloodthirsty men, loathsome foes. On Thee alone, Keeper of the world, I fix my mind, the steadfast love of my heart; and I will pray Thee, Father of angels, radiant Giver of happiness, that Thou, Judge of men, do not allot me among wicked persecutors, cursed workers of evil, the worst death upon earth.'

After these words there came to the prison a sacred glorious sign from heaven, like the bright sun; there it was made manifest that holy God granted aid. Then was heard the voice of the King of heaven, wondrous beneath the sky, the sound of the speaking of the glorious Lord; with clear voice He declared health and solace to His bold servant in bondage: 'I give to thee,

Matthew, My peace under the sky.   Be not over-fearful in soul, nor mourn in mind; I will stand by thee and free thee from these fetters and all the multitude who bide with thee in bondage. Paradise, the brightest of glories, the fairest abode of splendour, the happiest of homes, shall be revealed to thee in its radiance by holy powers.   There thou shalt be able to enjoy for ever thy desire for glory.   Endure the affliction of men; the time is not long in which the traitors, the sinful men, through guile will be able to torment thee with bonds of torture.   I will straightway send Andrew to thee for a protection and a comfort in this pagan city; he will free thee from this hostility.   There is a space of time, in truth just twenty-seven nights, until the season when thou mayest have done with distress, pass from humiliation into the protection of God, afflicted with sorrows, made glorious with victory.'   Then the holy Guardian of all creatures, the Creator of angels, departed to the celestial country.   He is King by right, a firm Guide in all places.

II

Then Matthew was once again mightily aroused.   The masking night glided away, quickly departed; light followed after, the dawn of day.   The warriors, the heathen fighting men, mustered in anger, thronged in troops under their shields—the armour rang, the spears rattled.   Their intent was to learn whether those who had dwelt for a while in the cheerless abode, fast fettered in prison, were living, to find out which one they might kill first for food after the appointed time.   Greedy for slaughter, they had set down with writing and reckoning the doom of the men, when they must become food for those lacking meat among the people.   Cold-hearted men made clamour; crowd pressed on crowd; ruthless leaders recked naught of right, of the mercy of God.   Often by counsel of the devil their minds were darkened, when they trusted in the might of the wicked.

Then they found the holy man, wise-minded, boldly awaiting in prison that which the bright King, the Prince of angels, willed to grant him.   Then the term of time had passed save for three nights, the appointed space, as the warriors had set it down in writing, when they thought to break the bones, speedily to separate body and soul, and then to portion out the flesh of the victim to warriors old and young, for food to the men and eager feasting.   They cared naught for his life, the greedy men of battle, for what should be appointed as to the spirit's fate after the torment of death. Thus after every thirty days they held council; great was their desire to rend with bloody jaws the bodies of men for food.

Then He who had established the world with mighty power forgot not how he dwelt in misery among strange people, bound with fetters, he who had often showed forth his love for the Hebrews and Israelites; also he had sternly withstood the magic arts of the Jews. Then from heaven the voice was heard in Achaia where the holy man, Andrew, was; he taught the people according to the way of life. Then the Glory of kings, the Master of mankind, the Lord of hosts, opened his heart and spoke thus in words to him who was bold in decision: 'Thou shalt go and bear thy life, seek out in a journey a place where cannibals inhabit the land, guard the country by murders. Such is the custom of that people, that they will allow life to no stranger in the land, when the wicked ones find the unhappy man in Mermedonia; there death, wretched slaughter of men, shall afterwards come to pass. I know that thy victorious brother lies there bound with fetters among the men of that city. Now there are yet three nights before he among that people must by a spear-thrust in conflict with the heathen, give up his spirit, ready to depart, unless thou come before that.'

Forthwith Andrew gave answer to Him: 'My Lord, Creator of the heavens, Ruler of glory, how can I perform a journey on a far way over the path of the deep as speedily as Thou sayest with Thy word? Thy angel can accomplish that easily. From heaven he knows the stretch of the seas, the salt ocean streams, and the swan road, the surging of the surf, and the terror of the water, the waves over the world. The foreign earls are not my friends, neither do I know aught of men's thoughts there, and strange to me are the highways over the cold water.'

Then the Lord everlasting answered him: 'Alas! Andrew, that thou wouldst ever be slow in setting forth. It is not hard for Almighty God to bring it to pass on earth that the city, the famed principality, with the citizens, should be removed hither to this country under the sweep of the sky, if the Lord of glory ordains it with a word. Thou canst not be slow in setting forth nor too yielding in mind if thou thinkest indeed to keep faith, true covenant, with thy Master. Be thou ready at the proper time; there can be no delay in the errand. Thou shalt accomplish the journey, and carry thy life into the clutch of hostile men, where battle will be offered thee by the tumultuous warring of the heathen, the fighting skill of men. At daybreak, even in the morning, thou shalt board the boat alone at the seashore and make thy way on the cold water across the sea. Bear My blessing wherever thou goest through the world.' Then the holy Ruler and Master, Lord of angels, Keeper of the earth, departed to seek His dwelling-place, the glorious home, where the souls of the just may enjoy life after the body's decay.

III

Then the errand was declared to the noble warrior in the city; his heart was not fearful, but he was unfaltering in the brave deed, resolute and bold, no whit a coward, eager for the fray, ready for God's warfare. Then at dawn with the break of day, he set out over the sand-hills to the seashore, bold in mind, and his thanes with him, walking on the beach. The ocean roared, the surges beat. The hero was joyful when in his bravery he found a broad-bosomed ship on the shore. Then radiant in the morning came the brightest of beacons, speeding over the sea, in holiness out of the darkness; over the waters shone the candle of heaven. There he found sailors, a glorious three, thanes, valiant men, sitting on the vessel, ready for the voyage, as if they had come over the sea. That was God Himself, the Lord of warriors, the eternal Almighty, with his two angels. They, the earls, were in dress like unto sailors, unto seafarers, when they toss on the cold water in ships upon a far journey. Then he who stood on the shore, eager to launch forth, greeted them, spoke in gladness: 'Whence have ye come, men of skill, sailing in ships, in the vessel, the excellent boat? Whence has the sea stream brought you over the tossing of the billows?'

Then Almighty God answered him, as though He, who awaited his speech, knew not what man it was, whom there at the seashore He talked with: 'We have come from afar from the race of the Mermedonians; the high-prowed vessel, the rapid sea steed, encompassed with swiftness, bore us by means of the flood on the whale road, till, sped by the sea, as the wind drove us, we reached the land of this people.'

Then Andrew answered Him humbly: 'Though I could offer thee few rings, costly treasures, I would fain ask thee to bring us to that people across the whale's dominion in the lofty ship, the high-beaked vessel; thy reward shall be with God, if thou art kindly to us on the voyage.'

The Guardian of princes, the Creator of angels, answered him again from the ship: 'Far-travellers cannot sojourn there, nor do strangers enjoy the land, but in that city they suffer death who venture thither from afar; and dost thou wish now to cross the wide sea that thou mayest lose thy life in strife?'

Then Andrew made answer unto Him: 'Dearest Master, desire drives us to that country, a high hope in our hearts to that famous city, if Thou wilt show us Thy kindness in the sea journey.'

The Lord of angels, the Saviour of men, answered him from the prow of the ship: 'Willingly, gladly, we will bear thee with us over the fish's bath even to the land where desire directs thee to go, when ye have made your payment, the appointed sum, as the ship-warders, the men on the boat, make agreement with you.'

Then hastily Andrew, friendless as he was, spoke to Him in words: 'I have not plated gold nor treasure, wealth nor food, nor wire ornaments, land nor twisted rings, to stir thy desire, thy worldly wish, which thou speakest of.'

Then the Lord of men, where He sat on the gangway, spoke to him upon the heaped-up shore: 'Dearest friend, how came it to pass with thee, that thou, stripped of treasures, wert minded to seek the hills by the sea, the boundary of ocean's streams, to come to the ship over the cold cliffs? Hast thou not bread for food to comfort thee, or a pure draught to sustain thee, on the ocean-way? Hard is his lot who for long travels the sea road.'

Then Andrew, wise in mind, unlocked his word-hoard in answer: 'It becomes thee not, since the Lord has poured out for thee wealth and food and worldly fortune, to search out an answer, an unkindly speech, in thy pride; better is it for each to address him who is eager to depart humbly with kindness, as Christ, the glorious Prince, bade. We His servants have been chosen as warriors. He is King by right, Lord and Creator of heavenly glory, one everlasting God of all creatures, for He, surpassing in victories, encompasses all with the strength of one, heaven and earth with sacred power. He Himself declared that, the Father of all peoples, and bade us go throughout the wide earth to win souls: "Go now through all parts of the world, even as far as the water surrounds it, or the plains stretch out their paths; proclaim the glorious faith throughout cities over the face of the earth; I will preserve you in peace. Ye need not take treasures on the journey, gold nor silver; I will provide you bounty of all good things according to your own desire." Now thou thyself mayest thoughtfully consider our journey; I shall straightway know what benefits thou wilt do us.'

Then the Lord everlasting answered him: 'If, as ye tell me, ye are servants of Him who raised up glory through the world, and have been faithful to what the Holy One commanded you, then I will bear you with joy over the ocean streams, as ye request.' Then bold-spirited, valorous, they mounted into the ship; the heart of each was gladdened on the sea journey.

IV

Then upon the surging waves Andrew began to pray the Prince of heaven for mercy for the sailors, and spoke thus in words: 'May the God of glory, the Master of mankind, grant thee thy wish in the world and happiness in heaven, as thou hast shown goodwill unto me on this journey.'

Then the holy man sat down hard by the helmsman, one noble man by another. I have never heard of a fairer ship laden with great treasures. Heroes sat in it, glorious princes, beauteous thanes. Then the powerful Prince, the eternal Almighty, spoke; bade His angel, the glorious servant, go and give meat; succour the destitute on the surging sea, so that they might easily bear their lot through the tumult of the waves. Then the whale mere was troubled and stirred; the swordfish sported, darted through the deep, and the grey gull wheeled about, greedy for slaughter; the candle of the sky grew dark, the winds rose, the waves dashed, the floods were fierce, the cordage creaked, the sails were soaked. The terror of the tempest rose up with the might of hosts; the thanes were afraid; none looked to reach land alive, of those who with Andrew sought the ship on the ocean stream. They knew not as yet who guided the sailing of the sea-floater.

Then the holy Andrew, a follower faithful to the Lord, when he had eaten, gave further thanks on the seaway, upon the weltering waters, to the mighty leader:

'May the true Lord, Author of light and life, Ruler of hosts, render thee reward for this food, and give thee sustenance, bread of heaven, as thou hast shown kindness, goodwill, towards me upon the ocean. Now my thanes, the young warriors, are cast down; the ocean roars, the pouring sea; the abyss is stirred, deeply troubled; the men are afflicted, the band of the brave ones mightily oppressed.'

The Creator of men answered him from the helm: 'Let us bring now our vessel, our ship, to shore over the sea, and let thy men, thy attendants, wait then on land till thou return.'

Then the heroes straightway gave him answer, thanes strong to endure; they would not agree to leave their loved teacher at the ship's prow and seek land for themselves: 'Whither shall we turn, lacking our lord, heavy at heart, bare of happiness, stricken with sins, if we desert thee? We shall be despised in every land, hateful to the peoples, when the sons of men in their valour hold debate as to which of them has always served his lord best in war, when hand and targe hacked by swords, suffered distress on the field of battle in the deadly play.'

Then the powerful Prince, the never-failing King, spoke, straightway lifted up His voice: 'If, as thou declarest, thou art a servant of Him who is throned in majesty, the King of glory, set forth thy secrets, how He taught men upon earth. Long is this journey over the yellow flood; comfort the minds of thy men. Long yet is the way over the waters, the land very distant to seek; the flood is mingled, the deep with the earth. God can easily send succour to sailors.' Then wisely with words he began to hearten his disciples, the glorious men: 'When ye set out on the sea, it was your purpose to venture your lives among the people of your foes and to suffer death for the love of the Lord, to surrender your souls in the land of the Ethiopians. I myself know that the Creator of angels, the Lord of hosts, protects us. Through the King of glory the water terror, the tossing flood, shall be rebuked and vanquished, grow more calm. So did it chance before this that we, riding the surge, made trial of the waves in a ship on the surf. The dread waterways seemed dangerous, the ocean streams beat on the cordage; the sea often spoke, wave unto wave. At times terror towered up over the ship out of the ocean's bosom into the hold of the vessel. There the Almighty, the Lord of mankind, abode in His brightness in the ship. Men grew fearful in heart; they desired safety, mercy, from the Glorious One. Then the company upon the ship began to cry out; straightway the King, the Lord of angels, rose up; hushed the waves, the surges of the water; rebuked the winds; the sea sank down, the size of the ocean streams grew moderate. Then our hearts leaped up when we beheld under the sweep of the sky winds and waves and the water terror grown timid in awe of the Lord. Wherefore I will tell you in truth that the living God never forsakes a hero on the earth if his courage fail not.' Thus the holy warrior spoke, wise in his ways; the blessed champion taught the thanes, heartened the heroes, until suddenly sleep fell upon them in their weariness beside the mast. The sea grew still; the working of the waves, the fierce tossing water once more passed away.   Then after terror the holy man's soul was made glad.

v

Then he who was sage in counsel started to speak; the man wise in mind laid open a treasury of words: 'Never have I found a better, a more skilful sailor, as it seems to me, a braver, shrewder mariner, more sober in speech.   I wish to beg yet one boon of thee, thou unknown hero, though I could give thee few rings, costly gifts, rich treasure; I would fain have thy good friendship if I could, glorious leader.   For that thou shalt receive grace, sacred joy in heavenly glory, if thou growest gracious of thy wisdom to those weary of seafaring.   Noble hero, I would seek help of thee in one thing, that, since the King, the Creator of men, has given thee glory and might, thou shouldst instruct me how thou dost control the course of the wave-floater drenched with the sea, the ocean steed.   It happens that I have been now and earlier sixteen times in a sea vessel, cold in my hands as we drove over the sea, the ocean streams—this is once more—yet I have never seen any man, glorious son of heroes, like unto thee, a pilot upon the prow.   The billow resounds, it beats upon the shores; this ship is exceeding swift; the foamy-necked one fares on; like a bird it skims the sea.   I know well that I have never seen on the ocean rarer skill in a sailor.   It is as if it stood still on the land, where storm nor wind can stir it, nor waterfloods break the high-prowed ship; yet it speeds on the sea, swiftly under sail.   Thou thyself art young, protector of warriors, not at all old in winters—yet, seafarer, thou hast in heart an earl's gift of speech; thou knowest a wise meaning for every word before men.'

The everlasting Lord answered him: 'Often it chances that we are making our way on a voyage in ships manned by sailors, over the sea in the steeds of ocean when the storm comes.   Sometimes we are sore beset on the waves, on the sea, though we survive, pass through the perilous journey.   The raging flood cannot grievously hinder any man against the Lord's will: but He who binds the waters, the dark billows, suppresses and scourges the power of their life.   He who set up heaven on high and established it with His hands, wrought and upheld it, filled with glory the bright radiant habitation, He shall righteously rule the peoples; thus the home of angels became blessed by His might alone. Therefore the truth is manifest, declared, known, and recognized, that thou art an excellent servant of the King throned in glory, because straightway the sea, the ocean's expanse, knew thee, that thou hadst the grace of the Holy Ghost. The sea once more retired, the tumult of waves; terror was hushed, the broad-breasted billow; the floods fell to rest when they perceived that God, who established the glory of heaven with His strong might, had compassed thee round with protection.'

Then with sacred voice the staunch warrior spoke, honoured the King, the Ruler of glory; and thus uttered words: 'Prince of mankind, Lord Saviour, blessed be Thou! Ever Thy glory lives! Both near and far Thy name is holy, adorned with glory throughout the nations, famed for forbearance. There is no man under heaven's vault, none of human race, who can relate or reckon how gloriously Thou, the Prince of peoples, the Comforter of spirits, givest Thy grace. Verily, Saviour of souls, it is manifest that Thou hast been gracious to this youth and hast honoured him, wise in understanding and words, with gifts while he is young. I have never found greater wisdom of mind in one of his years.'

Then the Glory of kings spoke to him from the boat; the Beginning and End boldly asked: 'Declare, thane wise in thought, if thou canst, how it came to pass among men that the impious ones with evil thoughts, the people of the Jews, uttered blasphemy against the Son of God. The wretched men, angry and wicked, believed not in their Creator, that He was God, though He showed forth many miracles to the multitudes, manifest and plain. Sinners could not recognize the royal Child who was born to protect and comfort mankind, all dwellers on earth. Speech and wisdom increased in the Lord, but in His prudence He never revealed any part of those marvels before proud people.'

Then Andrew gave answer unto Him: 'Dearest of men, how could it come to pass among the people, that thou hast not heard of the Saviour's power, how He, the Son of the Almighty, showed forth His grace far and wide throughout the world? He gave speech to the dumb, the deaf were made to hear; He cheered the heart of the lame and the leprous, those who had long been crippled, weary, sick, held in torments; throughout the cities the blind were given sight. Thus on earth He roused many men of various sorts from death with a word. Likewise He also manifested in His glory many marvels by the might of His power. In the presence of the multitude He consecrated wine from water, and for the bliss of men bade it change to the better kind. Likewise from two fishes and five loaves He fed five thousand men; the companies sat down, sad at heart; weary after wayfaring, they enjoyed the rest; they received food, the men on the ground, as was most pleasant for them. Now, dearest man, thou canst learn how the glorious Guardian loved us in life with words and deeds, and led us by teaching to that fair joy, where those who seek the Lord after death can dwell in happiness, blessed among the angels.'

VI

Again the Ruler of the wave unlocked His word-hoard; the man upon the gangway spoke boldly: 'Canst thou tell me, so that I may know the truth, whether thy Lord showed the wonders on earth, which He wrought no few times, openly where bishops and scribes and elders held council, deliberating together? It seems to me that in their hatred they plotted guile through deep error; doomed men hearkened too eagerly to the devil's promptings, to the angry traitor. Fate played them false, misled, and misguided them. Now speedily they shall suffer punishment, cursed among the cursed men, bitter burning in the slayer's embrace.'

Then Andrew made answer unto him: 'Verily I tell thee, that very often He wrought wonder after wonder before the rulers of the people in the sight of men; likewise the Lord of men did good secretly to the people, even as He turned His thoughts to peace.'

The Guardian of princes answered him: 'Canst thou, wise hero, man brave in mind, tell in words the miracles which He, fearless in might, showed forth, when often ye held secret converse with the Lord, the Ruler of the heavens?'

Then Andrew made answer unto Him: 'Dearest lord, why dost thou question me in wondrous words, and yet knowest through the might of wisdom the truth of all that has happened?'

Then still the Ruler of the wave spoke with him: 'I question thee not on the whale road in order to blame or censure, but my heart rejoices, flourishes in happiness, through thy speech abounding in excellence. Nor am I alone in that, for the heart is joyful, the spirit finds solace, in every man who far or near calls to mind how the Man wrought, the Son of God upon earth. Spirits departed; eager to leave life they sought heaven's joys, the home of angels, through noble strength.'

Quickly Andrew made answer unto Him: 'Now in thee I perceive truth, understanding of wisdom, skill granted by wondrous power (the breast in its wisdom blooms within with bright bliss)—now I will tell thee the beginning and end, according as I always heard the Prince's word and wisdom from His own mouth among men. Often great hosts, an exceeding multitude, gathered together at the Lord's command, where they hearkened to the Holy One's teaching. Then the Guardian of princes, radiant Giver of happiness, departed to another dwelling,[1] where many wise hall-rulers came to Him to the meeting-place, praising God; they ever rejoiced, men glad in heart, at the coming of the city's Defender. Thus it befell formerly that the triumphant Judge, the mighty Prince, went away; there were no more of the people, of His men, except eleven warriors accounted glorious; He Himself was the twelfth. Then we came to the capital city, where the Lord's temple was built, lofty and wide-gabled, famed among men, gloriously adorned. The chief priest with evil thought began to mock with insult, with scornful speech, opened his word-hoard, uttered contumely; he perceived in his mind that we followed the path of the Righteous One, performed His teaching; quickly he lifted up his voice full of hatred and lamentation: "Lo! ye are wretched beyond all men; ye go far journeys, endure many sufferings, ye obey now the teachings of a stranger contrary to the custom of the people; stripped of wealth, ye proclaim a prince, say in sooth that ye live daily with the Lord's Son. It is known to men whence that Prince's lineage sprang; in this land was He fostered, born a child among his kinsmen; thus, as we learn by report, His father and mother dwelling at home are called Mary and Joseph. To their family two other children have been born, brothers in kinship, sons of Joseph—Simon and Jacob." Thus the rulers of the people, men of ambition, thought to conceal the Lord's might. Wickedness came again, endless evil, where before it had sprung up.

[1] The phrase is vague; it may refer to Christ's house-to-house preaching.

VII

'Then the Prince, the Lord of men, departed, mightily strengthened, from the meeting-place with a band of followers to seek out a secret land. By many miracles, great deeds in the wilderness, He made known that He in His mighty power was rightly King over the world, Ruler and Creator of heavenly glory, one eternal God of all created beings. Likewise He showed forth other wondrous works in the sight of men.

'Afterwards He went once again with a great host, and He, the Prince of glory, stood in the temple. Speech arose throughout the great hall; sinners received not the Holy One's teachings, though He made known so many true tokens where they beheld them. Likewise He, the Lord of victories, saw beautiful wondrous works carved, likenesses of His angels on both walls of the hall, brightly adorned, fairly wrought. He spoke: "This is a likeness of the most illustrious of the tribes of angels who are in that city with the dwellers there; those in the joys of heaven are called Cherubim and Seraphim; firm of heart they stand before the face of the Lord everlasting, praise with their voices, with holy strains, the glory of the heavenly King, the protection of the Lord. Here is portrayed the countenance of the saints, angels in heaven carved on the wall by strength of hands." Again the Lord of hosts, the Spirit of heavenly holiness, spoke before the multitude: "Now I shall bid a sign appear, a miracle come to pass among men, that this likeness in its beauty should come to earth from the wall and utter a word, tell in true speech what is My lineage—thereby men shall have faith in My race."

'Then the wondrous work in the presence of the multitudes durst not neglect the Saviour's command, but the thing wrought of old sprang from the wall, so that it stood on the ground, stone apart from stone. Afterwards came a voice, loud through the hard stone; speech resounded, it was heard in words—the stone's action seemed wondrous to the resolute men—it taught the priests by clear tokens; in its wisdom it held sway over them and spoke: "Ye are wretched, tricked by the snares of miserable thoughts, or, troubled in mind, ye know not better; the immortal Son of God ye call man, Him who with His hands wrought land and sea, heaven and earth, and the raging waves, the salt ocean streams, and the sky above. This is the same Almighty God whom our fathers knew in days past; to Abraham, Isaac, and Jacob He gave grace, honoured them with riches, first declared unto Abraham the destiny of the glorious man, that from His race the God of glory should be brought forth. Now the event is revealed and manifest among you; now ye may behold with your eyes the God of victory, the Lord of heaven."

'After these words the multitude hearkened throughout the wide hall; all were silent. Then the eldest evil men—they perceived not the truth—began again to say that it was done by enchantment, by magic, that the bright stone spoke before men. Wickedness abounded in the men's breasts; fiery hate surged in their mind, the worm hostile to happiness, baleful poison. There the doubting heart, evil thought of men, encompassed with wickedness, was made manifest by blasphemy.

'Then the Prince bade the glorious work, the stone, to move from the place to the street, and go forth to tread the earth, the green fields; to bear, as it was taught, God's messages to the land of the Canaanites; to bid Abraham with his two descendants rise from the sepulchre at the King's word, to leave the tomb, gather their limbs together, receive spirit and youth, straightway appear, wise patriarchs, declare to the people Him whom they had perceived to be God by His power. Then it departed, as the mighty Prince, the Creator of men, had appointed it, over the paths through the land till it came to Mamre brightly gleaming, as the Lord bade it, where the bodies, the corpses of the patriarchs, had long time been buried. Then speedily it ordered Abraham and Isaac, Jacob, the third prince, to rise up from the ground at God's command, quickly from that sound sleep: it ordered them to make ready for the journey, to go at the Prince's command; they were to declare to the people who verily in the beginning created the earth all green and heaven above, where the Almighty was who established that work. No whit longer then durst they delay in fulfilling the glorious King's behest; then the three prophets went walking fearless through the land; they left the grave, the sepulchres, standing open; they wished to make known quickly the Father of creation. Then that people was seized with terror when the princes did honour in words to the Prince of glory. Straightway then the Guardian of the kingdom bade them once more seek in peace the joys of heaven for their happiness, and blissfully to enjoy it for ever.

'Now, dearest youth, thou mayest hear how He declared in words many marvels, yet men blind in heart believed not His teaching. Further, I know many a long glorious tale of what the Hero wrought, the Ruler of heaven, which thou, wise in thought, art not able to endure, to comprehend in thy heart.' Thus Andrew the livelong day praised in speech the teaching of the Holy One, till suddenly sleep fell upon him on the whale road beside the King of heaven.

VIII

Then the Bestower of life bade His angels bring the loved man over the tumult of the waves, bear him in their embraces over the sea, in joy to the Father's keeping, till sleep fell upon them weary of voyaging.   Borne through the air he came to land to the city which the King of angels had before revealed unto him in Achaia.   Then the messengers departed, blessed ones in ascent, to seek their native land.   They left the holy one sleeping in peace by the army road under the protection of heaven, biding in happiness the space of a night near the city wall by his enemies, until the Lord let the day-candle shine brightly.   Shadows vanished, dark under the clouds.   Then came the torch of the sky, bright light of heaven, gleaming over the dwellings.   Then the man resolute in war awoke, gazed on the field; in front of the city gates rose slopes, steep hills; round the grey stone stood buildings bright with tiles, towers, windy walls.   Then the wise man perceived that he had come in his journey to the race of the Mermedonians, as the Father of mankind Himself had bidden him, when beforehand He laid orders upon him.   Then he beheld his followers on the ground, men bold in battle, lying asleep by his side.   Straightway he began to waken the warriors, and spoke: 'I can tell you a manifest truth, that yesterday on the ocean flood a prince bore us over the sea.   The Glory of kings, the Ruler of the people, was in that ship; I knew His speech, though He had concealed his countenance.'

Then the noblemen, the young men, answered him with speeches, with spiritual mysteries: 'Easily we shall make known our journey unto thee, Andrew, that thou thyself mayest have wise understanding in thy thoughts.   Sleep fell upon us weary of the sea; then eagles came flying, proud of their pinions, over the surge of the waves; they carried off our souls while we slept, joyfully bore them in flight through the air, glad with clamour, gleaming and gentle; gladly they showed us favour, and joyously abode with us; there was unceasing song and the circuit of the sky, a fair throng of companies and a glorious multitude.   Angels in thousands stood outside around the Glorious One, thanes about their Prince; with hallowed voice they praised the Lord of lords in the height; joy was blissful.   There we perceived holy patriarchs and a great multitude of martyrs; they, noble warriors, sang praise sincere to the Lord of victory.   There David, a noble hero, the son of Jesse, king of the Israelites, had come with them into the presence of Christ; moreover we saw you, abounding in virtues, glorious heroes twelve in number, standing before the Son of God; dwellers in glory, holy archangels, served you; well is it for those men who may enjoy those delights.   There was heavenly bliss, glory of warriors, noble acting; none felt sorrow. Misery is appointed, torment prepared, for them who shall grow estranged from those joys, and go in misery, when they pass hence.'

Then the holy man's heart was greatly gladdened in his breast, after the disciples had heard the speech, that God was pleased to deem them so greatly worthy above all men; and the protector of warriors spoke these words: 'Now, Lord God, I have seen that Thou, Glory of kings, wert not distant on the ocean path when I went up into the ship, though I could not see Thee on the flood, Prince of angels, Comforter of souls.   Now be kind and gracious to me, Almighty Lord, radiant King!   I uttered many words on the ocean stream; now afterwards I know who bore me in honour over the floods in the wooden ship; He is the Comforter for the race of men.   Help is at hand there, favour from the Glorious One; success is granted to all men who seek Him.'

Then at the same time the Prince, King of all living things, was revealed plain before his eyes in the fashion of a boy; then He, the Lord of glory, spoke: 'Hail to thee, Andrew, with this faithful band, rejoicing in spirit!   I will protect thee, so that foul foes, hostile evildoers, may do no harm to thy soul.'

The wise hero fell then to earth, craved protection in words, questioned his friendly Lord: 'Master of men, Saviour of souls, how did I, sinning against Thyself, deserve that I was not able to perceive Thee, so good, on the seaway, where I spoke more of my words before the Lord than I should have done?'

Almighty God answered him: 'Thou didst not sin so greatly as in Achaia thou didst protest that thou couldst not go on distant ways, nor come to the city, accomplish the meeting in the space of three nights, according as I bade thee go over the tumult of the waves.   Thou knowest now more certainly that I can easily aid and help any of My friends in any land, wherever it pleases Me.   Rise up now quickly, straightway learn My will, blessed man; for the radiant Father will honour thee for ever with glorious gifts, power, and might.   Go thou into the city beneath the prison where thy brother is.   I know that Matthew is smitten with sword-strokes by the hand of evil men, thy kinsman encompassed with snares; thou shalt seek him, free the loved man from the hate of foes, and all those men who are with him foully bound by the evil fetters of strange men. Relief shall come quickly to him in the world and reward in heaven, as aforetime I said to himself.

IX

'Now, Andrew, thou shalt quickly venture into the grasp of foes; battle is to be thy portion; thy body shall be rent with wounds from hard sword-strokes; thy blood shall run forth in a stream like water. They cannot give thy life over to death, though thou suffer a blow, the stroke of sinful men. Endure that pain; let not the power of heathen men, fierce strife of spears, turn thee aside to desert God, thy Lord. Ever be eager for glory; let it dwell in thy memory how it became known to many men throughout many lands that unblest men mocked Me, bound with fetters; they taunted Me with words, struck and scourged Me; sinful men could not declare the truth by hostile speech. Then among the Jews I hung on the gallows—the cross was raised up—and there one of the warriors let out blood from My side, gore to the ground. Many miseries I endured on earth; therein I wished with kindly intent to set you an example, even as it shall be shown in this foreign land. There are many in this famous city whom thou wilt turn to the light of heaven through My name, though in days past they have wrought much wickedness.' Then the Holy One, King of all kings, went joyfully up to seek heaven, the pure home; there mercy awaits all men who can find it.

Then the warrior, bold in battle, remembered and was patient; with haste the resolute hero entered the city, upheld by courage; the man brave in heart, faithful to God, stepped on the street; the path guided him, so that none of the sinful men could perceive or see him. The Lord of victories had with His love encompassed the dear leader of the people in that place with protection. Then the nobleman, Christ's warrior, had drawn near the prison. He beheld the band of heathen gathered together, guards standing before the prison doors, seven of them together. Death took them all off; shamefully they died; sudden death seized the blood-stained men. Then the holy man in his thoughts besought the gracious Father, praised the glory of the King of heaven on high, the majesty of God. Straightway the door burst open at the holy Spirit's touch, and mindful of courage the hero, bold in battle, entered there; the heathen men were sleeping, drunk with blood; they stained the place of death. He saw Matthew in the prison, the bold hero in the place of darkness, uttering praise to God, glory to the Prince of angels. He sat there alone in the house of sorrow troubled by tribulations; then he saw under heaven his dear comrade, one saint the other; hope was renewed. He rose then to meet him, thanked God that they could ever behold one another unhurt beneath the sun. Peace filled both brethren, bliss was born anew; each with his arm enfolded the other, they kissed and embraced. They were both dear in heart to Christ; a light shone round about them, sacred and heavenly bright; their hearts within were stirred with joy. Then Andrew first began to greet with his speech the noble God-fearing comrade in prison; told him of battles, the fighting of hostile men: 'Now thy people are eager, men hither on . . .¹ deed, to seek the land.'

After these words the glorious thanes, both brethren, bowed in prayer, sent their petitions before the Son of God. Likewise the holy man in the prison greeted God and prayed to Him for aid, to the Saviour for help, ere his body should fall before the valour of the heathen; and then out of bonds away from the prison into the safety of the Lord he led two hundred and forty, duly numbered, saved from enmity—he left none there bound with fetters in the city prison—and there, moreover, to swell the throng he set free women full of fear, fifty less one. They were glad of the going; speedily they went; no whit longer did they abide to endure strife in the house of sorrow. Then Matthew went to lead the throng into God's keeping, as the Holy One bade him; he covered the multitude on their eager journeys with clouds, lest wicked persecutors, arch-enemies, should come to assail them with a flight of arrows. There the brave men, trusty comrades, held council together ere they parted into two bands; each of the earls heartened the other with the joy of the kingdom of heaven, warded off with words the torments of hell. Thus together the warriors, heroes bold in mind, excellent fighters, praised with hallowed voices the King, the Disposer of events, to whose glory an end shall never be set among men.

¹ There is a gap in the narrative here. Andrew and Matthew talk together, and Andrew restores Matthew's sight.

X

Then, glad in heart, Andrew went into the city where he had heard of the meeting of hostile men, the company of foemen, until he found by the path a brazen column standing near the street. Then he sat down by its side, cherished pure love, everlasting heavenly thought of the bliss of angels; thence he went to await in the city prison what war deeds should be ordained for him. Then great hosts, leaders of the people, gathered together; the throng of the faithless, heathen warriors, came with weapons to the fortress, where aforetime the captives endured hurt in the darkness of prison. In their hostility they had expected and desired to make food of the foreigners, the feasting appointed; their hope played them false when the angry spear-bearers in a troop found the prison door open, the work of hammers unclosed, the warders dead. Then hapless, reft of joy, they returned again to bear the ill tidings; they told the people that in the prison there they had found none remaining alive of the foreigners, the men of strange speech; but there the warders lay, stained with blood, dead on the ground, the bodies of the doomed men despoiled of life. Then many a ruler of the people grew afraid because of the heavy news, wretched, sad of mind, expecting hunger, the pallid table guest. They knew no better way than to devour the lifeless, the dead men, for food; for all the door-keepers together at one time the war-couch had been prepared by stern conflict.

Then I heard that the men of the city were speedily summoned; men came riding on horses, a troop of warriors brave on steeds, holding council together, proud of their spears. When the people were all gathered together to the place of council, then among them they let the lot direct which of them should first yield his life as food for the others;[1] they cast lots with hellish arts, they made count with idolatries among them. Then the lot fell even upon one of the chieftains who was a wise man in the throng of earls, in the van of the host. Quickly after that he was firm bound with fetters, hopeless of life. Then he, though brave in spirit, cried aloud in troubled speech; he said he would give his own son, his young child, into their power, to support life; quickly they received the offering with gladness. The people were full of desire, languishing for food; they had no joy

---

[1] In the Greek version of the story the Mermedonians are about to eat the dead warders when, in answer to Andrew's prayer, their swords fall and their hands are turned to stone.

in treasure, delight in rich stores; they were hard pressed by hunger, for the people's foe fiercely prevailed. Then many a warrior, man bold in battle, was stirred in heart concerning the youth's life. That grief for the violent deed was widely known, proclaimed throughout the city to many a man, that they sought the youth's death with a troop, with old and young warriors; that they had seized one life for the support of others. Quickly they, the heathen guardians of the temple, assembled there the army of citizens; clamour arose. Then the youth, fettered before the host, destitute of friends, began in sad voice to chant a song of sorrow, to crave safety; the wretched man could find no favour, protection from the people, that they would grant him life, existence; the warriors were set on violence; the edge of the sword in a hostile hand, keen, and hard in battle, stained with blood marks, must demand his life.

Then it seemed wretched to Andrew, the great evil grievous to bear, that he so guiltless should suddenly leave life. The hostility was bold and hard to face; the warriors, daring retainers, moved quickly, lusting after murder; they, the brave men, wished straightway to wound the youth's head, to destroy him with spears. God in holiness from on high guarded him against the heathen people; He bade the weapons of the men melt all away in the battle like wax, so that the wicked persecutors, the horrible foes, could do no hurt by the strength of swords. Thus the youth was freed from hostility, from affliction. Thanks be wholly to God, the Lord of lords, for He grants glory to all men who wisely seek succour from Him; there eternal peace is ever ready for him who can attain it.

XI

Then lamentation was raised in the city of men, loud outcry of the host; the heralds shouted, bemoaned the famine; weary they stood, afflicted with hunger. The gabled halls, the wine building, remained desolate; the men held no riches to enjoy in that bitter season; wise men sat apart in debate to ponder on the distress; they had no delight in their land.

Then one warrior often questioned another: 'Let him who has gracious counsel, wisdom in his heart, keep it not hidden! Now the time has come, exceeding great trouble; now is great need for us to hearken to the words of wise men.'

Then before the multitude the devil appeared, dark and foul

he had a cursed countenance. Then the dispenser of wickedness, the hell-limper, in his hostility began to betray the holy man, and spoke these words: 'Here over the far way has been brought within the city a certain nobleman of strange race; him I have heard called Andrew; he harmed you greatly when he led out from the fortress more men than was fitting. Now ye may easily avenge injuries on the doers; let the weapon's stroke, the sword hard of edge, cut the life's dwelling-place, the doomed man's body; go boldly, that ye may humble the enemy in fight.'

Then Andrew made answer unto him: 'Lo! rashly thou teachest the people, makest them bold to battle. Thou knowest the torment of fire, hot in hell, and thou stirrest the throng, the troop, to strife; thou art hostile to God, the Judge of men. Lo! thou devil's dart, thou increasest thy misery; the Almighty humbled thee hapless, and thrust thee into darkness where the King of kings covered thee with a fetter, and ever after they have named thee Satan, they who knew how to glorify the law of the Lord.'

Further the hostile one prompted the people to strife with words, with fiendish craft: 'Now ye hear the foe of men, who has wrought most injuries on this host. That is Andrew who disputes with me with wondrous words before the multitude of men.' [1]

Then a sign was given to the men of the city; men brave in battle leaped up amid the shouting of the host, and warriors pressed to the gates, bold under banners, with a great troop to the conflict, with spears and with shields. Then the Lord of hosts spoke a word, God strong in might said to His servant: 'Andrew, thou shalt do bravely; hide not from the throng, but make thy mind steadfast against trials. The time is not far distant when murderous men shall put torments upon thee, chill fetters. Show thyself, strengthen thy mind, make steadfast thy heart, that in thee they may perceive My power. They in their guilt cannot and are not able to give thy body over to wounds and death against My will, though thou suffer a blow, evil cruel strokes. I shall stand by thee.'

After those words came an exceeding great throng, false teachers in anger, with a shield-armed troop; quickly they bore him out, and there they bound the holy man's hands when the best of noblemen grew visible and they could behold the brave man among them with their eyes. There was many a man in the multitude of people on the battle-field eager for the fray. Little

---

[1] Andrew is invisible though his voice is heard.

they recked what requital should come to them after. Then the fierce enemies bade him be led over the land, dragged from time to time in the most terrible way they could devise. They pulled the dauntless man through the hill caves, the stout-hearted man round the rocky slopes, even as far as the ways stretch, old works of giants, within the city, streets paved with stones of varied colours. A tumult arose throughout the city houses, no slight uproar of the heathen host. The holy man's body was afflicted with wounds, wet with blood, his limbs broken; blood gushed out in surges, in hot gore. Within him he had unwavering courage: that noble heart was set apart from sins, though he must needs suffer so much pain from deep wounds. Thus the whole day until evening came the victorious one was chastised; pain again entered the man's breast, till the bright sun went gliding radiantly to its setting. The people haled the hated foe to prison; yet was he dear to Christ in heart; he was joyful in mind, holy in heart, his thought courageous.

XII

Then the holy man, the fearless earl, was encompassed by thoughts of wisdom the whole night in the darkness. Snow bound the earth with winter storms; the breezes grew chill with grievous hail showers; likewise rime and frost, grey warriors, laid fetters upon the land of men, the habitations of people. Freezing was the ground with cold icicles, the strength of the water shrank on the streams, the ice bridged the black sea road. The illustrious earl abode glad in heart, not forgetful of courage, bold and long-suffering amid afflictions through the chill winter night; he turned not in mind terrified by fear from what he began before—that he ever praised God most gloriously, honoured Him with words, till the jewel of the sky appeared in heavenly brightness. Then came a band of men, no small multitude, advancing eager for slaughter amid the clamour of the host to the dark prison. They bade the nobleman, the faithful hero, to be haled out quickly into the power of hostile men. Then again as before he was scourged with sore strokes the whole day; blood gushed in surges out of his body; it flowed in clots, in hot gore; the body, worn out by wounds, had no rest from affliction. Then came the sound of weeping, a cry issuing forth from out the hero's breast; the stream of the flood flowed forth, and he spoke:

'Now, Lord God, King of hosts, look upon my lot! Thou knowest and hast in mind the hardships of all. My Creator, in Thee I put my trust, that Thou, Saviour of men, eternal Almighty, in Thy kindness wilt never forsake me because of Thy power; likewise, whilst my life lasts on earth, I shall act so that I shall depart but little, Lord, from Thy gracious counsels. Eternal Author of well-being, Thou art a protector for all Thy people against the weapons of the foe; let not now the murderer of mankind, the leader of wickedness, with fiendish power mock and beset with slanders those who exalt Thy praise.'

Then the direful spirit, the wrathful traitor, appeared there; the devil of hell, cursed with torments, gave counsel to the warriors before the multitude, and spoke these words: 'Strike the sinful man, the people's foe, on his mouth, now that he speaks overmuch.'

Then again once more strife was stirred up, hate arose, until the sun went gliding to its setting under the high headland; dusky night masked and covered the steep crags; and the holy man, brave and eager for glory, was led to the house, to the dark building; the faithful one must needs abide for the space of a night in prison, in the unclean abode. Then with six others the dire monster, plotting evils, came to the hall, the foul prince of crime darkly shrouded, the devil deadly cruel, reft of glory.

He began then to speak words of insult to the holy man: 'What didst thou think, Andrew, of thy coming hither into the power of hostile men? Where is thy glory which proudly thou didst exalt, when thou didst humble the idols of our gods? Now for thyself alone thou hast claimed all the land and people, as thy Teacher did—He assumed royal dignity—whose name was Christ upon earth, while these things were allowed to be; Herod deprived Him of life, the king of the Jews vanquished Him in battle, reft Him of His realm, and committed Him to the cross, so that He sent forth His spirit on the gallows. Thus now I command my children, glorious thanes and disciples, to humble thee in war. Let the spear's point, the shaft stained with poison, pierce the doomed man's life; go boldly that ye may beat down the warrior's boast.'

They were fierce; straightway they rushed on him with eager clutches; God, the firm Guide, guarded him by His mighty power. After they perceived the cross of Christ, a glorious token, on his countenance, then they grew terrified, timid, fearful, and took to flight. The arch-enemy, the captive of hell, began again as before to chant a song of sorrow: 'What came

upon you so brave, my warriors, comrades in battle, that ye sped
so poorly?' Then the wretched man, the hostile ancient foe,
made answer unto him, and spoke to his father: 'We cannot
suddenly work hurt upon him, death by cunning; go thyself
thither. There forthwith thou wilt find battle, terrible fighting,
if thou durst venture thy life further against the solitary man.

XIII

'Dearest of earls, we can easily give thee better counsel for
the sword-play ere thou straightway do battle, raise the tumult of
war, whatever may befall thee in the conflict. Let us go back
that we may scorn him, fettered in bonds, mock his misery; have
speech duly pondered ready against the magician.'

Then afflicted with torments he spoke with loud voice, and
uttered these words: 'Long while, Andrew, thou hast dealt in
magic arts. Lo! thou hast beguiled and misled many men.
Now thou mayest no longer carry on the work; for thee are
torments decreed, dire according to thy deeds. Sad in spirit,
hapless, reft of comforts, thou must needs suffer hurt, grievous
death-agony. My warriors are ready for the battle-play, who
straightway in little time shall destroy thy life with their valorous
deeds. Who is there among men in the world so mighty as to
free thee from fetters against my will?'

Then Andrew made answer unto him: 'Lo! Almighty God,
the Saviour of men, can easily deliver me, He who long ago
fettered thee with fiery bonds amid sufferings where ever since,
bound in torture, thou hast suffered in exile, hast forfeited glory,
from the time that thou didst despise the word of heaven's King.
There was the beginning of evil; never shall the end of thy exile
come to pass. Thou shalt for ever increase thy sorrow; for thee
ever from day to day shall thy lot be more hard.' Then he who
long while since wrought the bitter strife against God turned in
flight.

Then at dawn with the breaking of day came the horde of the
heathen to seek the holy man with a troop of people; they bade
the patient thane to be led out for the third time; they purposed
straightway to weaken the brave man's heart; it could not come
to pass thus. Then hate was roused anew, grievous and cruel.
The holy man was sorely afflicted, cunningly bound, pierced by
wounds, while daylight lasted. Then, sad in spirit, he began to
call aloud to God, the bold man in his bondage; weary in heart he

lamented with hallowed voice and spoke these words: 'Never by the Lord's desire have I endured a harder lot under the vault of heaven wherever it fell to me to glorify the law of the Lord. My limbs are wrenched apart; my frame painfully broken, my body stained with blood; my wounds, gory gashes, gush forth. Lo! Ruler of victories, Lord Saviour, Thou didst grow sad among the Jews for the space of a day, when from the cross Thou didst call aloud to the Father, the living God, the Lord of creation, the Glory of kings, and spoke thus: "Father of angels, Creator of light and life, fain would I ask Thee, Why dost Thou forsake me?" And now for three days I have had to endure cruel torments. God of hosts, Nourisher of souls, I pray that I may commit my spirit into Thy own hand. Thou didst promise by Thy sacred word, when Thou didst begin to encourage us twelve, that the warring of hostile men should not hurt us, that neither a part of our body should be suddenly dismembered, nor sinew, nor bone be cast on the ground, nor a lock be lost from our head, if we were mindful to perform Thy bidding. Now my sinews are destroyed; my blood has flowed forth; my locks lie scattered over the land, my hair upon the earth. Far dearer to me is death than this agony of life.'

Then the voice of the glorious King spoke to him, uttered speech to the resolute man: 'Dearest friend, mourn not thy misery; it is not too terrible for thee. I keep guard over thee, encompass thee round with the power of My protection. Sway over all things in the world and triumph has been given unto Me. In truth many a man shall make that known on the great day in council, that it shall come to pass that this fair world, heaven and earth, shall perish together, ere any word which I speak by My mouth be brought to naught. Behold now thy track where thy blood shed a gory path by the breaking of thy bones, the bruising of thy body. Those who have wrought the greatest of grievous injuries may not do thee any more hurt by the stroke of spears.' Then the beloved warrior, obeying the words of the glorious King, looked back; he beheld blossoming groves bright with flowers standing where before he had shed his blood.

Then the protector of warriors spoke a word: 'Thanks and praise be to Thee, Ruler of nations, glory for ever in heaven, because Thou, my victorious Lord, hast not left me alone in suffering, a sojourner in a strange land.' Thus the hero praised the Lord with hallowed voice, till the bright sun, gloriously radiant, went gliding beneath the waves.

Then the fourth time the leaders, dread foes, led the nobleman to the prison; they would fain change the mighty thoughts, the mind, of the counsellor of men, in the dark night. Then the Lord God, the Glory of heroes, the Father of mankind, the Teacher of life, entered that prison, and then greeted His friend with words and uttered solace; bade him enjoy his body in soundness: 'Thou shalt by no means suffer pain any longer amid the slights of foemen.'

Then the man brave in might rose up, healed from grievous torments, gave thanks to God from his prison; his fairness was undefiled, neither was the fringe violently rent from his robe, nor a lock from his head, nor a bone broken, nor a bloody wound of hurtful kind, nor a part of his body wet with gore from a blow; but again as erstwhile by the glorious power he was offering praise and was sound in his body.

XIV

Lo! for a space now I have set forth in words, in a song, the story of the saint, the praise of what he wrought, an event famous and beyond my power. There is much to tell: his long study, that which he performed in life, everything from the beginning. A man on earth more learned in the law than I count myself shall find in his heart that from the beginning he knows all the hardships, the fierce fights, which he bravely endured. Yet we shall relate some few things more in the poem. It is an old tradition, how he endured exceeding many torments, grievous conflicts, in the heathen city. He beheld by the wall in the prison great pillars wondrous firm, columns standing, beaten upon by the storm, ancient work of giants. Mighty and brave, wise, wondrously sage, he spoke unto one of them, straightway uttered a word: 'Hearken, thou marble, to the commands of the Lord before whose face all creatures shall feel fear when they behold the Father of heaven and earth with the greatest of hosts seek mankind in the world. Let now burst forth from thy base floods, a stream of water, now that the Almighty King of heaven bids thee send forth speedily on this proud people wide-spreading water, a pouring sea for the destruction of men. Lo! thou art more precious than gold, than a gift of treasure; the King Himself, the God of glory, wrote upon thee, set forth in words, awful secrets, and in ten words the Lord strong in might set a sign of His just law; to Moses He gave it, as truthful men have afterwards kept it, brave followers, his kinsmen, God-fearing men, Joshua and Tobias.[1] Now thou mayest recognize that the King of angels adorned thee in days of old with gifts far more than all the race of gems. By His holy command thou shalt quickly make known if thou hast any understanding of Him.'

Then was there no further delay ere the stone split; the flood gushed forth, flowed over the earth; the foamy waves covered the earth at dawn; the deluge grew greater. After the day of feasting came fear; the warriors started up from sleep. The waters, deeply stirred, whelmed the earth; the host were terrified at the sudden peril of the flood; doomed to death, they perished; the onslaught swept away the young men in the sea by the salt wave. That was a burden of sorrow, a bitter beer-drinking; cup-bearers, servants, were not slow to come; there straightway from daybreak was drink enough ready for all. The water's power waxed greater; men made lamentation, old spear-bearers; fain would they have fled forth from the yellow flood; they wished to save their lives, to seek an abode in the mountain caves, a refuge in the earth. An angel who overspread the city with gleaming flame, with hot fierce surging, denied them that; fierce within there was the dashing sea; the company of men could not contrive to flee from the fortress. The waves towered higher, the billows made uproar; sparks of fire flew; the flood surged with waves. There within the city was not far to seek a sad measure sent forth; many a one in fear lamented the tribulation; they sang a song of death. The fearful flame grew plain to see, dire devastation, dread noise; the blasts of the fire in the air girdled the walls; mightier grew the waters.

There weeping of men was widely heard, hapless lamentation of mankind. Then one there, a wretched man, began to gather the people; unhappy, sad in mind, he spoke in sorrow: 'Now ye yourselves can perceive the truth, that wrongfully we put fetters, bonds of torment, upon the stranger in prison; fate harsh and cruel does us hurt; that is thus manifest here. Far better is it, as I truly believe, for us all with one mind to free him from fetters—haste is best—and pray the saint for succour, aid, and solace. Peace will straightway be prepared for us after sorrow, if we seek him.'

Then the behaviour of the people was manifest there to Andrew's heart; there the might of brave men, the strength of warriors, was made humble. The waters spread; the sea

[1] Why Tobias is mentioned here is not clear. It may be a mistake for Caleb. (See Numbers xiv. 6.)

flowed; the flood was eager, until the surging waves rose above the breast, up to the shoulders of the earls. Then the nobleman bade the flowing of the stream to cease, the storms to be stilled around the stony slopes. Bold, undaunted, he stepped out quickly; wise, precious to God, he came out from prison; straightway a street was opened ready for him through the watercourse; pleasant was the plain of victory; wherever his foot trod the ground became dry from the deluge. The citizens grew glad in heart, rejoicing in spirit. Then had succour come forth after sorrow; the sea grew still at the saint's command; the tempest paid heed; the sea road remained at rest. Then the hill, the dread cave, opened up, and let the flood, the yellow waves, spread thither; the abyss devoured all the rushing tumult. He caused not the wave alone to sink there, but also the worst of the host, fourteen bitter foes, went hastening to destruction in the wave under the depths of the earth. Then many a one standing behind these men grew terrified, timid; they looked for the slaughter of women and men, a more miserable time of bitter experiences, after the warriors, hostile in wickedness, guilty of murder, had perished beneath the ground.

Then with one mind they all said: 'Now it is manifest that the true God, King of all creatures, who sent hither this herald to the aid of the people, holds mighty sway. Now is great need to obey Him righteously with eagerness.'

XV

Then the saint began to gladden the men, to cheer the troop of warriors with words: 'Be not too fearful, although the band of sinful men have chosen destruction; they have suffered death and torments, according to their deeds; the light of glory is revealed to you in radiance, if ye think aright.' Then he sent his prayer before the Son of God, prayed the Holy One to aid the young men who aforetime in the sea had given up their lives in the grasp of the flood, that their spirits should not be brought, void of happiness, deprived of glory, into destroying torments, into the power of the fiends. Then that message was uttered in thought to Almighty God, the Prince of peoples, after the speech of the holy man; then He bade them all rise up unhurt, the young men from the ground, whom the sea had slain before.

Then, as I heard, many in assembly rose up there in haste from the dead, sons not fully grown; then body and soul were wholly united, though before they had swiftly lost their lives by the flood's sudden onslaught; freed from torments, they received baptism and the covenant of peace, a promise of glory, God's protection. Then the brave man, the King's builder, bade a church to be set up, a temple of God to be prepared, where the young men had arisen by the Father's baptism and the flood had sprung up. Then far and wide throughout the festive city men gathered together with a host of people, earls with one mind and their women with them; they said they would faithfully obey, boldly receive the bath of baptism at the Lord's will, and abandon idolatry and old altars. Then among the people baptism was given, nobly among the earls, and God's righteous law raised up to be obeyed in the land among the city-dwellers, and a church was consecrated. There God's messenger set one, a sage man, wise in word, in the shining city to be bishop of the people, and consecrated him before the company through his power as apostle for the good of men—he was called Platan—and boldly he charged them that they should zealously follow his teaching, win salvation. He said that his mind was eager to forsake the gold-city, the hall joy and treasure of men, the radiant halls of ring-giving, and to seek the ship by the surge of the sea. That was distress for the host to endure, that the leader of the people would no longer abide with them. Then the God of glory, the Lord of hosts, appeared to him on the journey, and spoke these words: [1] . . . 'people from their sins? Their mind is sad; they go mourning; they lament their grief, men and women together; weeping has come upon them, a mourning mood . . . hastening before Me. Thou shalt not forsake that flock in their joy so new, but establish My name firmly in their hearts. Protector of warriors, do thou sojourn for the space of seven nights in the festive city, in the halls decked with treasure; afterwards thou shalt fare forth with My favour.'

Then once more he, brave, bold in might, went to seek the city of the Mermedonians. The speech and wisdom of the Christians increased when they beheld with their eyes the glorious thane, the messenger of the noble King. Then he taught the people in the path of faith, gloriously encouraged them; guided an exceeding host of blessed ones to glory, to the holy home of the kingdom of heaven, where the Father and the Son and the Comforter in the glory of the Trinity hold sway for

[1] A short passage is missing here. God appears to Andrew and exhorts him to return to Mermedonia.

ever and ever over the heavenly habitations. Likewise the saint cast down the heathen temples, destroyed idolatry, and overthrew false belief. That was sore for Satan to suffer, heavy sorrow of heart, to see the multitude turn, glad of heart, by Andrew's gracious teaching from heathen temples to fair happiness, where a fiend, a hostile spirit shall never pass through the land.

Then according to the Lord's decree the days were fulfilled in number, as God had bidden him, which he was to pass in the pleasant city. Then, exultant in joys, he began to prepare and make ready for the sea; he was minded to seek Achaia once again by ship, where he suffered the passing of his spirit, death in battle. That was not repaid to the murderer with laughter, but he made his journey into the jaw of hell, and afterwards, outcast, destitute of friends, he possessed not solace. Then I heard that the men, sad in mind, with a multitude of people brought the dear teacher to the ship's prow; there many a one felt surging thought hot at his heart. Then they brought the keen warrior to the boat at the sea headland; then they stood weeping on the shore after him, whilst they could see the best of noblemen on the waves over the seal paths, and then they worshipped the Lord of glory, called aloud all together, and spoke thus: 'There is one eternal God of all creatures! His might and His power are famously honoured throughout the world, and His glory gleams over all on the saints in heavenly majesty, with beauty in heaven for ever and ever, eternally among the angels. That is a noble King!'

ELENE

[The story of St Helena's discovery of the Cross must have appealed to Cynewulf and his contemporaries not merely because it dealt with matters of interest to all Christians, but also because it was a tale of strange adventure in a distant land.]

I

WHEN in the course of years two hundred and thirty-three winters had been duly told off in the world since mighty God, the Glory of kings, the Light of the righteous, had been born in the world in human form,[1] then was the sixth year of Constantine's rule, since he, the battle prince, was raised up to be army leader in the kingdom of the Romans.[2] The protector of his people, valiant with the shield, was gracious to men. The prince's kingdom increased under the heavens. A true king was he, the war-guardian of men. God made him strong with glories and with powers, so that to many men throughout the world he became a delight; a scourge of the nations when he took up arms against his foes. Battle was offered him, the tumult of war. The people of the Huns and the glorious Goths gathered their hosts; the warlike Franks and Hugas set out; men were bold, ready for battle. Spears shone, woven mail-coats; with swords and shields they raised up the battle standard. Then were heroes plainly assembled and gathered together. The host of people went forward. The wolf in the wood howled a song of battle; he hid not the battle secret. The dewy-feathered eagle raised up its song in the track of the foemen. Hastily over the strongholds sped the greatest of armies with their hosts to war, the greatest the king of the Huns could anywhere summon to battle from his neighbouring warriors. The mightiest of armies went forth; the footmen were strong in their troops, so that the spear-warriors, staunch-hearted, encamped with the clamour of a multitude in a strange land on the Danube, hard by the surging water. They purposed to overcome the kingdom of the Romans, to plunder it with their

[1] What is really meant is the two hundred and thirty-third year since the Cross was buried.
[2] A.D. 312.

hordes.   There the coming of the Huns came to be known to the city-dwellers.   Then the emperor bade warriors be summoned with great haste to battle against the foe under a flight of arrows, to be led out to the fight under the heavens.   The Romans, men renowned in victory, were straightway ready with arms for the struggle, though they had a smaller host for the fight than rode round the valiant king of the Huns.

Then the shield clashed, the targe resounded; the king went forth with his troop, with his host, to the fight.   The raven screamed aloft, black and greedy for corpses.   The army was on the move, the trumpeters ran, the heralds made proclamation.   The steed trod the ground.   Quickly the multitude was gathered for the strife.   The king was afraid, troubled by terror, when he saw the strange people, the host of the Huns and Goths, so that he gathered his army by the water's edge, at the border of the Roman kingdom, a measureless multitude.

The king of the Romans felt sorrow of heart; lacking men, he looked not for victory; he had too few warriors, trusted comrades, brave men for battle, to face the greater host.   The army encamped, the earls around the prince, all through the night hard by the river, after they had first seen the marching of the enemy.

Then to the emperor himself in his sleep, when he slumbered amid his band, a vision was revealed and shown to him who was famed for his victories.   It seemed to him that there appeared in human form a man, beauteous, radiant, and bright of hue, more glorious than he had seen early or late beneath the sky. He started from sleep covered with his boar-helmet.   Quickly the messenger, the fair herald from heaven, addressed him, and called him by name—the shades of night vanished away:

'Constantine, the King of angels, the Ruler of events, the Lord of hosts, bade protection be proclaimed unto thee.   Fear not, though strange people threaten thee with terror, with dire battle.   Look to heaven to the glorious Guardian; there shalt thou find help, a token of victory.'

Forthwith he was ready according to the holy one's behest, opened his breast, looked up, as the messenger charged him, the lovely weaver of peace.   He saw upon the roof of the clouds the glorious cross in its beauty, gleaming with adornments, decked with gold; gems glittered.[1]   The bright tree was inscribed with letters brilliantly and clearly: 'With this sign shalt thou overcome the enemy in the perilous onset, thwart the

[1] Compare the vision in *The Dream of the Rood*.

hostile host.' Then the light departed, mounted up, and the messenger with it, to the hosts of the pure. The king, the prince of men, was the more joyous and the less sorrowful at heart by reason of that fair vision.

II

Then the protector of chieftains, ring-giver of men, war-chief of armies, Constantine, the glorious king, bade a sign be wrought in great haste like unto the cross of Christ, even as he had seen that token which before was shown to him in the heavens. Then at dawn with the break of day he bade the warriors awake and raise the war standard for battle and bear the holy tree before them, carry the sign of God among the foe.

The trumpets rang out loudly in front of the hosts. The raven rejoiced in the work; the dewy-feathered eagle beheld the going forth, the warring of fierce men; the wolf, the forest-dweller, lifted up its song. The terror of war was there. There was crashing of shields and press of men, hard striking and slaughter of hosts, when first they met the flying arrows. Upon that doomed people fierce foemen by the strength of their fingers sent forth flights of arrows, spears above the yellow shields, adders of war, in the midst of the enemy. Steadfast in mind they marched on; earnestly they pressed forward; they broke down the shields, thrust in their blades, hastened on, strong in battle. Then the banner was raised, the sign in front of the troops; the song of victory was chanted. The golden helmet, the spears, gleamed on the field of battle. The heathen perished; the barbarians fell. Forthwith the people of the Huns fled, when the king of the Romans in the midst of the fight bade the holy tree be raised. Far asunder the warriors were scattered. War carried off some; some barely escaped in that venture with their lives; some, half alive, fled to the fastness and saved their lives among the rocky cliffs; they dwelt in the land around the Danube; drowning in the river swept some away and ended their lives.

Then was the army of brave men gladdened; they pursued the foe from the break of day on till the evening; spears flew, the adders of war. The host was destroyed, the shield-troop of foemen. Few of the army of the Huns returned home. Then it was plain that the King almighty in that day's work had granted to Constantine victory, glorious honour, triumph under the heavens, by his rood-tree. Then the protector of armies departed home again, exulting in booty, distinguished in war—the battle had been decided. Then the defender of warriors, the king renowned in battle, with his band of followers came to seek his mighty dwelling and to visit his cities.

Then the guardian of warriors called the wisest men quickly to assembly, those who had learned skilful wisdom from ancient writings, who had stored the counsels of men in their thoughts. Then the prince of the people, the victorious king, in the presence of the vast host began to ask if there were any, old or young, who could truly tell him, declare in words who the God was, the Giver of success, 'of whom this was the sign, most radiant of tokens, which appeared unto me so bright, and saved my people, and granted me glory, victory against my foes, by that fair tree.' They could render him no answer, nor did they know very well how to speak clearly about that sign of victory. Then the wisest uttered words before the multitude, that it was the token of the heavenly King, and that there was no doubt thereof. When they who had been taught by baptism heard that, their hearts were light, their souls rejoicing, though they were few, that they could declare the gift of the Gospel before the emperor; how the Guardian of souls, the Glory of kings, honoured in the majesty of the Trinity, had been born, and how God's own Son had been hanged on the cross with cruel agonies in the presence of multitudes; how He had set free the sons of men, the sorrowing spirits, from the snares of the devil, and had given them grace by the same object which had appeared in His sight as a sign of victory against the onset of nations, and how on the third day the Glory of men, the Lord of all mankind, had risen from the grave from death, and ascended to heaven. Thus they spoke wisely of spiritual mysteries to the man renowned in victory, as they had been taught by Silvester. From him the prince of the people received baptism, and remained true thereto thenceforth for the term of his days according to the will of God.[1]

[1] Silvester, Bishop of Rome 314–35, did not baptize Constantine. The rite was performed by Eusebius, Bishop of Nicomedia.

III

Then the giver of treasure, the king bold in strife, was glad. A new joy had entered his heart. The Lord of heaven was his greatest solace and highest hope. Then day and night he began to tell forth eagerly God's law by the grace of the spirit, and in sooth he, the gold-friend of men, warlike, unflagging, devoted himself to God's service. Then the prince, the protector of the people, brave and bold, with the help of teachers, found in God's scriptures where the Ruler of the heavens had been wickedly hanged on the rood-tree in hate amid the clamour of a multitude, as the ancient foe with his wiles led them astray, seduced the people, the Jewish race, so that they hanged God Himself, the Prince of hosts. For that they must needs in humiliation suffer punishment for ever.

Then the praise of Christ was in the emperor's heart, and henceforth he forgot not that famous tree; and then he bade his mother travel the road to the Jews with a troop of people, zealously seek with a band of warriors where the glorious tree, the cross of the noble King, was hidden in its holiness under the earth. Helena was not minded to hold back from the journey, nor neglect the command of the giver of joy, her own son; but straightway the woman was ready for the longed-for journey, as the protector of hosts, of armoured warriors, had ordered. Then in haste the band of earls began to make ready for the voyage. The sea-horses stood ready at the shore of the sea, ocean steeds bound by ropes, lying on the water. Then the woman's journey was noised abroad when the company came to the surging wave. There many a proud man stood on the shore of the sea of the Vandals.[1] They pressed forward in succession, troop after troop over the paths; and then they loaded the wave-horses with coats of mail, with shields and spears, with armoured warriors, with men and women.

Then they let the high ships sweep foaming over the sea. Often the sides of the ship above the water caught the blows of the waves; the sea resounded. I have not heard before or since of a woman leading a fairer company on the ocean stream, on the sea road. There he who saw the voyage could watch the boat breaking over the seaway, speeding on under swelling sails, the sea-horse prancing, the wave-floater moving on. Blithe were the warriors, brave in heart; the queen rejoiced in the journey.

[1] The Mediterranean.

After the vessels with ringed prows had reached port in the land of the Greeks over the stretch of waters, they left the ships, the ancient vessels, at the wave-beaten sea-coast, held by their anchors on the surge, to await what should befall the men, until the warlike queen with her band of men should seek them again over the roads from the east. There were plainly seen on earls woven corslet and trusty sword, splendid armour, many a helmet, excellent boar-helmet. The spear-warriors, the men round the victorious queen, were ready for the journey. The bold fighters, the emperor's messengers, soldiers clad in armour, set forth eagerly into the land of the Greeks. There among the warlike band was seen the precious gem in its setting, the gift of the lord. The blessed Helena, fearless in thought, eager in heart, forgot not the prince's desire, that she should seek the land of the Jews across fields of battle with a trusty band of shield-warriors, with a troop of heroes. Thus in a short space it afterwards came to pass that that company, heroes renowned in battle, entered the city of Jerusalem with the mightiest following, warlike earls with the noble queen.

IV

Then she bade command be given to the wisest city-dwellers far and wide among the Jews, to every man, that speakers who could most learnedly set forth the secret of the Lord by true law should meet together. Then from far ways was gathered a mighty host, who could declare the law of Moses. Three thousand of the people were there picked out to give counsel. Then the beloved woman began to address the Hebrews with words:

'Well have I learned through the secret words of the prophets in God's scriptures, that in days past ye were dear to the King of heaven, loved by the Lord and daring in deeds. Lo! in your folly ye fiercely flung away all wisdom, when ye reviled Him who purposed to deliver you from damnation, from fiery torment, from bondage, by His glorious might. Ye spat with filth on the face of Him who by His precious spittle restored the light of your eyes and cured you of blindness, and often saved you from unclean spirits of devils. Ye condemned Him to death, who Himself had before raised up many of your people from death in the presence of men. Thus with blinded hearts ye confounded lying with truth, light with darkness, malice with mercy; ye

contrived crime with wicked thoughts. Wherefore the curse
lies heavy upon you for your guilt. Ye condemned the radiant
power, and have lived in error, with dark thoughts, to this day.
Go now quickly; with wisdom think of men exceeding wise and
skilled in speech, who, strong in virtues, do especially store in
their minds your law, who can truly tell me, render me before
you, the answer I seek from them for every marvel.'

Then downcast departed the men deep-versed in the law,
oppressed by terror, troubled with griefs; earnestly they sought
the wisest words of mystery, whether of good or evil, that they
might please the queen, as she required of them. Then they
found a thousand wise men gathered together, who best knew
old tradition among the Jews. They pressed then together in a
throng, where the emperor's kinswoman waited in majesty on
her throne, the stately warlike queen decked with gold. Helena
spoke and uttered words before the men:

'Hearken, ye sages, to the holy secret, to my words and
wisdom. Lo! ye have received the teaching of prophets, how
the Author of life, the mighty Lord, was born as a child. Of
Him Moses sang, the keeper of the Israelites, and spoke these
words:[1] "To you shall be born in secret a boy, glorious in
power, whose mother's womb shall not be made fruitful by
love of man." Of Him King David, the ancient sage, the father
of Solomon, the prince of warriors, chanted a noble song, and
spoke these words:[2] "I have foreseen God the Creator, the
victorious Lord; He, the Lord of hosts, the glorious Guardian,
was in my sight, on my right hand. Thenceforth I thought not
ever to turn away my eyes." So later with you the prophet
Isaiah, pondering deeply by God's spirit, declared before multi-
tudes:[3] "I raised up young sons, and brought forth children on
whom I bestowed wealth, sacred solace; but they scorned me,
hated me with enmity, had no forethought, understanding of
wisdom; even the miserable beasts which every day are driven
and beaten know their benefactors; in no wise do they vengefully
hate their friend who gives them fodder. But the people of
Israel would never know me, though I wrought many wonders
for them, while I sojourned on earth." Lo! we have heard
through holy books that God, the Lord, gave you stainless glory,
fullness of powers; He told Moses how ye should obey the King
of heaven, perform His behests. Soon that grew burdensome
to you, and ye resisted the right, rejected the bright Creator of

[1] The reference is perhaps to Isaiah vii. 14.
[2] Psalm xvi. 8.   [3] Isaiah i. 2–3.

all, the Lord of lords, and followed error against God's law. Now go forthwith, and find once again those who by skilful wisdom best know ancient writings, your code of law, that they may be able to give me answer out of their deep minds.'

V

Then sad at heart the proud men went away in a multitude, as the queen bade them; then they found five hundred picked men of the land, great in wisdom, who in their memories possessed greatest store of learning, wisdom in their minds. Again after a short space they, the city guardians, were summoned to the palace. The queen began to address them with words; she cast her glance over all:

'Often ye, miserable outcasts, have wrought a foolish deed, and scorned the scriptures, the counsels of your fathers; never more so than now, when ye have rejected a cure for your blindness, and denied truth and right, that the Lord's Son, the only begotten King, the Chief of princes, was born in Bethlehem. Though ye knew the law, the word of the prophets, ye would not in your sinfulness receive the truth.'

Then with one mind they made answer: 'Lo! we learned at God's ark the Hebrew law which our fathers knew in days past, nor do we well know why thou, lady, hast been thus sternly wroth at us. We know not the offence which we have committed among this people, or any great wrong ever against thee.'

Helena spoke and uttered words openly before the men; the woman made speech loudly before the hosts: 'Go now quickly, seek out far and wide those among you who have greatest wisdom, might, and intelligence, that they may boldly and honestly declare unto me all the things I seek from them.' Then they left the council, as the mighty queen, bold in the city, had charged them; sad at heart they pondered seriously; craftily they sought what the sin might be which they had committed among the people against the emperor, for which the queen blamed them.

Then one skilled in speeches, mighty in word—Judas was his name—spoke before the men there: 'Well do I know that she is minded to seek the tree of victory on which the Lord of men, free of all faults, God's own Son, suffered, whom, guiltless of every sin, our fathers in days past hanged on the high cross in their

hate. That was a terrible thought. Now is great need to set
our hearts firmly to proclaim not the murder nor reveal where
the holy tree was hidden after the tumult, lest the wise old
writings be destroyed and the counsels of our fathers renounced.
Not for long after that will the race of the Israelites, the religion
of our people, be able to rule the world any more, if this be
noised abroad; thus long ago did my valiant grandsire, a wise old
man—Sachias was his name—tell my father (who was called
Simon), his loved son, this very thing; he was leaving the world,
and spoke these words: " If it befall thee in the days of thy life to
hear wise men asking about the holy tree, and raising dispute
about the victorious cross on which the true King, the Lord of
heaven, the Child of all peace, was hanged, then, my dear son,
do thou speak forth quickly ere death take thee. Thenceforth
the people of the Hebrews, for all their wisdom, can never hold
sway, rule men, but the glory and valour shall live for ever and
ever of them who, filled with joy, praise and worship the King
who was hanged."

VI

'Then straightway I rendered answer to my father, to the old
man versed in law: "How should it come to pass in the world
that our fathers with angry mind should lay hands on the Holy
One to take His life, if they knew before that He was Christ, the
King in heaven, the true Son of God, the Saviour of souls?"
Then my parent rendered me answer; my father, wise in heart,
spoke: "Young man, perceive God's mighty power, the
Saviour's name. By no man can He be told of in words. One
cannot search Him out on earth. I was never inclined to have
part in the plots which this people made, but ever I held myself
apart from their guilt, and wrought no shame to my soul. Often
I earnestly opposed the iniquity, when wise men held debate,
sought in their minds how they should hang the Son of God, the
Guardian of men, the Lord of all angels and men, most noble of
Sons. Miserable men of such folly could not put Him to death,
as before they had expected, afflict Him with pangs, though He,
the victorious Son of God, did for a space on the cross yield up
His spirit. Then afterwards the Ruler of the heavens, the Glory
of all glories, was taken down from the cross; three nights after
that He stayed in the grave, in the place of darkness; and then on
the third day He rose up alive, Light of all light, Prince of angels,

and revealed Himself, radiant in glory, the true Lord of victories, unto His disciples.

'"Then after a time thy brother received baptism, bright faith. Then Stephen[1] for his love of God had stones cast upon him; nor did he return evil for evil, but with fortitude he interceded for his old foes, prayed the King of glory that He should not avenge upon them the evil deed, that in hate they had reft him of life, though innocent and sinless, by the counsels of Saul, just as in his hostility he condemned many others of Christ's people to death. Yet afterwards God showed him mercy, so that he became a comfort to many of the people. Afterwards the God of created things, the Saviour of men, changed his name; and later he was called St Paul; and there was no greater teacher of the law or better man under the sheltering sky, of those whom woman or man brought into the world, though he ordered Stephen, thy brother, to be slain with stones on the mountain. Now, my loved man, thou mayest perceive how merciful is the Lord of all, though often we commit offence against Him, wound Him with our sins, if straightway afterwards we feel repentance for the evil deeds, and again forsake wrongdoing. Wherefore truly I and my dear father afterwards believed in these glad tidings, that the God of all glories, the Guide of life, had suffered loathly torment because of the great need of mankind. Wherefore, dearest youth, I tell thee in secret counsel never to be guilty of taunting speech, hatred, nor blasphemy, hostile utterance against God's Son. Then shalt thou deserve to have eternal life, greatest of guerdons, given thee in heaven."

'Thus in bygone days my father, a man wise in utterance, taught me, still a youth, with his words, instructed me with true speeches—his name was Simon. Now ye clearly know what may seem best to your mind to declare, if this queen questions us about that tree; now ye know my heart and thought.'

Then the wisest in the company of men spoke to him with words: 'We have never heard any man, any other thane, among this people, save thee now, speak in this wise about an event so secret. Thou, skilled in old learning, do as seems best to thee, if thou art questioned amid the band of men. He has need of wisdom, of cautious words and the shrewdness of a sage, who shall render answer to the noble woman in assembly before this company.'

[1] The martyr Stephen is here made contemporary with Constantine.

VII

Words increased with much speaking; men on every side, some hither, some thither, deliberated, reflected, and thought. Then came the company of men to the assembly. The heralds made proclamation, the emperor's messengers: 'This queen summons you, ye men, to the palace, that ye may truthfully tell what ye have decided together. Ye will require counsel, wisdom of mind in the meeting-place.' They were ready, the guardians of the people, sad at heart, when they were summoned by stern command; they went to the court to show their artful strength. Then the queen began to address the Hebrew men with words, to ask the soul-weary ones about the ancient scriptures, how erstwhile in the world the prophets, men of holy souls, sang of God's Son, of where the Prince, the true Son of God, suffered for love of our souls. They were stiff-necked, harder than a stone; they would not truthfully reveal that secret, nor in their bitter hostility give her any answer of what she sought from them, but in their hearts they strongly opposed every word which she asked; they said that neither early nor late had they ever heard aught of that sort in their lives.

Helena spoke, and answered them in anger: 'Truthfully I will tell you who stand before me, and as I live there shall be no lie in it, if ye longer persist in this falsehood with treacherous deceit, a funeral fire, hottest of surging blasts, a darting flame, shall consume you on the mountain, and destroy your bodies, so that your falsehood shall bring death upon you. Ye cannot prove those words true which now for a while ye have wrongfully cloaked under sinful coverings. Ye cannot keep the thing hidden, conceal the secret powers.' Then they looked for death, fire, and the end of life; and there then they put forward one very skilled in speeches—Judas was the name given him among his companions—him they gave up to the queen; they said he was exceeding wise:

'He can declare the truth unto thee, reveal secret events, the law from the beginning on to the end, according as thou dost ask him. He is of noble race in the world, wise in the art of speech, and the son of a prophet, bold in council. It is his nature to have wise answers, skill in his heart. He will reveal unto thee by his great power before the multitude of men the gift of wisdom as thy heart craves.'

She let every man depart in peace to his own dwelling, and kept Judas alone as a hostage; and then earnestly begged him to reveal the truth concerning the cross which long since had been hidden in its burial-place; and called him apart. Helena, the glorious queen, spoke to that lone man: 'Two fates are ready for thee, either life or death, as thou preferrest to choose. Say now quickly which of those things thou wilt accept.'

Judas replied to her; he could not escape sorrow, avert deadly enmity. He was in the queen's power: 'How can it come to pass with him who in the wilderness treads the moorland, weary and starving, gripped by hunger, and to his sight there appear both together a loaf and a stone, hard and soft, that he shall take the stone to ward off hunger and heed not the loaf, betake himself to want and scorn food, despise the better when he can have either of the two?'

VIII

Then the blessed Helena rendered him answer openly before the men: 'If thou wishest an abode in heaven with the angels, victorious reward on high, and life on earth, tell me quickly where the cross of the heavenly King rests in holiness under the ground, which now for a while ye have hidden from men because of the wickedness of the murder.'

Judas spoke; sad was his mind, his heart troubled; and grief awaited him either way, whether he rejected the glorious joy of heaven and this present kingdom under the sky, or pointed out the cross: 'How can I find that which was so long ago in the course of years? Many years have passed, two hundred or more have been counted. I cannot tell, since I know not the number. Many wise and good sages who lived before us have since passed away. I was born afterwards in later days. I do not know that which is unknown to me; I cannot find in my heart what came to pass so long ago.'

Helena spoke in answer to him: 'How has it happened among this people, that ye bear in mind such manifold things, all the heroic deeds which the Trojans wrought in battle? That famous battle was much further back in the course of years than this noble happening. Ye can clearly tell me forthwith what was the number of all the men in the slaughter, of spear-men who fell dead under the wall of shields. Ye set down in writing the graves under the rocky slopes, and also the place and the number of years.'

Judas spoke—sorrow pressed upon him: 'My lady, perforce

we remember war near at hand, and set down in writing the stress of battle, the deeds of men; but we have never heard this revealed to men by any man's mouth save here now.' To him the noble queen rendered answer: 'Too strongly dost thou strive against truth and right concerning the tree of life, and even now thou didst speak truly to thy people about the victorious cross, and now thou turnest to lying.' Judas answered her, said that he had spoken in sorrow and very much in doubt; he feared wretched evil was to fall upon him.

Quickly the emperor's kinswoman spoke to him: 'Lo, we have heard that it was revealed to men by holy scriptures, that the King's noble Child, God's spiritual Son, was hanged on Calvary. Thou shalt tell me fully about the place, even as the writings say, where the spot on Calvary is, before destruction and death take thee for thy sins, so that afterwards I may purify it according to Christ's will, as a help unto men, so that holy God, the mighty Lord, the Giver of glory to hosts, the Succourer of souls, may satisfy the earnest thought of my life and my desire.'

Judas, steadfast in mind, spoke to her: 'I know not the place, nor know I aught of the ground, nor of the fact.' Helena spoke in wrathful mood: 'I swear by God's Son, by God who was crucified, that thou shalt be killed with hunger before the face of thy kinsmen, unless thou forsake falsehoods, and plainly tell me the truth.'

Then she commanded him to be led away by a band, and for his guilt to be thrust alive into a dry cistern—the servants delayed not—where for the space of seven nights, void of happiness, he lay in sorrow, imprisoned, afflicted with hunger, clasped with fetters; and then on the seventh day, weakened by pains, weary and starving—his strength was lessened—he began to call out: 'I entreat you, by the God of heaven, to raise me from these sufferings, who am made miserable by hunger's attack. Gladly will I reveal that holy tree now that by stress of hunger I can no longer hide it. So severe is this bondage, so heavy this misery, and so terrible this torment as the days go by, I cannot endure, nor longer conceal the tree of life, though erstwhile I was possessed by folly, and too late I myself recognized the truth.'

IX

When she who ruled men there heard that, noted the man's demeanour, she quickly charged them to raise him from confinement, and from prison, from the narrow dwelling. Straightway they did that with speed, and mercifully brought him up from the dungeon as the queen bade them. Then resolute they strode to the place upon the hill where erstwhile the Lord, the Ruler of heaven, the Son of God, was hanged on the cross, and yet he, though humbled by hunger, knew not clearly where the holy cross dwelt in its grave, buried in the ground by the fiend's cunning, long time secure in its bed, concealed from men. In his helplessness he at once lifted up his voice, and spoke in Hebrew:

'God the Saviour, Thou who dost possess power of judgment, and hast wrought by Thy glorious might heaven and earth and the surging ocean, the wide sweep of the sea and all creation; and hast measured out with Thy hands the whole world and the sky; and Thyself, Lord of victories, sittest above the most noble race of angels, who sweep through the air in a mighty host encircled by light;[1] the race of men cannot rise there in the body from the ways of earth among the radiant company, the servants of heaven. Thou, holy and heavenly, didst create them and appoint them to serve Thee. Of those of that order in eternal joy six are named who are also folded round with six wings; fairly they shine in their adornments. There are four of them who in their flight ever gloriously perform their service before the face of the everlasting Judge, ceaselessly sing in glory with clear voices the praise of the heavenly King, loveliest of songs, and utter these words with pure voices—they are called the cherubim:[2] "Holy is the holy God of archangels, the Lord of hosts. Heaven and earth are full of his glory, and all his mighty power is clearly proclaimed."[3] There are two among them in heaven—a victorious race—who are named seraphim. They must keep paradise and the tree of life sacred with flaming sword.[4] The sharp blade shakes and quivers, and the inlaid sword, terribly sure in its grasp, flashes varied hues. O Lord God, Thou shalt have sway over that for ever, and Thou hast cast out from heaven Thy sin-stained, rash foes who work iniquity.[5] Then the accursed company was doomed to fall into

---

[1] See Psalms xcv. 5; xcix. 1; cii. 25; Isaiah xl. 12.
[2] See Isaiah vi. 2; Ezekiel i. 5, 25–8.   [3] See Isaiah vi. 3.
[4] See Genesis iii. 24.   [5] See Revelation xii. 9.

the abodes of darkness, into destroying torments. There now
in the surging fire, whelmed in darkness, they suffer the anguish
of death in the dragon's embrace. He strove against Thy
authority, for which he, full of all foulness and abhorred, must
needs suffer in torments, must endure bondage. He cannot
oppose Thy word there; he, the source of all sin, is fast in tor-
ments, fettered in agony.   If, Lord of angels, it be Thy will that
He should rule, who was on the cross and was born into the
world as a Child by Mary, He, the Prince of angels (if He had
not been Thy Son void of sin, He would never in His days have
wrought so many true marvels in the world; Thou, Ruler of
men, wouldst not have raised Him from the dead so gloriously
before the people, if He had not been Thy Son in glory through
the bright Virgin), do Thou now, Father of angels, show forth
Thy sign. As Thou didst hearken to the holy man, Moses,
when he prayed, when Thou, mighty God, didst reveal to the
man at that glorious time under the rocky slope Joseph's bone,[1]
so, Lord of hosts, if it be Thy will, I pray Thee by that radiant
One, that Thou, Creator of souls, reveal to me that golden
treasure which has long been hidden from men. Now, Author
of life, let a pleasant smoke mount up from the place rising
through the air under the sweep of the sky. I shall believe the
better and fix my heart the more firmly, an unfaltering hope, on
the crucified Christ, that He is truly the Saviour of souls, eternal,
almighty, King of the Israelites; that He holds glorious sway in
heaven for ever without end over the everlasting mansions.'

X

Then a vapour rose up from the place, smoke under the skies.
Then was the man's heart exalted. Worthy and wise in the law,
he clapped both his hands towards heaven. Judas spoke, wise
in thought: 'Now in truth I myself have learned in my hard
heart that Thou art the Saviour of the world. Thanks without
end be to Thee, God of hosts, who sittest in glory, for that
Thou through Thy glory hast revealed secret events to me, so
wretched and sinful. Now, Son of God, King of hosts, since I
know that Thou hast been revealed and brought forth as the
Glory of all kings, I will pray Thee, O God, to be no more
mindful of my sins which I wrought not seldom. Let me,
mighty God, abide among the people of Thy kingdom with the

[1] See Exodus xiii. 19.

throng of the holy, in the bright city where my brother Stephen is honoured in glory, because he failed not in faith towards Thee, though he was crushed by stones cast upon him. He has the reward of warfare, endless happiness. His marvels which he wrought are set forth in books and writings.'

Then glad in mind, resolute in zeal, he fell to digging in the earth, under the turf, for the glorious tree, till he found it, buried twenty feet down, hidden in darkness under the steep cliff. There he came on three crosses together concealed in the ground, in that dreary abode, just as the band of cruel men, the race of the Jews, had covered them with earth in days gone by. They stirred up hatred against the Son of God, as they would not have done, unless they had hearkened to the counsels of the author of sins. Then his heart was exceedingly rejoiced, his mind cheered, his soul inspired, by that holy tree, when he saw the sacred token under the ground. With his hands he laid hold on the glorious cross of gladness, and raised it up from its grave before the host.

The strangers went their way, the chieftains into the city. Then zealous men in their boldness set up the three triumphant crosses to be seen in the presence of Helena. The queen rejoiced in heart at the work, and asked then on which of the crosses the Son of God, the Giver of gladness to men, had been hanged: 'Lo! in holy books we have heard it declared with proofs, that two suffered with Him, and He Himself was the third on the rood-tree. The sky grew all darkened in that dread hour. Say, if thou canst, on which of these three the Prince of angels, the Guardian of glory, suffered.'

Judas could not tell her clearly—he knew not for certain— the triumphant cross on which the Saviour, the victorious Son of God, had been raised up, but he commanded the trees to be set up amid acclamation in the midst of the glorious city and to remain there until the King almighty revealed unto them a marvel before the hosts concerning that glorious tree. The men renowned in victory, wise in counsel, sat down, raised their voices in song around the three crosses till the ninth hour; they had gloriously found a new gladness.

Then a multitude came there, a great press of people; and brought a dead man, a lifeless youth, on a bier with a throng of men pressing round—it was then the ninth hour. Then Judas was greatly gladdened there in his heart. Then he bade them set the dead man, the body bereft of life, the lifeless one, on the earth, and he, the revealer of right, wise in heart, pondering deeply, lifted up in his embrace two of the crosses over that lifeless corpse. It remained dead as before, the body fast where it lay; the limbs were cold, held by miserable constraint. Then the third one was raised up in its holiness. The corpse had been waiting till the Prince's rood was raised over him, the cross of heaven's King, the true sign of victory. Straightway he rose up, alert in spirit, body and soul united. There glad praise was poured forth among the people. They honoured the Father, and praised the true Son of God in words. Glory and thanks from all creatures be to Him for ever.

XI

Then were borne in on the people's mind, as they ever shall be, the marvels which the Lord of hosts, the Leader of life, wrought to save mankind. Then the lying fiend darted up in the air there. The devil of hell, the dread monster, his mind full of evil, began then to speak: 'Lo! what man is this who because of an ancient strife again destroys my followers, increases the old hate, plunders my possessions? An endless quarrel is this. Sinful souls can no longer dwell under my sway, now that a stranger has come whom I believed before to be fast bound in sins; he has robbed me of all my rights, of my treasures. No fair fate is that. The Saviour, who was fostered in Nazareth, did me many a hurt, injurious wrongs. When He had but grown from childhood, He drew my possessions to Him. Now I cannot succeed in any of my rights. His kingdom is wide flung over the world; my domain has diminished under the heavens. No cause have I to mock the cross with scorn. Lo! the Saviour has often shut me in that narrow abode in grievous sorrow. Erstwhile I was heartened by Judas,[1] and now once again by Judas I am humiliated, reft of benefits, outcast, and friendless. Yet I shall be able by crimes to come again from the home of felons. I shall raise up against thee another king [2] who will persecute thee, and he will not heed thy teaching, but will follow my ways of sin, and send thee then to the darkest and worst torments; so that, afflicted with agonies, thou shalt strongly strive against the crucified King whom before thou didst obey.'

Then Judas, wise in thought, a hero dauntless in battle, answered him—the holy spirit came mightily upon him, glowing

[1] Judas Iscariot.   [2] Julian the Apostate, Roman Emperor, 361-3.

love, his mind stirred by a prophet's sagacity—and full of wisdom he spoke these words: 'Thou, with thy mind full of sins, hast no cause to renew anguish so bitterly and stir up strife, thou foul lord of sin; the mighty King, who with His word has raised many dead men, will hurl thee, contriver of sin, down to the depths, into the abyss of torments, stripped of glory. Know thou the more clearly that in folly thou didst forsake the brightest radiance and the love of God, fair gladness; and since then thou hast dwelt in a fiery bath, ringed round with torments, burnt by the flame, and there for ever shalt thou, in thy hostility, suffer punishment, misery without end.'

Helena heard how the fiend and her friend strove together, the glorious and the evil, one side against the other, the sinful and the blessed. Her heart was gladdened to hear the hellish foe, the author of sins, vanquished; and then she wondered at the man's wisdom, how he in such short space and so ignorant had ever become so full of faith and so fraught with knowledge. She thanked God, the glorious King, that through the Son of God her desire had been fulfilled in both things, both in seeing the victorious cross and in the faith, the glorious Grace, which she so clearly saw in the man's bosom.

XII

Then the great tidings of the morning were noised abroad among the people, spread far and wide among men, proclaimed through the cities, which the ocean encircles, in every town, to the terror of many who would fain have kept secret the law of God, that the cross of Christ, buried long since in the earth, had been found, best token of triumph, which late or early had been raised up in holiness under the heavens; and to the Jews, hapless men, it was the greatest of griefs, the most hateful of fates, that they could not in the face of the world avert it, the joy of Christians.

Then the queen sent word throughout the troop of warriors quickly to prepare messengers for a journey; they must needs seek the lord of the Romans across the high sea and tell the warrior himself the greatest of glad tidings, that by the grace of God the victorious token had been discovered, found in the earth, which long before had been hidden as a vexation to holy men, to Christian people. Then at the great news the king's heart was gladdened, his soul rejoiced. Then there was no

lack of men in the city to question those who had come from afar
in golden corslets. He felt the greatest delight in the world, a
rejoicing heart at the glad tidings which messengers brought to
him, the leader of the army, from the east, how the men with the
triumphant queen had made a safe journey over the swan road to
the land of the Greeks. The emperor ordered them to prepare
in great haste again for a journey. The men tarried not, as soon
as they heard the answer, the prince's behest. He bade the
warlike men give greeting to Helena, if they, bold-hearted
heroes, could cross the sea safely and journey unharmed to the
holy city. Constantine also bade the messengers charge her to
build a church, a temple of God, for the weal of them both there
on the mountain slope, on Calvary for Christ's sake, to aid men,
where was found the sacred cross, most famous of trees which
dwellers on earth have heard of in the world. She accomplished
it thus, when the friendly men brought many welcome tidings
from the west over the world of waters.

Then the queen bade them seek out far and wide men trained
in arts, the best who could work most rarely in fitting stones, to
build God's temple in that place. As the Keeper of souls
counselled her from heaven she ordered the cross to be overlaid
with gold and gems, with the most costly precious stones; they
decked it with cunning arts, and enclosed it with clasps in a
silver case. There the tree of life, the most excellent trium-
phant cross, remained afterwards inviolable in its virtues.
Succour is ever ready there for the sick in all torments, in strife
and sorrow. There they straightway find aid, divine grace,
through the holy thing.

Likewise Judas after due time received baptism and was
purified, faithful to Christ, dear to the Lord of life. His faith
grew firm fixed in his heart, after the Comforter had made His
abode in the man's breast, stirred him to repentance. He chose
the better part, the bliss of heaven, and fought against the worse,
against idolatry, and put down heresies, unrighteous law. The
eternal King, the Lord, God the mighty Ruler, was gracious
unto him.

XIII

Then he, who many times before had for long greatly scorned
the light, was baptized; his soul was kindled to the better life,
turned towards heaven. Verily, fate decreed that he should

come to be so full of faith and so dear to God in the world, pleasing to Christ. That was made manifest when Helena bade Eusebius, bishop of Rome,[1] exceeding wise, to be brought to the council to the holy city to aid in the deliberations of men, so that he might place Judas in the priesthood in the city of Jerusalem as bishop for the people, chosen for his knowledge for God's temple by the grace of the spirit; and with wise thought she afterwards renamed him Cyriacus. The name of the man in the city was henceforth changed to that better one—'the Saviour's faith.'[2]

Helena's heart was yet very mindful of the glorious event in regard to the nails which had pierced the Saviour's feet and His hands likewise, with which the Ruler of the heavens, the mighty Prince, had been fastened on the cross. The Christian queen began to ask questions concerning them; prayed Cyriacus that he, by the power of the spirit, might further fulfil her will in the wondrous matter; that he by glorious grace might make revelation, and she uttered these words to the bishop; boldly she spoke:

'Protector of men, thou hast rightly revealed to me the precious tree, the cross of the King of heaven, on which the Succourer of souls, God's own Son, the Saviour of men, was hanged by heathen hands. My eagerness for knowledge lets not my mind forget the nails. Fain would I thou shouldst find them, still buried deep and secretly in the earth, hidden in darkness. My mind shall ever mourn, grieve in sadness and not be at rest, till the Father almighty, the Lord of hosts, the Saviour of men, the Holy One from on high, grant my desire, by the finding of the nails. Now do thou quickly, with all humility, O noblest herald, send thy petition to that bright realm, to the Joy of heaven; pray the Glory of warriors, the King almighty, to reveal unto thee the treasure under the earth, which still remains hidden, concealed from men, unknown.'

Then the holy bishop of the people, inspired in heart, made a firm resolve; glad in mind he went with a company of men who praised God; and then Cyriacus earnestly bowed down his head at Calvary; he hid not his heart's secret. In all humility he called unto God by the strength of the spirit; prayed in this new trouble the Ruler of angels to reveal to him the unknown thing, the exact place where he might expect to find the nails. Then

[1] This is Pope Eusebius. He is confused here with Eusebius, Bishop of Nicomedia.
[2] The name really means 'of the Lord.'

the Father, the Comforter, caused a sign to mount up, where they beheld it, in the form of fire, where by men's counsels, by secret cunning, the most precious nails had been hidden in the earth. Then all at once came a darting flame brighter than the sun. Men saw their Giver of joy show forth a marvel, when the nails deep down in the ground shone brightly, gleaming below from confinement, like the stars of heaven or gems of gold. The people rejoiced, the host was exultant; all with one heart glorified God, though, lured by the devil, they had long been in error before, turned away from Christ. They spoke thus:

'Now we ourselves see the token of triumph, the true miracle of God, though aforetime we fought against Him with false-hoods. Now the course of events has come to light and has been revealed. May the God of the heavenly kingdom on high have the glory thereof.'

Then he, the bishop of the people, who had turned to repent-ance through the Son of God, was once again gladdened. Troubled with fear, he took the nails, and brought them to the venerable queen. Cyriacus had wholly accomplished the woman's will, as the noble one had commanded him. Then there was sound of weeping, hot gush of tears on cheek, not at all from grief. Tears fell on the nails of twisted wire. The queen's desire was gloriously fulfilled. She knelt down in joyous faith; she honoured the gift, gladly exulting, which was brought to her as a solace in her sadness. She thanked God, the Lord of victories, that she now knew the truth which long before from the beginning of the world had often been pro-claimed as a comfort to the people. She was filled with the gift of wisdom; and a holy heavenly spirit dwelt within her, filled her breast, her noble heart. So the almighty, triumphant Son of God thenceforth guarded her.

XIV

Then earnestly with secret ponderings of the spirit she began in her soul piously to seek a way unto glory. Verily, the God of hosts, the Father in heaven, the King almighty, helped the queen to achieve her desire in the world. The prophecy had been uttered before by sages from the very beginning as after-wards it came to pass in all things. By the grace of the spirit the queen of the people earnestly began to seek very closely how she might best and most gloriously use the nails for the joy of men, and what was the Lord's will therein. She bade then be brought swiftly to conference a man exceeding prudent, sage in mind, whose counsel she well knew through its wise strength; and began to ask him what seemed best to his mind to do in that matter; and accepted his advice as a command. Boldly he spoke to her: 'Most noble queen, fitting it is that thou shouldst keep God's command, the holy mystery, in mind, and zealously fulfil the King's behest, since God, the Saviour of men, has given thee triumph for thy soul and skill of wisdom. Bid these nails be fixed on the bridle as a bit for the steed of the noblest of the kings of earth who hold cities.[1] That shall become renowned to many throughout the world, when in the fight he shall be able therewith to vanquish every enemy, when men bold in battle, warriors with swords, seek war on both sides, where they strive for victory, foe against foe. He shall have success in war, victory in battle and everywhere peace, safety in fight, who bears the bridle before him on the white horse, when proved men, renowned in battle, bear shield and spear to the fray. For all men this shall be an invincible weapon in battle against warriors. Of it the prophet spoke, sage in his skill. His mind pierced deep, his wise understanding. He spoke these words: "It shall be known that the king's steed, among the brave, is honoured with the bit, with the bridle-rings. That token shall be called holy unto God and the brave man who guides that horse shall be distinguished in war."'

Then Helena wrought all that with speed before men; she bade them adorn the bridle of the chieftain, of men's giver of rings; she sent the glorious gift as an offering to her own son over the stream of ocean. Then she commanded the best of mankind she knew among the Jews to come together to the holy city, to that place. Then the queen began to teach the band of loved men that they, sinless in their lives, should firmly hold to the love of God and also to peace, friendship between them- selves, and should obey the counsels of the leader, the Christian customs, which Cyriacus, learned in books, proclaimed to them. The bishopric was fairly established. Often to him from afar came the lame, the crippled, the feeble, the halt, the blood- stained, the leprous and blind, the poor, the sad in heart; always they found in the bishop salvation and healing for ever. More- over Helena, when she was ready to journey again to her home,

---

[1] So fulfilling, according to some of the Church Fathers, the words of Zacharias (xiv. 20): 'In that day that which is upon the bridle of the horse shall be holy to the Lord.'

bestowed on him precious gifts; and then charged all those in the kingdom who praised God, men and women, that with mind and might and thoughts of the heart they should honour the glorious day on which the holy cross was found, most famous of trees which have grown up from earth, sprouting forth with leaves.   Spring had passed away then to the first of May; it was only six nights till the coming of summer.[1]

For all men who remember the festival of the most precious cross under the skies, on which the most mighty Lord of everything stretched His arms, may the door of hell be shut, that of heaven unclosed, the everlasting kingdom of the angels opened, joy eternal, and their lot assigned them with Mary.

xv

Thus, I, aged and about to depart hence because of this frail body, have woven the art of words and have wondrously gathered my matter, have pondered at times and sifted my thought in the anguish of the night.   I knew not clearly the truth about the cross till wisdom by its glorious strength revealed to the thought of my mind a larger view.   I was stained by deeds, bound by sins, pained by sorrows, bitterly bound, beset by troubles, before the mighty King, to comfort me in my old age, taught me in glorious manner, bestowed fair grace, and poured it into my mind, revealed it in its beauty, enlarged it once and again, unbound my body, opened my heart, unlocked the art of song which I have used gladly, with joy, in the world. Not once but often, before I had revealed the marvel concerning the radiant tree, I pondered on the tree of glory, as I found it in the course of events, set forth in books and writings concerning that sign of victory.   Always till then the man had been beaten by surges of sorrow; a smouldering Torch (C) was he, though he received treasures in the mead hall, apple-shaded gold.   He bemoaned the Evil (Y), he, the comrade of Sorrow (N); he suffered distress, cruel secret thoughts, though for him the Horse (E) measured the mile-paths, proudly ran, decked with adornments.   Joy (W) is lessened, and pleasure, as the years pass; youth has departed and the pride of old.   The splendour of youth was once Ours (U).   Now in due time the old days have gone, the joys of life have fled, even as Water (L) glides away, the moving floods.   Wealth (F) is fleeting for all men

[1] 3rd May is the day of the Invention of the Cross.

under heaven; the adornments of the earth vanish under the clouds like the wind when it rises loud before men, goes among the clouds, fares on in fury, and on a sudden grows still again, close shut in its prison, oppressed by might.

Thus all this world shall pass away, and the dire flame shall also destroy those likewise who were brought forth therein, when God Himself with a host of angels comes to pass judgment.[1] Every man shall there hear the truth about all of his deeds from the mouth of the Judge, and pay a penalty likewise for all words spoken aforetime in folly, and bold thoughts.[2] Then in the fire's embrace He shall divide in three all people who have ever lived on the wide earth. The righteous, the band of the blessed, men eager for glory, shall be topmost in that fire; thus they, a multitude of brave men, shall be able to endure and easily suffer without distress. He will wholly temper for them the flare of the flame, as shall be easiest and most pleasant for them. In the middle the sinful, those who are tainted with wickedness, men sad at heart, shall be punished, covered with smoke in the hot surge. The third part, accursed evildoers, false persecutors, shall be held fast in the fire because of their former deeds; the multitude of the merciless ones shall be in the grip of the flames. From their house of torment they shall come not afterwards into the mind of God, the King of glory, but they, fierce enemies, shall be cast from the surge of battle into the abyss of hell. To the two kinds of men shall be dealt different fates. They shall be able to see the Lord of angels, the God of victories. They shall be purified, set apart from sins, like pure gold, which is all purged of every foulness by the fire of the furnace, purified and melted. So shall each of those men be freed and cleansed of every guilt, of great sins, through the fire of judgment. Afterwards then they shall be able to enjoy peace, eternal prosperity. The Lord of angels will be merciful and kindly unto them because they abhorred every wickedness, sinful deeds, and with their words called on the Son of God. Wherefore now they shine in beauty, like unto the angels; they enjoy the heritage of the King of heaven for ever. Amen.

[1] See 2 Peter iii. 10–12.   [2] See Matthew xvi. 27; xii. 36.

THE DREAM OF THE ROOD

[*The Dream of the Rood* is the most beautiful of Old English religious poems. The radiant vision, the simple devout wonder of the dreamer, the pathos of the Crucifixion as told by the Cross are unmarred by the set lifeless phrases so common in Old English religious verse. The authorship of the poem has been much discussed. Before the poem was discovered in the *Vercelli Book*, some lines were found and deciphered on an old stone cross at Ruthwell, near Dumfries. These lines, which correspond to certain portions of the poem, were ascribed to Cædmon, but the arguments which supported this theory have been discredited. A good case has been made out for regarding Cynewulf as the author, though there is no certainty in the matter. In style and mood *The Dream of the Rood* offers many resemblances to the known poems of Cynewulf, and *Elene* shows his interest in the cross as a subject for poetry]

Lo! I will declare the best of dreams which I dreamt in the middle of the night, when human creatures lay at rest. It seemed to me that I saw a wondrous tree rising aloft, encompassed with light, the brightest of crosses. All that sign was overlaid with gold; fair jewels were set at the surface of the earth; there were also five upon the cross-beam. All the angels of God, fair by creation, looked on there; verily that was no malefactor's cross, but holy spirits gazed on Him there, men upon earth and all this glorious universe.

Wondrous was the cross of victory, and I, stained with sins, stricken with foulness; I saw the glorious tree joyfully gleaming, adorned with garments, decked with gold; jewels had fitly covered the tree of the Lord. Yet through that gold I could perceive the former strife of wretched men, that it had once bled on the right side. I was all troubled with sorrows; I was full of fear at the fair sight. I saw the changeful sign alter in garments and colours; at times it was bedewed with moisture, stained with the flowing of blood, at times adorned with treasure.

Yet I, lying there a long space, beheld in sorrow the Saviour's cross, till I heard it speak. Then the most excellent tree began to utter words:

'Long ago was it—I still remember it—that I was cut down at the edge of the forest, moved from my trunk. Strong foes took me there, fashioned me to be a spectacle for them, bade me raise up their felons. Men bore me on their shoulders

there, till they set me on a hill; many foes made me fast there.
I saw then the Lord of mankind hasten with great zeal that He
might be raised upon me. Then I durst not there bow or
break against the Lord's behest, when I saw the surface of the
earth shake; I could have felled all the foes, yet I stood firm.

'Then the young Hero—He was God almighty—firm and
unflinching, stripped Himself; He mounted on the high cross,
brave in the sight of many, when He was minded to redeem
mankind. Then I trembled when the Hero clasped me; yet I
durst not bow to the earth, fall to the level of the ground, but I
must needs stand firm.

'As a rood was I raised up; I bore aloft the mighty King, the
Lord of heaven; I durst not stoop. They pierced me with
dark nails; the wounds are still plain to view in me, gaping
gashes of malice; I durst not do hurt to any of them. They
bemocked us both together. I was all bedewed with blood,
shed from the Man's side, after He had sent forth His Spirit.
I have endured many stern trials on the hill; I saw the God of
hosts violently stretched out; darkness with its clouds had
covered the Lord's corpse, the fair radiance; a shadow went
forth, dark beneath the clouds. All creation wept, lamented
the King's death; Christ was on the cross.

'Yet eager ones came there from afar to the Prince; I beheld
all that. I was grievously troubled with sorrows, yet I bowed
to the hands of men in humbleness with great zeal. There they
took Almighty God, lifted Him from the heavy torment; the
warriors left me standing, covered with blood; I was all stricken
with shafts. Then they laid Him down, weary of limb; stood at
His body's head; there they looked on the Lord of heaven; and
He rested there for a space, tired after the mighty strife. Then
in sight of the slayers men began to fashion Him a tomb; they
hewed it out of bright stone; they placed therein the Lord of
victories. Then, unhappy in the eventide, they began to sing a
dirge, when they were about to depart in their sorrow from the
glorious Prince; He rested there alone.

'Yet for a long space we stood there in our place streaming
with blood after the voice of warriors had risen up. Cold grew
the corpse, fair house of the Soul. Then they began to cut us
all down to the earth; that was a dread trial. They buried us in
a deep pit. Yet there the followers of the Lord, friends, found
me out; (then they raised me from the ground), decked me with
gold and silver.

'Now, my loved man, thou mayest hear that I have endured

bitter anguish, grievous sorrows.   Now the time has come when far and wide over the earth and all this splendid creation, men do me honour; they worship this sign.   On me the Son of God suffered for a space; wherefore now I rise glorious beneath the heavens, and I can heal all who fear me.

'Long ago I became the severest of torments, most hateful to men, before I opened to mankind the true path of life.   Lo! the Prince of glory, the Lord of heaven honoured me then beyond the trees of the forest, even as Almighty God also honoured his mother Mary herself above the whole race of women.

'Now I bid thee, my loved man, to declare this vision unto men; reveal in words that it is the glorious tree on which Almighty God suffered for the many sins of mankind and the old deeds of Adam.

'There He tasted death; yet God rose up again with His mighty power to help men.   Then He ascended to heaven; hither again will the Lord Himself make His way to this world to seek mankind on the day of judgment, Almighty God and His angels with Him, when He who has power of judgment will judge each one according as he merits in this fleeting life.   No one can be without fear there at the word the Lord says: He will ask before the multitude where the man is who for God's sake would taste bitter death, as He aforetime did on the cross; but then they will be afraid, and think little of what they begin to say to Christ.   No one need be terrified there who erstwhile bears in his breast the best of signs, but each soul which desires to dwell with the Lord must through the cross seek the kingdom which is far from earth.'

Then glad at heart I worshipped the cross with great zeal, where I was alone with none to bear me company.   My soul was eager to depart; I felt many yearnings within me.   Now I have joy of life that I can seek the triumphant cross alone more often than all men, do it full honour.   Great is the desire for that in my heart, and to the cross I turn for help.   I have not many powerful friends on earth, but they have gone away hence from the joys of the world, have sought the King of heaven, live now in heaven with God the Father, dwell in glory; and each day I look for the time when the Lord's cross, which erstwhile I saw here on earth, will fetch me from this fleeting life, and bring me then where there is great gladness, joy in heaven, where God's people are placed at the feast, where there is bliss unending; and will set me then where I may thereafter dwell in glory, enjoy happiness fully with the saints.   May the Lord, who here on earth suffered aforetime on the cross for the sins of men, be a friend unto me; He has redeemed us and has given us life, a heavenly home.

Hope was born anew with blessedness and joy for those who before endured the burning.   The Son was triumphant on His journey, mighty and successful, when He, the Master almighty, came with the throng, the company of spirits,[1] into God's king-dom—to the gladness of the angels and all the saints who before dwelt in heaven in glory, when their Lord, Almighty God, came where his home was.

[1] Those whom Christ redeemed when He descended to hell.

THE PHOENIX

[Resemblances between *The Phoenix* and Cynewulf's acknowledged poems
have led some to accept him as the author of this work, but there is no
certainty in the matter. The first half of the poem—describing the Earthly
Paradise, the beauty of the bird, its flight to the palm-tree in Syria when full
of years, the building of its nest, its death and new birth—is derived from a
Latin poem, *De Ave Phoenice*, which has been attributed to Lactantius. But
the English poet works freely. He expands, omits, and changes; he gives to
his poem a thoroughly Christian tone which is not in the Latin. The
remainder of the poem, in which the phoenix is taken as a symbol of the
Christian life in this world and the next, and also as a symbol of Christ, is not
based on Lactantius. The poem embodies very old beliefs and traditions.
In Egypt the phoenix was regarded as a symbol of the rising sun and of
resurrection. The account in Herodotus is that the bird flies from Arabia
to the temple in Heliopolis (the City of the Sun). It carries its father,
plastered up in myrrh, and buries him in the temple. This comes to pass
about every five hundred years. In other versions of the story the bird is
burned to ashes on the altar of the temple, and from the ashes rises to new life.
Pliny, in his *Natural History*, says there is only one phoenix alive at a time and
that it is burned in its nest. From its corpse comes a worm which changes
into the new phoenix. It is this version which is used in Lactantius and in
the English poem. Early Christian writers adopted the phoenix as a symbol
and proof of resurrection, and also as a symbol of Christ. The phoenix
survived the Middle Ages and is often found in the Elizabethans. Shake-
speare, for example, uses the old story when he wishes to praise Elizabeth and
her successor:

> Nor shall this peace sleep with her; but as when
> The bird of wonder dies, the maiden phoenix,
> Her ashes new-create another heir
> As great in admiration as herself,
> So shall she leave her blessedness to one—
> When heaven shall call her from this cloud of darkness—
> Who, from the sacred ashes of her honour,
> Shall star-like rise, as great in fame as she was,
> And so stand fix'd.]

I

I HAVE heard that far hence in the east is the noblest of lands,
famous among men. The face of the land is not to be found
across the world by many of the earth's dwellers, but by God's
might it is set afar off from evildoers. Lovely is all the land,

dowered with delights, with earth's sweetest scents; matchless is that water-land, noble its Maker, proud, rich in power; He created the country. There often to the blessed the delight of harmonies, the door of heaven is set open and revealed. That is a fair field, green forests spread beneath the skies. There neither rain, nor snow, nor the breath of frost, nor the blast of fire, nor the fall of hail, nor the dropping of rime, nor the heat of the sun, nor unbroken cold, nor warm weather, nor wintry shower shall do any hurt; but the land lies happy and unharmed. That noble land is abloom with flowers. No hills or mountains stand there steeply, nor do stone cliffs rise aloft, as here with us; nor are there valleys, or dales, or hill caves, mounds or rising ground; nor are there any rough slopes there at all. But the noble field is fruitful under the sky, blossoming in beauty. That radiant land is twelve fathoms higher (so wise sages in their wisdom tell us in their writings from hearsay) than any of the mountains, which here with us rise aloft in brightness under the stars.

Gentle is that plain of victory; the sunny grove gleams; pleasant is the forest. Fruits fall not, bright are the blooms; but the trees stand ever green as God bade them. Winter and summer alike the forest is hung with fruits; the leaves under the sky shall never wither away, nor the fire ever do them hurt, before a change comes over the world. When long ago the torrent of water, the sea flood whelmed all the world, the circuit of the earth, then by God's grace the noble field stood secure from the rush of wild waves, no whit harmed, happy, undefiled. Thus it shall bide in blossom till the coming of the fire, the judgment of God, when the graves, the tombs of men, shall be torn open. There is no foe in the land, nor weeping, nor woe, nor sign of grief, nor old age, nor sorrow, nor cruel death, nor loss of life, nor the coming of a hateful thing, nor sin, nor strife, nor sad grief, nor the struggle of poverty, nor lack of wealth, nor sorrow, nor sleep, nor heavy illness, nor wintry storm, nor change of weather fierce under the heavens; nor does hard frost with chill icicles beat upon anyone. Neither hail nor rime falls on the ground there; nor is there a windy cloud; nor does water come down there, driven by the gust; but there the streams, wondrously splendid, gush welling forth; they water the land with fair fountains; winsome waters from the midst of the forests, which spring ocean cold from the soil, sometimes go gloriously through the whole grove. It is the Lord's behest that the beautiful flowing water should cross that glorious land twelve times. The groves are hung with blossomings, with fair fruits; there the ornaments of the forest, holy under heaven, never fade; nor do the yellow fruits, the beauty of the trees, fall to the ground there; but the branches on the trees there are always splendidly laden, the fruit ever new. On the grassy plain green stands the brightness of groves, joyfully decked by the Holy One's power; the forest keeps its colour unfading. There the sacred fragrance fills that land of joy. That shall never suffer change till He who shaped it in the beginning bring the old, long-established work to an end.[1]

II

A bird wondrous fair, mighty in its wings, which is called the Phoenix, dwells in that wood. Alone there it holds its abode, its brave way of life; never shall death do it hurt in that pleasant place while the world endures. There it is said to gaze on the sun's going and to come face to face with God's candle, the gracious jewel, to watch eagerly till the noblest of heavenly bodies rises gleaming over the waves of the sea from the east, the ancient work of the Father, radiant sign of God, shining in its adornments. The stars are hidden, whelmed under the waves in the west, quenched in the dawn; and the dark night departs with its gloom. Then the bird, mighty in flight, proud of its pinions, gazes eagerly at the ocean, across the waters under the sky, till the light of the firmament comes gliding up from the east over the vast sea.

So the noble bird in its changeless beauty by the water-spring dwells by the surging streams. There the glorious creature bathes twelve times in the brook before the coming of the beacon, heaven's candle; and even as many times, at every bath, cold as the sea, it tastes the pleasant waters of the spring. Then after its sport in the water it rises proudly to a lofty tree, whence most easily it can see the movement in the east when the taper of the sky, the gleaming light, shines clearly over the tossing waters. The land is beautified, the world is made fair, when the glorious gem, most famed of heavenly bodies, passing over the sweep of the sea, pours light on the land throughout the world.

[1] The legend of an Earthly Paradise such as that described here is ancient and widespread. Compare, for instance, with this passage Genesis ii; *Odyssey*, Book vii; Dante's *Purgatory*, xxviii.

As soon as the sun towers high over the salt streams the grey bird goes in its brightness from the tree in the grove; swift in its wings, it flies aloft, pours forth harmony and song to the sky. Then so fair is the way of the bird, its heart uplifted, exulting in gladness, it sings a varied song with clear voice more wondrously than ever a son of man heard under the heavens since the mighty King, the Creator of glory, established the world, heaven and earth. The harmony of that song is sweeter and fairer than all music, and more pleasant than any melody. Neither trumpets, nor horns, nor the sound of the harp, nor the voice of any man on earth, nor the peal of the organ, nor the sweetness of song, nor the swan's plumage, nor any of the delights which God hath devised to gladden men in this dreary world can equal that outpouring. Thus it sings and chants, blissfully glad, till the sun has sunk in the southern sky. Then it is silent and falls to listening; it lifts up its head, bold, safe in thought; and thrice it shakes its feathers swift in flight; the bird is mute.

Ever it notes the hours twelve times day and night, as it is decreed, so that it, the dweller in the grove, may there possess the plain in gladness and enjoy happiness, life and delights, the beauties of the land, until it, the guardian of the forest grove, has lived for a thousand years of this life. Then aged, old in years, the grey-feathered one is weighed down; the glory of birds flees from the green earth, the blossoming land; and then seeks as its dwelling and home a vast tract in the world where no men live. There in its might it holds sway over the race of birds, supreme in the troop; and for a while it dwells in the wilderness with them. Then mighty in flight, swift in its pinions, pressed down by years, its goes flying westwards. Birds press round the noble one; each is intent to serve and follow the famous lord, until with a countless train it comes to the Syrians' land. There on a sudden the pure bird parts from them, so that it inhabits a desert place in the shade in a forest grove, covered and concealed from the throng of men. There in the wood it bides and dwells on a lofty tree firm-rooted, under the vault of heaven; men call the tree 'Phoenix' on earth from the name of the bird.[1] The glorious King, the Lord of mankind, has, I have heard, granted to the tree, that of all trees which tower aloft on the

---

[1] The Greek word φοῖνιξ means both palm-tree and phoenix. Confusion sometimes resulted. In Job xxix. 18 ('Then I said, I shall die in my nest, and I shall multiply my days as the sand'), the Hebrew word translated by *sand* also meant phoenix. Probably the author meant phoenix. In the Septuagint the word was translated by φοῖνιξ, and in the Vulgate this appears as *palma*.

earth this one is brightest in blossom. Nothing bitter may cruelly hurt it, but, ever guarded, it shall bide unscathed while the world endures.

III

When the wind is hushed and the weather is fair, and the jewel of heaven shines clear in its holiness, when the clouds are scattered, and the masses of water lie calm, when all storms are stilled under the sky, and the candle of the sky gleams from the south, and sheds light and warmth upon men, then it begins to build in the branches, to fashion its nest. Great eagerness has it, through the urging of its mind, to change old age for life, to lay hold on youth. Then far and near it gleans and gathers the sweetest things, pleasant plants and blossoms of the wood for its dwelling, every sweet odour of pleasant plants which the glorious King, the Father of all creatures, created upon the earth, sweetest under heaven, for the glory of mankind. It bears the bright treasure within the tree, where fair and beauteous the wild bird fashions its house in the wilderness on the tall tree, and dwells there itself in its lofty station, and in the leafy shade surrounds its body and wings on every side with sacred odours and the noblest blossoms of earth; it perches ready for flight. When the jewel of the sky, the sun in the summertime, shines most hotly above the shade, and goes its appointed course, o'er-looks all the world, then its house is heated by the cloudless heaven; the plants grow warm, the pleasant dwelling gives out sweet odours; then in the glow the bird is burnt with its nest in the fire's embrace. The pile is kindled; then flame enfolds the sad creature's dwelling; fiercely it hastens, the yellow flame consumes; and the Phoenix, aged with long years, is burnt; then fire falls on the frail body. The life, the spirit of the fated creature, is about to fare forth; then the funeral fire burns flesh and bone. Yet after due time life returns to it anew once more, when the ashes after the surging flame begin to draw together again, shrunk to a ball. When the brightest of nests, the abode of the valiant bird, is wholly destroyed by fire, its corpse has grown cold, its frame is shattered, and the burning dies away. Then out of the pile, in the ashes, the likeness of an apple is afterwards found. From it grows a worm, wondrous fair, as if it had been brought forth from eggs, bright from the shell. Then it grows up in the shade, so that at first it is like the eagle's young, a fair fledgling. Then yet further it happily flourishes, till in stature it is like an old eagle, and after that in rich array of plumage, brightly bedecked as it was in the beginning. Then its flesh is all fashioned anew, born again, set apart from sins. Somewhat as men at the harvest bring home for their sustenance the fruits of the earth, pleasant food, ere the coming of winter, at reaping-time, lest a downpour of rain destroy them under the clouds; therein they find benefit, the pleasure of feasting, when frost and snow cover the earth in winter garments with mighty power. From those fruits the wealth of men shall again spring forth by the nature of grain, which is first sown merely as a seed; then the sun's brightness, the symbol of life, in the spring brings forth worldly treasure, so that the fruits, the rich produce of the earth, are born again by their own nature. Thus the bird, grown old after years, renews its youth, clothed in flesh. It does not take food, meat on the earth, except that it eats a little honey-dew which often falls at midnight. Thereby the brave bird fosters its life, until once more it seeks its ancient abode, its own dwelling.

IV

When the bird, proud of its plumage, grows up among the plants, when its life is renewed, young, full of grace, then, swift in limb, from the dust it gathers its body, the remnant of the burning, which the fire destroyed before. Artfully it collects the bones, crumbled after the stress of the fire; and then puts together again bones and ashes, the leavings of the flame; and spreads with plants that spoil of death, richly arrayed. Then it is driven to seek its own home once more. Then with its feet it lays hold on the relics of the fire, clutches them with its claws; and joyously seeks again its home-land, sunny haunts, happy native country. All shall be made anew, its life and feathery dress, as it was in the beginning, when first victorious God placed it in the noble plain. It brings there its own bones, the ashes too, which the surge of fire embraced before on the funeral pile.

Then the valiant bird buries the bones and ashes all together in that water-land. The sign of the sun is renewed for him, when the light of the sky, brightest of jewels, the best of noble stars, shines up from the east over the sea. The bird is ever fair of hue, bright with varied shades in front round the breast;

green is its head behind, wondrously mingled, blended with purple. Then the tail is beautifully divided, part brown, part crimson, part artfully speckled with white spots. The wings are white at the tip and the neck green, downward and upward; and the beak gleams like glass or a jewel; bright are its jaws, within and without. Strong is the quality of its eye and in hue like a stone, a bright gem, when by the craft of smiths it is set in a golden vessel. About its neck like the round of the sun is the brightest of rings woven of feathers. Of rare beauty is the belly beneath, wondrous fair, bright and gleaming. The covering above, over the bird's back, is joined together with rich array. The legs and yellow feet are overgrown with scales. The bird is wholly peerless in aspect, like a peacock of fair growth, of which writings speak. It is not sluggish nor slothful, dull nor torpid as some birds who wing their way slowly through the air, but it is speedy and swift and very alert, fair and winsome, and gloriously marked. Eternal is the Lord who grants it that bliss.

Then it departs from this country to seek the plains, its ancient abode. As the bird flies, it is seen by people, by many men throughout the world. Then they assemble in troops from south and north, from east and west; they come from far and near in hosts where they behold the Creator's grace fairly manifest in that bird, as the King of victories at the beginning bestowed a rare nature upon it, adornments fair beyond the race of birds. Then men throughout the earth marvel at its beauty and stature; and their writings set it forth. They shape it in marble with their hands, whenever the day and the hour reveal to men the splendours of the bird swift in flight.

Then the race of birds press round on all sides in bands; they come from distant ways; they praise in their song, they exalt the brave bird with loud voices; and thus they circle that sacred bird with a ring, while they fly in the air. The Phoenix is in the midst, thronged round by hosts. The people behold; they gaze in wonder at how the faithful band, flock after flock, honour the wild bird, mightily proclaim it and make it known for king, how they bring the loved prince of the people, the noble one, with joy to his dwelling, until the solitary bird, swift of wing, flies off, so that the melodious band cannot follow it. Then the delight of men seeks its homeland away from this part of earth.

V

Thus the blessed bird after the hour of death visits once more its old country, the fair land. Sad at heart, the birds return from the warrior again to their dwelling. Then the noble creature is young in its haunts. Only God, the Almighty King, knows what its sex is, female or male; none of mankind knows, save God alone, how wondrous are the rulings, the fair decree of old, concerning that bird's birth. There the blessed one in the forest groves may take pleasure in its abode, in the gushing streams; it may dwell in the plain till a thousand years have passed. Then comes the end of its life; the funeral pile covers it, the kindled fire. Yet, strangely stirred, it returns wondrously to life. Wherefore it recks not of languishing death, the sore torment of dying, for it knows that after the stress of the fire new life, existence after death, is always its portion, when quickly it is transformed in shape of a bird, grows young again once more from the ashes under the sheltering sky. In itself it is both son and dear father, and ever also the heir again of its old relics. The mighty Prince of mankind granted that it should so wondrously become again the same that erstwhile it was, clothed with feathers, though fire take it off.

Thus each of the blessed makes choice for himself through dark death of eternal life after tribulation, so that after his lifetime he may enjoy God's grace in lasting joys; and ever afterwards as reward for his deeds dwell in that world. The nature of this bird is very like the chosen ones, the followers of Christ. It shows forth unto men how they with the Father's help may possess in this time of danger bright joy under heaven, and in the home on high gain noble bliss. We have learned that the Almighty created man and woman by His marvellous might; and then He set them in the fairest of earth's places, which the sons of men call Paradise. They lacked no happiness there in that new delight, whilst they were willing to observe the Eternal One's behest, the command of the Holy One. There hatred did them hurt, the ancient foe's malice, who offered them food, fruit of the tree, so that in their folly they both ate of the apple; against God's command they tasted what was forbidden. Then bitter sorrow came upon them after the eating, and on their children also; a sorry feast was that for their sons and daughters; their greedy teeth were grievous unto them. Retribution followed guilt; they bore the wrath of God, bitter dire grief;

and their children since have suffered sorrow because they ate that food against the Eternal One's command.   Therefore they were destined, heavy at heart, to forsake their pleasant abode because of the serpent's hate.   Grievously it beguiled our parents then in past days with deceitful spirit, so that far from thence in this valley of death they sought their abode, a more drear dwelling.   From them the better life was hidden by darkness, and the holy ground fast closed by the fiend's cunning for many years, until the King of glory, the Joy of mankind, the Consoler of the weary and our only Hope opened it once more for the holy by His coming hither.

VI

Like unto that, by what scholars tell us in words and writings set forth, is this bird's way of life, when, grown old, it forsakes its dwelling and home-land and is stricken with age.   Weary-hearted, weighed down with years, it departs to where it finds the lofty shelter of the forest in which with twigs and choicest herbs it fashions a new abode, a nest in the grove.   Great eagerness has it, that, young once again, it may lay hold on life after death after the fire's blast, be renewed in youth, and seek its old home, its sunny haunts, after its fiery bath.   So those who went before us, our parents, turned their backs on the fair plain and the glorious abode in its beauty, went a far journey into the power of the wicked, where foes, wretched creatures, often did them hurt.   Yet there were many who under the heavens obeyed the Lord well in holy ways, in glorious deeds, so that God, the great King of heaven, was gracious in heart unto them.   That is the high tree in which now His holy ones have their dwelling; none of the old foes can do them any hurt there with venom, with show of malice in this perilous time.   There by glorious deeds God's warrior fashions himself a nest against every onset when he gives alms to the poor, to those bereft of good things, and calls God the Father to aid him; he hastens forth from this fleeting life, quenches sins, black deeds of evil, holds God's law, unafraid in his heart; and seeks prayer with pure thoughts, and bows his knee in piety to the ground, shuns every evil, terrible guilt, through fear of God.   Glad at heart he longs to achieve the greatest number of good deeds; God, the Ruler of victories, the Lord of hosts, is his guardian at all times.   These are the herbs, the fruits of plants, which the wild bird gathers far and wide under the sky for its dwelling, where it fashions its nest wondrously firm against every onset.

So now in their habitations the warriors of God work His will with heart and might, attempt glorious deeds; the eternal Almighty will grant them blessed guerdon for that. From those plants a dwelling-place shall be fashioned in the heavenly city as a reward for their deeds, because day and night with fervent minds they let not holy counsel grow cold in their hearts; they praise the Lord with pure faith; they choose their Loved One rather than worldly wealth; nor does the hope of long possessing this fleeting life bring joy unto them. Thus a worthy man by his zeal shall earn joy everlasting, a heavenly home with the King on high, till the end of his days comes, when death, the ravenous foeman, mighty in weapons, lays hold on the life of every man, and swiftly sends the frail bodies, bereft of their souls, into the earth's embrace, where for long they shall be covered with the ground till the coming of the fire. Then a great host of mankind shall be gathered together; the Father of angels, the true King of victory, the Lord of hosts, will hold assembly, will judge according to right. Then shall all men on earth be raised up, as the mighty King, the Prince of angels, the Saviour of souls, sends forth His behest with the blast of the trumpet over the wide world. Dark death shall be done with for the blessed by the might of the Lord. They shall go in glory, press forward in throngs, when this world, because of its guilt, burns in fire, consumed by the flame. Everyone shall feel fear in his heart when the fire ruins the fleeting riches of the land, and the flame wholly devours the treasures of earth, greedily clutches the apple-shaped gold, ravenously swallows the wealth of the land. Then in that revealing time the fair and gladsome meaning of this bird shall be made plain to men when the Lord shall raise up all in their graves, gather the bones, the limbs, and the body also and the spirit of life, before Christ's knee. Gloriously the King, the beauteous Jewel of heaven, shines on the holy from His high throne. Well shall it be for him who in that dread time may please God.

VII

Then will bodies cleansed from sins move with glad hearts; souls will turn to the frames which held them, when the fire mounts high to heaven. The dread flame will be hot for many, when everyone, righteous and sinful, the soul with the body, from his earthy grave shall seek God's judgment, stricken with fear. The fire shall march onward; it shall consume sins. There the blessed after their time of suffering shall be clothed with their works, their own deeds. These noble ones are the pleasant plants wherewith that wild bird girdles its own nest without, so that on a sudden it burns with fire, is consumed under the sun, and itself therewith; and then after the flame it once more renews its life. So everyone of mankind clothed in flesh shall be beautiful and renewed in youth, who of his own will here brings it to pass that the King of heaven in His might will be merciful at that meeting, when holy spirits shall shout aloud and righteous souls shall lift up a song, and the pure and chosen praise the King's majesty; voice after voice shall rise to heaven with the fragrance of their good deeds.

Then shall the souls of men be tested, brightly cleansed by the burning fire. Let none of the race of men think that I make my song, write my poetry, of false words! Hearken to the wisdom of Job's songs. By the inspiration of his spirit, stirred in his breast, gloriously honoured, he boldly spoke and uttered these words:[1] 'I scorn not in the thoughts of my heart to choose a bed of death in my nest, to go wretched hence, a man sore wearied, on the long journey, covered with clay, into the clasp of earth, mourning my past deeds; and then after death by grace of God after resurrection I may be able like the bird Phoenix to possess life anew, delights with God, where the precious company praise the Loved One. Never shall I be able to see the end of that life, of light and mercies. Though my flesh fall to decay in its earthy dwelling, a delight to the worms, yet the God of hosts will deliver my soul after death, and rouse it to glory; the hope of that never fails in my heart, for I hold firm to a constant joy in the Prince of angels.'

Thus in days long past the wise man, sage in heart, the prophet of God, sang of his resurrection into life everlasting, so that we might more clearly perceive the glorious token that the bright bird offers in its burning. After the fire it gathers the remnants of the bones, the ashes, and embers all together. Then the bird brings them in its feet to the Lord's abode, towards the sun, where afterwards they dwell many years, shaped anew in stature, wholly young again. There in that land none threaten them with harm. So now after death by

[1] The passage which follows is a paraphrase of Job xxix. 18 and xix. 25, 26. For the reference to the phoenix in Job, see the preceding note (p. 242).

the might of God souls shall set forth with the body, fairly adorned, like unto that bird, in joy, with fragrant perfumes, where the true sun shines in its beauty over the hosts in the heavenly city.

VIII

Then high above the vaults of the sky the Saviour Christ shall shine on the righteous. Fair birds shall follow Him born again in beauty, gladly exulting in that happy home, chosen spirits, for ever and ever. There the hostile, shameless fiend cannot with malice evilly hurt them, but there for ever they will live, robed in light, as the bird Phoenix, in God's safe keeping, beauteous in glory. The works of each one shall gleam brightly in that glad abode before the face of the Lord everlasting, ever in peace, like the sun. There a radiant crown wondrously fashioned of precious stones shall rise over the head of each of the blessed. The heads shall gleam, gloriously covered; a princely diadem shall adorn with rare beauty each of the righteous brightly in that life, where lasting joy, eternal and renewed, never passes away; but girt round with glory they shall dwell in beauty amid fair adornments, with the Father of angels. No sorrow shall fall on them in those abodes, no misery, or poverty, or troubled days, hot hunger nor bitter thirst, suffering nor old age; the excellent King shall grant them every good thing. There the band of spirits shall praise the Saviour and proclaim the power of the heavenly King, chant God's praise. The peaceful troop shall make melody with loudest outburst, clear-sounding round the holy throne of God. Gladly the worthy ones with the angels shall bless the best of Princes in unison, thus:

'Peace be to Thee, true God, and skill of wisdom, and thanks be to Thee, who sittest in glory, for all the good gifts granted of late! Great beyond measure is the strength of Thy might, exalted and holy. Father almighty, Majesty of majesties, the heavens are beautifully filled with Thy glory, above with the angels and also on earth. Thou who didst shape the beginnings of things, protect us! Thou art the Father almighty, the Lord of heavens on high.'

Thus speak the doers of right, purified of evil, in the glorious city; the company of the righteous declare His Majesty, sing the Saviour's praise in heaven, to whom alone belongs eternal honour henceforth without end. There was never origin for Him, nor a beginning of His blessedness, though in the state of a child He was born here in the world. Yet the greatness of His power, glory indestructible, remained in its holiness high above the heavens, though He was doomed to suffer on the cross the agony of death, grievous torment. On the third day after the death of His body He received life again by the help of the Father. Thus does the Phoenix, young in its dwelling, betoken the power of the Son of God, when from its ashes it rises again to the life of life, strong in its limbs. Thus the Saviour brought us succour, life without end, by the death of His body. Thus the bird loads its two wings with sweet and pleasant plants, with fair fruits of the earth, when it is driven forth. These are the words, the utterance of holy men—as the Scriptures tell us—whose hearts are urged on to heaven, to the God of mercy, to the joy of joys. Then to God, to the Lord, as an offering, they bring the fragrant perfume of their words and deeds into that glorious realm, into that pure life. Praise be to Him for ever and ever and fullness of glory, honour, and power in the heavenly kingdom on high. He is rightly King of the world and of heaven, girt round with glory in the fair city.

The Author of light has granted us that here we may earn, win by good deeds, delights in heaven. There we may seek out the most spacious realms and sit in lofty seats, live in the joy of light and peace, dwell in gracious abodes of gladness, enjoy happy days, ever behold the Prince of victory merciful and mild, and, happy among the angels, sing His praise with endless worship. Alleluia.

PHYSIOLOGUS

[These poems on the panther and the whale (and also a fragmentary poem on a bird—perhaps a partridge) follow *The Phoenix* in the *Exeter Book*, and resemble it in their use of natural history for purposes of moral instruction. These poems belong to a very popular branch of medieval literature. The earliest form of these accounts of birds and beasts was probably in Greek, but the original Greek *Physiologus* or *Bestiary*, as it is usually called, has been lost. There are versions in many languages. The work probably originated in Egypt, and was the result of a genuine, if not very critical, interest in the facts and marvels of nature. The allegorical applications were, it would seem, added later. The excuse for comparing the panther to Christ was found in Hosea v. 14, where the Septuagint version reads: 'I am become as a panther to Ephraim.' The whale is called Fastitocalon in the English poem. In earlier versions the creature was a turtle and was named Aspidochelone. In course of time the name became corrupted, and the whale replaced the turtle. The rough surface of the animal, mentioned in the poem, better suits the turtle. These strange old beliefs about birds and beasts are referred to by some Elizabethan and later writers. Dryden reminds us that

> 'The Panther's breath was ever fam'd for sweet';

and Milton compares the fallen Satan to

> 'that sea beast
> Leviathan, which God of all his works
> Created hugest that swim the ocean stream.
> Him, haply slumbering on the Norway foam,
> The pilot of some small night-foundered skiff,
> Deeming some island, oft, as seamen tell,
> Moors by his side under the lee, while night
> Invests the sea, and wished morn delays.'

Sindbad's adventure on the whale island will, of course, be remembered.]

THE PANTHER

Many are the kinds of creatures beyond count throughout the world, of whom we cannot rightly tell the lineage or know the number, so widely are the numerous multitudes of birds and beasts which move on the earth scattered through the world, even as the water, the roaring sea, the swell of the salt waves, girds this glorious earth. We heard tell of the strange nature of one of the beasts, that he bides in distant lands, in a dwelling very famous among men, holds his domain amid the mountain caves. That beast is called Panther by name, as the sons of men, men of wisdom, set forth in writings concerning that solitary wanderer. He is a friend to all, bounteous in kindness, except to one monster, with whom he ever lives in hostility by reason of all the evils which he can effect. That is a strange animal, wondrously beautiful with all colours. As men, holy men, say that Joseph's coat was brilliant with colours of every hue, of which each shone wholly more bright and beautiful than the other among the children of men; so the animal's hue in its brilliance shines wondrously with all bright and beautiful colours, so that each flashes more marvellous, more excellent and fair, than the others, with always rarer beauty.

He has a strange nature, mild and slow to wrath. He is gentle, loving, and kind; he will not work any harm on anyone, except on the venomous monster, his ancient foe, of whom I spoke before. Ever pleased with plenty when he receives food, he seeks rest after the feasting, a hidden place in the mountain caves; there the mighty warrior for the space of three nights slumbers at rest, sunk in sleep. Then valiant, magnified in strength, he rises up on the third day quickly from sleep; a melodious sound comes forth, sweetest of songs from the beast's mouth. After the voice a perfume issues forth from the place, an odour more pleasant, sweeter, and stronger than all smells, than the flowers and blossoms of plants, more excellent than all the adornments of earth. Then from cities and royal seats and from halls many bands of men go on earth's pathways with hosts of people; javelin-fighters in troops, made ready in haste—animals also—after the voice has spoken go to the smell.

Thus the Lord God, the Ruler of joys, is benignant to all other creatures, to every man, except one monster, the author of venomous evil; that is the ancient fiend whom He bound in the abyss of torments, fettered with fiery chains, laid under dire constraint;[1] and on the third day He rose from the grave after He, the Prince of angels, the Bestower of victories, had suffered death for us for three nights. That was a sweet smell, fair and pleasant throughout the whole world. Then righteous men through the whole sweep of earth's plains hastened in hosts on every side to the perfume. Thus spoke St Paul in his wisdom: 'Manifold are the unstinted good things in the world which the Father almighty and the sole Hope of all creatures above and below bestows on us as a gift and for the fostering of life.' That is an excellent perfume.

---

[1] This refers to Christ's descent into hell between the Crucifixion and the Ascension.

THE WHALE

Now by my wit I will also speak in a poem, a song, about a kind of fish, about the mighty whale. He to our sorrow is often found dangerous and fierce to all seafaring men. The name Fastitocalon is given him, the floater on ocean streams. His form is like a rough stone, as if the greatest of seaweeds, girt by sand-banks, were heaving by the water's shore, so that seafarers suppose they behold some island with their eyes; and then they fasten the high-prowed ships with cables to the false land, tie the sea steeds at the water's edge, and then undaunted go up into that island. The ships remain fast by the shore, encompassed by water. Then, wearied out, the sailors encamp, look not for danger. On the island they kindle fire, build a great blaze; the men, worn out, are in gladness, longing for rest. When he, skilled in treachery, feels that the voyagers are set firmly upon him, are encamped, rejoicing in the clear weather, then suddenly the ocean creature sinks down with his prey into the salt wave, seeks the depths, and then delivers the ships and the men to drown in the hall of death.

Such is the wont of demons, the way of devils, that by secret power they betray men by their behaviour and persuade them to the ruin of fair deeds, lure them as they will, so that they grievously seek solace from foes, till they make firm choice to dwell with the faithless one. When the foe, false and malicious, knows from the quick torment that any men are firm fixed on his round form, he afterwards by cunning sleight slays them in their pride and wretchedness, who work his will here in wickedness. Hidden by a helmet which makes him unseen, he, void of virtues, suddenly seeks hell with them, the bottomless surge under the misty gloom; even as the mighty whale who whelms the seafarers and ships.

He, the proud voyager, has another habit, yet more wondrous. When on the ocean hunger harries him, and the creature feels a craving for food, then the warden of the ocean opens his mouth, his wide lips. A pleasant smell comes from within, so that other kinds of fish are betrayed thereby; they swim swiftly to where the sweet smell issues forth. They enter there in a thoughtless throng, till the wide jaw is filled. Then suddenly the fierce jaws snap together, enclosing the plunder. Thus is it for every man who in this fleeting time most often looks heedlessly upon his life; he lets himself be snared by a sweet smell, a false desire, so that is he guilty of sins against the King of glory.   After death the cursed one opens hell for them who, unmindful, have evilly followed the false joys of the flesh.   When the malicious one, cunning in evil, has brought them in that fastness to the lake of fire, those who, loaded with sins, call unto him, and who formerly in their life-days eagerly hearkened unto his counsels, then he snaps his fierce jaws firmly together after the slaughter, the doors of hell.   They who enter there can never have return nor escape nor passage out any more than the fish of the sea can leave the whale's grasp.   Wherefore certainly it is best for us in haste to please well the King of glory, Lord of lords, and ever fight against fiends by words and deeds, so that we may see the King of glory.   Let us ever seek grace and salvation from Him in this transitory time, so that for ever and ever we may enjoy heaven in glory with One so beloved.

GUTHLAC

[St Guthlac (673?–714) was of Mercian stock. After a military youth he became a monk at the age of twenty-four, and after some time spent in devotion and study he felt the desire to become a hermit. In 699 he took up his abode at Croyland in the desolate fen country of Lincolnshire, where he remained for fifteen years. He died in Easter week, 714 or 715, and according to his wish, was buried in his own little church. The body was later placed in a shrine, and over it Æthelbald, who became King of Mercia in 716, raised the building which afterwards became Croyland Abbey.

There are two poems in Old English on the life of Guthlac. *Guthlac* A was probably written during the lifetime of the saint or shortly after his death. It is probably based on oral tradition. *Guthlac* B follows the Latin *Vita Guthlaci* by Felix of Croyland.]

A

I

THERE are many ranks of men throughout the world under heaven who are numbered among the holy; accordingly we can rightly belong to any of them if we will observe the holy commands. A wise man may now enjoy the happiness of fortunate times, and yet have wishes for his spirit's course hereafter. The world is troubled, the love of Christ grows cold; many tribulations have arisen throughout the world, as long ago God's messengers declared in words and set it all forth by prophecy as now it comes to pass.

The world's abundance of all sorts grows old and all kinds of produce lose their beauty: the latter time of all seeds is less in power. Wherefore man need not look for recovery for this world, that it shall bring us fair delight to offset the afflictions which we now endure, before all the creatures which in six days He established shall come to an end, which now bring forth their kinds great and small under the heavens. This world is divided in parts. The Lord sees where they dwell who keep His law; every day He beholds the laws which He established by His own word fade and depart from the justice of the world. He shall find many; but few shall be chosen.

Some wish to bear the fame of good men by words, and perform not the works; earthly wealth, which shall depart from every earth-dweller, is more to them than that life everlasting, the highest of joys. Wherefore now they despise the hearts of the holy men who fix their thoughts on heaven; they know that that land remains for ever for all that host who serve God throughout the world, and they desire to merit that precious home. Thus these worldly treasures shall be bartered for that glorious possession, when they over whose heads inclines the fear of God yearn for that. They are chastened by that highest majesty; they pass this life in obedience to commandments, and wish and hope for the better one afterwards. They purchase glory, give alms, solace the poor, are generous of their true treasures, are kindly with gifts to those who own less, serve the Lord daily. He beholds their deeds.

Some dwell in deserts; seek and inhabit of their own accord homes in dark places; they wait for the heavenly home. Often he who grudges them life brings hateful fear upon them, shows them terror, at times empty splendour; he, the crafty slayer, has power over both; he persecutes lone-dwellers. Angels stand before them ready with the weapons of the spirit; they forget not to give aid; they protect the lives of holy men; they know their gladness is with God. These are the tried warriors who serve the King who never withholds the reward from them who are faithful in love.

II

Now we can tell what was lately made known to us by means of holy men, how Guthlac governed his heart according to the will of God, rejected all evil, earthly excellence, turned his thoughts on high to his home in heaven. He had joy in that, after He who prepares the path of life for souls had shed light upon him and given him divine grace, so that he went to dwell alone in a mountain abode, and humbly gave all his wealth to God, which in youth, it is said, he devoted to the joys of the world. A holy guardian from heaven beheld him, who earnestly strengthened that pure heart in spiritual good.

Lo! we have often heard that the holy man in his youth loved many dangerous things. The time was to come, however, in God's judgment, when He should cause an angel to appear to Guthlac, so that his sinful lusts should abate. The time was drawing near; two guardians kept watch about him, the angel of the Lord and the dread spirit, who strove together. Many times they gave teachings to his mind no whit alike; the one told him that all earthly things beneath the sky were fleeting, and praised the lasting possessions in heaven where the souls of saints enjoy the delights of the Lord in triumphant glory; He eagerly grants reward for their deeds to them who will gratefully receive His gifts and forsake the world more utterly than the life everlasting. The other urged him to seek at night a band of thieves and by boldness to strive for the world, as outcasts do, who reck not for the life of the man who brings plunder to their hands, if by that they may win booty.

Thus they urged him on both sides until the Lord of hosts put an end to the strife to the glory of the angel. The fiend was put to flight; afterwards the Comforter remained to aid Guthlac, loved him and taught him with ever more earnestness, so that the delights of the land grew dear to him, the dwelling on the mountain. Often dread came there, terrible and strange, the malice of old foes mighty in cunning. They appeared before him; and there aforetime they had set up many abodes. Thence they departed, far-wandering, shorn of glory, flying in the air. That spot was hidden from men, until the Lord revealed the hill in the grove, when the builder came who raised a sacred abode there, not because he cared for life's unstable wealth, but that he might protect that land fairly for God, when he, Christ's warrior, vanquished the fiend. He was tempted in the times of men who remember, who still honour him for his spiritual wonders and keep up the fame of his wisdom that the holy servant won by his valour when he dwelt alone in the secret place, where he uttered and exalted the praise of God. Often in speech he declared God's messages to those who loved the ways of the martyrs, when the spirit had revealed to him the wisdom of life, so that he denied his body pleasures and worldly joys, soft seats and days of feasting, also idle delights of the eyes, vainglorious dress. The fear of God was too much in his mind for him gladly to receive human glory.

III

Guthlac was good; he bore divine joy in his soul; he attained the salvation of eternal life. The angel was near him, a faithful protector to him, who with a few others dwelt in the waste land. He became an example there to many in Britain, when, bold in fight, the blessed warrior went up the mountain; earnestly he girt himself with spiritual weapons. He blessed the ground; first he raised up the cross of Christ as his help. There the warrior overcame many perils. Many of God's servants became active there; wherefore we ascribe Guthlac's precious lot to God. He gave him victory and artful wisdom, mighty protection, when the multitude of fiends came with dangerous shooting to make onslaught. In their envy they could not leave him, but brought many temptations against Guthlac's spirit. Help was near him; the angel upheld him mightily, when they in anger threatened him with dread surge of fire, stood about him in troops. They said that he must needs burn on the mountain and the flame consume his body, that his sufferings would prove wholly a sorrow to his kinsmen, if he himself would seek no more the bliss of men afar from strife, and joyfully observe the claims of kin with better skill among mankind, and let striving be.

Thus he who spoke for the whole host of fiends angered him. Guthlac's soul was not afraid thereof, but God gave him strength against fear, so that the guilty band of the old enemy suffered shame. The evildoers were full of rage; they said that Guthlac alone, besides God, had wrought them the greatest of sufferings when from pride he seized on the mountains, where aforetime they, hapless foes, were permitted to have their abode at times after torments, when weary from wanderings they came to rest for a space; they enjoyed the quiet which was granted to them for a little while.

The secret spot, empty and desert, uninhabited, stood in God's mind; it awaited the coming of a better guardian. Therefore the old enemies felt terror, for they must now endure misery constantly; they may not enjoy their abode on earth, nor does the air lull them for the rest of their limbs; but, unprotected, they lack homes. Sorrowfully they lament; they long for death; wish that God by the stroke of death would put an end to their sufferings.

They could not injure Guthlac's soul, nor by a hard blow part his soul from his body, but with cunning lies they raised up tribulations. They ceased from laughter; they grieved in sorrow when the stronger guardian vanquished them in the field. The exiles were forced, sorrowing, to yield up the green mountains. Yet still God's foes uttered insults against him, promised verily that he should suffer death if longer he awaited a sterner encounter, when they should come with a greater host who grieved little for his life.

Guthlac answered them; he said they had no cause to boast of their deeds against the might of God: 'Though ye promise me death, He who governs your distresses will save me from onslaughts.   God alone is almighty; He can easily guard me; He will protect my life.   I will tell you many truths; unaided, I can hold this spot against you without difficulty.   I am not so destitute, as I stand before you, with no band of men; but a greater share of divine mysteries dwells and grows within me which gives me support.   I shall easily build here house and shelter for myself alone.   My teaching comes from heaven; wherefore I little doubt that an angel is leading me to fair success in words and deeds.   Go now, accursed, disheartened, from this place whereon ye stand; flee afar off.   I desire to gain security from God; my spirit shall not fall into error with you, but God's hand shall mightily guard me.   Here shall my earthly dwelling be, no longer yours.'

IV

Then clamour was raised.   The outcasts stood about the mount in hosts; shouting arose, the cry of the woeful; many spokesmen of the fiends called out, gloried in their sins:

'Often we have seen between the seas the customs of people, the violence of proud men, who led their life amid change; we have not found throughout the world greater pride in any man. Thou dost declare thou wilt wrest our abode from us; thou art God's pauper!   Whereon wilt thou live, though thou hold the land?   No one will sustain thee here with food; hunger and thirst will be hard foes unto thee, if thou goest alone from thy land like the wild beasts; that is a mad venture!   Give up this spot!   No one can give thee better counsel than all this host. We will be kindly unto thee, if thou wilt hearken unto us, or again we will seek thee in thy unreadiness with a greater host, so that no one will need to lay hands upon thee, nor thy body to fall by the strokes of weapons.   We can destroy this dwelling with our feet; the people will press in with troops of horses and with armies.   They will be angry, who will lay thee low; they will trample and tear thee and vent their wrath, bear thee off leaving tracks of blood, if thou dost resolve to await us.   We shall assail thee with onslaughts.   Crave refuge; go where thou mayest look for friends, if thou hast any care for thy life.'

Guthlac was ready; God made him strong in answer and in

courage. He changed not for their words, but proclaimed sorrow for his foes; well he knew the truth:

'Wide is this wilderness, many the places of exile, hidden abodes of hapless spirits; faithless are they who abide in these dwellings. Though ye summon out all of them, and also set up opposition, ye shall make a vain venture with your angry persecution: I purpose not to bear a sword, a worldly weapon, against you with wrathful hand; nor shall this ground be taken for God by bloodshed. But I purpose to please my Christ by an offering more precious! Now that I have ascended this land ye have offered me with vain words many dwellings. My heart is neither frightened nor fearful, but He who governs the works of all mighty things holds me safe above mankind. There is nothing I prize which I look for from you, nor can ye do me any hurt. I am the servant of God; often He comforts me by an angel. Wherefore unsatisfied longings come upon me but little, or cause me sorrow, now the divine Protector guards me; my hope is with God. Nor do I care for worldly wealth, nor desire great possessions with my heart; but every day by the hand of man God supplies my needs.'

Thus did he, who stood against many, bear himself proudly; the glorious warrior, nobly upheld by the strength of angels. Thence the host of fiends all departed. Nor was it for long space that they purposed to yield to Guthlac.

He had strength and humility; he abode on the mountain, had pleasure in his dwelling; forsook the desires of fleeting joys. He did not shut himself off from mercy towards men, but prayed for the weal of every soul, when in the desert he laid his head on the ground. His heart was kindled with a glad spirit from heaven. Often he pondered—an angel was near him—how his body might have least to do with the joys of this world. He failed not in faith by fear of the wretched creatures, nor did he neglect the time when he should toil for his Lord so that slumbers or sluggish mind robbed him of vigour at his rising up.

Thus shall a warrior ever fight for God in his heart and often hold his spirit in fear of him who is eager to persecute every soul, when he may bind it. They always found Guthlac firm in God's will, when they who dwelt in the hidden haunts came flying fiercely by darkness of night to find whether his joy in the land was lessened. Fain were they that a craving for human love should come upon his heart, that he should depart again to his own land. That was not his intent, when the angel greeted him most earnestly in the wilderness and gave him grace, so that no desire should keep him from God's will, but he dwelt in his Teacher's keeping.   Often he uttered speech:

'Verily it behoves him, whom the Holy Spirit guides at will and whose work He strengthens, whom He invites with gentle words, to whom He promises rest after life, to hearken to his Leader's teachings, nor let the old foe turn his heart again from God.   How shall my spirit come to safety unless I yield God an obedient mind so that the thoughts of the heart . . .[1] that soon or late an end shall come to your power of afflicting me wondrous sore.   Nor can my body keep out death from this fleeting life, but it shall perish as all this earth on which I stand here. Though ye with hostile thoughts attack my flesh with surging fire, with greedy flame, ye shall never turn me from these words, whilst my understanding lasts.   Though ye torment it with pains, ye may not touch my soul, but ye will bring it to a better state.   Wherefore I will endure what my God gives me for my portion.   Death gives me no grief; though both my bones and blood should turn to earth, the undying part of me will pass into bliss, where it shall enjoy a fair dwelling.   The abode on this mountain is not more excellent nor greater than serves for a man who daily in tribulations performs the will of God.   Nor shall the Lord's servant love greater worldly wealth in his heart than is fit measure for him alone, so that he may sustain his body.'

Then again as before the malice and hostility of the ancient fiends was aroused.   A second clamour resounded with no slight noise, when the cry of the sad spirits rose aloft.   Ever the praise of Christ grew and dwelt in Guthlac's good heart and the God of hosts guarded him on earth, as He keeps every living being safe when the higher spirit is strong in virtue.   He was one of those; he strove not for the world, but he set the joys of his heart in heaven on high.   Who was greater than he, that single warrior and champion, made manifest to our days, so that for his sake Christ showed more wonders in the world?

V

He fended him against the horrible attacks of foes, of wretched spirits.   They were fiercely eager to attack him with greedy clutches.   God willed it not that his soul should suffer that agony in his body; yet He granted that they should lay hands upon him, and that peace should be kept with them.

[1] Gap in the manuscript.

Then they raised him high in the air, gave him powers greater
than mankind, so that before his eyes he saw all the doings of
men in monasteries under the sway of holy guardians who lust-
fully devote their lives to vain possessions and riches, splendid
robes, as is the wont of youth, where the fear of the Lord is not
felt.   The fiends had there no cause to rejoice, but their success,
which for a short space was granted unto them, they quickly
reaped, so that they could no longer afflict his body with tor-
ments; nor did he receive any hurt from what they had done to
injure him.   They brought him then from the air to the dearest
dwelling on earth, so that once more he mounted the hill in the
grove.   The slayers lamented; they mourned in grief that a son
of man should o'erwhelm them in miseries, and should come
alone, so poor, bringing tribulations on them, if they could not
wreak vengeance on him with heavier afflictions.   Guthlac set
his hope in heaven, trusted in salvation; he had survived the
onset of the fiends.   The first temptation of the wretched spirits
was vanquished.   The warrior abode on the mountain in glad-
ness; his happiness was with God.   It seemed to his heart that
he was blessed among mankind, who guarded his one life, so that
the fiend's hand should do it no hurt at the end of all when God's
decree brought him to death.   Yet revilers, remembering their
afflictions, still promised miseries unto him with bitter speeches
of anger.   Grace was made manifest when God rewarded
Guthlac's valour with mercies, because he had striven unaided.
The accursed spirit spoke unto him in words:

'We had not needed to torment thee thus hard, if thou hadst
been willing to hearken promptly to the counsels of friends,
when thou didst first come to this struggle, hapless and
wretched; when thou didst vow that the holy Spirit would easily
shield thee from sufferings, because of the token which turned
the hand of man from thy noble face.   Many live in that guise,
given over to guilty deeds; they have nothing to do with God,
but they gladly delight their bodies with pleasant foods.   Thus
do ye pay honour to God with foolish rejoicing.   Much do ye
hide from men which ye think in your heart; your acts are not
secret, though ye do them by stealth.   We took thee up in the
air, removed from thee the pleasures of earth, wished that thou
thyself shouldst see that we told thee the truth.   Thou hast been
put to all this torment because thou couldst not turn it aside.'

Then it had come to pass that God wished to give him a
reward after his sufferings, because he had welcomed martyr-
dom in his heart.   He bestowed on him wisdom in the thoughts

of his heart, a steadfast mind. Mightily upheld, he made a stand against many of his ancient foes, told them to their sorrow that they must needs give up the green plain in defeat:

'Ye are scattered. Guilt rests upon you. Ye cannot pray God for any good thing, nor humbly seek mercy. Though for a little space He allowed you to have power over me, ye would not receive that patiently, but angrily raised me up so that from the air I could see the buildings of countries. The light of the sky was revealed to me in its radiance, though I suffered grief. Ye counted it shame to me that I lightly regarded the loose rules and wild hearts of young men in God's temples. Ye wished thereby to mock the praise of the saints, sought out the worse, and judged not the better according to their deeds. Nevertheless they shall not be hidden. I will tell you the truth now. God created youth and the joy of men; they cannot in their first zest have the ways of old age, but they delight in the pleasures of the world, till length of years comes upon their youth, so that the spirit loves the appearance and presence of an elder age, which in seemly fashion many throughout the world conform to in their ways: men display wisdom to the people, leave pride, when the spirit flees from the lasciviousness of youth. Ye do not distinguish that, but ye tell of the sins of the guilty; ye wish not to celebrate the spirit and virtue of righteous men; ye rejoice in sins; ye look not for solace that ye may win relief from these exiled wanderings. Often ye are among thieves; punishment for that comes from heaven. Then He sends me, He who for us lived as a man, He who settles the length of every life.'

Thus spoke the holy warrior. The martyr was sundered from the sins of mankind. He must needs suffer a further share of pain, though God governed his torments. Lo! that seemed a marvel to men, that He would allow the wretched spirits to touch him further with their eager clutches, and yet that came to pass. It was a still greater thing, that He Himself sought the world and shed His blood at the hands of murderers. He had sway over both life and death, when He gladly endured in lowliness the hatred of persecutors on earth. Wherefore it is fitting now that we should celebrate the deeds of the righteous, render praise to God for all the examples by which the Scriptures reveal His wisdom unto us by His wondrous works.

Grace abode with Guthlac by divine strength. It is a great
matter to tell everything from the beginning which he endured
in his valour. The Father almighty Himself set His messenger
against secret deadly foes, where his soul became pure and
suffered temptation. It is widely known throughout the world,
that his heart was happy in God's will: yet there is much to be
told of what he himself suffered under the close bonds of the evil
spirits. He ever scorned well those things which hurt the soul;
he trusted in help from the Lord, the Guardian who kept that
heart safe, so that faith in his breast wavered not, and lamenta-
tions hurt not his soul; but the staunch heart abode in its holi-
ness until it had come through its trials.

Bitter were the afflictions; fierce were the fiends. They all
vowed an end to his life; they, the upholders of sin, could not
pass judgment of death upon him, but the soul stayed in the
body awaiting a fitter time. Well they saw that God was
minded to save him from afflictions and to pass heavy judgment
upon their harrying. Thus God, the only Almighty, can easily
guard each of the blessed against sufferings. Nevertheless, the
outcasts, angry and wrathful, brought him, the glorious warrior,
the holy son of the Sacrament, to hell's gate, where the doomed
spirits of sinful men after death's agony first seek entrance to
that dread dwelling, the deep abysses down under cliffs. They
terrified him, cruelly threatened him with hostility, terror, and
hatred, with a perilous journey, as is the wont of fiends, when
they purpose to snare the souls of the righteous by sins and
cunning devices. They began fiercely to torment God's warrior
in soul; earnestly they vowed that he should pass into that grim
place of terror, depart humbled to the dwellers in hell, and there
suffer burning in bonds. With bitter speeches they, wretched
creatures, purposed to draw God's champion to despair. It
could not be thus. The sorrowful creatures, hateful to Christ,
spoke fiercely to Guthlac:

'Thou art not seemly, nor wholly proved a servant of God,
nor declared a good champion by words and deeds, holy in
heart. Now thou shalt go deep down to hell, have not at all
God's light in heaven, the lofty mansions, a dwelling in the sky,
because thou hast wrought too many sins and iniquities in the
flesh. Now we will give thee thy reward for every trans-
gression, where it shall be most loathly for thee, in the cruellest
anguish of the soul.'

The blessed man, Guthlac, answered them, with the strength of God in his soul:

'Do even thus, if the Lord Christ, the Author of life and light, the Ruler of hosts, will let you lead one who craves His protection into the loathly flame. That is in the power of the King of heaven, Christ the Saviour, who humbled you and drove you into bondage, into close confinement. I am His humble obedient servant, His patient follower. I shall wholly accept in every way the judgment of Him alone, and will ever be subject to Him zealously in my thoughts, faithfully obey my Saviour with virtue and honour, and give Him thanks for all the gifts which God first created for angels and dwellers on earth; and with glad heart I bless the Author of life and light, and day and night in fitting fashion sing praise unto Him, worship in my heart the Keeper of the heavenly kingdom. Never shall it be granted to you from on high by the favour of heaven, that ye may utter praise to God, but ye in death shall sing with lamentation of surging sorrow; ye shall have wailing in hell and not holy worship of the heavenly King.

VII

'I will honour the Judge in my days by words and deeds, will love Him whilst I live.' (Thus learning and reverence bring forth fruitful speech in them who perform His will by their deeds.) 'Faithless are ye; so long have ye lived in exile, plunged in fire, grievously misled, reft of the sky, void of gladness, consigned to death, encompassed with sins, with no hope of life, that ye might ever be cured of your blindness. In days long past ye readily despised the fair creation, the spiritual joy of heaven, when ye rejected holy God. Ye were not allowed to dwell in happiness for ever, but for your pride ye were shamefully thrust in your guilt into the undying fire, where ye must endure death and darkness, lamentation for ever: ye shall never know relief from that. And I trust in the Author of life, in the eternal Ruler of all creatures, that He, the Saviour of men, in His mercy and might will never forsake me, because of the brave striving with which in my body and soul I have long fought for God by mysterious, manifold powers. Wherefore I trust in the most radiant majesty of the Trinity, who in His counsels holds heaven and earth in His hands, that ye, in your anger, shall never be able by your onsets to draw me into torments, ye, my murderous foes and foul enemies, dark and discomfited. Of a truth my breast is pleasantly filled by bright faith and by love of God; my heart is kindled towards that better home, radiantly lighted towards the most precious everlasting abode, where in the glory of the Father is a land fair and joyous. Then the brightness of light, nor the gladness of life before the Saviour in God's kingdom shall never be given unto you because of your pride, which by vain boasting rose overweening in your heart. Ye expected and wished in your hostility to become like the Creator in glory; then a worse fate came upon you, when the Lord in His anger plunged you into that dark torment, where afterwards the fire mingled with venom was kindled for you, your joy taken from you by terrible decree, the fellowship of the angels. So now it shall be for ever and ever, that ye shall endure the surging flame of damnation, of blessing no share. Shorn of your glory, ye need not hope that ye in your sinfulness can with cunning wiles thrust me into darkness, nor hurl me down into the blazing fire, into the house of hell, where your abode is appointed, never-ending gloom, unceasing strife, fierce torment of soul, where ye must needs suffer death in sorrow, and I shall possess blissful joys with angels in the heavenly kingdom on high, where is the true King, the Help, and Salvation of mankind, and troops and retinues.'

Then came God's holy messenger from heaven, who in speech proclaimed unto the wretched spirits terror from heaven above, bade them bring quickly the guiltless, glorious warrior unharmed out of misery, so that the most precious spirit might joyfully pass prepared into God's keeping. Then the company of fiends were stricken with fear; the illustrious one, the dear servant of God, spoke; he shone with the brightness of day. The dauntless guardian, rich in his powers, had Guthlac's spirit in his keeping; he fettered the servants of darkness with afflictions, laid distress upon them and earnestly charged them:

'Let there not come upon him the breaking of a bone, nor a bloody wound, bruise of body, nor any harm from that which ye may do to his hurt; but set him unscathed where ye found him. He shall hold sway over the place; ye cannot wrest from him his dwelling. I am the judge; God bade me quickly declare that ye should heal all his pains with your hands and afterwards be obedient to his authority. I shall not hide my face before your host; I am God's servant; I am one of the twelve whom He, when in man's form, cherished in His heart as most faithful. He sent me hither from heaven; He saw that ye on earth in your enmity tormented his follower. He is my brother; his suffering was a sorrow to me. I shall bring it to pass where my friend dwells in his refuge (for I wish to keep friendship with him now that I can help him), that ye shall often behold my presence. Now I purpose to seek him out frequently; I shall bring his words and his work to the knowledge of God; He shall know of his deeds.'

VIII

Gladdened was Guthlac's soul when Bartholomew had declared God's message. Ready obedient stood the thralls who fully heeded the holy one's command. Then God's warrior in his glory set out on the loved journey to that pleasant spot of earth. They bore him along and kept him from hurt; they raised him with their hands and guarded him from falling. Gentle and smooth was their going under the fear of God. He who had built the dwelling came in triumph to the mountain. Many kinds of creatures blessed him with fervent voices; the birds in the trees declared by signs the blessed man's return. Often he had held food for them, when in their hunger they flew round his hand, greedily eager. They were glad of his safety. Thus that gentle heart held itself apart from the joys of mankind, served God, took delight in the wild beasts, when he had rejected the world. Peaceful was the scene of victory and new the abode, pleasant the jargoning of birds, blossoming the land; cuckoos proclaimed the spring. Blessed and single-hearted, Guthlac could enjoy his dwelling. The green field stood in God's keeping; the guardian who came from heaven had driven the fiends afar off. What fairer pleasure has come to pass in the life of man which our fathers could call to mind, or which we ourselves have since known? Lo! we are witnesses of these wonders; all these things happened within our times. Wherefore none of the race of men on the earth need doubt that, for God brings about such things to strengthen the life of souls, lest the weaker hearts should not accept the testimony, when they have truth in their sight.

So the Almighty loves all bodily creatures under heaven, the nations of men throughout the world. The Lord wishes that we should ever eagerly acquire wisdom, so that His truth, in return for His gifts which He gives and sends us in mercy and for our understanding, may work upon us. He prepares for souls pleasant paths through life, clearly ordained. Verily, that is not the slightest of things that love makes manifest, when in man's heart it raises spiritual grace. So by His power He exalted Guthlac's days and deeds. The noble man was firm set against sins to the terror of the fiends; there afterwards he failed not at all in his promise. Often he humbly sent up his speech to God, let his prayer go to the realm of light, thanked God that he could dwell in torments, till through God's will the better life should be granted him.

Thus Guthlac's soul was carried in angels' embraces to heaven; they brought it there lovingly before the face of the eternal Judge. To him was a guerdon given, a seat in heaven, where for ever and ever he might dwell secure, abide in gladness. The Son of God, the mighty Lord, the holy Protector, the Keeper of heaven, is his kindly Guardian. Thus the souls of the righteous may rise to the everlasting abode, to the kingdom of the skies, those who in words and deed perform here in their lifetime the lasting teachings of the King of heaven, earn on earth life immortal, a home on high. They are those who have taken the eucharist, chosen warriors, dear to Christ; they bear clear faith in their breasts, holy hope, pure hearts; they do honour to the Lord. Their thoughts are wise, ever ready to turn to the Father's home. They prepare a house for the soul, and with wisdom vanquish the fiend, and check sinful lusts in their breasts. Brotherly love they eagerly practise, according to God's will. They mortify themselves; they adorn their souls with holy thoughts; they fulfil the command of the heavenly king on earth. They love fasting; they ward off wickedness and turn to prayer; they strive against sins, hold fast the truth and right. They sorrow not after death, when they pass into the holy city, and go straight on to Jerusalem, where for ever in joy they can earnestly look upon God's face in peace with their sight. There it stands fair and glorious in truth, for ever in the joyous band of the living.

B

I

IT is known far and wide to the races of men, noised abroad among the people, that the God of created things, the Almighty King, created the first of mankind from purest earth. Then was a new beginning for the race of men, joyous creation fair and gladsome.

[The story of man's fall is told in about sixty lines. There have, however, always been some striving to do God's will; such was Guthlac.]

Books tell us how Guthlac through God's will became blessed in England. He made choice of eternal strength and help; far and wide his wondrous works grew renowned, famed throughout the cities in Britain; how often, by God's might, he cured many sad men of grievous torments, who sorrowing in pain, in the grip of disease, downcast in heart came to seek him from far places. Ever they found solace, help, and healing ready there from God's warrior. There is no man who can tell, or who knows the number of all the miracles which by God's grace he wrought here in the world for men.

II

Often the deadly horde of devils, reft of happiness, came in a host to the dwelling, thronging in bands, where the holy servant, steadfast in valour, held his abode. There with many voices in the wilderness they lifted up clamour of many sorts, loud warcry, bereft of beauty, empty of joys. God's warrior, the bold leader, valiantly resisted the hosts of fiends. The hour was not slow to come, nor the delay long for the wretched spirits, till the workers of evil wept aloud, howled in defeat, uttered loud sounds. Raging at times like wild beasts they shouted together; at times the foul evil foes turned again to human form with the greatest of clamours; at times the accursed faithless ones, wretched creatures crippled by fire, changing again to the shape of a serpent, spewed out venom. Ever they found Guthlac ready, shrewd in thought; he endured in patience, though the multitude of fiends threatened him with slaughter. At times the race of birds driven by hunger flew to his hands, where they found food ready, and honoured him with fervent voices. At times again human messengers humbly sought him, and there the eager travellers found help, ease of heart, in the place of triumph from the holy servant. There was not even one who departed again downcast, unhappy, hopeless; but the holy man by his noble power healed every man, both body and soul, men sorrowing in heart, who, being stricken, sought him in their need, whilst the Guardian of life, eternal, almighty, was pleased to grant that he should here enjoy happiness, life in the world. Then the end by death of the strife and miseries on earth was close at hand; fifteen years after he had chosen his abode in the wilderness, then the comforter was sent from above, in holiness from on high to the blessed preacher. His heart glowed within him, eager to be gone. On a sudden sickness fell upon him; yet valiant, unterrified, glad in his stronghold, he awaited the fulfilling of the radiant promises. After nightfall hard pressed was his body; his mind was enfeebled. The glad spirit was eager to go forth. The Father of angels purposed not to let the sinless one dwell for long after that in this wretched life of the world, for he by his works and deeds here in his life had done his pleasure with unflagging zeal. Then the Almighty showed the power of His hand where His holy servant dwelt bravely, secretly in glory, dauntless and valiant. Hope was born again, bliss in his breast. His body was consumed by disease, bound by inward fetters, his frame torn apart; his limbs were afflicted, seized by pains. He knew the truth, that Almighty God in His mercy had sought him from on high. Stoutly he strengthened his heart against the encircling danger of fiends' attacks. Yet was he not afraid; nor did the strength of disease, nor the wrench of death trouble his mind. But the praise of God burned in his breast, glowing love triumphant in his soul, which constantly vanquished every pain. He felt not regret for this fleeting life, though his body and soul, a wedded pair, should break their loved union. Days passed on, the nights with their covering darkness. The time was at hand when he must fulfil his fate, win glory by the coming of death, even the same which long ago our fathers boldly encountered, as the first of mankind did before them.

III

Then Guthlac's strength was exhausted in that sad time, his heart very strong, steadfast in valour. Dire was the disease, burning and raging: his breast swelled inwardly; his body was on fire. The drink was made ready which Eve prepared for Adam at the beginning of the world. The fiend first gave the woman to drink, and she afterwards poured forth the bitter cup for Adam, her loved husband; whereby their sons since have cruelly paid the penalty for what was wrought in the past, so that since the beginning there has been none of mankind, no man on earth, who could ward off and escape the dread draught of death's deep cup; but at that cruel time the door uncloses itself, opens the entrance. No one who dwells in the flesh, mighty or humble, can resist that with his life, but it assails him with greedy clutches. So the lone one who brings sorrow, the foeman greedy for slaughter, had then after nightfall drawn near unto Guthlac, close to his side.

One servant dwelt with him, who visited him daily. Then pondering deeply, wise in heart, he went to God's temple, wherein he knew was the preacher of the land, the most loved chosen teacher, and then he entered to speak with the blessed man. He wishes to hearken to the holy man's teachings, to the kind man's speech. Then he found his master stricken with disease. That fell heavily on his heart; grief weighed upon him, great sorrow of mind. Then his servant began to question:

'My friend and master, father, guardian of thy friends, how is thy life tormented, closely assailed? Never before, dearest master, have I found thee thus worn out. Hast thou still power of speech? It seems to my mind that weakness from the onsets of disease this last night troubled thee, afflicted thee with wounds. That is the keenest of griefs to my heart till thou dost comfort my mind and soul. Knowest thou, noble master, what shall be the end of this disease?'

Then after a while he spoke to him; he could not at once draw up breath. The dread illness had made in him its dwelling. Boldly he spoke; blessed in his courage, he rendered answer:

'I declare that suffering came upon me, agony pierced in, tore my body this dark night. My limbs are afflicted, seized by pains. This lodging for the soul, this doomed body, shall bide in the grave, fast in the bed of death, covered by its earthy house, the limbs stretched upon the clay. The foe draws nigh,

eager for the struggle. The delay till soul and body part will
not be longer than the space of seven nights by appointed time,
so that on this eighth, the approaching day, my life will go to
seek its close. Then shall my days on the earth be done with,
my sorrow lessened, and then I can win my reward at God's
knees, new gifts, and for ever and ever henceforth follow the
Lamb of God amid lasting joys. Now the soul is ready to go
thither, eager to set out. Now thou hast full knowledge of the
death of my body. Long is this tarrying in the life of the world.'

Then there was weeping and wailing; sad was the youth's
soul, mournful his mind, when he heard that the holy one was
about to depart. He felt grief heavy in his heart for his lord
because of the dread tidings. Gloom filled his breast: his
mind was troubled, because he saw his lord about to leave. He
could not refrain, but, suffering affliction, he let hot tears gush
forth, drops well out. Fate could keep life, the dear treasure,
in the doomed one no longer than had been decreed for him.

IV

He who was holy in spirit perceived the languishing heart of
the sorrowful man. Then the protector of men, cheerful, dear
unto God, began to hearten his disciple, to address with words
his most loved friend:

'Be not sad, though this disease consume me inwardly. No
hardship is it for me to suffer the will of God, of my Lord; nor
in this time of illness do I sorrow in my heart because of death;
nor do I greatly fear the hostile horde of fiends. The first-born
of iniquity cannot impute to me sin, evil, frailty of the flesh;
but in the fire, whelmed in surging sorrows, they shall bewail
their anguish, lament their exile, stripped of all things they
desire in the abode of death, of all good things, of love and
forgiveness. My dear son, be not too sad in soul! I am girt for
the journey, eager to take a dwelling on high as a guerdon, to
gaze on the Lord of victories in everlasting gladness according to
my deserts. My dear son, it is not suffering or grief for me that
I shall seek glorious God, the King of heaven, where are peace
and gladness, the joy of the just; where the Lord is present
whom I have zealously pleased by my ponderings, by my deeds
in this mournful time with my heart and strength. I know the
flawless reward, the holy guerdon on high which is for all time,
there where my hope is to seek it. My soul struggles forth

from the body to lasting joy in bliss. This abode to me is neither pain nor sorrow; I know that a lasting reward awaits me after my body's decay.'

Then the saint ended his speaking, the valiant sage. He had need of rest in his weariness of spirit. The sky grew dark over the sons of men; a number of nights in their blackness had gone by over men. Then the day came on which the living, eternal Almighty Lord joyfully rose in the body, when He, the Glory of all glories, rose up from death, from the earth, in His might in the Easter-tide, carried up to heaven the greatest of hosts when He mounted up from hell. Thus the blessed man, gentle and moderate, at that glorious season, gladly rejoicing in that bright day, bravely made an effort of strength with difficulty. The delight of men, staunch, wise, rose up as quickly as he could, wearied by his great torments; he began then to fix his mind on pure faith. Pondering deeply in meditations, he made an offering, according to the will of the Lord, in God's temple, and began to preach the gospel to his disciple by the grace of the spirit, as became a master; to speak with convincing signs and wondrously to make strong his mind in the glory and joy of the radiant realm, in such way as never in his life, early or late in this fleeting existence, had he heard teaching such as that, nor the mystery of God set forth so profoundly by the mouth of a man of spacious mind. It seemed to him that it was the speech of a divine angel from the joys of heaven, of a mighty minister, far rather than the teaching of any man, of any human creature on earth. That seemed to him the greatest of marvels, that such wisdom dwelt here in the breast of any man, of any of the sons of men. All his words and wisdom were profound, and the man's exhortation, his heart and strength, which the Lord of angels, the Succourer of souls, had bestowed on him.

v

Then four days passed away while the servant of God, afflicted with disease, tormented with agonies, bravely endured. He felt not grief, a sorrowing soul, a downcast mind, because his spirit must go hence. Death drew nigh; came with stealthy pace, strong and stern; it sought the soul's lodging. The seventh day came to men since the darting shafts in warring showers pierced in hot, nigh to his heart; unlocked his life's treasure which they sought with cunning keys. Then the wise man, the servant, the attendant, went to seek the noble man in the sacred dwelling; found then his faultless master holy in spirit in God's temple, lying down, about to leave life, whelmed in surges of pain. That was the sixth hour at midday; the end of life was at hand then for his lord. Closely assailed with afflictions, pierced by the arrows of death, he could hardly draw breath, speak with his voice. Then sad in mind, dispirited and weary in soul, he greeted the dying man, weary but glad in heart; prayed him by the mighty Creator to speak, if he could command utterance, bring forth speech, that he would declare to him in discourse, reveal by his words, what faith he had in his condition, in his state of life in that unknown disease before death should lay him low. The blessed man rendered him answer, one loved man to another, though he, the dauntless man, could draw breath but slowly:

'My dear son, now is it not very distant from the last day of my life, from the wrench of death, so that not long after this thou shalt hear my last words in this life, counsel never empty of reward. Be faithful to all the covenant and friendship, the words we two spoke, thou dearest of men.' 'Never, my master, when thou art in need will I let love and friendship grow faint.' 'Be thou prepared for the going forth, when body and limbs and the spirit of life shall part their union through the wrench of death. Do thou hasten, thereafter, and tell my most dear sister of my setting out on the long journey to fair delight, to the eternal mansion. And also declare unto her in my words, that I denied myself her presence all the time of this earthly life, because I wished that we might see one another again in eternal joy in the glory of heaven before the face of the eternal Judge free from sins. There our love shall stand true; there in the radiant city we may for ever enjoy our desires, happiness with the angels. Do thou tell her also to bury this body on the mountain, close round with clay in the darkness the soulless frame, where it shall bide afterwards for a space in its earthy house.'

Then the servant's mind was greatly troubled, cruelly afflicted, at his master's words, when he clearly knew that death, the end of life for his lord, was not far off. Then in haste he began to speak in words to his friendly master:

'Dearest of men, of all mankind, delight of the people, I entreat thee by the Keeper of souls to lighten the sorrow of my heart. The end is not distant of which I have been told by thy prophetic speech.   Often my sad soul, sorrow pressing on the heart, my mind grieving in the anguish of the night, admonished me, and I durst never question thee, my father, my solace. Always when the jewel of heaven, the joyous candle of men, sloped towards the west, the radiant sun on the eve of setting, I heard in the eventide another man in council with thee.   Sad at heart I heard the speech of the lord, the unknown messenger, who often came, the discourse of the man, the talk of the stranger wise in the dwelling, 'twixt dawn and dark night and also in the morning.   Verily I know not yet, till thou, my master, reveal it further to me by thy speech, whence are his comings.'

VI

Then after a long space the blessed one rendered answer to him he loved, as well as he, devoid of strength, could slowly command his breath:

'Lo! my friend, thou speakest words unto me, dost question me as I die, of what before I would never in my life utter even to any man on earth, to anyone among the people, save now to thee, lest men and women should have marvelled at it and told it forth in mockery, spread it in songs, while I was alive.   Verily, I myself in my life was never minded by boastful speech to harm my soul's well-being, nor ever to draw down the wrath of God my Father.   My victorious Lord, the Life-Giver of peoples, has ever sent me, since first a year ago I began to dwell in my second hermitage, a holy spirit, an angel from heaven; he, a mighty servant of God, has sought me in his triumphant strength every evening and again in the morning, and healed all my pains, my grief of mind.   And the glorious messenger of joy enclosed in my breast the gift of wisdom far more manifold than any man may know in this life, which it is not granted to me to reveal to any living men on earth, so that no man should be able to hide from me what he secretly cherished in the thoughts of his heart, when he was in the sight of my eyes.   Ever have I hidden from all men in my heart to this day, thou dearest of men, the glorious coming of the angel.   Now for love of thee and the companionship that long we have held together, I will not let thee after my death ever be sad, weary, sick at heart, plunged in surging griefs. I shall always hold friendship with thee.   Now the soul hastens from the breast to true bliss; the time is not distant.   This frame grows feeble, my body suffers sorrow; eager to go forth, the soul speeds to its everlasting home, to the better abode. Now I am greatly worn out with pain.'

Then he sank down to the wall, bowed his head, braced yet his courage within him, drew breath at times, brave in his strength. From his mouth issued the sweetest of odours, as in the summer-time the blossoming plants in some places, flowing with honey, firm fixed in their stations, smell sweetly through the fields. So did the holy one's breath mount up the livelong day on till evening. Then the glorious splendour sought its setting; the black northern sky was dark under the clouds; it wrapped the world in mist; covered it with darkness; night came rushing down over the world, over the land's adornments. Then came the greatest of lights in holiness from heaven, shining clearly, radiant over the city-dwellings. He who was destined bravely awaited his end in blessedness, pierced by the arrows of death. An excellent glorious light shone bright about the noble man the livelong night; the shadows drew off, dispersed through the air. The gleaming splendour, the heavenly candle, stayed round that sacred house from the dusk of evening till dawn; the glowing sun came from the east over the deep sea path. The saint rose up, blessed, mindful of valour; spoke to his servant, the illustrious one to his true comrade: 'It is time that thou shouldst go and mind well the messages; and bring in haste, as before I charged thee, the message to the loved woman. Now the soul is very ready to leave the body, longing for joys divine.'

Then having eaten the eucharist, the glorious food, he humbly raised up his hands; likewise he opened his eyes, the holy jewels of the head; looked then, glad in heart, towards the heavenly kingdom, towards the reward of grace; and then sent forth his spirit, beauteous by its acts, into the joy of heaven.

VII

Then Guthlac's soul was brought in blessedness on high; angels bore it to lasting joy. The body grew cold, lifeless beneath the sky. Then the light, brightest of beams, shone there; that sign was all about that holy house, a heavenly gleam, rising from the earth like a fiery tower, set up straight to the vault of the heavens, seen under the sky brighter than the sun, than the splendour of noble stars. Troops of angels sang a song of triumph; there was music in the air, heard under the heavens, the rejoicing of saints. So the abode was filled with gladness, with sweet odours and heavenly wonders; the old dwelling of the blessed one filled within with the sound of angels. Fairer and more pleasant it was there than voice can tell in the world, how the odour and music, the heavenly harmony and the holy song were heard, the great glory of God, outburst after outburst. The island trembled, the ground was troubled. Then the servant, reft of courage, was frightened; the man hastened in distress to board a boat, urged on the steed of the waves. The ship sped under the sorrowful man. Hot shone the sky, radiant over the houses. The sea-wood hastened, nimble, quick on its course; the water-horse darted with its cargo to the haven, so that the sea-floater after tossing in the waves trod on the land, ground on the sand. He bore grief hot at his heart, a sad mind, a weary soul; he who knew that his master, his dear friend, reft of life, was left behind. The cry of lamentation grievously called that to his mind; tears gushed forth in streams, burning drops; and in his breast he bore great grief. He must needs take the ill tidings, too true, to the maiden. Sad at heart, he came there where the virgin was, the glorious saint. He did not conceal what had come to pass, the death of the destined one. Reft of his friend, he chanted a dirge and spoke these words:

'Courage is best for him who most often must endure great ills, seriously ponder on grievous parting from a master, when the time comes destined by fate. He knows that who must needs grieve with sad heart; he knows that his gracious giver of treasure is buried. He shall turn away thence, hapless, sorrowing; he shall be empty of gladness who most often endures hardships in his sad soul. Verily, small cause have I to rejoice at his death! My lord, prince of men, and thy brother, support of the weary, dearest of kinsmen, protector of his friends, the best between the seas which we have ever heard of, born as a child among men in England, has passed from worldly joys by decree of God to the majesty of heaven, to seek an abode, a dwelling on high. Now the earthly part, the ruined body, bides on a bed of death in the dwelling, and the heavenly part has gone from the body to seek its triumphant reward in God's splendour; and he bade me tell thee that ye two might possess a common home for ever in everlasting joy with the peaceful band, a glorious guerdon for your deeds, might enjoy in gladness, happiness, and bliss. My victorious lord also, when he was about to depart, bade me tell thee that thou, dearest of maidens, shouldst cover his body with earth. Now thou knowest my mission fully. I must needs go hence, sad at heart, downcast, with heavy mind . . .[1]

[1] The end of the poem is incomplete in the manuscript.

THE SOUL'S ADDRESS TO THE BODY

[The soul's anger at the sinful body is a very common subject in medieval literature. The grimness of the poem is a common mood in Old English poetry. The fragment describing the gratitude of the saved soul to the body for its self-denial on earth is a much rarer theme.]

I

VERILY it behoves every man that he himself should ponder his soul's state, how sound that is, when death comes, sunders the union which existed before, body and soul. Long is it after that till the soul receives from God Himself either bale or bliss, even as the body won for it erstwhile on earth. The spirit, the soul, shall come, loud in its sorrows, always on the seventh night, for three hundred years, to find the body which long since it wore, unless ere that the great King, Almighty God, the Lord of lords, will bring the end of the world. Then, most woeful, it will cry in a cold voice; the soul will speak sternly to the dust:

'What hast thou done, sorrowful one? What affliction hast thou caused me; the foulness of earth falls all to ruin, like unto clay. Little didst thou think what thing thy soul should afterwards become when freed from the body. What hadst thou to blame in me, accursed? Lo! thou didst little think to be the food of worms, when thou didst follow all the lures of pleasure; now in the earth thou shalt feed worms. Lo! in the world before little didst thou think how long this lasts. Lo! the Lord almighty by His own hand sent thee a soul by an angel from the heavens on high from His majesty and bought thee with the holy blood; and thou didst bind me with grievous hunger and fetter me with hell-torments. I dwelt within thee; compassed by flesh I could not come out of thee, and thy sinful lusts lay heavy upon me, so that full often it seemed to me that it would be thirty thousand years till thy death-day; ever with pain I waited till we two should part. Verily the end now is not over-good. Thou wert proud in thy food and glutted with wine; thou wert gloriously daring, and I was athirst for the body of God, for spiritual drink. Wherefore here in life, when I was forced to dwell in thee in the world, thou didst not think that thou wert sorely troubled by flesh and sinful lusts; and upheld by me; and I was a soul sent to thee from God.   Thou didst never guard me with the lust of thy desires against hell-torments so grievous; thou shalt suffer the disgrace of my shame on the great day when the Only Begotten shall gather together all the race of mankind.   Thou art not more dear as a comrade to any living man, neither mother, nor father, nor any kinsman, than the dark raven, since I passed out from thee alone, by the hand of Him who formerly sent me.   Henceforth they cannot take from thee the golden ornaments, neither gold nor silver, nor aught of thy gauds, nor thy bride's circlet, nor thy wealth, nor any possessions which formerly thou didst own.   But here thy bones shall bide, stripped bare, snatched away from sins; and I thy soul against my will shall often seek thee, revile thee with words, as thou didst unto me.   Now art thou dumb and deaf; thy joys are naught; yet perforce I shall seek thee by night, stricken with sins, and straightway leave thee again at cock-crow, when holy men lift up a song of praise to the living God, and seek my abode which thou didst appoint me here, and my cruel dwelling-place; and here many earthworms shall gnaw thee, dark creatures, ravenous and greedy, grievously rend thee. Thy follies are fled which here on earth thou didst flaunt before men.   Wherefore it would be better for thee by far, than that all the wealth of the world were thine save thou didst give it to God Himself, if thou at the beginning hadst become a fowl, or a fish in the sea, or toiled for food as a beast on earth, as cattle wandering in the field without wisdom, or the fiercest of wild animals in the wilderness, if God had thus willed it, and even though thou hadst been the basest of worms than ever thou hadst become a man on earth or ever received baptism, when thou must answer for us both on the great day, when the wounds shall be revealed to men which long ago sinners wrought in the world.   Then will the Lord Himself, the Creator of the heavens, hear the deeds of every man from the speech of all men's mouths, requital for wounds; but what wilt thou say then to the Lord on the Day of Judgment?   Then shall there be no joint so small in a limb, but for each separately thou shalt pay the penalty when the Lord is stern at the Judgment.   But what shall we twain do when He has made us to be born once again? Then together we shall suffer such miseries as formerly thou didst decree for us.'

Thus it reviles the body; then it must needs depart, afflicted by deeds, seek the abyss of hell, by no means the joys of heaven. The dust lies where it was; it can return no answer, nor offer then any refuge, aid, or solace to the sorrowful soul.

The head is cleft, hands disjointed, jaws gaping, mouth rent open; sinews are slackened, the neck gnawed through, fingers decayed, feet broken; zealous worms strip the ribs; thirsty for blood, they drink the corpse in swarms; the tongue is torn in ten parts for the pleasure of the hungry; wherefore it cannot wisely exchange words with the unhappy spirit. The worm is called glutton, whose jaws are sharper than a needle; it ventures to the grave first of all, so that it tears the tongue, and pierces the teeth, and from above eats through the eyes into the head, and opens the way for other worms to food, to high feasting, when the weary body grows cold which erstwhile for long he guarded with garments. Then it is the food and sustenance of worms in the earth. To every wise man that may be a warning.

II

More joyous is it then when the holy soul, encompassed by solace, goes to the flesh; that message is found happier for the heart. Gladly with delight it seeks the body wherein long since it dwelt. Then the spirits, wise, triumphant, utter good speeches, and in truth thus gladly they greet the body: 'Dearest friend! though the eager worms are yet busy about thee, now I thy soul have come, fairly adorned, to my Father's kingdom, surrounded with mercies. Alas! my lord! could I but take thee with me so that we twain should behold all the angels, likewise the glory of the heavens, as erstwhile thou didst appoint for me! Thou didst fast on earth, and didst fill me with God's body, the drink of the spirit; if thou wert in poverty, thou gavest me abundance of things I craved. Wherefore no cause hast thou to be ashamed of what thou gavest me, when the sinful and the righteous are sundered on the great day; nor needst thou repent in the meeting-place of men and angels of all thou didst give me in life. Thou didst humble thyself before men and exalt thyself to eternal joy; wherefore, dearest of men, regret lies ever heavy on my heart, for that I know thee to be in these miseries, a food for worms. But it was God's will that thy portion should thus ever be the hateful grave. I would tell thee then not to be troubled, for we two shall be gathered together at God's Judgment. Then afterwards we can rejoice, and be exalted in heaven; we need not be troubled at the Lord's coming, nor have grievous sorrow at heart as to our answer, but we ourselves can exult in our deeds at the Judgment, in what merits were ours.   I know that thou in the world wert gloriously exalted of this . . . [1]

---

[1] The end of the poem is missing.

DOOMSDAY

[This impressive poem is adapted from a Latin poem, *De Die Judicii*, which has been attributed to Bede and also to Alcuin. The English poem, however, is nearly twice as long as the Latin and is in no way a slavish translation.]

Lo! I sat alone within a grove covered with foliage, amidst a wood, where the streams made music and ran in the midst of a meadow, even as I say. Pleasant plants also grew there and bloomed amid the throng in the excellent field, and the trees of the forest tossed and murmured. The sky was troubled with the dread strength of the wind, and my poor mind was all in distress. Then of a sudden, in terror and sadness, I began to sing these gloomy verses, even such as thou mightest speak when mindful of sins, of the vices of life, of the long time, of the coming of dark death to earth. I felt fear too of the great judgment for my evil deeds here on earth, and also I dreaded the eternal wrath for myself and for each sinful one before God Himself, and how the mighty Lord will part all mankind and pass sentence by His secret power. I remembered too the glory of the Lord and of the holy ones in the heavenly kingdom; likewise the evil and torments of the wretched. I remembered this within myself, and I mourned exceedingly, and mourning I spoke, distressed in mind:

'Now I pray all ye veins quickly to open wide your gushing springs hot upon my cheeks in tears. Then in my sin I strike hard with my fist, I beat my breast in the place of prayer and lay my body on the ground, and I invoke all the agonies which I have deserved. Now I entreat you earnestly to hold not back because of tears, but vex the sad face with weeping, and straightway shed salt drops upon it; and lay bare sin to the eternal Lord. Nor let aught remain there in the heart's recess of miserable guilt, that is not clear as day; let that which was hidden, everything of breast and tongue and flesh, be also disclosed with open words. This is the only salvation for a wretched soul and the best of hopes to the sorrowing, that by weeping here he should make known his wounds to the heavenly Physician. He alone can cure guilty crimes with good and swiftly unbind the prisoners; nor will the Lord of angels with His right hand harshly bruise the careless heart, nor will Christ the Ruler quench with water the faint smoke of frail flesh. Did not the thief who with Christ was killed on the cross show thee sharply by example how much avails and how glorious is that true repentance for sins and transgressions? The thief on the cross was guilty and sinful, all weighed down with crimes; nevertheless, when near unto death he made his prayer unto God from the thoughts of his breast. Quickly he gained salvation and succour with words few but full of faith, and passed in at the peerless gates of Paradise with the Saviour. Ah, unhappy mind, I ask thee why dost thou tarry so long that thou dost not show thyself to the Physician? Or thou, sinful tongue, why art thou silent? Now thou hast ready time for forgiveness, now the almighty Guardian of the heavenly kingdom will hear thee gladly with attentive ears. But the day is coming when God will judge the whole world. Thou alone must render account with words to God the Creator and rightly account to the mighty Prince. I counsel thee to hasten the more with tears of repentance and forestall the wrath of the eternal Judge. O flesh, why dost thou not purge away thy grievous sins by a pouring forth of tears? Why dost thou not pray for bathings and plaster for thyself, for the medicine of life from the Prince of life? Thou must cry now, shed tears, while there is time and a season for weeping. Now it is wholesome that men should weep here and do penance to please God. God's Son is glad if thou dost bear grief and dost judge thyself for sins on earth. The God of heaven will not avenge on any man wrongs and transgressions more than once. Thou must not scorn lamentation and weeping and the ready time for forgiveness. Let not thy heart forget also how great is the torment which the wretched will have for their former deeds, or how dread and terrible a King in His high majesty will here judge all people according to their former deeds, or what portents will begin to appear and declare Christ's coming on earth. The whole earth shall shake; the hills also shall fall and perish, and the coverings of graves shall bow and melt, and the dread roar of the raging sea shall greatly trouble the minds of men. Heaven above also shall be all black and overcast; quickly it shall grow dark and dim of hue and a black chaos. Then the stars shall fall, losing their places, and the sun shall forthwith grow dark in the morning, nor shall the moon have any power to scatter the darkness of the night. And then down from heaven shall come those who betoken death; they shall terrify the wretched. Then shall come the heavenly hosts, a strong band roused up. Whole troops of angels shall leap about and circle the Eternal One, the glorious Lord, with power and majesty. Then the Ruler of heaven radiant as the sun shall sit on the high throne, glorified with His crown. On a sudden we shall be brought before Him, coming from all sides to His presence, so that each may receive judgment from God Himself according to his deeds. O man, I pray thee remember how great shall be the terror then before the judgment seat of the Lord. He shall stand heartless and timid, confused and confounded, powerless, fearful. Then from the shelter of the sky all the hosts of angels shall surround the Eternal One. At once there shall be a great summons, and all the race of Adam shall be called thither, of dwellers on earth who were ever fostered in the world, or whom a mother bore in human form, or those that were or were to be or were at all about to be counted. Then on that day the secret thoughts of all shall be revealed to all, all that the heart thought of evil, or the tongue uttered in malice, or the hand of man wrought of wickedness, of things on earth, in dark caves; all the sins in the world which anyone was ashamed to betray or declare to any man. Then that which man long hid shall be open to all together equally and laid bare. Besides all this, all the upper air shall be also filled with venomous flame; the fire shall sweep over all, nor will there be aught to stop it, nor shall a man be able by any means to stand against its strength. All that seems boundless to us beneath the sweep of the sky shall be equally filled with red flame. Then the fiery blaze shall blow and crackle; red and wrathful, it shall rush and hasten to prepare torment for the sinful. Nor shall the avenging flame hold back, or do mercy to anyone there, unless he be cleansed here from filth and then come thither greatly purified. Then many tribes, countless peoples, shall violently beat their sinful breasts with the fist because of their evil lusts. There the needy and the kings of peoples, poor and rich, shall all be afraid. There the poor and the wealthy shall have one law; therefore they shall all together feel fear. That raging flood shall flash with fire and cruelly burn the poor souls; and worms shall swiftly tear and rend the hearts of sin-guilty ones. Nor can any man there be bold near his Judge because of honourable works, but terror shall run alike through all, heart-searchings and bitter lamentation, and there all the wicked host shall stand, stiffened like stone, awaiting misery. O flesh, what art thou doing? What art thou busy with now? How canst thou at that time lament thy distress? Alas! thou art now serving thyself, and art living here gladly in lust, and dost urge thyself with the strong goads of pride. Why dost thou not fear the fiery terror, and greatly dread the torments for thyself which God ordained long ago for devils, for accursed spirits, as reward for their sins? These in their vastness surpass the thought and speech of every man. There can be no power of speech that can relate in discourse to any on earth the dire penalties, the foul places, in the fiery abyss amid the grim torment in hell. There for sorrow are mingled together flaming vapours and grievous ice, exceeding hot and cold, in the midst of hell. Sometimes eyes shall weep there without measure; he shall be filled with misery because of the fire of the furnace. Sometimes also the teeth of men shall chatter because of great cold. This bitter change—wretched men will for ever and ever wander therein amid dark black nights and the misery of boiling pitch and vapour. No sound stirs there save violent weeping and lamentation—naught else. Nor shall the face of any creature be seen there save the tormentors who afflict the wretched. Nor shall aught be found there save fire and cold and loathsome foulness. They will not be able to smell aught except immensity of stench. There the wailing lips shall be filled with flame-darting blaze of hateful fire, and ravening worms shall rend them and gnaw their bones with burning tusks.

'Besides all this, the unhappy breast shall be terrified and tormented with bitter care, because sinful flesh in this perilous time wrought so many sins for itself that it was destroyed in prison. The dread eternal torments are there; there no little spark of light shines for the wretched. Nor goodness, nor peace, nor hope, nor stillness gives cheer, nor the multitude of men at all. Solace shall flee away, nor shall there be any help there which can give protection against bitter things. Nor shall sight of any gladness be found there; there shall be horrible terror and fear and grievous gnashing of teeth in sorrow. Everywhere there shall be cruel sadness, old age and wrath and weariness and sin there too. Souls in the flame, in the dark den, shall burn and run to and fro. Then the hurtful joys of this world shall pass away hence, wholly depart. Then drunkenness shall pass away with feasts, and laughter and play shall go together, and lust also shall depart hence, and greed shall depart afar off. Lust and each wanton desire shall hasten in guilt into the darkness. And unhappy powerless sleep, slothful with slumber, shall slink behind. Then in the dark bitter flames the wretched shall see what is not yet allowed. What is dearest in life shall then be loathed; and verily sins shall turn that weary heart to dwell among sorrows and grief.

'Ah! he shall be happy and more than happy and happiest of creatures for ever and ever who can well avoid with happiness such destruction, and can at the same time, blessed in all the world, serve his Lord. And then he may possess the kingdom of heaven; that is the greatest of joys. Night or gloom never darkens there the beaming of the heavenly light. Sorrow comes not there, nor pain, nor worn-out age; nor is any toil found there, or hunger, or thirst, or unhappy sleep; nor is there fever there, or illness, or sudden pestilence, nor crackling of fire, nor hateful cold. Sadness is not there, nor weariness, nor ruin, nor care, nor cruel torment. Nor is there lightning there, nor hateful storm, winter, nor thunder, nor any cold, nor keen hail showers there with snow. Nor is poverty there, nor loss, nor dread of death, nor misery, nor sloth, nor any grieving. But peace reigns there together with happiness and goodness and everlasting God, glory and honour, also worship and life and fair concord.

'Besides all this, the eternal Lord provides them gladly with all good things, honours and receives them all in His presence. And the Father also blesses, glorifies, and graciously regards them, fairly adorns and nobly loves them, and sets them high on a heavenly throne. His gracious Son, the Giver of victory, bestows everlasting guerdon on each, heavenly ornaments. That is a glorious gift. Among the excellent host of angels and the bands and companies of the holy ones there they shall be joined among the nations, amidst the patriarchs and holy prophets. The messengers of Almighty God are there with glad hearts in the cities. And amid red masses of roses there they shall shine for ever. A virgin band of the stainless ones, decked with blossoms, most radiant of companies, shall wander there. God's excellent beloved will lead them all, the woman who for us gave birth to the Lord, the Creator, on earth. That is Mary, the pure virgin, best of maidens. She, most blessed of all, will lead with a noble host through the bright shining realms of the glorious Father, between Father and Son, and amid the eternal peace on high, in the kingdom of the Counsellor, the Lord of heaven. What hardship can there be here in life, if thou wilt speak truth to him who asks, to compare with that, that thou mayest eternally dwell without change among that host, and in the blessed seats of those on high enjoy gladness henceforth without end?'

RIDDLES

[There are various authors of Latin riddles—Symphosius, Aldhelm of Malmesbury, Bishop of Sherbourne, Tatwine, Archbishop of Canterbury, Eusebius, Abbot of Wearmouth, and others. The relation of the Old English riddles in the *Exeter Book* to these Latin riddles has been a good deal discussed. Out of all the riddles—nearly a hundred in number—comparatively few owe much to Latin riddles on the same subjects. Generally speaking, the Old English poet develops his theme in his own way. The so-called First Riddle which we now know by the name of *Wulf and Eadwacer* was formerly interpreted to give the solution 'Cynewulf,' and on this theory the authorship of all the riddles was ascribed to Cynewulf. This view is no longer tenable, and the authorship of the riddles is unknown. It is probable they are not all from one hand, nor of the same date. It is likely that the majority were written down in the eighth century. In merit the riddles vary greatly. Some are merely obscure or ingenious; the text of some is so imperfect that we can know neither their worth nor meaning. But not a few show remarkable skill in workmanship. There is description of nature as in the riddles on the *Storm*, charming fancy as in those on the *Swan* and the *Book*, sympathy for animals as in the vivid poem on the *Badger*, and above all many traces of old folklore and intimate pictures of English life before the Norman Conquest.]

STORM ON LAND

WHO of men is ready-witted and wise enough to say who drives me forth on my journey, when I arise in my strength, exceeding furious, when I resound in my might? Sometimes I move with malice through the land, burn the people's halls, spoil the houses; the smoke rises up, grey over the roofs; there is noise on earth, the death-pang of men. When I stir the wood and the flowery groves, when, covered with water, sent by the high powers to drive afar in my roving, I fell the trees, I bear on my back what erstwhile covered the forms of dwellers on earth, flesh and spirits together in the water. Say who it is who covers me, or what I, who bear those burdens, am called.

STORM AT SEA

AT times I go, as men do not expect, to seek the earth, the bottom of the sea, beneath the press of the waves. The ocean is roused, the foam tossed; the whale mere roars, it rages loudly; the surges beat the shores, strongly they cast stone and sand on the high slopes, seaweed and wave, when I, struggling, covered by the ocean, stir the earth, the vast depths of the sea. Nor can I escape the covering of water ere He allow me who is my guide on every journey. Say, wise man, who draws me from the embraces of the sea, when the surges again grow still, the waves gentle, which erstwhile covered me.

STORM

At times my Prince confines me fast, then sends my broad bosom beneath the fertile plain and forces me to stop, drives me in my might into darkness, casts me into a narrow place, where the earth sits hard on my back. I have no escape from that tribulation, but I stir the home of men; gabled halls tremble, dwellings of men; walls shake high above the house-holders. The air seems quiet over the land and the water silent, till I break forth from prison, even as He guides me, who formerly at the beginning laid bonds upon me, chains and fetters, so that I may not escape from that power which shows me my paths.

At times from above I must rouse the waves, stir the surges, and drive the flint-grey flood to the shore. The wave struggles foaming against the cliff; the dark mountain rises above the deep; behind, moves a second dark sea, mixed with the ocean, so that they meet the high hills by the seashore. There is the ship full of clamour, the shouting of mariners; quietly the high stone cliffs abide the strife of the waters, the dashing of the waves, when the towering surge presses on to the rocks. There the ship must look for hard struggle, if the sea bear it with its freight of souls in that dread time, so that it shall be robbed of its power and ride in foam, its life beaten out on the ridges of the waves. There is shown to men the terror of those whom I in my strength must obey on my rough path. Who shall set that at rest?

At times I rush through what rides on my back, dark clouds, scatter far and wide the water-streams, at times let them once more glide together. It is the greatest of uproars, of noises over cities, and loudest of crashes, when one cloud comes sharp against another, edge against edge; dark creatures, hastening over men, sweat fire, and crashes move, dark with mighty din, above the multitudes; they march in battle, they pour dark pattering wet from their bosom, moisture from their womb. The dread legion moves in battle; terror arises, a great fear in mankind, horror in cities, when the pallid, stalking demons shoot with keen weapons. The fool fears not the spears of death; yet he dies, if the true Lord speeds the arrow, the swift shaft, downwards from the whirlwind straight upon him through the rain; few escape whom the weapon of the swift visitant reaches. I contrive the beginning of that strife, when I go forth in the battle of the clouds to force a way through the press in my vast might over the bosom of the torrent; the towering battalions burst with uproar; then once more I stoop under the cover of the air near earth, and load my back with what I have been admonished by the power of my Prince. Thus I, a strong servant, make war at times; at times under the earth; at times from on high I stoop beneath the waves; at times from above I rouse the sea, the surges; at times I mount up, I drive the racing clouds; widely I travel, swift and violent. Declare what my name is, or who shall raise me when I may not rest, or who shall hold me in when I am still.

SHIELD

I AM a solitary dweller, wounded with a knife, stricken with a sword, weary of battle deeds, tired of blades. Often I behold war, fight a dangerous foe; I look not for comfort, that safety may come to me out of the struggle, before I perish entirely among men; but the forged brands strike me; the handiwork of smiths, hard-edged, exceeding sharp, bite me in the strongholds. I must await a more grievous encounter. Never could I find in the city the race of physicians, of those who healed wounds with herbs, but my sword wounds grow wide by deadly blows day and night.

SUN

THE true Ruler of victories, Christ, set me in the fight. Often I burn living creatures; close to the earth, I afflict countless races with distress, although I touch them not when my Lord bids me fight. Sometimes I gladden the minds of many; sometimes I console from very far off those whom I make war upon; yet they feel both the hurt and the help, when over the deep tumult I better their life once more.

SWAN

SILENT is my garment when I tread the earth or inhabit the dwellings or stir the waters. Sometimes my trappings and this high air raise me above the abodes of men, and the power of clouds then bears me far and wide over the people. My adornments resound loudly and make melody; they sing clearly when I am not near the flood and the earth—a travelling spirit.

NIGHTINGALE OR JAY

I SPEAK with many voices through my mouth, sing with modulated notes; often I change my voice, I cry aloud, I hold my melody, nor do I refrain from laughter. Aged bard of the evening, I bring to men joy in cities when I cry with varying voice; they sit in silence, quiet in the dwellings. Say what is my name who, like a female jester, loudly mimic a player's song, announce to men many welcome things with my voice.

CUCKOO

[The cuckoo is described as deserted by its own parents before its birth and adopted by another mother. The young cuckoo grown strong shows its ingratitude by ejecting the other young birds from the nest.]

FATHER and mother gave me up dead in these days, nor was life or stir yet within me. Then one, a kinswoman very gracious, began to cover me with garments, held and guarded me, covered me as honourably with a protecting robe as her own child, till beneath her bosom, as my destiny was, I became mighty in spirit among those who were no kin of mine. The beautiful kinswoman afterwards fed me, till I grew up, could set out more widely on journeys; she had the fewer of her own dear sons and daughters by what she did thus.

NIGHT

The riddle seems to refer not only to darkness but also to night revels. 'The dearest of treasures' is perhaps the sun. An alternative solution is wine.]

GREY is my garment; adornments bright, red, and shining are in my raiment. I lead astray the stupid, and urge the foolish on to rash journeys; others I hinder from a useful journey. I know not at all why they, thus maddened, deprived of mind, led astray in deed, praise my crooked ways to everyone. Woe to them for their custom, when the High One brings the dearest of treasures, if they cease not from folly ere that.

HORN

[The horn speaks of its earlier life on the head of the living ox, and then of its existence as a magnificently decorated horn to hold wine or to summon men to battle by land or sea.]

I WAS an armed warrior. Now the proud young champion covers me with gold and silver, with curved and twisted wires. Sometimes men kiss me; sometimes I summon pleasant companions to battle with song; sometimes the steed bears me over the ground; sometimes the sea-horse carries me, bright with ornaments, over the surges; sometimes a maiden ring-adorned fills my bosom; sometimes I must lie stripped, hard and headless, on the tables; sometimes I hang, decked with trappings, fair on the wall, where men drink; sometimes warriors bear on the steed the noble war ornament; then, gleaming with treasure, I must draw in breath from a man's bosom; sometimes with my utterance I invite proud men to wine; sometimes I must rescue with my voice booty from foes, rout the plundering enemies. Ask what is my name.

BADGER

MY neck is white, my head yellow, also my sides; I am swift in my going, I bear a weapon for battle; on my back stand hairs just as on my cheeks; above my eyes tower two ears; I walk on my toes in the green grass.   Grief is doomed for me if anyone, a fierce fighter, catch me in my covert, where I have my haunt, my lair with my litter, and I lurk there with my young brood when the intruder comes to my doors; death is doomed for them, and so I shall bravely bear my children from their abode, save them by flight, if he comes close after me.   He goes on his breast; I dare not await his fierceness in my hole—that were ill counsel —but fast with my forefeet I must make a path through the steep hill.   I can easily save the life of my precious ones, if I am able to lead my family, my beloved and kin, by a secret way through a hole in the hill; afterwards I need dread not at all the battle with the death-whelp.   If the malignant foe pursues me behind by a narrow path, he shall not lack a struggle to bar his way after I reach the top of the hill, and with violence I will strike with war darts the hated enemy whom long I fled.

ANCHOR

Often I must war against the wave and fight against the wind; I contend against them combined, when, buried by the billows, I go to seek the earth; my native land is strange to me.   If I grow motionless I am mighty in the conflict; if I succeed not in that they are stronger than I, and straightway with rending they put me to rout; they wish to carry off what I must keep safe.   I foil them in that if my tail endures and if the stones are able to hold fast against me in my strength.   Ask what is my name.

BALLISTA

[The riddle describes the engine of war which casts out darts and other missiles.   The wires may refer to the ropes with which the ballista was wound.]

I am the guardian of my family, an enclosure firm with wires, filled within with noble treasures.   Often by day I spit out terror of spears; the greater my fullness, the greater the success. The master beholds how the war darts fly from my womb. Sometimes I swallow dark brown weapons, bitter points, deadly poisoned spears.   My stomach is serviceable, the foison of my

womb is fair, precious to proud men. Men forget not what
passes through my mouth.

SWORD

I AM a wondrous creature, shaped in strife, loved by my lord,
fairly adorned; my mail-coat is motley; also a bright wire lies
round the gem of death which my master gave me, who some-
times in his wanderings guides me myself to the fight.   Then I
bear treasure through the bright day, the handiwork of smiths,
gold through the dwellings.   Often I slay living men with the
weapons of war.   The king decks me with treasure and silver,
and honours me in hall, nor withholds the word of praise,
voices my virtues before the people, where they drink mead.
He confines me close pent; sometimes again lets me go at large,
me, weary of journeying, mighty in battle.   Often at the hands
of his friend I have injured others fiercely; far and wide I am
outlawed, accursed in my weapons.   I have no cause to hope
that, if any hostile man assails me in fight, a child will avenge me
on the life of the slayer; nor will the family from which I sprang
become magnified by my offspring, unless I, lacking a lord,
can leave my possessor who gave me rings; if I obey my lord,
do battle, as formerly I did, for my prince's pleasure, my destiny
is decreed, that I must lack the getting of children; I can have
naught to do with a bride, but he who formerly laid fetters
upon me still denies me that joyous play.   Wherefore I must
enjoy the treasures of heroes in singleness.   Often I, foolish
with ornaments, anger the woman, frustrate her desire; she
speaks an evil word to me, claps her hands, chides me with
words, cries out an ill thing; I care not for the contest.

PLOUGH

[The 'foe of the wood' is probably the iron of the ploughshare which in the
      form of an axe destroys the tree, or it may be the farmer who turns forest
      into ploughed land.   The former life of the wooden part of the plough
      as a tree is recalled.   The two 'cunning points' are the coulter and the
      share.]

MY nose is downward; I go deep and dig into the ground;
I move as the grey foe of the wood guides me, and my lord who

goes stooping as guardian at my tail; he pushes me in the plain, bears and urges me, sows in my track. I hasten forth, brought from the grove, strongly bound, carried on the wagon, I have many wounds; on one side of me as I go there is green, and on the other my track is clear black. Driven through my back a cunning point hangs beneath; another on my head fixed and prone falls at the side, so that I tear with my teeth, if he who is my lord serves me rightly from behind.

MONTH

[The sixty men are sixty half-days. The eleven horses are accounted for in one theory by taking the month of December as the subject of the riddle. December has seven holy days, and these, with the four Sundays (the white horses), make up the required number. If the riddle refers to December, the opposite shore which the men wish to reach is the New Year.]

SIXTY men came riding together on horses to the shore; the horsemen had eleven horses of peace, four white horses. The warriors could not pass over the sea as they desired, but the flood was too deep, dire the press of waves, high the banks, strong the currents. Then the men began to mount the wagon, and they loaded their horses together under the pole. Then the wagon bore forth the horses, the steeds and earls, proud with ashen spears, to the land across the water's abode; an ox did not draw it thus, nor the strength of asses, nor a road-horse; nor did it swim on the flood, nor go on the ground beneath its guests, nor did it stir the sea, nor fly in the air, nor return backwards; yet it brought the warriors over the stream from the high shore, and their white horses with them, so that they, the brave ones, stepped up on the other bank, the men out of the wagon and their horses in safety.

BOW

[Final b was changed to f in Old English about the middle of the eighth century. If we substitute b for f in 'Agof' we get 'Agob,' and this reversed gives 'Boga,' which is the word for bow.]

'AGOF' is my name reversed. I am a wondrous creature, shaped in conflict. When I bend and from my bosom the

poisonous arrow passes, I am eager to sweep away that deadly
evil far from me. When the master who contrived that torment
for me releases my limbs, I am longer than before, until, fraught
with destruction, I spit out the very baleful poison which earlier
I swallowed. That which I speak of there parts from no man
easily; if that which flies from my womb touches him, he buys
that drink of death with his strength, complete atonement firmly
with his life. When unstrung I will obey no one, unless cun-
ningly bound. Say what is my name.

JAY

[The runic letters properly arranged give the word 'Higora,' which means jay
or magpie.]

I AM a wondrous creature, I vary my voice; sometimes I bark like
a dog; sometimes I bleat like a goat; sometimes I cry like a
goose; sometimes I scream like a hawk; sometimes I mimic the
grey eagle, the laugh of the war-bird; sometimes with a kite's
voice I speak with my mouth; sometimes the song of the gull
where I sit in my gladness. They call me G, also A, and R; O
gives aid and H, and I. Now I am named as these six letters
clearly signify.

BOOK

[This interesting riddle describes the making of a book. The skin of which
the parchment is to be made is softened in water, dried, scraped, folded,
written on by a quill ('the bird's delight') which swallows the ink ('tree-
dye'), bound, illuminated with red, and made ready to serve men for
their profit and delight.]

A FOE deprived me of life, took away my bodily strength; after-
wards wet me, dipped me in water, took me out again, set me in
the sun where I quickly lost the hairs I had. Afterwards the
hard edge of the knife cut me, with all impurities ground off;
fingers folded me, and the bird's delight sprinkled me over with
useful drops; it made frequent tracks across the dark brim,
swallowed the tree-dye, part of the stream, again moved on me,
journeyed on leaving a dark track. Afterwards a man covered
me with binding, stretched skin over me, adorned me with gold;

and so the splendid work of smiths, circled with wire, decked me. Now the ornaments and the red dye and the glorious possessions make renowned far and wide the Protector of multitudes, in no wise the torments of hell. If the sons of men will use me they will be the safer and the more victorious, the bolder in heart and blither in thought, the wiser in mind; they will have the more friends, dear ones and kinsfolk, true and good, worthy and trusty, who will gladly increase their honour and happiness, and lay upon them benefits and mercies and hold them firm in embraces of love. Ask what is my name, useful to men; my name is famous, of service to men, sacred in myself.

MEAD

[The wings which bear the mead are those of bees from whose honey the mead is made.]

I AM cherished by men, found far and wide, brought from the groves and from the city heights, from the dales and from the downs. By day wings bore me in the air, carried me with skill under the shelter of the roof. Afterwards men bathed me in a tub. Now I am a binder and scourger; straightway I cast a young man to the earth, sometimes an old churl. Straightway he who grapples with me and struggles against my strength discovers that he must needs seek the earth with his back, if he forsakes not his folly ere that. Deprived of strength, doughty in speech, robbed of might, he has no rule over his mind, feet, nor hands. Ask what is my name, who thus on the earth in daylight bind youths, rash after blows.

BEER

[The riddle gives a detailed account of how the barley is treated to make beer, and of the joys which the drink brings to men. The death referred to in the closing lines may mean the drunken sleep of the men, or the death of the barley which becomes potent in its new function. The riddle may be compared with Burns's famous poem on John Barleycorn.

A PART of the earth is fairly adorned with the hardest and with the keenest and with the bitterest treasures of men, cut, polished, turned, dried, bound, twisted, bleached, softened, decked, made

ready, led from afar to the doors of men; joy of living creatures
is in it, and remains and endures, of those who with long life
behind them enjoy their desires and do not speak against it;
and then after death fall to declaiming and many fashioned
mouthing.   Wise men should ponder much what that creature
is.

MOON AND SUN

[The subject of the riddle is the hostility of sun and moon.   The moon is
   described as bearing between its horns light won from the sun, and when
   she is about to establish her place in the heavens the sun appears, and the
   moon departs westward, vanquished.]

I SAW a wondrous creature, a radiant air-vessel artfully adorned,
bringing booty between her horns, spoil homewards from the
foray.   She wished to build herself a bower in the stronghold,
set it up with skill, if so it might be.   Then came a wondrous
creature over the mountain-top—he is known to all dwellers on
earth—snatched the spoil and drove the wanderer to her home
against her will.   Thence she departed westward on a journey
of vengeance; she hastened forth.   Dust rose to the heavens;
dew fell on the earth; night went hence.   No man afterwards
knew where the creature journeyed.

SHIP

[The generally accepted solution is *ship* which moves on its keel (the 'one
   foot'), which is braced by beams ('many ribs'), and which has a hole in
   the deck ('mouth').]

THIS world is beautified in various ways, decked with adorn-
ments.   I saw an artful work go forth, excellent in journeys,
grind against the sand, move with a cry; the strange creature
had not sight nor hands, shoulders nor arms; the curious thing
must move on one foot, go quickly, pass over the plains; it had
many ribs; its mouth was in the midst, useful to men; it brings
to the people provision in plenty, bears food within it, and each
year yields to men a gift of which men, rich and poor, make use.
Tell, if thou canst, O sage, wise in words, what that creature is.

ICEBERG

[The iceberg is described as sailing through the waves with joyous, destructive energy. Its mother is water, but, since it can turn again to water, its daughter also is water.]

THE monster came sailing, wondrous along the wave; it called out in its comeliness to the land from the ship; loud was its din; its laughter was terrible, dreadful on earth; its edges were sharp. It was malignantly cruel, not easily brought to battle but fierce in the fighting; it stove in the ship's sides, relentless and ravaging. It bound it with a baleful charm; it spoke with cunning of its own nature: 'My mother is of the dearest race of maidens, she is my daughter grown to greatness, as it is known to men, to people among the folk, that she shall stand with joy on the earth in all lands.'

RAKE

I SAW a creature in the cities of men who feeds the cattle; it has many teeth; its beak is useful; it goes pointing downward; it plunders gently and returns home; it searches through the slopes, seeks herbs; always it finds those which are not firm; it leaves the fair ones fixed by their roots, quietly standing in their station, gleaming brightly, blowing and growing.

COAT OF MAIL

THE dewy earth, wondrous cold, first brought me forth from its womb. I know in my thoughts I am not made of the fleeces of wool, of hairs, through excellent skill. Woofs are not wound round me, nor have I warp, nor does a thread of mine resound through the thrust of many strokes, nor does the whirring shuttle move in me, nor shall a weaver's rod smite me from anywhere. Silkworms, who deck the yellow precious web with adornments, did not weave me with the strength of the fates. Yet far and wide over the earth before men they will call me delightful. O thou skilled in cunning thoughts, learned in words, tell in true speech what is this garment.

BELLOWS

The bellows are blown up by the man, whose labour is wasted if the air a once escapes. Air is both the father and son of the bellows.

I SAW the creature; its belly was at the back, mightily swollen; a servant was behind, a strong man; and he had endured much when its fullness flew out through its eye. It does not always die when it must yield its store to the other, but revival comes again to its bosom, its breath is exalted; it creates a son, it is its own father.

BULLOCK

[The bullock is pictured as drinking in life at the four udders of its mother, from which the milk gushes. If it lives it breaks the ground with the plough; when dead, its hide forms thongs.]

I SAW a creature of the weaponed kind; greedy of the joy of youth, he allowed as a gift to himself four life-saving fountains to spring forth clearly, to gush in fitting fashion. A man spoke; he said to me: 'The creature, if he lives breaks the downs; if he dies, he binds the living.'

CREATION

This, the longest of all the riddles, is a translation, sometimes free and sometimes defective, of Aldhelm's Latin riddle, *De Creatura*. The end of the riddle is lacking.]

ETERNAL is the Creator who now rules this earth with sustaining power and governs this world; mighty is the Monarch and rightly King, Master of all; He rules and governs earth and heaven even as these He encompasses. He created me wondrously in the beginning when He first established this earth; bade me dwell long at my vigil, so that I never sleep after, and suddenly sleep comes upon me, my eyes are closed in haste. The mighty Lord everywhere guides this earth with His power; so I at the Ruler's word include all this world. I am so timid, that a spectre, swift moving, can boldly terrify me, and I am everywhere bolder than a boar, when enraged he stands at bay; none of the warriors upon earth can prevail against me save only God who governs and rules this high heaven. I am much fairer in fragrance than is incense or the rose, which in its pleasure springs so peerlessly from the soil of the earth; I am more delicate than it; though the lily is loved by men, bright in its blossom, I am better than it; so too perforce I always over-power the perfume of spikenard with my sweetness everywhere. And I am fouler than this dark fen which here reeks of disease. I guide all things under the sweep of the sky, according as my loved Father taught me in the beginning, that I must rule rightly thick and thin; hold the likeness of each thing everywhere. I am higher than heaven; the high King bids me behold His precious hidden things. I too see everything under the earth, the evil foul dens of malignant spirits. I am older by far than this world or this earth could become, and yesterday I was born a babe from my mother's womb, renowned among men. I am fairer than adornments of gold, though man gird it about with wires; I am meaner than this foul wood or this seaweed which lies here cast away. I am everywhere broader than the earth, and wider than this green wold; a hand can enclose me, and three fingers can with ease clasp me all about. I am harder and colder than the hard frost, the fierce rime, when it comes to earth; I am hotter than the darting shining light, the fire of Vulcan. I am yet sweeter on the palate than the bread of bees mingled with honey; I am also more bitter than is wormwood which stands grey in the copses. I can eat more mightily and hold my own with an ancient giant in gorging; and I always can live happily, though I never see food. I can fly faster than ever could pernex [1] or eagle or hawk; there is no zephyr or coursing wind which can sweep so swiftly everywhere; the snail is speedier than I, the earthworm more nimble and the fen-frog faster in his journey; the son of the dung whom we call the weevil is more rapid in his going. Far heavier am I than the grey stone or the great mass of lead; I am much lighter than this little worm which goes here dry-foot on the flood. I am harder than flint which drives this fire out of this strong hard steel; I am far softer than down which is wind-blown here in the air. I am everywhere broader than the earth and wider than this green wold. I easily embrace everything at a distance, curiously

---

[1] The translator misunderstood Aldhelm's phrase, 'plus pernix aquilis' (swifter than eagles), and has taken the Latin adjective to be the name of a bird.

woven with wondrous power.   There is no other creature below me in this mighty earthly life; I am above all beings whom our Ruler created, who alone can mightily tame me with eternal power, so that I shall not be puffed up with pride.   I am greater and stronger than the mighty whale which views with dim vision the depth of the sea; I am more powerful than he; likewise am I slighter in my strength than the hand-worm which the children of men, the sages, dig with a knife.   I have no fair locks on my head, delicately curled, but am bald far and wide; nor could I enjoy eyelids, nor brown hair, but the Creator deprived me of all; now curled locks grow wondrously on my head, so that they can shimmer very curiously on my shoulders. I am larger and stouter than fattened swine, the grunting pig, which, dark-coloured, lived joyously rooting in the beech-wood, so that he . . .

SOUL AND BODY

['The noble guest' is the soul; its servant and brother is the body.   The earth is mother and sister to both—mother, because man's body is made from her; sister, because she was made by the same father—God.]

I KNOW a noble guest cherished in his excellent dwelling, whom grim hunger cannot harm nor hot thirst, old age nor illness.   If the servant tends him kindly, he who must ever go on the journey, they shall find in safety in their home food and gladness appointed for them, countless kindred; sorrow, if the servant obeys his lord badly, his master on the journey.   Nor will one brother fear another; when, hasting away, they both leave the bosom of one kinswoman, mother and sister, they both suffer. Let the man who will, set forth in fitting words what the stranger is called or the servant of which I speak here.

BOOKWORM

A MOTH ate words.   That seemed to me a strange event, when I heard of that wonder, that the worm, a thief in the darkness, should devour the song of a man, a famed utterance and a thing founded by a strong man.   The thievish visitant was no whit the wiser for swallowing the words.

CHALICE

[The sacred gold vessel brings thoughts of Christ to the minds of men during the celebration of Communion.]

I HEARD of a bright ring interceding well before men, though tongueless, though it cried not with loud voice in strong words. The precious thing spoke before men, though holding its peace: 'Save me, Helper of souls!' May men understand the mysterious saying of the red gold, the magic speech; may wise men entrust their salvation to God, as the ring said.

FIRE

WONDROUSLY is the warrior brought forth on earth from two dumb creatures for the use of men, created gleaming, which foe bears against foe for his hurt. A woman often binds it in its great strength. It obeys them well, serves them greatly, if maidens and men tend it with due measure, feed it well. It is exalted for the benefit of their joy in life. Cruelly it requites him who lets it grow to be proud.

PEN AND FINGERS

[The four creatures are the thumb, two fingers and the pen, which once had supported the swift bird and now was dipped in the ink. The 'struggling warrior' is the arm and the 'rich gold' may refer either to the gold of the ink-pot or to the illuminated page of the manuscript.]

FOUR curious creatures I beheld travelling together; swarth were their tracks, their marks very black. The support of the swift ones was quick in its course; it flew in the air, dived under the wave. Restlessly suffered the struggling warrior who points their paths to all four over the rich gold.

FLAIL

I saw two hard captives carried into the dwelling under the roof of the hall; they were companions fettered fast together by strait bonds. Close to one of them was a dark-haired slave-woman who controlled both of them fast in bonds in their course.

BATTERING RAM

[The battering-ram's former life as a tree in the forest and its later destructive duties, when its massive head makes a breach in wall or gate, are vividly described.]

I saw the tree tower up in the wood glorious with branches; that tree was in joy, a growing timber. Water and earth fed it well, until, grown old in other days, it was sorely stricken in its downfall, silent in bonds, its wounds fettered over, adorned in front with dark trappings. Now by the might of its head it clears the way for another malicious foe. Often together, mid storm, they have plundered the hoard. The second was swift and restive if the former fell into danger. No one could venture to grapple with it.

SWALLOWS

[Gnats, starlings, and other solutions have also been suggested for this charming little poem.]

THIS air bears over rocky slopes little creatures who are very black, swarthy, dark-coated. Valiant in song, they move in flocks, they cry loudly; they tread the woody promontories, at times the city houses of the children of men. Name them yourselves.

REED

[This beautiful little poem first describes the reed growing by a lonely shore, then taken by men and fashioned into a flute or whistle to give music in hall, or into a pen which may write a secret message. The poem immediately precedes *The Husband's Message* in the *Exeter Book*, and it has been very plausibly suggested that it forms the beginning of that poem and is, in fact, not a riddle at all.]

BESIDE the shore and near the strand,
Right where the sea beats on the land,
I, rooted, dwelt in my old place;
And few there were of human race
Who saw my solitary abode,
But every morn the brown wave flowed,
And with its watery clasp me caught.
And little had I any thought
That it should ever be decreed,
That o'er the bench where men drank mead,
I, mouthless once, should speak and sing,
Or soon or late. A wondrous thing
To mind which cannot understand
How point of knife and strong right hand,
The man's mind coupled with the blade,
Pressed me purposely and made
Me give a message without fear
To thee with no one else to hear,
So that no other men e'er may
Tell far and wide the words we say.

CREATION

[A free treatment of part of the larger riddle on the same subject.]

I AM greater than this world, less than a hand-worm, lighter than the moon, swifter than the sun. All the floods of the sea are in my embraces and the bosom of this earth, the green fields. I touch the depths, I plunge beneath hell, I mount above the heavens, the abode of glory; far I extend over the dwelling of angels; I fill the earth, the whole world and the streams of ocean far and wide with myself. Tell my name.

OYSTER

THE sea fed me, the water-covering enveloped me, and waves covered me, footless, close to earth. Often I open my mouth to the flood; now some man will eat my flesh; he cares not for my covering, when with the point of a knife he tears off the skin from my side and afterwards quickly eats me uncooked also. . . .

HORN

[The horn is slung across the shoulder, at other times it is filled with mead ('what grew in the grove') and is handed to men in the hall; its harsh note sounds in battle, and it is given as a reward to the gleeman for his song.]

I AM the noble's shoulder-companion, the warrior's comrade, loved by my lord, the king's associate. Sometimes the fair-haired queen, the earl's daughter, lays hand on me, though she is noble. I bear in my bosom what grew in the grove. Sometimes I ride on the proud steed at the head of the host; harsh is my tongue. Often I render reward for his words to the singer after his measure. Good is my nature, and I myself am black. Tell my name.

WEATHERCOCK

I AM puff-breasted, swollen necked, I have a head and lofty tail, eyes and ears and one foot, a back and hard beak, a high neck and two sides, a rod in the middle, a dwelling above men. I endure misery when he who stirs the forest moves me and torrents beat upon me in my station, the hard hail and rime; and frost comes down and snow falls on me, pierced through the stomach, and I . . .

FISH AND RIVER

MY abode is not silent, nor I myself loud voiced; the Lord laid laws upon us, shaped our course together; I am swifter than he, stronger at times, he more laborious; sometimes I rest; he must needs run on. I ever dwell in him while I live: if we are parted death is my destiny.

ONE-EYED SELLER OF GARLIC OR ONIONS

A CREATURE came where many men, wise in mind, were sitting in the meeting-place; it had one eye and two ears and two feet, twelve hundred heads, back and belly, and two hands, arms, and shoulders, one neck and two sides. Say what is my name.

KEY

My head is forged by a hammer, wounded with pointed tools, rubbed by the file. Often I gape at what is fixed opposite to me, when, girded with rings, I must needs thrust stoutly against the hard bolt; pierced from behind I must shove forward that which guards the joy of my lord's mind at midnight. At times I drag my nose, the guardian of the treasure, backwards, when my lord desires to take the stores of those whom at his will he commanded to be driven out of life by murderous power.

GNOMIC POETRY

[Gnomic poetry consists of sententious sayings of different kinds. Sometimes a general truth is stated, a simple observation based on human experience; sometimes a moral maxim is laid down. Such poetry is found in the early stages of many literatures. Between two and three hundred lines of Old English gnomic poetry have come down to us. They show no great beauty, except in the famous passage about the Frisian wife welcoming her sailor husband, but they are interesting as illustrating an early stage in poetic development. This kind of sententious writing is frequently found elsewhere in Old English verse. In *Beowulf*, in the lyric poems such as *The Wanderer*, and elsewhere, we can see the tendency to generalizations of the kind found in the purely gnomic poetry.]

I

QUESTION me with wise words; let not thy thought be hidden, the mystery that thou mayest know most thoroughly. I will not tell thee my secret if thou concealest thy wisdom and the thoughts of thy heart. Wise men must needs exchange proverbs. Man shall first fittingly praise God, our Father, because in the beginning He bestowed on us life and transitory will; He will remind us of those gifts. Man shall dwell on earth; the young shall grow old. God is everlasting for us; fates change Him not, nor does disease or age vex Him, the Almighty, at all; nor does He grow old in spirit, but He is still as He was, a Prince long suffering. He gives us thoughts, differing minds, many languages. Many an island far and wide encloses many living races. The Lord, Almighty God, has raised up for mankind spacious domains, as many peoples as customs. Sage shall hold meeting with sage; their minds are alike; they ever settle strife; they teach peace, which miserable men took away before. Counsel shall be with wisdom, justice with wise men, a good man with good men. Two are consorts. A woman and a man shall bring a child into the world by birth. A tree on earth shall suffer in its leaves, lament its branches. The ready man shall depart, the doomed man shall die and every day fight at parting from the world. The Lord alone knows whence the death comes which departs hence from the land. He increases children, whom early illness takes; thus there come to be on earth so many of the race of men; there would not be a limit of progeny on earth if He who created this world did not decrease them. Foolish is he who knows not his Lord, since death often comes unlooked for. Wise men save their souls, righteously maintain their truth. Happy is he who prospers in his home; hapless he to whom his friends are false. Never shall he be happy whose store fails; he shall be bound for a space by distress. The guiltless heart shall be glad. The blind man shall suffer the loss of eyes; clear sight shall be taken from him; they cannot behold the radiant heavenly bodies, sun nor moon. That will be grief for him in his mind, sorrowful since he alone knows it, nor looks for his sight to come again. The Lord gave him that torment; He can give him a cure, health of eye, if He knows him to be clean of heart. The weak man needs a leech. One shall teach the young man, strengthen and urge him to know well, until one has subdued him. Let him be given food and clothing till he be brought to understanding. He shall not be rebuked as a child before he can declare himself. Thus shall he prosper among the people, so that he shall be firm of purpose. A man shall rule with a strong mind. The sea often brings a storm, the ocean in stormy seasons; fiercely they begin to hasten, the dun waves afar off, to the land; yet may it stand fast. The walls shall oppose resistance to them; they both feel the wind. As the sea is serene when the wind wakes it not, so peoples are peaceful when they have settled a dispute; they sit in happy circumstances and then hold with comrades. Bold men are mighty by their nature. A king is eager for power. Hateful is he who lays claim to land, loved is he who gives more. Majesty shall go with pride, bold men with brave ones; both shall straightway do battle. The earl shall be on the war-horse's back; the host shall ride in a company, the foot-troop stand fast. It is meet that a woman be at her table; a roving woman causes words to be uttered; often she defames man with her vices. Men speak of her with contempt; often her cheek fades. A shamed man shall walk in the shade; a pure man's place is in the light. Hand shall be laid on head,[1] treasure shall abide in its resting-place; the throne shall stand ready, when men divide it. Greedy is he who receives the gold; the man on the high seat will satisfy him. There shall be reward, if we will not tell lies, from Him who has decreed us this mercy.

[1] This may refer to some ceremony between lord and vassal. Perhaps the chief laid hand on the warrior's head when he gave him treasure.

II

Frost shall freeze, fire consume wood; earth shall grow, ice form a bridge; water shall wear a covering, wonderfully lock up the sprouts of earth. One shall unbind the fetters of frost, God very mighty; winter shall depart, good weather come again, summer brightly hot. The ocean shall be unquiet. The awful path of the dead is longest secret. Holly shall go to the fire. The property of the dead man shall be parted. Glory is best. A king shall buy a queen with goods, with beakers and bracelets; both shall first be generous with gifts. Battle, warfare, shall be strong in the earl, and the woman shall thrive, beloved by her people, be cheerful of mind, keep counsel, be liberal with horses and treasures, everywhere at all times before the band of comrades greet first the protector of the nobles with mead, present straightway the first goblets to the prince's hand, and shall know wise counsel for them both together, the householders. The ship shall be nailed, the shield bound, the linden targe light.

Dear is the welcome one to the Frisian wife when the ship comes to rest. His vessel has come, and her husband is at home, her own provider; and she bids him come in, washes his sea-stained garment and gives him fresh clothes. Pleasant it is for him on land whom his love constrains. A wife shall keep faith with her husband; often she defames man with her vices; many a one is steadfast in mind, many a one is prying; she loves strange men when the other travels afar. Long is the sailor on the voyage; yet ever shall one await a beloved, await what he cannot hasten for. When again chance is given him, he comes home if he lives uninjured, unless the sea stays him. The ocean holds him in its hands. A maid is the delight of her owner. A wealthy man will sell his property, a king his dwelling, to the sailor when he comes sailing. He enjoys wood and water when a dwelling is granted him; he buys meat if he needs more, ere he grows too weary. He who eats too rarely is ill; though he is brought into the sun, he cannot endure the open air, though it is warm in summer. He is overcome, he may soon perish, if he knows not someone to keep him alive with food. One shall nourish strength with meat. He who thinks to hide it shall conceal a murder underground, down beneath the earth; that is no seemly death when it is kept secret. The hapless man shall bow down; sickness shall languish; justice shall flourish. Wisdom is most useful; evil most useless, which the wretched one obtains. Good is powerful and belongs to God. Thought shall be held in, hand controlled; the pupil shall be in the eye, wisdom in the breast where man's thoughts are. Every mouth craves meat; meals shall duly come. Gold is fitting on the man's sword, rare triumphant raiment, treasure on the woman; a good minstrel for men, spear-battle for heroes, war in resistance to protect the dwellings. The shield shall be for the warrior, the shaft for the spoiler; the bracelet shall be for the bride, books for the scholar, the Eucharist for holy men, sins for the heathen. Woden wrought idols; the Lord wrought heaven, the spacious skies; that is a mighty God, the King of truth Himself, the Saviour of souls, who gave us all that we live by and afterwards at the end rules all mankind; that is the Lord Himself.

III

A man shall utter wisdom, write secrets, sing songs, merit praise, expound glory, be diligent daily. A good man is mindful of a good and tame horse, known and tried and round of hoof. No man acquires too much. Well shall one keep a friend in all ways; often a man passes by the village afar off where he knows he has no certain friend. Unfriended, unblest, a man takes wolves for companions, a dangerous beast; full often that companion rends him. There shall be terror of the grey wolf; a grave for the dead man. It is grieved by hunger; it goes not around that [1] with lamentation; the grey wolf weeps not indeed for the slaughter, the killing of men, but ever wishes it greater. A bandage shall be bound round; vengeance shall be for the brave man. The bow shall be for the arrow; to both alike shall man be a companion. Treasure becomes another's; a man shall give gold; God may give goods to the rich and take them away again. A hall shall stand, grow old itself. A tree which lies low grows least. Trees shall spread out and faith increase; it springs up in the breast of the merciful. A false man and foolish, venomous and faithless, God cares not for him. The Lord created many things which came to be long ago, bade them be thus henceforth. For every man wise words are fitting, the song for the singer and wisdom for the man. As many men as

[1] The grave.

there are in the world, so many thoughts are there; each has his own heart's longing; yet the less for him who knows many songs and can play the harp with his hands, he has the gift of his music which God has given him. Hapless is he who must needs live alone; fate has decreed that he shall dwell friendless; it were better for him had he a brother, that they both were the sons of one man, of an earl, if they both should attack a boar or bear; that is a very fierce beast. Ever shall these warriors bear their armour and sleep together; never shall one mar their peace by tale-bearing ere death part them. They two shall sit at the chess-board while their anger passes away; they forget the shaping of harsh destinies; they have sport at the board. The idle hand of the gamester is at leisure long enough when it casts the dice but seldom in the broad ship, unless it is running under sail. Weary shall he be who rows against the wind; full often one blames the timid with reproaches, so that he loses courage, draws his oar on board. Guile shall go with evil, skill with things fitting; thus is the die stolen. Often they bandy words before they turn their backs on one another. The resolute man is everywhere ready.[1] Hostility has been among mankind even since the earth swallowed the blood of Abel. That was not the hatred of a day from which wicked drops of blood sprang far and wide, great evil to men, to many people pernicious hate. Cain slew his own brother whom death carried off; far and wide was it known then that lasting hate injured men, so citizens.[2] They were busy with strife of weapons far and wide throughout the earth; they devised and tempered the harmful sword. The shield shall be ready, the dart on its shaft, the edge on the sword and point on the spear, courage in the brave man. Helmet shall be for the bold man, and ever the soul of the base man shall be a treasure most paltry.

IV

A king shall rule. Cities are to be seen afar off, cunning work of giants, which are on this earth, wondrous work of wall-stones. Wind is swiftest in the sky; thunder is loudest at seasons. The glories of Christ are great. Fate is strongest. Winter is coldest; spring most frosty; it is longest cold; summer

[1] Ready, perhaps, to foil his cheating opponent in the game, or ready for the dispute which results from the cheating.
[2] The text may be corrupt here.

most fair with sunshine; the sun is hottest; autumn most
glorious; it brings to men the fruits of the year which God sends
them.   Truth is plainest; treasure is most precious, gold for all
men, and the aged man the wisest, old in years gone by, who
before endured many things.   Woe is wondrous clinging.
The clouds go on their way.   Good comrades shall urge a young
noble to battle and the bestowal of rings.   Courage shall be in a
man.   The sword shall endure battle against the helm.   The
hawk, though wild, shall abide on the glove.   The wolf shall
dwell in the grove, a wretched recluse; the boar shall dwell in the
wood, strong in the might of his tusks.   The good man shall
gain glory in his land.   The dart shall be in the hand, the spear
bright with gold.   The gem shall stand in the ring, high and
broad.   The stream shall mingle in waves with the ocean.   The
mast, the sail-yard, shall be at rest in the boat.   The sword shall
lie in the bosom, excellent iron.   The dragon shall dwell in the
cave, old, splendid in ornaments.   The fish shall bring forth its
kind in the water.   The king shall give out rings in hall.   The
bear shall dwell on the heath, aged and terrible.   Water shall
flow from the hill, earth-grey.   The army shall be gathered
together, a band of glorious men.   Faith shall be in an earl,
wisdom in a man.   The wood shall bloom with blossoms on
earth.   The hill shall stand green on the earth.   God shall
dwell in the heavens, the Judge of deeds.   The door shall be in
the hall, wide mouth of the building.   The boss shall be on the
shield, firm guard of the fingers.   The bird shall sport in the air.
The salmon shall go darting in the pool.   The shower in the
skies shall come into this world mingled with wind.   The thief
shall go in dark weather.   The demon shall dwell in the fen,
alone in the land.   The woman, the virgin, shall by secret craft
seek her friend, if she does not wish to prosper among the people
so as to be bought with rings.   The ocean shall surge with salt;
cloud and flood, mountain streams, shall flow about every land.
Cattle on the earth shall bring forth and teem.   The luminary
shall shine brightly in the heavens as the Lord commanded it.
Good against evil, youth against age, life against death, light
against darkness, army against army, one foe against another,
injury against injury, shall strive round about the land, avenge
hostility.   Ever shall the wise man ponder on the struggle
round about this world.   The felon shall be hanged, shall fairly
pay for committing crime before against mankind.   The Lord
alone knows whither the soul shall afterwards pass and all the
spirits who turn to God after the day of death.   They await

judgment in the Father's embrace. The future state is secret and hidden; the Lord alone knows, the Father who saves. No one returns hither under our roofs who may truly tell men here what is the Lord's decree, the abodes of those who have triumphed, where He Himself dwells.

THE ARTS OF MEN

MANY new gifts are ever seen on earth which living beings hold in their minds, according as the God of hosts, the Lord mighty in strength, deals unto men, bestows special gifts, sends them far and wide by His own power, and of them each among the people may receive a part. There is no man in the world so hapless, nor so needy, so weak in thought, nor so dull-minded, that the beneficent Giver strips him of all skill of mind or of mighty deeds, wisdom in thought or in speech, lest he should despair of all things he did in life, of every benefit. God never decrees that anyone shall become so wretched. No one by wise skill shall rise to glory among the people so mightily in this life that the Protector of peoples by His holy grace will send hither to him, let come under his sole sway, all wise thoughts and worldly wisdom, lest he in pride, full of glorious favours, should lose fit restraint of mind and then despise the less fortunate. But He who has power of judgment scatters variously to dwellers throughout this world the bodily powers of men. To one on earth here He grants goods, worldly treasures. One is poor, an unfortunate man; yet he is wise in arts of the mind. One receives more bodily strength. One is beautiful, fair in form. One is a poet skilled in songs. One is eloquent in words. One is a pursuer in hunting of glorious beasts. One is prized by men of power. One is bold in war, a man skilled in battle where shields clash together. One can in the council of sages devise a decree for the people, where many wise men are gathered together. One can marvellously plan the making of all high buildings; his hand is trained, skilful and deft, as fits the workman, to set up a hall; he knows how to join firmly the spacious building against sudden downfall. One can play the harp with his hands; he has the cunning of quick movements on the instrument. One is a swift runner; one a straight shooter; one skilled in songs; one swift on the land, fleet of foot. One guides the prow on the yellow wave; the leader of the host knows the watery path over the vast sea, when mighty mariners with nimble strength wield the oars by the ship. One is skilled in swimming; one an artful workman in gold and gems when a protector of men bids him set a jewel with splendour. One, a cunning smith, can make many weapons for use in war, when he shapes a helmet or short sword or corslet, gleaming blade or the round shield; he can join them firmly against the flying spear. One is pious and charitable, virtuous in his ways. One is a nimble servant in the mead hall. One is well versed in horses, learned in the arts of steeds. One with strong heart patiently endures what he must needs. One knows laws where men seek counsel together. One is clever at chess. One is witty at the wine-drinking, a good lord of the beer. One is a builder, good at raising a dwelling. One is an army leader, a bold general. One is a councillor. One is a servant with his lord, the more bold at need. One has power to endure, a steadfast mind. One is a fowler, skilled with the hawk. One is daring on horseback. One is very swift, enjoys rare sport, the faculty of mirthful deeds before men, sprightly and agile. One is kind, has a heart and speech pleasant unto men. One earnestly ponders in his heart here the needs of the soul, and makes choice of God's favour above all worldly wealth. One is fearless in fighting the devil, is ever ready in the battle against sins. One has skill in many a church service, can loudly exalt with songs of praise the Lord of life; he has a high clear voice. One is book-learned, skilled in lore. One is deft with his hands in writing words. There is no man now on earth so artful in mind, nor so mighty in strength, that all these arts should be put upon him alone, lest boastfulness should do him hurt, or his heart should be puffed up by fame, if he alone above all men had beauty and wisdom and success in deeds. But in various ways He prevents mankind from boasting and bestows His gifts to one in virtue, to one in skill, to one in beauty, to one in war; to one man He gives a gentle heart, a kindly mind; one is loyal to his master. Thus fittingly the Lord scatters His gifts far and wide. Ever may He have the glory thereof, splendid praise, who gives us this life and shows His gentle heart unto men.

THE FATES OF MEN

FULL often it comes to pass by God's power that man and woman bring forth a child into the world and deck him with many-coloured garments, train him and caress him, till the time comes and it happens in the course of years that the young limbs and members are grown strong. Thus the father and mother foster and feed him, bestow gifts on him, and adorn him. Only God knows what the years will bring to him when he grows up.

To one unhappy man it chances that his death comes with sorrow in youth; the wolf shall eat him, the grey heath-stepper. Then the mother mourns his death; such things are not in man's power. Hunger shall destroy one; tempest shall drive one afar; the spear shall slay one; war shall kill one. One shall pass through life blinded, grope with his hands; one, lame in foot, sick with sinew wounds, shall lament his pain, mourn his fate, heavy in heart. One in the forest shall fall, wingless, from a high tree; yet does it fly, sports in the air, till the growth of the tree is no longer there. Then, reft of life, sad in mind, it sinks down to its roots, falls on the earth; its life has departed. One shall perforce go on foot on far paths and bear his needs with him, and on a dewy track tread the perilous land of alien people. He has few of living men to entertain him; the friendless man is everywhere hated because of his miseries. One shall swing on the broad gallows, hang in death, until the body, the frame, is bloodily destroyed. There the raven pecks his eyes, the dark-coated one rends the corpse, nor can he keep the hateful flying foe from that malice with his hands; his life is gone, and, powerless to feel, past hope of life, he endures his fate, pale on the tree, surrounded with a deadly mist. His name is accursed. Fire shall destroy one on the pyre, the fierce flame, the cruel glowing blaze, shall devour the fated man, then his parting from life comes swiftly. The woman weeps who sees the flames cover her child. The sword's edge takes the life of one on the mead bench, a drunkard in his wrath, a man sated with wine; too hasty were his words before. One at the beer-drinking by the cup-bearer's hand shall become excited with mead; then he knows not how to check his mouth with his mind, but full

318

miserably he shall leave life, suffer great misery, reft of joys, and men call him a self-slayer, and talk of the drinking of him who was roused by mead.   One shall by strength of God make an end of all his misery in youth and later in old age become happy, enjoy days of gladness, and receive wealth, treasures, and the mead goblet among his kinsmen, as far as any man can keep possession for all time.

Thus mighty God variously bestows, grants, and assigns to all over the face of the earth, and orders their destinies; to one wealth; to one a portion of suffering; to one joy in youth; to one success in war, mighty war-play; to one a blow or stroke, radiant glory; to one skill at the dicing-board, cunning at chess; some scribes become wise.   For one a wondrous gift is wrought by goldsmith's work; full often he hardens and well adorns the corslet of the king of Britain, and he gives him broad land as a guerdon; gladly he receives it.   One shall gladden men gathered together, delight those sitting on the benches at the beer where the joy of the drinkers is great.   One shall sit at his lord's feet with his harp, receive treasure and ever swiftly sweep the strings, let the plectrum, which leaps, sound aloud, the nail with its melody; great is the desire for him.   One shall tame the wild bird in its pride, the hawk on the hand, till the falcon grows gentle.   He puts foot-rings upon it, feeds it thus in fetters, proud of its plumage, wearies the swift flier with little food, till the foreign bird grows subject to his food giver in garb and act, and trained to the youth's hand.   Thus wondrously the God of hosts throughout the world has fashioned and bestowed the arts of men and ruled the destiny of everyone of mankind on earth.   Wherefore now let everyone render all thanks to Him because He cares for men in His mercy.

JUDITH

[Unfortunately only the closing sections of this poem have survived. It is a work of remarkable power and beauty. The exultation with which the poet describes the overthrow of Holofernes and his host may have been inspired by the struggle of the English against the Danes.]

. . . She did not lose faith in His gifts on this far-spreading earth; then truly she found protection there in the famous Prince when she most needed the favour of the highest Judge, that He, the Lord of creation, should guard her against the greatest danger. The glorious Father in heaven bestowed that boon on her because she never failed in firm faith in the Almighty. Then Holofernes, as I heard, eagerly sent forth a bidding to wine, and dressed up dainties wondrously sumptuous. The prince of men bade all the eldest thanes come; the shield-bearing warriors attended in great haste; the chiefs of the people came to the mighty leader. It was on the fourth day that Judith, wise in thought, a woman of fairy beauty, first sought him.

X

Then they went to sit down at the banquet, exulting to carousal, all his companions in evil, bold corslet warriors. Often down the benches there deep bowls were borne, brimming beakers, too, and goblets for the guests. Daring shield-warriors, doomed to death, laid hold on them, though the leader, the dread master of men, had no thought of his fate. Then Holofernes, gold-friend of men, grew merry with the pouring out of wine; he laughed and called aloud, clamoured and made outcries, so that the children of men could hear from afar how he of stern mood stormed and shouted; proud and fevered by mead, he often urged the guests on the benches to bear themselves bravely. Thus the wicked one, the stern giver of treasure, drenched his officers all day in wine, till they lay swooning; he vanquished all his veterans with drink as if they were stricken by death, void of all virtue. Thus did the prince of men order the guests to be plied until the dark night drew near the children of men.

Then, steeped in malice, he ordered the blessed maid to be brought with speed, laden with rings, adorned with circlets, to his bed. Quickly, the retainers did as their prince, the chief of corslet warriors, bade. Straightway they stepped to the guest-house where they found wise Judith; and then the shield-warriors promptly led the noble maid to the lofty pavilion, where the mighty man was ever wont to rest at night, Holofernes abhorred by the Saviour. There was a fair curtain, all golden, hung round the leader's couch, so that the evil man, the prince of warriors, could look through on each of the sons of men who entered there, and no man on him, unless the proud man bade one of his mighty warriors draw nearer him to hold council. Quickly then they brought the wise woman to the couch; then, troubled in mind, the men went to proclaim to their lord that the holy virgin had been led to his pavilion.

Then the renowned ruler of cities grew jubilant in his heart; he thought to stain the radiant woman with pollution and foulness. The glorious Judge, the Prince of majesty, was not minded to let that come to pass, but He, the Lord, the Master of warriors, kept him from that thing. Then the fiendish wanton with evil intent went to seek his bed with a band of followers, where forthwith in one night he was to lose his life. Then the unsparing sovereign of men had reached on earth his violent death, such a one as he had deserved while he dwelt in this world under the canopy of the clouds. Thus, fuddled with wine, the chieftain fell in the midst of his couch, as if he had no wits in his mind; the warriors passed out of the chamber with utmost haste, men sated with wine, who had brought the traitor, the hateful tyrant, to his bed for the last time.

Then did the Saviour's glorious servant ponder deeply how she might most easily spoil the monster of life, before he awoke with foul lust. Then the Creator's handmaiden, with curling tresses, grasped a sharp sword hardened in the storms of battle, and with her right hand drew it from the scabbard. Then she began to call upon the name of the Lord of heaven, the Saviour of all who dwell upon earth, and she spoke these words:

'I pray to Thee, God of creation, Spirit of comfort, Son all powerful, Glory of the Trinity, for Thy mercy in my need. Now is my heart greatly kindled and mournful my mood, sorely stirred with sorrows; give me, O Lord of heaven, victory and true faith, that with this sword I may cut down this dealer of sudden death; grant me my salvation, O stern Prince of men; never had I greater need of Thy mercy. Avenge now, O Lord of might, noble Giver of glory, what angers my mind, kindles my heart.'

Then the highest Judge straightway inspired her with courage, as He does all men here who seek His aid in a right mind and true faith. Then her heart grew large; hope was renewed in the holy maid. Then she grasped the unbeliever hard by his hair; with her hands she drew him towards her to his shame, and with cunning laid the malicious one down, the hateful man, as she best could contrive to do with the caitiff. Then the maiden with curling tresses struck the hostile foe with gleaming sword, so that she cut his neck half through; and, drunken and stricken, he lay in a swoon. He was not yet dead, wholly lifeless; the undaunted woman once again fiercely smote the heathen hound, so that his head rolled forth on the floor. The foul carcass lay dead behind; the spirit departed elsewhere under the deep cliff, and there it was humbled, bound for ever in torment, surrounded with serpents, fettered with agonies, held fast in hell-fire after death. Nor need he hope, engulfed in gloom, that he may leave that hall of serpents, but there he must dwell for ever without end in that dark home, empty of joy.

XI

Judith then had won illustrious fame in fight, as God granted unto her, the Prince of heaven, who gave her victory. Then the wise maiden swiftly brought the warrior's head all bloody in the bag in which her servant, a fair-cheeked woman of excellent virtue, had fetched thither the food for them both, and Judith gave it then all gory into her hand, to her attendant, the prudent woman, to bear home. Forwards they fared thence, the two valorous women, until, bold-hearted, they passed clear of the host, the triumphant maidens, so that they could clearly behold Bethulia, the walls of the fair city shining. Then, ring-adorned, they sped their steps, till, glad of heart, they had reached the rampart gate. Warriors were sitting; watchmen were keeping guard in the stronghold, as Judith, the maiden of wisdom, the woman of valour, had bidden the sorrowing people before, when she went on her venture. Then had the loved one come again to her people, and then the wise woman quickly commanded one of the men to come to her from the far-spreading fortress and admit her with speed through the rampart gate, and she spoke these words to the victorious people:

'I am able to tell you a thing of note, that no longer you need sorrow in soul. God, the glorious King, is gracious unto you. That has been made manifest far throughout the world, that glorious success is coming to you in splendour, and that exaltation has been granted after the afflictions you long have endured.'

Then the citizens were glad when they heard how the holy maiden spoke over the high rampart. The people rejoiced, the host hastened to the fortress gate, men and women together, old and young, in troops and throngs, in swarms and crowds; surged and ran in thousands towards the maiden of the Lord. The hearts of all men in the mead city were made glad when they learned that Judith was come again to her home, and then in haste they let her in with reverence. Then the wise maiden, decked with gold, bade her heedful handmaid uncover the warrior's head and show it all bleeding for a sign to the citizens of how she had sped in battle. Then the noble woman spoke to all the host:

'Victorious heroes, chiefs of the people, here you can clearly behold the head of the most hateful heathen warrior, of Holofernes now dead, who most among men dealt us out death, bitter sorrows, and was minded to do yet more; but God did not grant him longer life to lay afflictions upon us. With God's help I reft him of life. Now I wish to pray all of you citizens and shield-bearing warriors to fit yourselves forthwith for fight. When God the Creator, the merciful King, shall send from the east the shining light, bear forth the shields, the bucklers before your breasts and the corslets, the gleaming helms, into the thick of the foe; lay low the leaders, the fated chiefs, with bloody blades. Your enemies are doomed to death, and you shall gain glory, fame in the fight, as the mighty Lord has shown you by my hand.'

Then the band of bold men was quickly made ready, men brave in battle; the valiant men and warriors marched out, bore banners of victory; they set straight forward to the fight, heroes beneath their helmets, from the sacred stronghold at break of dawn; the shields rang, resounded loudly. The lean wolf in the wood rejoiced at that, and the dark raven, the bird greedy for slaughter; both knew that the warriors purposed to provide them with a feast of fated men; and behind them flew the dewy-feathered eagle, hungry for food; dark-coated, horny-beaked, it sang a song of war. The men of battle marched on, warriors to the strife, protected by shields, hollow linden targes—they who erstwhile had borne the flaunting of foreigners, the taunt of the heathen. All the Assyrians were rigorously requited for that at the spear-play when the Hebrews under their banners had come upon the camp. Then keenly they shot forth showers of arrows, adders of war, from their bows of horn, strong shafts; the raging warriors loudly stormed, cast spears into the press of brave men; wroth were the heroes, the dwellers in the land, against the hateful race; sternly they stepped forward; stout of heart, they harshly aroused their ancient foes overcome by mead. The men with their hands drew from the sheaths the brightly adorned blades with trusty edges; fiercely they smote the Assyrian warriors, contrivers of evil; they spared no living man of the host, mean or mighty, whom they could overcome.

XII

So all morning the clansmen pursued the foreign people, until those who were angered, the chief guardians of the host, perceived that the Hebrews had violently shown them the stroke of the sword. They went to declare that in words before the eldest thanes, roused up the warriors and in terror announced to them sudden tidings, a morning alarm to men overcome by mead, dread play of swords. Then forthwith, as I heard, heroes doomed to perish shook off sleep, and sad men pressed in crowds towards the pavilion of the evil one, Holofernes. They meant straightway to make known the battle to their lord, before the terror, the might of the Hebrews, came down upon him. All supposed that the prince of men and the fair maid were together in the beautiful tent, Judith the noble and the lecher, terrible and fierce. Yet there was not one of the earls who dared awaken the warrior, or seek to find out how the soldier had fared with the sacred maiden, the virgin of the Lord. The troop drew near, the host of the Hebrews; they fought hard with keen swords; fiercely with blood-stained brands they made requital for ancient quarrels, for old grudges. The glory of the Assyrians was destroyed in that day's work, their haughtiness made humble. The men stood round their prince's pavilion, exceeding bold but gloomy in mind. Then all together they, without God to believe in, began to shout, to call loudly and to gnash their teeth, grinding their teeth in sorrow. Then their glory was past, their success and deeds of prowess. The earls wished to waken their friendly lord; they did not succeed. Then tardily and late one of the warriors grew so bold as to venture undaunted into the tent, so strongly need drove him. Then he found his bestower of gold lying pale on the bed, reft of his spirit, despoiled of life. Then forthwith he fell cold on the ground; fierce in heart, he began to tear his hair and his robe also, and spoke these words to the warriors who in sadness remained there without:

'Here is our ruin revealed and shown to be at hand, that now in tribulation the time has come upon us when we must perish together, fall in fight. Here lies our ruler, headless, hewn by the sword.'

Then, sad of soul, they cast their weapons down; despairing, they hastened to flee. At their back fought a powerful host, until the greatest part of the army were stretched on the field of victory, laid low by war, hewn by swords, a delight to the wolves and also a joy to birds greedy for slaughter. Those who lived fled from the shields of their foes. Behind them went the army of the Hebrews, honoured with victory, made glorious with fame; the Lord God, the Almighty Prince, gave them fair help. Then the valiant heroes hastily wrought a passage with their blood-stained blades through the press of foemen; they hacked the targes, cleft the roof of shields. The fighters were enraged in the conflict, the Hebrew men; the warriors lusted exceedingly at that time after battle. There fell to earth the greater part of Assyrian nobility, the hateful race; few came alive to their native land. Valiant men turned back, warriors in retreat, amid carnage, reeking corpses. The dwellers in the land had a chance to spoil the most hateful ones, their ancient foes now lifeless, of bloody booty, beautiful ornaments, shields and broad swords, brown helmets, precious treasures. The guardians of their country had gloriously conquered their foes on the field of battle, put their old enemies to sleep with swords; those who were most hateful to them of living nations lay on the field.

Then all the tribe, most famous of peoples, proud, curly-haired, bore and brought to the fair city of Bethulia for the space of a month helmets and hip-swords, grey corslets, war-trappings of men decked with gold, treasures more splendid than any man among the sages can tell. The warriors won all that by courage, bold in battle under the banners by the wise counsel of Judith, the valorous virgin. The warlike earls brought to her from the pursuit the sword and blood-stained helmet of Holo-fernes as a guerdon, likewise wide corslets decked with red gold and all the wealth and private property that the stern prince of warriors possessed, rings and bright treasures; they gave that to the fair woman of wisdom.   Judith ascribed the glory of all that to the Lord of hosts who endued her with honour, fame in the realm of the world and likewise reward in heaven, the meed of victory in the splendour of the sky, because she ever held true faith in the Almighty.   At the end she doubted not at all of the reward which long while she had yearned for.   Therefore glory for ever be to the dear Lord who in His own mercy created the wind and the airs, the skies and spacious realms, and likewise the fierce streams and the joys of heaven.

THE BATTLE OF BRUNANBURH

[The poem celebrates a victory won in 937 by Æthelstan against Constantine, King of Scotland, allied with the Strathclyde Welsh and the Norwegians. The site of Brunanburh is uncertain; perhaps it is on the Solway Firth. Tennyson's translation of the poem is well known.]

IN this year King Æthelstan, the lord of earls, ring-giver of men, and his brother also, Prince Eadmund, won in battle everlasting glory with the edges of their swords at Brunanburh. The sons of Eadweard split the shield wall, hewed the linden targes with forged brands; as befitted their descent from noble kinsmen, often in fight they guarded their land, treasure, and homes against every foe. Enemies fell, Scots and seafarers sank doomed; the field grew slippery with the blood of men when the sun, the famous light, glided over the earth in the morning, the bright candle of God, the eternal Lord, until that noble creation sank to rest. There many a warrior lay destroyed with spears, many a Northman and Scot likewise pierced above his shield, weary, sated with war. The West Saxons in bands pursued the hateful troops all day, hewed the fugitives sorely from behind with swords ground sharp. The Mercians refused not the hard hand-play to any heroes who, fated to the fight, sought land with Anlaf in the bosom of the ship over the surging waves. Five young kings lay low on that field of battle, put asleep by swords, likewise seven earls of Anlaf and a countless number of the host, seamen and Scots. There the leader of the Northmen was put to flight, driven to the prow of the boat with a small troop; the galley hastened to sea; the king went out on the dark flood, saved his life. Also there the crafty one, Constantine, went fleeing north to his native land; the old warrior had no cause to exult at the meeting of swords; he was reft of his kinsmen, deprived of friends on the battle-field, slain in fight, and he left his son destroyed with wounds on the place of slaughter, the young man in battle. The grey-haired man, the old crafty one, had no cause to vaunt of the striking with swords, and no more had Anlaf. They had no cause to laugh with the remnants of their host that they had the better in warlike deeds in the clash of standards on the battle-field, the meeting of javelins, the struggle of men, the conflict of weapons, which they played on the field of slaughter with the sons of Eadweard.   Then the Northmen departed in their nailed boats, bloody survivors of javelins, humiliated, on Dingesmere [1] over the deep water to seek Dublin, Ireland once again.   Likewise both brothers together, king and prince, sought their own land, the country of the West Saxons, exulting in war.   They left behind them the dark-coated, swart raven, horny-beaked, to enjoy the carrion, and the grey-coated eagle, white-tailed, to have his will of the corpses, the greedy war-hawk, and that grey beast, the wolf in the wood.   Never yet before this was there greater slaughter on this island of an army felled by the edge of the sword such as books, old learned men, tell us of, from the time when Angles and Saxons came up from the east hither, sought the Britons over the broad seas, when proud workers of war overcame the Welshmen and gallant earls seized the land.

[1] This may not be the name of a place.   The right translation may be 'the loud-sounding sea.'

THE BATTLE OF MALDON

[The battle between the English and the Danes, described in the poem, was fought in 991 at Maldon, on the Blackwater (Panta), in Essex. The entry in the Chronicle says: 'This year Ipswich was ravaged and after that very shortly was Byrhtnoth the ealdorman slain at Maldon.' The invaders were between two branches of the river and were thus separated from the English host, composed of the Essex levy under Byrhtnoth. When the tide ebbed, Byrhtnoth, in proud confidence, allowed the Danes to cross, and the English were completely defeated. The poem was apparently written very soon after the battle. Though a fragment, it is a magnificent record of heroism. Its spirit is best expressed in the words of Byrhtwold, the old companion: 'Thought shall be the harder, heart the keener, courage the greater, as our might lessens.']

. . . It was broken. Then he commanded each of the warriors to leave his horse, to drive it away and to go forth, to think of his hands and of good courage. Then the kinsman of Offa first found out that the earl was not minded to suffer cowardice. Then he let the loved hawk fly from his hands to the wood, and went forward to the battle. Thereby one might know that the youth would not weaken in the fight when he grasped the weapons. Eadric also wished to attend his leader, his prince, to battle. Then he began to bear his spear to the fight. He had a good heart while with his hands he could hold shield and broad sword. He achieved his boast, that he should fight before his prince.

Then Byrhtnoth began there to exhort his warriors. He rode and instructed; he directed the warriors how they should stand and keep their station, and bade them hold their shields upright firmly with their hands and be not afraid. When he had fairly exhorted those people, then he alighted with his men where he best wished, where he knew his most trusty household troops were. Then the messenger of the Vikings stood on the shore, called out fiercely, spoke with words; he boastfully announced to the earl where he stood on the bank the message of the seafarers:

'Bold seamen have sent me to thee, bade me say to thee that thou mayest quickly send rings as a defence; and it is better for you that ye should avert with tribute this rush of spears than that we, so hardy, should deal out battle. We need not destroy

329

each other, if ye will consent to that. We will establish a truce with that gold. If thou who art mightiest here wilt agree to disband thy men, wilt give to the seamen at their own judgment money for peace and accept a truce from us, we are willing to embark with that tribute, to go to sea, and keep peace with you.'

Byrhtnoth spoke; he grasped the shield; he brandished the slender spear of ash. He uttered words; angry and resolute, he gave him answer: 'Dost thou hear, seafarer, what this people say? They will give you darts for tribute, poisonous spears and ancient swords, gear which will profit you naught in the fight. Messenger of the seamen, take word back again, say to thy people far more hateful tidings, that here stands a noble earl with his troop who will defend this land, the home of Æthelred, my prince, the people, and the ground. The heathen shall fall in the battle. It seems to me too shameful that ye should embark with our tribute with impunity, now that ye have come thus far hither to our land. Nor shall ye win treasure so lightly; point and edge shall reconcile us first, grim battle-play, ere we yield tribute.'

Then he commanded shields to be borne, the warriors to go, so that they all stood on the river bank. One troop could not come at the other there by reason of the water; there the flood came flowing after the ebb-tide; the streams ran together; they were impatient to clash their spears. There they stood in array beside the stream of Panta, the battle-line of the East Saxons and the ship-army. Nor could one of them injure the other, unless anyone received death from the arrow's flight. The tide went out; the pirates stood ready, many Vikings eager for battle. Then the protector of heroes commanded a warrior, stern in fight, to hold the bridge; he was called Wulfstan, bold among his race—he was the son of Ceola—who with his spear struck the first man who there most boldly stepped upon the bridge. There stood with Wulfstan warriors unafraid, Ælfere and Maccus, two brave men. They would not take to flight at the ford, but they firmly kept guard against the foe as long as they could wield weapons. When they beheld that and clearly saw that they found the guardians of the bridge fierce there, the hostile strangers began then to practise deceit. They asked to be allowed to approach, to go over the ford, to lead their soldiers. Then the earl began in his pride to yield the hateful people too much land. Then the son of Byrhtelm began to call over the cold water; the warriors listened:

'Now is space granted to you; come hither to us quickly,

warriors to the battle. God alone can tell who will hold the place of battle.'

Then the slaughterous wolves, the horde of Vikings, passed west over Panta. They cared not for the water; they bore shields over the gleaming water; the seamen carried targes to land. There Byrhtnoth stood ready with his warriors to oppose the enemy; he commanded the war hedge to be made with shields and that troop to hold out stoutly against the foes. Then was the fight near, glory in battle; the time had come when doomed men must needs fall there. Then clamour arose; ravens wheeled, the eagle greedy for carrion; there was shouting on earth. Then they let the spears, hard as a file, go from their hands; let the darts, ground sharp, fly; bows were busy; shield received point; bitter was the rush of battle. Warriors fell on either hand; young men lay low. Wulfmær was wounded; he, the kinsman of Byrhtnoth, his sister's son, chose a bed of slaughter; he was sorely stricken with swords. There requital was given to the Vikings. I heard that Eadweard slew one with his sword stoutly; he withheld not the stroke, so that the fated warrior fell at his feet. For that his prince gave thanks to him, to the chamberlain, when he had opportunity. Thus the brave warriors stood firm in battle; eagerly they considered who there could first mortally wound a fated man with spear, a warrior with weapons; the slain fell to the earth. They stood steadfast; Byrhtnoth incited them; he bade each warrior give thought to war who would win glory against the Danes. Then he who was hardy in battle advanced; he raised up the weapon, the shield for a defence, and stepped towards the man. Thus the earl went resolute to the churl; each of them planned evil to the other. Then the seafarer sent a spear of southern make, so that the lord of warriors was wounded. He thrust then with the shield, so that the shaft burst; and that spear broke, and sprang back again. The warrior was enraged; with a spear he pierced the proud Viking who gave him the wound. The warrior was skilful; he let his lance go through the man's neck. His hand guided it, so that he reached the life of his sudden enemy. Then hastily he darted another, so that the corslet burst; he was wounded in the breast through the coat of ring-mail; the poisonous spear stood at his heart. The earl was the gladder; then the brave man laughed, gave thanks to God for that day's work which the Lord had granted him. Then one of the warriors let fly a javelin from his hand, from his fist, so that it went forth through the noble thane of Æthelred. By his side stood a youthful warrior, a stripling in the fight; full boldly he, Wulfstan's son, the young Wulfmær, plucked the bloody spear from the warrior. He let the exceeding hard spear go forth again; the point went in, so that he who erstwhile had sorely smitten his prince lay on the ground. Then a warrior went armed to the earl; he was minded to seize the bracelets of the man, the armour and rings and ornamented sword. Then Byrhtnoth drew the sword from the sheath, broad and gleaming edged, and struck at the corslet. One of the seafarers hindered him too quickly and destroyed the earl's arm. Then the sword with golden hilt fell to the ground, nor could he hold the hard brand, wield the weapon.

Then the old warrior yet spoke these words, encouraged the fighters, bade the valiant comrades go forth; nor could he then longer stand firm on his feet; he looked to heaven: 'I thank Thee, O Lord of the peoples, for all those joys which I have known in the world. Now, gracious Lord, I have most need that Thou shouldst grant good to my spirit, that my soul may journey to Thee, may pass in peace into Thy keeping, Prince of angels. I entreat Thee that devils may not do it despite.' Then the heathen men hewed him, and both the men who stood by him, Ælfnoth and Wulfmær, were laid low; then they gave up their lives by the side of their prince.

Then they who were not minded to be there retired from the battle. There the sons of Odda were the first in flight; Godric fled from the battle and left the valiant one who had often given him many a steed; he leaped on the horse which his lord had owned, on the trappings, as was not right, and both his brothers, Godrinc and Godwig, galloped with him; they cared not for war, but they turned from the fight and sought the wood; they fled to that fastness and saved their lives, and more men than was at all fitting, if they had all remembered the rewards which he had given them for their benefit.[1] Thus erstwhile Offa once said to him in the meeting-place, when he held assembly, that many spoke bravely there who would not endure in stress.

Then the people's prince had fallen, Æthelred's earl; all the hearth companions saw that their lord was laid low. Then proud thanes, brave men, went forth there, eagerly hastened. Then they all wished for one of two things—to depart from life or to avenge the loved one. Thus the son of Ælfric urged them on, a warrior young in years. He uttered words; Ælfwine spoke then; boldly he said: 'Remember the times when often

[1] Compare the cowardice of Beowulf's men in his fight with the dragon.

we spoke at the mead-drinking, when on the bench we uttered boasting, heroes in hall, about hard strife. Now he who is brave may show it in the test. I will make known my lineage to all, that I was of a mighty race among the Mercians. My old father was called Ealhelm, a wise alderman, prosperous in the world. Thanes shall not reproach me among the people, that I wish to leave this army, to seek my home, now my prince lies low, hewn down in battle. That is the greatest of griefs to me; he was both my kinsman and my lord.' Then he went forth; he forgot not the feud; he smote one pirate in the host with spear, so that he lay on the earth, slain by his weapon. Then he began to admonish his friends, companions, and comrades, that they should go forth.

Offa spoke; he shook his spear-shaft: 'Lo! thou, Ælfwine, hast admonished all the thanes as is needed. Now that our prince lies low, the earl on the earth, it is the task of all of us, that each should exhort the other warrior to fight whilst he can grasp and hold a weapon, a hard brand, a spear, and good sword. Godric, the cowardly son of Odda, has betrayed us all. Very many men believed when he rode on a horse, on the proud steed, that it was our lord. Wherefore here on the field the army was divided, the shield array broken. May his enterprise fail for putting so many men to flight here.'

Leofsunu spoke and raised his shield, his targe in defence; he spoke to the man: 'I promise that I will not flee hence a footstep, but will go forward, avenge in fight my friendly lord. The steadfast heroes about Sturmere [1] shall have no cause to taunt me with words, now that my friend has fallen, that I journey home lacking a lord, turn from the fight; but the weapon, spear and brand, shall take me.' He went very wrathful, fought staunchly; he scorned flight.

Dunnere spoke then, shook his spear, a humble churl; he cried out over all, bade each man avenge Byrhtnoth: 'He in the host who thinks to avenge the prince cannot waver nor mourn for life.'

Then they went forth; they recked not of life. Then the retainers began to fight stoutly, fierce bearers of spears, and prayed God that they might avenge their friendly lord and work slaughter on their foes. The hostage began to help them eagerly; he was of a stout race among the Northumbrians, the son of Ecglaf; his name was Æscferth. He wavered not at the war-play, but often he urged forth the dart; at times he shot on

[1] A lake or fen in Essex, or the mouth of the Stour.

to the shield; at times he wounded a man. Ever and again he dealt out wounds whilst he could wield weapons.

Then Eadweard the tall still stood in the line of battle, ready and eager. With words of boasting he said that he would not flee a foot's length of land or move back, now that his leader lay low. He broke the wall of shields and fought with the men until he worthily avenged on the seamen his giver of treasure ere he lay among the slain. Likewise did Ætheric, the brother of Sibyrht, a noble companion, eager and impetuous; he fought earnestly, and many others also split the hollow shields; the bold men made defence. The border of the shield broke and the corslet sang a terrible song. Then in the fight Offa smote the seaman, so that he fell to the earth, and there the kinsman of Gadd sought the ground. Quickly was Offa hewn down in the battle; yet he had accomplished what he promised his prince, as erstwhile he boasted with his giver of rings, that they should both ride to the stronghold, unscathed to their home, or fall amid the host, perish of wounds on the field of battle. Near the prince he lay low, as befits a thane.

Then there was breaking of shields; the seamen advanced, enraged by war. Often the spear pierced the body of a fated man. Then Wistan went forth, the son of Thurstan; he fought with the men; he slew three of them in the press ere Wigelin's son was laid low among the slain. There was a stern meeting; the warriors stood firm in the struggle; fighters fell, wearied with wounds; the slaughtered dropped to the earth. Oswold and Ealdwold, both the brothers, exhorted the men all the while; they bade their kinsmen with words to bear up there in the stress, use their weapons resolutely. Byrhtwold spoke; he grasped his shield; he was an old companion; he shook his ash spear; full boldly he exhorted the warriors: 'Thought shall be the harder, heart the keener, courage the greater, as our might lessens. Here lies our leader all hewn down, the valiant man in the dust; may he lament for ever who thinks now to turn from this war-play. I am old in age; I will not hence, but I purpose to lie by the side of my lord, by the man so dearly loved.' Godric, the son of Æthelgar, likewise exhorted them all to fight. Often he let fly the spear, the deadly dart, against the Vikings, as he went foremost in the host. He hewed and struck down until he fell in the battle; that was not the Godric who fled from the fight.